A Lonely Death

ALSO BY CHARLES TODD

The Ian Rutledge Mysteries

A Test of Wills

Wings of Fire

Search the Dark

Watchers of Time

Legacy of the Dead

A Fearsome Doubt

A Cold Treachery

A Long Shadow

A False Mirror

A Pale Horse

A Matter of Justice

The Red Door

The Bess Crawford Mysteries

A Duty to the Dead

An Impartial Witness

Other Fiction

The Murder Stone

A Lonely Death

Charles Todd

HARPER LUXE

An Imprint of HarperCollinsPublishers

A LONELY DEATH. Copyright © 2011 by Charles Todd. All rights reserved. Printed in the United States of America. No part of this book may be used or reproduced in any manner whatsoever without written permission except in the case of brief quotations embodied in critical articles and reviews. For information address HarperCollins Publishers, 10 East 53rd Street, New York, NY 10022.

HarperCollins books may be purchased for educational, business, or sales promotional use. For information please write: Special Markets Department, HarperCollins Publishers, 10 East 53rd Street, New York, NY 10022.

FIRST HARPERLUXE EDITION

HarperLuxe™ is a trademark of HarperCollins Publishers

Library of Congress Cataloging-in-Publication Data is available upon request.

ISBN: 978-0-06-201772-7

11 12 13 14 ID/OPM 10 9 8 7 6 5 4 3 2 1

California has a wonderful list of indepen-
dent mystery book stores—we salute them
all in dedicating A Lonely Death to Ed
Kaufman and the staff of "M" is for Mystery
in San Mateo. With great affection, we rec-
ognize a lifetime of loving the mystery and a
second career as a bookseller supporting it—a
man with a great sense of humor and infinite
knowledge.

And because they shared Rutledge almost from
the beginning, we say farewell to two faithful
companions. . . .

Going on fifteen is old for a Golden, but Lin-
da's Simba, a rescue, was loved by all who met
him, and he returned that love with a deep and
extraordinary devotion. We said good-bye on
May 29, 2010. Letting go is the last great gift
of love. Simba filled such a chasm of emptiness
when we lost Biedermann and Cassandra that we
knew he was meant for us. That joyous smile and
a heart wide enough to encompass cats and dogs
and people were his hallmarks. We shall not look
upon his like again.

Going on fifteen isn't old for a cat. Fluff, another rescue, ten pounds of elegant long gold and white Persian fur, was a diva who offered love on her own dear terms. A North Carolinian by birth, she spent the second half of her life in Delaware, but never forgot her roots. She brought such happiness with her, and was content to sit by the computer as I worked. She put up a gallant fight against the cancer that slowly took her from us, and died on her own terms, surrounded by her family, on June 30. To Martha and Marla, who gave her into our keeping, our eternal gratitude. It wasn't easy parting with her, but they knew she would be safe with us. In return, she brightened our lives in so many small ways that we were hers from the start. Bless her for all she was and all she gave.

Sleep well, dear ones.

1

Northern France, Early June 1920

The sod had grown over the graves, turning the torn earth a soft green, and the rows of white crosses gleamed brightly in the morning sun. Except for the fact that a fallen soldier lay beneath each wooden marker, it was pretty there under the blue bowl of the French sky, peaceful finally after four tumultuous years of war. Even the birds had come back, picking at the grass for seeds, insects, and worms.

The man watched them, those birds, and was reminded of a line from *Hamlet,* that somehow had caught a schoolboy's imagination and then lingered in a corner of his adult mind—that a worm may feed on a king. Had these fed on lesser dead?

Many had been hastily buried where they fell, others in mass graves. Sorting the dead for proper burial had been gruesome at best. Many had never been identified. Walking down the rows now, looking at names, remembering burial details, broken bodies, bits of them, endless lines of them, he wondered if he was changed by them.

No, on the whole, he thought not. The war had been a part of the fabric of his life, and he had endured it, survived it, and was still steadfast in his purpose.

He stopped, his gaze sweeping the crosses. It was the living who concerned him now. A few had escaped him, but there were still eight left. And he was ready.

Were they?

Not that the state of their souls troubled him overmuch.

He turned his back on the cemetery, striding toward the Paris taxi that had brought him out here. And as he did, the slanting June sun warmed his shoulders.

Listening to the sound of his footfalls, he realized that he hadn't bargained for the silence here. He wondered if those lying beneath the crosses savored it after the noise of battle. Or was it unnerving?

There was a train to Calais tonight. Another from Dover to London. But he was in no hurry.

A good dinner first, if he could find one, a bottle of wine, and then a sound night's sleep.

As the taxi turned and drove back the way it had come, he leaned his head against the cracked leather of the seat and closed his eyes.

2

London, July 1920

C hief Inspector Cummins walked into Scotland
Yard at half past nine, went directly to his office,
and set about finishing packing his books. It was his
last day, and he wanted no fanfare. An injury sustained
in the line of duty had put an end to his career.

"And not a day too soon," he said to Inspector Ian
Rutledge who had stepped in to wish him well. "I
should have left at the end of the war. But I found one
excuse after another to stay on. This case pending, that
case passing through the courts. And here I still am,
well past my time." He looked up, another stack of
books in his hand. "No regrets."

"I feel responsible—" Rutledge began, but Cummins cut him short.

"Nonsense. I knew what I was doing. I hadn't reckoned on the toll the years had taken, that's all. I wasn't

quite fast enough. At fifty-five, one still believes one is thirty until he looks in his mirror as he shaves."

"Will you be content in Scotland, after the bustle of London?"

"My God, yes. And if I'm not, my wife will tell me that I am." Cummins reached for the roll of tape to seal that box and then turned to fill another. "When do you intend to marry? Don't leave it too long. I'll be a grandfather, next month."

Rutledge laughed, as he was meant to do. "You've left behind a splendid record. We'll be living up to it for decades to come."

Cummins set the books down on a corner of his cluttered desk and looked around the office. The shelves were nearly empty, the desk as well, and the photographs had been removed from the walls. He took a deep breath and said pensively, "Yes, well. I enjoyed the hunt, you see. More than I should have done. All the same, there was one case I never solved. I was a little superstitious about it, if you want the truth. I kept the folder on my desk for years, telling myself I'd get to the bottom of it, sooner or later. I even dreamed about it sometimes, when I was tired. What bothered me most was not knowing whether the dead man was a sacrifice or a victim. And if his murderer had ever killed again."

"A sacrifice?" It was an odd choice of words for a man like Cummins.

Cummins glanced sheepishly at Rutledge. "It was what struck me as soon as I saw the man. That he was left there for a purpose. A warning, if you will. Or a sacrifice of some sort. Not religious, I don't mean that kind of thing . . ." He broke off, then shrugged, as if to make light of what he'd said. "It was the setting. It made me fanciful, I dare say."

"When was this?"

"Long before your time. It was Midsummer's Eve, 1905." Cummins turned away and walked to the window, where sunlight had just broken through the morning clouds and was turning the wet pavements from a dull gray to bright pewter. "Some fifteen people had come to Stonehenge dressed as Druids. Unbleached muslin, handmade sandals, staffs of peeled oak boughs. Mind you, I doubt they knew much about ancient druidism, but they'd come to watch the sun rise and chant nonsense, and feel something—God knows what. Anyway, they walked to the stones, sang and marched, drank a little homemade mead—honey laced with rum, we were told later—and waited for sunrise."

Cummins paused, staring not at the view outside his window but back into a past he reluctantly remembered, and Rutledge thought, *He's not going to finish it. It cuts too deep.* Still, he waited quietly, ignoring the dull rumble of Hamish's voice in the back of his mind.

Finally Cummins went on, as if compelled. "They were misguided, playing at something they didn't understand. But harmless enough, I suppose. At length the sun rose. One of the women told me later that it was magnificent. Her word. She said the dark sky turned to opal and rose, then purest gold. As they watched, the rim of the sun appeared on the eastern horizon. She said that what followed was unbelievable—a shaft of light came spilling across the dark earth and touched her face. She said she could feel it. Just as the schoolmaster had told them. He was the one who talked them into this silliness. But even he was taken by surprise."

Losing his train of thought, Cummins turned and said, "Where was I? Oh, yes. This young woman—her name was Sarah Harmon—was still staring at what she called the stone of sacrifice. That's what the schoolmaster had told them it was called. It stands along the eastern avenue between the main section of Stonehenge and the horizon. Do you know it?"

"Yes. I do."

"Hmm. She was trying to recapture a little of the emotion she'd felt when the sun struck her face, and then she noticed something odd about that stone. It was light enough, by then, you see. When she began screaming, everyone turned toward her, startled. She pointed to the stone. They could just make out something there and rushed down the avenue to find a man strapped to it. He was dead. Even they could see that, and when they held up their lanterns for a better view, they realized he'd been stabbed." Cummins cleared his throat. "He was strapped to the dark side. Not toward the light."

"Hadn't they seen anything? Anyone?"

"Apparently not. I questioned them for hours. The body could have been out there before ever they arrived. In the dark, they wouldn't have noticed."

"They didn't know the victim?"

"They swore they didn't."

"Not even this schoolmaster, who'd lured them out there? It would have been a perfect cover for murder."

"Terrence Nolan? He was as frightened as the rest of them. And in the end, I believed them. I expect the murderer, whoever he was, had counted on no one finding the victim for days. As for the dead man, he was young—thirty to thirty-five at a guess—and he was wearing only a scrap of cloth, like a loincloth— there was no clothing at all, no marks on the body, nothing through which we could identify him. Even the bit of cloth was a cheap cotton that could be bought anywhere. It took us six weeks to discover his name."

"Who was he?" Rutledge asked, intrigued.

"One Harvey Wheeler. He came from Orkney. A ne'er-do-well, according to the authorities there. His father had gone to Kirkwall to run the post, and Harvey grew up rather wild and unruly, a truant from school, roaming the island at will and never sorry for his escapades. His parents gave up trying to control him, apparently, and he went missing in 1902 after a brush with the police. It was thought he'd come south into Scotland. At any rate, he reappeared in Edinburgh in late 1903, and then left a step ahead of the police, who were after him for attempting to defraud a woman he'd met there. That was the last anyone had heard of him until he was found dead on Salisbury Plain. Why anyone would wish to kill him is still a mystery. It must have had to do with the missing two years of his life, although it always struck me as odd that someone like Harvey Wheeler should end that way. As murders go, it didn't fit."

"Were you certain of the identification?"

"As certain as may be. When Edinburgh took an interest in the description we'd passed around, we sent along a photograph. That was when they recommended we contact Orkney. They in turn felt it was very likely that our corpse was this young man. His father was dead by that time, and his mother too ill to be shown the photograph. But the Kirkwall police had no doubts. And so he was buried in a churchyard on the outskirts of Winchester. No one saw any point in sending the body north. That was the end of it. His murderer was never found." Cummins paused, looking toward the window, as if it held the answer, before bringing his gaze back to Rutledge. "It was an odd inquiry from start to finish. I never felt comfortable with it. I'd have liked to go to Kirkwall myself, but the Orkney Islands are at the northern tip of Scotland, and the Yard felt it was money wasted to send me there. All the same, I'd have liked to know more about Harvey Wheeler. What brought him into England, for one thing, and where he might have lived on this side of the border."

"The murder weapon never turned up?"

"We searched the area, every inch of it. We came to the conclusion that the murderer carried it off with him. It could be anywhere—thrown from a bridge, buried in a dustbin, returned to wherever it had come from. There would be no way to know, would there, that it had anything to do with a crime? What was odd was the coroner found a tiny flake of flint in the wound. The feeling was it was on his clothing and driven in by the force of the blow. That led us to believe two facts: that he was dressed when he was killed, although his clothing was never found, and that he must have come from a part of England where flint was readily available. And that covered a good bit of ground."

"Was he killed there at Stonehenge?"

"Very likely not. There was no sign of a struggle. Unless of course Wheeler was drugged and carried there. Still, the coroner found no evidence of his being either drugged or knocked unconscious prior to his death. And there wasn't enough blood at the site." Cummins hesitated. "It was his face, I think, that disturbed me as much as the rest of it. A handsome enough man, fit and well made, more a gentleman than Wheeler appeared to be. Or perhaps that was his charm, and why he nearly succeeded in defrauding that widow. How many more women were there that we never heard of?"

"I can understand why Wheeler's murder has remained fresh in your mind."

"That, and the fact that it was the only case I failed to solve to my own satisfaction." Cummins made a wry gesture and smiled. "Sheer arrogance, of course. I took pride in my record, all the same. The men used to call me Cautious Cummins. But it was always my way, to work out each detail until I could make a case out of the pieces. You remind me of myself as a young inspector, you know." The smile widened. "I bequeath you this albatross of a case. If you ever solve it, let me know." He went back to packing. "Don't let Bowles lay the blame for my going on you, Rutledge," he warned. "Because he will try. He has it in for you, he has from the day you returned to the Yard after the war. I don't know precisely why, but he's been instrumental in blocking promotions and failing to give you proper credit where it was due. He's mean and vindictive. I've never liked him, and I'm not about to pretend now."

"Warning taken," Rutledge said, surprised that Cummins would speak so bluntly.

"I should finish this," the Chief Inspector said, glancing around the room. "Two more boxes should do it, I think. I'm not one for prolonging the inevitable." He put out his hand, and Rutledge took it in a firm grip. "I wish you well, Ian."

"Thank you, sir. I hope your retirement will be a happy one."

Rutledge walked to the door and was on the point of opening it when Cummins said, "Inspector. I would have no objection to hearing from you from time to time." And then his attention returned to the half dozen books in his hands.

As Rutledge strode down the passage toward his own office, his footsteps loud on the bare boards, he wondered if he would look back at the end of his career and remember a case the way Cummins had lived with his.

"Aye, but first ye must survive long enough to leave the force on your ain twa feet," Hamish said, his voice seeming to follow Rutledge the short distance to his own room.

Hamish was his penance for what he'd done in the war: a voice that was relentless and unforgiving, like the guilt that haunted him. In life Corporal Hamish MacLeod had been the closest thing Rutledge had had to a friend during the darkest hours of the Somme Offensive, despite the vast difference in rank between them. The young Highlander would have made sergeant if he'd survived the battle. He was a natural leader, the sort who cared for his men and understood the tactics of war. But that had been his undoing. Refusing a direct order on a battlefield had led to a firing squad. It wasn't cowardice, it was an unwillingness to lead tired and dispirited men in another useless charge against a well-concealed machine gun nest. Yet even knowing as well as Hamish did what it would cost in lives, knowing that it was impossible to dislodge the enemy, Rutledge had had no choice but to give the order to try one more time in an effort to clear out the nest before the main attack began along the entire line. The few sacrificed for the sake of the many. And then as an example to his men, he'd had no choice but to give the order to fire that had ended Hamish's life. Military necessity, but in human terms, despicable to Rutledge's already battered mind.

After days of endless fighting that had killed thousands of good men for mere inches of ground and did nothing to bring the war nearer its inevitable end, this one death had seemed insupportable. A decision made at HQ, a decision that appeared sound and workable to officers far from the fighting, officers who didn't have to look exhausted men in the face and ask them to climb over the top one more time and die to satisfy a strategy that was broken before it had even begun, had resulted in a bloodbath that was incomprehensible. Hamish MacLeod had simply given that bloodbath a personal face.

Dr. Fleming had explained it best—though it was no comfort to Rutledge to hear it: "You couldn't accept that one man's death. And so you refused to let him die. He's every young soldier you tried to keep alive and failed. He's your expression of guilt for that failure, and he will be in your head as long as that guilt lasts. Or until you die and take Hamish MacLeod with you to the grave."

Guilt or not, Hamish's voice sounded as clear as if it had come from a foot or so behind Rutledge's shoulder, where Hamish had so often stood and fought. And explanations did nothing to ease the strain of knowing the voice was there, that it would speak or not as it chose, and there was nothing on God's earth to prevent it or keep others from hearing it, even when Rutledge knew they could not. He could never be certain of anything except that Hamish had never forgiven him, just as he had never forgiven himself— even though he had never been given any choice in the matter. Hamish had taken that away too and left Rutledge to cope alone. And yet never alone.

Trying to shut out the soft Scots words in his mind, Rutledge tried to settle to the papers on his desk, and after a time he managed to concentrate on them. He knew he would miss Cummins. There were already rumors that Inspector Mickelson would be promoted to fill his place.

3

Eastfield, Sussex, on the Hastings Road, July 1920

Eastfield was neither particularly charming nor particularly important, historically or politically. It had begun as a hamlet where the road out of Hastings climbed the bluffs, leveled out, and turned eastward. A large field at that point had served as grazing for tired oxen and horses either before their descent into the town below or after their ascent from it. This common field had eventually been encircled by the huts of providers of services—a tavern to feed the drovers, a smithy to see to torn hooves, and a brothel to ease a man's other needs. The new-built abbey at Battle had soon taken the hamlet in hand, to save the souls of its inhabitants and to charge a small fee for the hitherto free grazing.

At the dissolution of the monasteries, the tiny village had passed into the keeping of a crony of Henry VIII's, hardly aware of the change in ownership. By 1800, descendants of that crony had fallen on hard times, and the village found itself forgotten, though the field for grazing still served those going to and from Hastings. The fees were now collected by a self-appointed squire, who was no more than a jumped-up yeoman who saw his chance to prosper, and no one thought to formalize the new status of Eastfield in any fashion.

It began to flourish in Victoria's reign, selling its produce and wares to the hungry fishermen and residents of the little port where the valley broke through the ridge and swept down to the water's edge, and as Hastings grew, so did Eastfield.

By 1880, it boasted changes that brought in more revenue—the small firm that had built tackle, fish boxes, and other furnishings for the fishermen found that the newly acquired taste for sea bathing had brought hotels in its wake, and hotels needed a better quality of furniture to serve those who expected fine accommodations. The second stroke of good luck occurred when the Pierce brothers decided to locate their brewery in three buildings at the far end of the Hastings Road. An exiled Frenchman set up a small Latin school in the middle of the village and made a good living educating the sons and daughters of those who could now afford it.

The brewery, the furniture making, and the Latin School gave the village an air of success. The Misses du Toit, thoroughly English daughters of the school's founder, changed their name to Tate on the death of their father, and in 1913 passed charge of the school to a niece, Mrs. Farrell-Smith, a young widow.

By 1900, Eastfield had doubled in population and in 1914 took great pride in furnishing a company of its sons to fight for King and Country in the Great War.

They had received a letter of commendation from the King himself, and the brewery produced a beer it called The Rose of Picardy, which unexpectedly became very popular among soldiers and then ex-soldiers, making the Pierce Brothers Brewery, under its Arrow label, famous throughout Kent, Sussex, and Surrey.

Content with their ordinary lives, the villagers of Eastfield saw no reason why their future shouldn't be as peaceful as their past.

And then on a Friday night, in July 1920, that illusion was shattered.

William Jeffers had no inkling of his fate when he walked into The Conqueror Pub in a back street of Eastfield.

The sign was swinging gently in the late evening breeze, squeaking a little in its iron frame. On one side of it, a vast, painted armada of Norman ships was shown anchored in an English bay—there was debate as to whether it was intended to portray Hastings or Pevensey—and on the other side, a victorious William raised his painted sword high to celebrate his famous victory over King Harold at Senlac Hill.

The haze of tobacco smoke was already thick as the barkeep hailed the newcomer with a smiling greeting. Jeffers rarely came to drink in the pub. He was a farmer and had little time in the evenings and less money to waste in conviviality. But it had become a regular thing each year for him to mark the anniversary of the wound that had ended his military career and nearly cost him his life.

Jeffers settled himself at a corner table with his first pint, and for the rest of the evening proceeded to drink as much as he could hold.

He left half an hour before closing, making his way toward the church.

The light was fading, and he sat on the low stone wall surrounding the churchyard until he had watched the sun set and the long shadows deepen into night. He was not a praying man, but he found himself saying a prayer for the dead. Most of the dead on his mind weren't lying here in St. Mary's, they were in France, but it would do.

At length he stood up and made his way to the outskirts of the village, where Abbey Street met the Hastings Road. He was only slightly tipsy, he told himself. He had to rise at half past four in the morning to milk the cows, but this anniversary was more important than duty. The hole in his chest was just a rough and ugly scar now, but it sometimes ached, as if it hadn't healed. Four years. The flesh had surely forgot the pain and the terror and the weakness from loss of blood. But the mind hadn't. The mind never forgot. And so he tried to drink himself into oblivion.

He never quite got there.

He tripped on a stone, recovered his balance, and walked on. The farm was barely a mile away, but tonight the road seemed twice as long. Overhead the stars were so bright he felt he could hear them. His grandfather always said to him when he was a lad, "Listen to the stars, Willie. Can you hear them? Just listen."

And he would listen, over the ordinary night sounds of rats in the feed bins or a stoat hunting in the hedgerow, a horse moving in its stall. He could have sworn he heard them.

A stone rattled on the road behind him, and he turned to see what was there. Nothing but his imagination. At this hour of the night, he had the road to himself.

His mind was clouded with the beer he'd drunk. His wife would have something to say about that. He shook his head to clear it, but it was no use.

He tripped again, and swore.

A voice quietly called his name. Jeffers whirled to see who it was, peering through the darkness, but for the life of him he couldn't bring the pale face into focus.

"Do I know you?" he asked after a moment.

"You did. Once."

"Sorry. I don't remember."

"Never mind. It doesn't matter."

Jeffers nodded. "Coming this way?"

"No. Good night."

He turned and plodded on, leaving the man standing there. He wanted his bed, now. The beer was making him sick.

Something flashed briefly in the starlight, seeming to fly over his head. And then it had him by the throat, and he was fighting for breath, twisting and shifting furiously, but the thing at his throat bit all the harder, and in the end it was no use.

William Jeffers was the first man to die.

Three nights later, Jimmy Roper was in his barn, sitting up with a colicky cow. Dandelion had always been prone to the ailment, with a temperament that was easily unsettled, but she was his best milker and worth the trouble to keep her healthy. Her calves carried that trait, and she had done much to improve the quality of the dairy herd.

He was tired. It had been a long day, and it would be longer still before he could seek his bed. But he had learned patience after taking over the farm from his ailing father. One waited for cattle and for crops and for time to shear. One waited for sun and for rain and for a still day to harvest. If he'd had a choice he would have worked at the brewery, but as an only son, he had had to fill his father's shoes.

He heard the squeak of the barn door and leaned around the edge of the stall, to see who was there. "Pa? Is that you? I told you I'd come to your room as soon as I saw to things here."

There was no answer. His father shouldn't have walked that far. He'd be out of breath, shaking.

Roper got to his feet, feeling a tingle in one leg from crouching there by Dandelion until his foot had gone to sleep under him. Picking up his lantern, he walked down the aisle, past the stalls where his three horses dozed, undisturbed by their temporary neighbor's restlessness, and saw that the outer door was open several inches—but there was no one inside the barn after all. Had his father had a fainting spell?

Crossing quickly to the door, he peered outside and saw that someone was standing a little distance away in the shadow of the cowshed. Not his father, then—this was someone taller, straighter, younger. He could just make out the man's features, but they meant nothing to him. Someone needing work, then. In the past six months he could have hired a dozen men like this, walking the roads, footsore and hopeful. But the farm could barely keep his own family and that of one laborer, and he had come to hate turning hope into hopelessness. He put off the moment of decision.

"Looking for me?" Roper asked, then went on quickly. "Sorry, I'm attending a cow. Can it wait?"

"It can wait," the man said. "Go back to your cow."

Roper nodded and left the door ajar, out of courtesy.

Dandelion was on her feet when he got back to her stall, mouthing the hay he had put in the manger for her, looking at him with what he swore was mischief in her dark eyes. "You just wanted company, then, did you?" he said, scratching her between her horns. "Too good for the yard, that's what you are." He'd long suspected that it was true—she had been sickly in her first year and kept in the stall where she was petted and made much of, and even now preferred the barn. "All right, you can stay here the night, but I'm going to bed." He stepped back, studying her for a moment to be sure she was recovered.

One of the horses snorted, moving uneasily in his stall. And then Roper was startled by a sound just behind him. Before he could turn, something flashed before his eyes, bright in the lantern's glow, tightening around his throat before he could put up his hands to protect himself. It cut into the skin with such force he could feel blood trickling down his neck. Dandelion jerked away, moving to the back of the stall, the whites of her eyes showing her fear, but he was beyond worrying about her, fighting for his life with the breath left in him. Strong as he was, the man behind him had a fearsome strength. And then Roper was on his knees on the hard-packed earthen floor, aware that he didn't have a chance in hell. A last fleeting thought as he died was for the lantern, and a dread that it had overturned in the struggle.

And Jimmy Roper became the second victim.

The third to die was the son of the present owner of the Pierce family's brewery. It occupied three stone buildings that had once belonged to the abbey and had fallen into ruin. But the abbot had built well, and Pierce's grandfather had bought them, renovated them, and made his fortune from them. The brewery stood on the inland side of Eastfield, where the road up from Hastings turned toward Battle, and in the beginning the family had occupied quarters in the third building, but expansion had put paid to that, and prosperity had brought them a fine house on Abbey Street.

That was a generation ago, and Tyrell Pierce, Anthony's father, had become a man to reckon with in the community. Anthony himself had come home from the war with one leg, but that hadn't prevented him from taking his place in the firm, continuing his rise through the ranks from the driver of the dray to assistant to the brewmaster. His father was a strong believer in an owner's intimate knowledge of each position in the yard and in the brew house.

On this night—the third since Jimmy Roper's death—Anthony Pierce had gone back to the brew house to look at one of the temperature gauges on the new kettle. It had been playing up and must either be repaired or replaced on the morrow. The foreman had tinkered with it earlier, with no success, and after dinner Anthony had strolled down to have a go at it, certain that it could be salvaged. His father had spoken to a supplier in London who had informed him that it would require three days to find and ship the new gauge, and that would mean that the current batch of mash would have to be dumped, at a loss.

He had always liked the smell of the brew house, almost a sour odor, rich and thick on a warm night. The door was never locked, and lighting his lantern, he walked in, climbed to the first floor, and went to the bench where the foreman had left his tools. Setting the lamp there, he walked over to study the offending piece of equipment.

After working with it for some minutes, he stepped back. There was no hope of repairing it. The foreman had been right. If it went now, they would just have to absorb the loss of this one kettle, clean it out, and wait for the new gauge to arrive before starting it up again. Twelve more hours, that's all they needed. And if luck was with them . . .

He shook his head, and then put his tools back on the bench.

Anthony Pierce had served as an officer in the war and was accustomed to leading men. He was popular enough with the brewery workers, and when he heard the outer door on the ground floor open with its familiar scraping sound, he called out, "I'm up here. Is that you, Fred? It's hopeless. I'll drive to London tomorrow myself, and see if I can expedite replacing the damned thing."

But the man who appeared on the stairs, his footfalls steady on the treads, was a stranger, not the brewmaster. Pierce frowned, said, "This building is closed to outsiders. Is there something you wanted?"

The man said, "Not really. I thought you might remember me."

Thinking the man was looking for work, Pierce said, "Is it help you need?"

"No. I'm here for old time's sake."

"Well, I'm just closing up. Walk down with me." He limped toward the man, wondering for a moment if he'd served with him. But the face wasn't familiar at all. And although he was dressed plainly, his clothes were of good quality. Not money then—he wasn't looking for work.

When Pierce reached the wooden stairs, the man moved aside. "You've got a new leg, I see. Why don't you go first?"

Pierce was reluctant, but he said only, "All right," and started down, one hand on the rail. He could hear the footfalls of the man behind him, almost pressing on his heels, and he felt a sudden unease. He told himself it was only because the cursed leg was new and he was still nervous about falling.

They had reached the ground floor, and Pierce crossed to the heavy door, his hand already out to push it wide, when he realized that there was something wrong. He was on the point of turning to order the other man to precede him into the alley between the brew house and the storage sheds when he saw the wire flash in front of his eyes.

He put up a good fight for a man with one false leg. But of course it was no use. He was no match for his murderer. The last thing he heard was a harsh whisper almost in his ear, and then nothing.

When the first of the workmen arrived the next morning, he was lying on the stone floor within a few feet of the door, his body already cold.

4

Rutledge found a letter waiting for him in his flat. As he picked up the envelope from the floor, he recognized the handwriting at once. Setting his hat on the table by the door, he crossed to a window, opening the envelope as he went and pulling out the single sheet inside. He could feel the tension in his mind that was Hamish, and tried to ignore it as he spread the sheet wide.

There was no salutation.

I'm writing to say good-bye. My decision has been made and by the time you read this, there will be no turning back. I have tried, Ian. But the war changed me, it changed my family, it changed everything, and finding my way again to what I knew before isn't possible. I went to Dr. Fleming, as you suggested, but he couldn't help me. I think after so much time, there's no real answer to be had. But he is a good man, and he did his best for me. I want you to know that. I have seen to financial matters, my wife will be taken care of, and I think she will be relieved not to have to deal with me. The nightmares are worse, and encroaching deafness from the guns is a frightful thing. It isolates a person, and I was already isolated. My wife must shout at me to ask the simplest questions, and even so I can barely hear her voice. Tenderness is impossible, and she sleeps in another room now so that I won't keep her awake with my tossing and turning and the screams I don't remember in the morning, but she does. We hardly knew each other when we married in 1914, and we never had a chance to build that common ground that might have seen us through. I'm tired, Ian, I can't tell you how tired. And this is the only way to peace I can see. Forgive me, if you can. Pray for me if you will. But know that I will be happier out of this misery, and I have not decided that lightly. Fare thee well, my friend. I hope that you will see your way clear where I have not. You didn't marry your Jean after all, and that may be your salvation. I have watched

someone I believed I loved more than life itself
withdraw a little more each day, until there's only
hurt and confusion left. It would break my heart, if
it weren't already broken. So good-bye, and may
God have mercy on both of us.

It was signed *Max.*

Rutledge stared at the letter in his hand, and then slowly reread it. It was dated two days ago. Too late. Far too late.

Maxwell Hume had been a captain of artillery whom Rutledge had come to know well at the start of the war. A career man, he was an experienced and able officer, liked by his troops and his superiors. Early in the war, the two men had shared their first leave, staying in a shell of a château, unable to find transportation to Paris or London—five days where their friendship had been cemented with laughter and more than a little wine salvaged from the destroyed cellars. The time had passed quickly, both men still able to see in the other an odd reflection of himself as he was before the war. And yet they had been as different as night and day. Max had possessed a mad sense of humor—"All artillerymen are mad. Just look at Napoleon"— while Rutledge had been blessed with a level head that kept both of them from breaking their necks in Max's impromptu dares amongst the chimney pots or on the half-missing stair-case or wherever else his wild fancy took them.

They had convinced an elderly woman from the nearest village to cook for them and do their washing, closed their eyes to the minor pilfering that went with her, and dug through the ruins of a once-fine library to pass their evenings reading. It was the only time in all the war that Rutledge had been able to put aside what he had seen and done and felt. The certainty that the fighting would be over in the first year still blinded men, even when they began to realize it wasn't true. And then came the Somme, and madness on a level that was intolerable.

Rutledge had always suspected that it was Max Hume's guns that had fallen short and taken out his own salient the night that Hamish MacLeod had gone before the hastily collected firing squad. But he had never said anything about it when next they met. Hume, like Rutledge himself, was a changed man by that time, terse and fallible and near to breaking. Some things were better left unsaid.

And yet, he thought in some fashion that Max knew the truth, and that it was the last straw in what had been a fine career.

Setting the letter aside, Rutledge went to the cabinet beneath the other window and poured himself a drink.

He silently toasted Hume, and then went to his bed-room to pack. Rosemary would need him now, and he had no choice but to go and do what he could.

"Aye." Hamish was there in his mind, as he always was in times of upheaval or stress. "But will the lass want you there?"

The viewpoint was unexpected. Rutledge heard himself saying aloud, "I was Max's friend. It's the least I can do."

"Aye. All the same, ye'll remind her of the war. And she'll no' thank ye for that."

Half an hour later, having told the Yard where to find him, he had set out for Gloucestershire and Hume's home just over the border.

It was late when he got there, and he found lodg-ing in the small hotel that stood on the main street of the town. He had hoped to arrive in time to speak to Rosemary that evening, but the drive had taken longer than he'd anticipated.

He had never been to Chaswell. It was a pretty little town, and Max had spoken of it often, but after the war neither man was fit for casual visits, although they had stayed in touch desultorily by letter.

The next morning, he went to Hume's house. It was set back from the road, a low wall surrounding the front garden and two steps leading to the grassy walk up to the door.

Before he'd lifted the crepe-hung knocker, the door opened, and Rosemary Hume stood on the threshold, staring up at him with haunted eyes. Rutledge said, "I've come to do what I can."

She flung herself into his arms and wept on his shoulder. It was the only time he was to see her cry. Pulling away at last, she wiped angrily at her tears before he could offer her his handkerchief. In the background he could hear voices, but she pulled the door closed behind her, to shut them away, and said, "He shot himself. He went to the far side of the churchyard, and shot himself, where I wouldn't be the first to see him. And when they came to tell me that he was dead, I wanted to take up that revolver and shoot him again. The fool. The poor, wretched, damned fool."

"He wrote to me. But by the time the letter came, it was too late."

"He left only a brief message for me. He told me he loved me too much to drag me down into his despair, and he asked my forgiveness. That was all," Rosemary told Rutledge. "After what we'd endured together, what we had tried to salvage out of his despondency, all he could leave me were a few dozen words. I deserved more, Ian, I deserved to know what he was planning and why. I could have accepted it then, hard as it would be, because I was included. But I was shut out." She was a small, slim woman with fair hair and very dark blue eyes. There were heavy circles under them, now, with grim lines about her mouth.

Rutledge, who had broken such news to other people more often than he could count, said, "Rosemary. It's natural to be angry with Max. All the same, I don't think he could have borne telling you that he'd failed. That's how he had seen it, his failure. And so it was a private matter because of that."

"You've been a policeman too long, Ian," she answered him coldly. "I was his wife, for God's sake. What does it say in the Bible? Something about a man and a woman cleaving together? And in the marriage vows? Forsaking all others? I shall never forgive him. Until the day I die, I shall never forgive him."

She swung the door open at that juncture, and led him inside.

Hamish reminded him, "Ye didna' believe me . . ."

Rutledge tried to ignore him as he walked into the room where friends and family had gathered. There were twelve to fifteen people sitting and standing, talking together quietly. Rosemary made the introductions, although Rutledge knew several of the former Army officers. Her parents were there, but Max's parents had died during the war, leaving only a distant cousin who had been gassed at Ypres. He was sitting in a chair by the double windows that led to the gardens, struggling to breathe and talk, finally falling silent, his face strained.

Rutledge hadn't met Reginald Hume before this, and as they shook hands, he remembered Max saying something about his cousin having been schooled in England, although he'd returned to Scotland to live.

"Inherited the family pile on the Isle of Skye, filled it with books, and prefers them to people. That's why he didn't come south for my wedding. I shan't be surprised if he misses my funeral as well." It had been said in jest.

There were voices in the kitchen, where food was being collected as friends and neighbors brought dishes along with their sympathy.

The day dragged on, and at one point, Rutledge found himself speaking to the rector of St. Paul's, Chaswell's church.

"Scotland Yard, are you?" Mr. Gramling asked. When Rutledge nodded, he went on, "I understand you are here in your capacity as a friend, not as a policeman? Good. Then you'll be pleased to hear that I've determined that Captain Hume died while his mind was overcome by his suffering. Wounds take many forms," he said to Rutledge with a perfectly straight face. "I see no reason why he may not be buried in holy ground."

"I'm glad to hear it," Rutledge responded. It was something that had been on his mind most of the afternoon. There would of course be an inquest. Someone else had brought that up. But he had hoped for Rosemary's sake that it would be reasonably considerate of her feelings. "I hope that I shan't be required to give evidence." Hume's letter was still in his pocket. He had no intention of reading it aloud at an inquest.

"I see no reason to impose on your personal grief," Mr. Gramling agreed, understanding Rutledge's unspoken message. "He regularly attended services with his wife, even when he couldn't hear what was being said. I could consider that a proof, if we need it, that he was sound of mind and spirit. Mr. Hume did not fail in his duty to the church, and the church will not fail in its duty to him."

"I consider that very enlightened of you," he said, and Gramling smiled.

He was a short, stout man with heavy shoulders. Just beginning to gray, he had deep-set dark eyes under thick eyebrows, lending him a sinister look until he smiled. "I don't hold with judging my flock. I see no reason to usurp God's right." He paused, then added, "Max and I spoke from time to time. Often on a tablet of paper I kept in my desk. I burned the sheets afterward. I considered him a friend."

They stood there talking about the war and the past, and then Rosemary called to Rutledge, asking him to help Reginald up the stairs to lie down for a while.

He was a pale shadow of his cousin. Thinner, fairer, his features less well defined because of his suffering. Each breath was a testament to his will to live. If asked, Rutledge would have thought that Reginald was the more likely of the two men to end his own life. But there was a tenacity in his face that gave it its intense character. He thanked Rutledge as he sank back against his pillows. "I came for Rosemary's sake," he managed to say. "Not for Max's. He told me he would not expect to see me at his graveside."

"Rosemary will need your strength."

"I've loved her as long as I've known her," Reginald said. "Max was aware of that. He knew I would have come for her sake if not his."

"Rest, while you can," Rutledge said. "I'll see that she's all right."

He left the room, the sound of Reginald's raucous breathing following him even after he had pulled the door closed behind him. On the stairs he found Rosemary sitting on one of the treads, out of sight on the landing. He thought she was crying, but she was simply sitting there, quietly staring into space. She turned as she heard his footsteps, and said, "Is he all right?"

"He's resting. It's for the best."

She nodded. "He got a letter too."

"Did he?" He had said as much, but Rutledge hadn't asked him the contents.

"Everyone but me."

She stood up resolutely and walked down the stairs without looking back.

The funeral the next day was well attended, although most of the people there had known Rosemary Hume most of her life, and Max Hume only for the past eight years, four of them interrupted by war. Rutledge was glad to see that she would have support after he had left. The service was simple, stressing the qualities of the man they were gathered to bury. And then it was time to follow the wooden coffin to its final resting place.

Rutledge watched it being lowered gently into the ground, and as he took up a handful of earth to cast into the grave in his turn, Hamish said, "It willna' be you, lying here. It's no' the answer."

But it had been in his mind, and Hamish knew it.

No. Not yet, he silently answered as the earth spilled from his fingers to land softly on the coffin lid. And then he was following Rosemary and Reginald Hume back through the churchyard, to where his motorcar was ready to carry them to the house.

A police constable stood by the bonnet, and he nodded to Rutledge as he came through the gates of the churchyard. Rosemary was settling Reginald in his seat, trying to save his energy for the meal already waiting at the house. She looked up to say something to Rutledge just as the constable stepped forward.

"Inspector Rutledge?"

"Yes, I'm Rutledge."

"A message from Scotland Yard, sir. Will you proceed with haste to Sussex. The village of Eastfield, just above Hastings. It's a matter of some urgency."

Rutledge glanced at Rosemary Hume. "I'll see my friends home first," he said. The inquest was that afternoon. Rosemary had asked for it to wait until after the funeral. He knew she expected him to be present.

She said, tentatively, "Ian?"

"I'll put in a call to the Yard. This may not be as urgent as it appears."

She shook her head. "It's better if you go."

Surprised, Rutledge said, "But I thought—" and broke off.

"I have my family now, and my friends. I don't need Max any longer. I don't need Max's friends."

He was on the point of arguing when he caught Reginald's eye. There was a warning there.

After a moment Rutledge said, "Yes, I understand. But you know how to find me if you should change your mind."

"I won't," she said with finality. And when he had delivered his passengers at the Hume house, Rosemary offered him her hand as he stood ready to help her out of the motorcar. "Thank you for coming, Ian. It was very kind of you. Maxwell loved you in his way. I think because you understood better than the rest of us. Thank you for that, as well."

And she turned to offer her support to Reginald, her back to Rutledge.

Reginald's face was expressionless. But as he shook Rutledge's hand, he said, "I'm glad you were here. Keep in touch, will you? I have a feeling about things sometimes. I'd like to hear from you."

Rosemary had gone ahead to open the house door and was out of earshot as Reginald spoke the last words. And then she was back, taking his arm as she steadied him on the short walk to the house.

Rutledge saw them inside, and then turned to drive to the police station.

But the constable—his name was Becker—had no more information than the brief message he had passed on to Rutledge.

"The hotel sent someone to find me," he explained. "It was a Sergeant Gibson on the line. I asked him if there was any further information to pass on to you, but he said that someone in Eastfield would explain all you needed to know. I was to tell you privately that the Chief Superintendent had not been at the Yard when the message from Eastfield had come through. And it was too urgent to await his return."

Rutledge said, "My things are at the hotel. I'll be packed and ready to leave in ten minutes."

"I've taken the liberty, sir, to ask Samantha if she will put up sandwiches for you. It's a long way. There will be a bottle of cider as well."

Rutledge thanked him. And in fewer than the ten minutes he was on his way, the sandwiches in a small basket beside him. It was necessary to drive past the Hume house on his way out of town. The windows were open to the summer heat, and through them he could see silhouettes of people moving back and forth inside.

He felt a surge of something, he couldn't have said what, and then returned his attention to the road.

And all the long way, Hamish kept him company, his voice just audible above the rushing of the wind. But it was not a pleasant companionship. As often happened in times when Rutledge's mind was occupied, the voice found the chinks in Rutledge's armor and probed them with a sure knowledge of what Rutledge least wished to hear.

It dwelt for a time on Max's life and then the manner of his death, moving on to the woman who swore she hated her husband, but who had wept, bereft, on Rutledge's shoulder before she could get herself in hand.

At one point as he drove eastward, Rutledge had stopped along a road in Hampshire to offer a lift to a woman trudging back to her village with her marketing in a basket. He had needed to hear a human voice, someone who knew nothing of him or his past. She was grateful for his kindness, and he set her down in front of her cottage without telling her how she had briefly lightened the darkness in his mind.

It was as if Hume's death by his own hand had foreshadowed his own.

5

Rutledge spent the night on the road, driving into Eastfield in the early hours of the next morning. A watery sun had risen, and he could see that there had been a heavy rain in the overnight hours. Puddles stood about in spots, and a pair of farmyard geese were noisily bathing in what appeared to be an old horse trough, filled now with rainwater.

He found the police station halfway down the high street, tucked into a small building between an ironmonger's and a milliner's shop. He left his motorcar on the street, and went inside.

The constable sitting at the desk across from the door looked up, his attention sharp and questioning, as if dreading to hear what this new arrival had to say.

The look of a man, Hamish was noting, who expected more trouble than he was prepared to deal with.

Rutledge gave his name and added, "Scotland Yard."
The constable's expression changed to intense relief.

"Constable Walker, sir. I wasn't expecting you, sir,
not for another hour or more," he responded, coming
around the desk to meet him. "The Yard told us you
were in Gloucestershire and hoped to leave shortly.
You made good time." A wry grin spread across
the man's plain face. "I'm more than happy to turn
this inquiry over to you. In all my experience I've
seen nothing like it. Nor has Inspector Norman, in
Hastings, I'll be bound. A shocking business. We never
expected one murder, sir, much less three. Sergeant
Gibson told us he was sending one of the Yard's most
experienced men. Whatever I can do to help, you can
count on me, sir."

Rutledge was surprised to hear Gibson singing his
praises. He found himself wondering why. They had
always had a guarded relationship, drawn together
more because of their mutual dislike of Chief Superintendent Bowles than because of any friendship between
them.

"Thank you, Constable," Rutledge began, hoping to
cut short Walker's effusive welcome, but the man was
already moving past him to the door.

"If you'll just follow me, sir? I promised to take you to Mr. Pierce as soon as you arrived. He'll tell you what you need to know. His son was the third victim."

"I don't think it's wise to speak to Mr. Pierce until you've given me a picture of what's happened, why I'm here." Rutledge followed him as far as his motorcar and stopped there, facing Walker.

The man turned to him, uncertain. "They didn't tell you anything at the Yard? But I explained to the sergeant I spoke with—"

"That may well be. But as you say, I was in Gloucestershire, and I was ordered to come here directly."

Walker stared at him. "I thought—" He recovered quickly and said, "It was Mr. Pierce who asked the Chief Constable if he would bring in the Yard. The Hastings police wanted to take over the inquiry, you see, and Mr. Pierce felt they wouldn't address his son's death as he would have wanted it done. It was cold-blooded murder, sir. It has turned Eastfield on its ear. Three men in nine days. All three of them garroted, and no sign of the murder weapon. William Jeffers, then Jimmy Roper three nights later, and three nights after that, Anthony Pierce. A farmer, a dairyman, the son of a brewer. One walking home, minding his own business and left dead in the road. One sitting with a sick cow in his own barn. And one at the brewery looking to repair a faulty gauge." He went on earnestly, "Who is killing these men? How does he know where to find them alone? And why these three? Worst of all, who is next? Me? My neighbor's son? The man who hires out for harvesting crops?"

Rutledge had listened closely, a frown on his face.

"Three dead. And no apparent connection among them? Except that they were alone at the time of their murder? And killed with the same type of weapon?"

"Well, there's the war, sir," Walker admitted. "And they're of an age, having fought in France together. Please, if you will, sir, speak to Mr. Pierce."

Rutledge agreed, although with reluctance. It was not usual to have a civilian passing on the details of an inquiry. But he could see, from Walker's anxious face, that Pierce was a man to be reckoned with in Eastfield, and until he knew just exactly what he was dealing with, it might be as well to see what Pierce had to say.

Leaving the motorcar where it was, they walked to Drum Street and the tall, mellowed brick facade of the brewery buildings. A large gold arrow had been affixed to the front of the main building under the name PIERCE BROTHERS, and Rutledge realized that this was the beer famous in three counties for its Rose of Picardy label.

They found the senior Pierce in his office, an old-fashioned but elegantly styled room in oak, with paintings of the founders on the walls and a large marble hearth that held pride of place to one side of the partners' desk by the windows.

A tall man stood up as Rutledge and Walker were admitted by an elderly clerk.

Scanning Rutledge's face, he came forward and said to Walker, "Good morning, Constable."

"This is Inspector Rutledge, Mr. Pierce. From Scotland Yard, as you requested."

Pierce held out his hand, and Rutledge shook it, saying, "I'm told you would prefer to tell me what's been happening here in Eastfield." He had kept his voice neutral, neither accepting Pierce's authority to do any such thing, nor disputing it.

Pierce led them to the chairs set out before the empty hearth. "I apologize for that, Mr. Rutledge. Constable Walker here has handled events so far with his usual skill, and I am grateful for that. It's just that I have a very personal stake in finding this madman. Two days ago my own son was his third victim. That doesn't make Anthony any more important than the other two victims, but William Jeffers's wife and Jimmy Roper's father aren't able to speak for themselves at this time. Their loss was as devastating as mine, but they are alone in their grief, and I have a staff at my disposal to see me through the next few weeks."

"I understand," Rutledge answered, without committing himself. Pierce was a man used to giving orders, and it was possible that Mrs. Jeffers and Jimmy Roper's father were grateful that he was taking charge.

Clearing his throat, as if to dispose of all emotion before he began, Pierce said, "The first Constable Walker, here, knew of Jeffers's death was sometime after midnight when a goods van, driven by one Sammy Black, came through Eastfield on his way to Hastings. He'd had a problem with his van and was several hours late as it was. Soon after passing the church, he saw something in the middle of the road. To use his own words, he said that it looked like a bundle of old rags lost off a dustman's cart. But he slowed, because there wasn't sufficient room to pass on either side, and he was wary about driving straight over the rags. He'd served as a driver in the war and was accustomed to watching out for unexploded ordnance in his path. By that time his headlamps had reached the bundle and he could see it more clearly. He realized it was someone lying in the road, and he stopped to see if it was a drunkard or if the man had been struck by another vehicle.

"He got out of his van, and walked over to what lay in the road, getting in the way of his own headlamps and having to step aside. Now he had no doubt the man was dead. His eyes were open, and there was a great deal of blood around his neck. At first Black believed that the man had cut his own throat. Unwilling to leave him there, Black finally decided to protect his body by leaving the van in the road, and he walked back into Eastfield to find the police station."

He turned to Constable Walker. "Have I got that right, Constable?"

"Yes, sir. It's exactly what he'd written in the statement he signed."

"Then perhaps you'd like to take up the account at this point."

"I sometimes sleep on a cot in the room above the station, Mr. Rutledge, my wife being dead for some years. I heard Mr. Black banging on the door, as I had only just gone to bed. I opened the window and called out to him, asking what the problem might be. He told me he'd just discovered a dead man in the road and would I come at once? I asked if he was certain the man was dead. He told me he'd seen enough dead men in the war, and he was certain. All the same, I took the time to summon Dr. Gooding, and he brought his trap with him, in the event we needed it. We reached the body, and Mr. Black drew his van to one side. Both Dr. Gooding and I had brought a lamp with us, and we could see fairly clearly. Mr. Black was right, the man was dead, and as the light reached his face, both of us recognized him at the same time. Dr. Gooding leaned closer, and then straightened up, looking up at me. 'He's been garroted,' he said, shock in his voice, and I bent over to see for myself. It was the only explanation—the wire had cut deep and yet it was clear from Jeffers's face that he had been strangled. Mr. Black at this point had gone back to his van, and I believe he was sick by some bushes along the verge. Knowing that this was a heavily traveled route from about four o'clock in the morning until first light, we cast about to see if we could find anything of importance. Dr. Gooding in particular wanted to find the ligature that had been used. But there was nothing to find. Just the body in the middle of the road. The doctor did say that Mr. Jeffers had been dead for some time, an hour or more at a guess."

His account had been vivid, where Pierce's had been factual, without personal feelings coloring it. But Rutledge could see that Walker, whose quiet village must seldom produce violence of any kind, had been appalled by the brutality of Jeffers's death.

"Dr. Gooding had brought a blanket, and we wrapped the body in it and I helped to set it in the cart. I drove back with Mr. Black, and the doctor took the body to his surgery. Mr. Black gave me his statement, and I found that Mrs. Sanders, across from the hotel, had spent a restless night and had seen the goods van come down the street just when Mr. Black had said it came, and it was very likely that his statement of finding the body when he did was true. I went back to the scene later and still found nothing that would tell me who or why murder had been committed."

Walker paused. Rutledge thought that if the constable had been in his own office he would have got to his feet and begun to pace. There was more on his mind than the death, and Rutledge waited patiently to hear the rest of the story.

"Dr. Gooding came to see me at half past ten," Walker went on reluctantly. "He asked me to come with him to the surgery. I found that he'd removed the victim's clothing, and it was obvious that he had been garroted, although neither Dr. Gooding nor I had ever seen a case before. But that was not what he wanted me to see. He had probed the mouth of the victim and found that inside it, almost dried to his tongue, was an identity disc."

Rutledge turned to stare at him. "From the war?" he asked in surprise.

"Yes, sir. From the war. I recognized it. But it wasn't Mr. Jeffers's disc, if he ever had one. There was another name on it. One I didn't know—" He reached into his pocket and brought out an oiled cloth, setting it on the low table in front of the hearth before unwrapping it.

Inside were three flat fiberboard discs. In the war, both the Army and soldiers themselves had come up with ways to identify the dead and wounded, but none of them had been successful enough to see widespread use. Some men had simply sewn their names in their uniforms, a time-honored method. A variety of discs had been introduced as well, some on string, some on thin rope. These particular discs had an interesting history.

Stamped from thin layers of compressed wood fibers, they came in pairs and were worn around the neck on a thin length of rope. If a man was killed, one of the discs was placed in his mouth for the burial detail to use in marking his grave. The other of the pair was collected and sent back with his kit, eventually ending up with his family.

But the war had been over for nearly two years. Why would such a disc be placed in the mouth of a murder victim?

Hamish, who had been quiet for a time, said quite clearly, "Revenge."

Rutledge suppressed a start, for it seemed that the soft Scots voice had echoed around the room, obvious to everyone. But when neither of the other men responded to it, he said after a moment, "There are three discs here."

"One was also found in the mouth of Jimmy Roper, who was sitting with a cow suffering from colic when he was killed. There was no one else in the barn, no sign of forced entry, and no one in the house—Roper's father or the maid who kept house and cooked for the two men—had heard anything," Pierce answered. "As for my son, he was discovered on the ground floor of the brewery, just by the stairs. Dr. Gooding examined his mouth there and then, and found the third one." Rutledge could hear the undercurrent of rage in the quiet voice.

Rutledge looked closely at the names on the discs. One belonged to a corporal in a Yorkshire regiment, the second to a Welsh sapper, and the third to a private from Cheshire. Turning to Pierce, he asked, "Was your son an officer?"

"Yes, of course."

"Officers weren't issued identity discs," he pointed out. "I wonder if these men survived the war?" He shook his head. "Three different regiments. What could these three soldiers have had in common with three men living quietly here in Sussex?"

"That's precisely why I asked the Yard to step in. We need to learn what we can about these soldiers if we're to answer the question. I'm sure you must know someone in the War Office who can find out for us. Where they served, and if their paths ever crossed."

Rutledge did know such a man but had no intention of applying to him for answers. But Sergeant Gibson would have his own way of looking into the matter.

"Tell me about their war records—Jeffers's, Roper's, and your son's. Were they ever involved in any trouble during the fighting? Discipline, misconduct, brawling?"

"Nothing of the kind," Pierce retorted curtly. "They all served honorably. My son was an officer in the same regiment as a company of men who enlisted together from Eastfield, but he never commanded them. As it happened, they were in two different sectors of the Front."

"Their paths never crossed?"

"I can't say never with complete certainty, but I don't recall my son ever speaking of encountering them. He'd have said something in his letters, asking me to relay the message to their families. He was that sort, thoughtful and responsible. There are others of that same company still alive, we could ask them."

"Two of the company died in France," Walker added. "One missing. And the rest came home."

It was not the case generally. Men who served together as a rule died together. The Eastfield Company had been very lucky.

Rutledge turned back to the discs. What were they intended to represent? Hamish had called it revenge, but how? Why?

Pierce was saying, "I know regiments were split up—sometimes sent to bring up the strength of other regiments. But it seems unlikely that there's a military connection. Still, these discs say otherwise."

Rutledge turned to Walker. "Was there any trouble among these local men? Have you heard any rumors of hard feelings, of unsettled issues?"

"I have not," Walker said with confidence. "My own nephew served with them." And then his attention was focused on Rutledge. "My God. Are you suggesting that the killing hasn't stopped? Should I be warning my nephew and the others that they could be in danger as well?"

"If these murders have to do with the Eastfield Company, then why did my son have to die?" Pierce demanded, almost cutting across the constable's question.

"I can't tell you the reason for that. Not yet," Rutledge answered him, and then to Walker, he added, "It will do no harm to have a word with these men. But if the killer is a local man, why the identity discs belonging to these outsiders?" He paused, weighing the discs in his hand, then asked, "Was the Eastfield Company—or your son, sir—ever on burial detail?"

Pierce shook his head. "I'm sure Anthony wasn't."

"I don't believe so," Walker answered. "But I'll ask. Are you saying that's where these other discs came from?"

"It's possible. But we won't know until we find out who these men are. And why their names are connected with three murders here."

"I'd rather believe it was one of them than one of ours," Walker said.

Pierce took a deep breath. "I don't care who it is. I want it stopped. I want this murderer brought to justice."

"Then why did you refuse to let the Hastings police step in?" Rutledge asked.

"Ah, that. I've had words with Inspector Norman in the past. Oh, not over anything of this nature, not murder. But my younger son, Danny, was troublesome in his day, and Inspector Norman wanted him clapped up in prison until he'd learned the errors of his ways. I refused to let Norman bully me or my son. And in the end, Danny won a medal for bravery, presented by the King himself, at Buckingham Palace. The same arrogance, as Norman called it when Danny was fourteen, saved the lives of dozens of men. Danny charged a machine gun nest single-handedly, and held the German detail at gunpoint until he could be relieved. They were taken prisoner. If he hadn't stopped them from firing, God knows how many of our men would have been killed."

"Where is Daniel now?" Rutledge asked.

Pierce flushed. "I don't know. He came back from the war, spent two weeks with us here in Eastfield, and then disappeared one night. We haven't heard from him since. I blame Inspector Norman there. Not two days after Danny came home, Norman was on my doorstep wanting to know if Danny had been part of a group of men who had robbed the owners of a small hotel and their dinner guests. He claimed that the description of one of them could have fit Danny quite easily."

"Did your son have an alibi?"

The flush deepened. "He didn't need one. His word was good enough."

But once a troublemaker, always a troublemaker, in the eyes of the police.

Walker stirred uneasily, as if he'd been caught in the crossfire between Pierce and the Hastings police.

Dropping the subject of Daniel Pierce, at least for the moment, Rutledge asked who had found the bodies of the other two victims.

Walker said, "It was the housekeeper at the Roper farm. She thought Jimmy might still be sitting with Dandelion. Instead she found his body just outside the stall. And young Mr. Pierce was discovered by the foreman, coming in to work the next morning. He thought the killer might still be in the brew house, and sent his men to search, armed with whatever weapons they could lay hands to, while he stayed with the body and one of the other men came for me."

"But there was no sign of an intruder."

"No, sir. Whoever he was, he hadn't broken in."

"Who survives Jeffers and Roper?"

"Mrs. Jeffers, his wife. And Roper's father—he's old, frail."

Rutledge turned to Pierce. "Your son Anthony wasn't married?"

"The young woman he would have married at the end of the war died in the Spanish flu epidemic in 1918. Of late, Anthony had been friends with Mrs. Farrell-Smith. She's head mistress at the Misses Tate School. It's a well-established institution here in Eastfield. A good many people from outside the village—Battle, Hastings, as far away as Rye—send their children here. Anthony attended it himself until he was twelve. The Tate sisters were still alive then."

"Have you seen any strangers here in Eastfield? Has anyone asked for Jeffers, Roper, or Pierce?"

"I spoke to any number of people—in the hotel, the shops, the pubs, the restaurants," Walker said, shaking his head. "And there hasn't been anyone here that we didn't know. And that's what's most worrisome. I'd always thought of a garrote as being a French weapon. But the only Frenchman in Eastfield is in the churchyard, and he's been there these thirty years and more."

Ten minutes later, when Rutledge and Constable Walker had taken their leave of Pierce, Rutledge waited until they were well out of earshot of the brewery and any of its workers before asking, "What do you think became of Daniel Pierce?"

"Daniel?" Walker repeated, and then looked away. "I don't know. He just—left. In the middle of the night. If you want to know what I think, he didn't wish to be a burden on his father. The Pierces have enjoyed a fine reputation all through the years. And Anthony was a good man, best suited to being the heir in temperament. Not one to carouse and come home drunk in the middle of the night, singing bawdy songs as he walked down the street."

"Pierce seems to believe his son changed."

"Yes, well, a father would, wouldn't he? But I've made inquiries from time to time—on my own, sir, not officially. And there's been no word of him in the towns where I know the police. So perhaps he has."

"Why should you search for him?" Rutledge asked, his curiosity aroused.

Walker flushed, the question catching him unprepared. After a moment he said, "I've always had a soft spot for young Daniel, sir. I was not my father's favorite child either."

And yet Rutledge had gathered the impression that Daniel *was* his father's favorite. Something in the timbre of his voice had betrayed the elder Pierce. "Still, the question that has to be asked is, was he jealous enough of his brother that in the end, he would kill two innocent men in order to cover his tracks when he killed Anthony Pierce?"

Walker sighed. "I don't think Daniel was the sort to want to be tied to a brewery for the rest of his life. I wouldn't have been surprised if he'd made a career of the Army. I remember how excited he was just before the war about Shackleton's journey to the Antarctic, and how pleased he was that the King encouraged Shackleton to go on with his plans even after war was declared." Changing the subject without appearing to, he pointed toward an ornate four-story building ahead.

"That's The Fisherman's Arms Hotel. A little grand to call it that, but it's comfortable. They're keeping a room for you. I took the liberty of asking them, after I was told the Yard was sending someone to Eastfield."

Rutledge thanked him. "I'll go and register. But as soon as possible I want to see the statements you've collected thus far, and then speak to Dr. Gooding."

"It's best to catch the doctor after his midday meal. One o'clock? Will that suit you?"

"Yes, I'll come for you then," Rutledge answered as they reached his motorcar. Walker turned the crank for him, and he drove on to the hotel. There was space to park in the small yard to the far side, and the woman at the desk smiled when he gave his name.

"We've been expecting you, Mr. Rutledge," she said, as if he were a valued guest and not a policeman in their midst. He rather thought that Pierce's name had been used to secure a better choice of room.

Hamish said as Rutledge climbed the stairs to the second floor, "Ye ken, Mr. Pierce doesna' want the Hastings police called in for fear they'll look for his ither son."

"Yes, that's very likely," Rutledge agreed. "Scotland Yard has no prejudices."

The room faced the street rather than the yard, and it was large, airy, and comfortable. Rutledge set his valise in the wardrobe and went to the pitcher of cool water on the stand between the windows, where he washed his hands. As he was reaching for a towel to dry them, he heard a commotion in the street and looked out to see what was happening.

Constable Walker was speaking to an elderly man crippled by arthritis, leaning heavily on his cane. He looked tired, distraught, and very angry.

The man was repeating at the top of his lungs, "I want him buried, do you hear? Decently, next to his mother, where he belongs. I don't care what the police have to say about it, I want my son."

Walker tried to placate him, but there was nothing he could say that would satisfy the old man.

Hamish said, "Roper's father."

Very likely, Rutledge thought. Walker had described him as old and frail.

Pushing away from the window, Rutledge hurried out of the room and down the stairs. When he reached the street, Walker was still patiently trying to persuade the elder Roper to return to his farm.

Rutledge walked up to them, introduced himself to Roper, and with a nod to Walker, said, "I'm here from Scotland Yard. In fact I only arrived this morning. If you will give me three days, I'll see that your son's body is released to you. But I want to be sure that

I know everything I need to know in order to find his murderer. Will you give me those three days?"

Roper turned to him, his eyes wet with tears. "Three days, you say?"

"Three days," Rutledge acknowledged.

"That's reasonable." Roper turned to go, finally satisfied.

Rutledge stopped him. "Did your son have any enemies, do you know? Someone who was jealous of him, who held a grudge of some sort, or had quarreled with him recently?"

Roper laughed, a harsh and breathless sound. "Jimmy had his hands full at the farm and caring for me. There was no time for jealousy or grudges or quarrels. Whoever it was should have killed me—I'm past being useful. But no, it was Jimmy was taken. Even the Germans had spared him, except for his damaged leg. I told him when he came home that he could give them the damned leg, it was his hands and his brain the farm needed. He was unhappy, then, moping about for weeks. I had to tell him, didn't I, that the leg was of no account? And to his credit, he came to his senses and set about making the farm pay again. And we'd have done it too, if he hadn't been killed! We'd have seen our way clear in another year, turned a profit even. That's gone with Jimmy, and I've put a father's curse on whoever killed him. I hope he suffers as I've suffered, and knows the fires of hell before ever he gets there." He gripped his cane fiercely, as if he could see himself bringing it down on the head of his son's murderer. But the outburst had exacted its toll, and Roper's face was drawn with the effort it had required.

"How did you get here?" Rutledge asked, taking note of that.

"I walked. No one would come and tell me what was happening."

Walker said, his eyes meeting Rutledge's over the stooped man's head, "It's no little distance to the farm."

Rutledge said, "My motorcar is just there, in the hotel yard. Drive him home."

"I'll do that, sir. Thank you." Walker touched Roper's arm. "This way, if you please, sir."

It was easy to see that Roper was torn between maintaining his dignity and allowing himself to be driven. After a moment, his aching bones made the decision for him. "I'd take that as a favor," he answered and let Walker lead him to where Rutledge had left his motorcar.

Rutledge watched him go.

It was easier for a policeman to consider the victim as another case until he met the family and friends of the deceased and began to learn to see the dead through their eyes. It was always a turning point. And now he had met first Pierce and then Roper.

It had also served to emphasize the difference in status between the first two victims—farmers both—and Anthony Pierce, the son of a man of position and wealth. What's more, one was married, two were not. What did those three have in common? The war? But two had served together and one had not. Was it the fact that all three had survived? But according to Walker, so had a number of others. Including his nephew.

What linked these three men?

Hamish said, "Yon identity discs in their mouths."

6

Rutledge had eaten his meal and was finishing his tea when Walker came to take him to meet Dr. Gooding.

The doctor's surgery was within walking distance, a rambling house that had been divided into two halves, one for his practice and the other for his living quarters.

Three women were just leaving the surgery as the two men opened the gate and started up the flag-stoned walk leading between borders in which flowers were blooming profusely. They noticed the man with Constable Walker straightaway, and Rutledge could all but hear the speculation racing through their minds. He could also imagine their conversation as soon as they were out of earshot.

Walker said, "The tallest of those women was married to one of the Eastfield Company that marched off together to fight the Kaiser. Mrs. Watson. Her husband was killed in the third week of the fighting after they reached the Front." He opened the surgery door for Rutledge, and added, "The rest led charmed lives for nearly five months before George Hopkins bought it."

"Roper had a bad leg?"

"Machine gun. He could hardly walk when he came home, but you'd not have known it now. Barely a limp. Pierce lost his to gangrene from a foot wound. He wasn't fitted with a new limb until last year. It took that long for the stump to heal. Jeffers was shot in the chest but lived."

The surgery door led into a cramped waiting room, empty now. Dr. Gooding was coming out of his office and looked up as the two men entered.

"Good afternoon, Constable," he said to Walker. "I was just going through to my luncheon. We're running late today." He was a man of slender build, with a receding hairline and a strong jaw.

"This is Inspector Rutledge, sir. From Scotland Yard. He'd like to speak to you about the dead men."

Gooding cast a glance at the clock sitting on the mantelpiece but said, "Yes, of course."

He took them into his office and gestured to the chairs opposite his desk. Sitting down again, he reached for a sheaf of papers set to one side of the blotter, passing them to Rutledge. "These are my reports on the bodies. Constable Walker has copies."

Rutledge glanced through them. "All three men were garroted? And all three had the army discs in their mouths?"

"Yes, that's correct. To tell you the truth, I'd never seen a case of garroting before, but of course I had no difficulty in recognizing at once what had been done when I examined Jeffers. My guess is that something like piano wire must have been used. It was strong, strong enough to cut through the flesh of the throat in each case, causing bleeding. I should think a man wielded it. Jeffers was inebriated, but he would not have been easy to kill. And the same goes for Roper, despite his leg. A woman couldn't have held on to the garrote, given the struggles of the three men. It was well after dark when they were attacked. And each was in a place where his death wasn't likely to be witnessed. Jeffers along the road on the outskirts of Eastfield, Roper in his barn, and of course Pierce in the main brewery."

"Were they stalked, do you think?"

Gooding shook his head. "They weren't prepared. That wire came over their heads, and there was an end to it. If they had believed they were in any danger, they might have got a hand up in time to try to defend themselves. It wouldn't have changed the outcome, they might have lost a finger, or at least their hands would have been noticeably damaged. And this wasn't the case."

It was a very concise report. But then the doctor's luncheon was waiting.

Rutledge said, "Do you know of any particular connection among the victims? Or any trouble they may have had with anyone else in the village?"

"I'd say Roper and Jeffers knew each other better than either of them knew Anthony Pierce. As boys, all three of them attended our village grammar school together, but when the Pierce brothers were sent away to public school, my guess is that they very likely lost touch. As for trouble, Walker here can answer that better than I could. If you're asking if they came here, yes, from time to time, but never anything more than childhood ailments and the occasional scrapes and bruises from climbing trees or a rough game of football."

"After the war, was there any sort of hard feelings amongst the survivors of their company? Something that happened in France, perhaps, and not finished there?"

"If there was, they never came to me to patch them up." He hesitated. "Daniel—Daniel Pierce, that is— may have been the sole exception to that. Two days before he disappeared, I saw him in the street, and there was a bruise on his left cheek. He didn't mention it and neither did I. It didn't appear to be anything serious."

"I've heard he was something of a troublemaker when he was young." It wasn't precisely what Pierce had told Rutledge But he was interested in hearing Gooding's point of view.

"A troublemaker? That's a little harsh. Who told you that?" Gooding asked, frowning. "You don't suspect he has had anything to do with these murders!"

"How well did he know Roper and Jeffers?"

"Probably no better than Anthony did. I always had a feeling that his escapades were nothing more than an attempt to impress his brother and the others. The youngest trying to prove his mettle."

"What sort of escapades?" Rutledge pressed. He could sense that Walker was uncomfortable now, but he ignored him.

"He probably thought it was quite a lark, the things he got up to. One summer three or four boys dressed in sheets and moved about the churchyard one moonless night. They gave the sexton's wife and two young people courting in the church porch one hell of a fright. On Guy Fawkes night, they made their own bonfire—the old mill on the edge of town. It was a shambles anyway, no one lived there. They torched it. Still, it could have caused a general conflagration if the wind had blown the sparks about. There were demands that the ringleaders spend a night in jail. Cooler heads prevailed, and they were marched home under escort."

"These hardly seem to be boyish pranks to me."

Walker said, "I was here then. They weren't intending to do harm. On the other hand, the summer before the mill incident, there was a near drowning. The father of the boy in the witch's chair was asked if he wished to press charges, but his son wouldn't hear of it. He told me they'd drawn lots to see who would play the witch. They'd been reading about the Reformation in school. And the pond wasn't deep enough to drown the boy, but they hadn't accounted for his being tied to a chair and took fright when his head went under."

"Does this boy still live here in Eastfield?"

"Oh, no, sir," Walker answered. "He hasn't for these past fifteen years. His father was a bookkeeper at the furniture maker's, and as I remember, he found another position in Staffordshire, closer to his late wife's family."

Which brought him full circle to Daniel.

"Did Daniel serve with the rest of the Eastfield Company?"

"Like his brother, he qualified as an officer, and he chose to join the sappers."

Remembering what Walker had told him about Daniel's taste for adventure, that made perfect sense to Rutledge. It had been dangerous work, tunneling under German lines to lay charges. The miners were often buried alive when the powder went off prematurely or the tunnel supports failed, or they were killed going back inside to find out why the tunnel hadn't blown on schedule.

"Anything else you can tell me about the three men?" Rutledge asked.

"Jeffers was very drunk. He wasn't an habitual drinker, mind you. It was just his habit to mark the anniversary of his war wound by going to the pub and taking on as much beer as he could hold. He told me once how close he'd come to dying, and he couldn't quite put the fear of that behind him."

"Then all three of the dead men had been wounded in France."

"Yes, I've received copies of their medical records. Nothing suspicious there, if that's what you're asking me. I suspect the anniversary was not as important to the killer as the opportunity to catch Jeffers alone on a dark road."

Rutledge turned to Walker. "Did you ask at the pub, was there a stranger there that night? Or anyone who showed undue interest in Jeffers?"

"Only the regulars, as it happened. And everyone knew it was Jeffers's night to remember. They generally left him to it."

Dr. Gooding pointedly glanced at the clock again, and Rutledge thanked him for his time.

He left Walker at the police station after picking up copies of the statements the constable had taken prior to his arrival, and went back to the hotel to read them.

As he walked into Reception, the man behind the desk said, "Mr. Rutledge? You have a visitor, sir."

Surprised, Rutledge asked who it was.

But the clerk said only, "He's waiting in the room beyond the stairs."

Rutledge thanked him and went on to the door of the room used sometimes as a parlor for hotel guests or as a dining room for small private groups.

The man standing there, looking out a side window toward a small garden, turned as he heard Rutledge come in. He was tall and thin, with a long face and brown hair flecked with gray.

"Inspector Rutledge?" he asked, his eyes scanning Rutledge with intent interest. "I'm Inspector Norman, from Hastings."

They shook hands, and then Rutledge got to the point. "I've been sent here in your place. I hope you have no objections."

"Not really, although I'm not happy to have a murderer loose so close to Hastings. I hope your appearance on the scene doesn't drive him to greener pastures."

Rutledge smiled. "Indeed. Know anything about Eastfield that would be useful to an outsider coming in?"

"Only that it's never been a problem. The usual village troubles—a fight now and again, petty theft, neighbors upset over real or imagined trespass, domestic quarrels where someone is hurt. A lorry accident or two over the years. They're mostly peaceful, and Walker is a good man. He keeps his patch quiet. Still, all three men were in the war. And I wouldn't be surprised if that's your connection."

"There was an entire company from Eastfield. But Anthony Pierce wasn't one of them."

"No, I'd heard he asked not to be given charge of men he knew. Very wise of him, in my opinion. Harder to keep order and discipline if you grew up with your men."

"Or sometimes easier," Rutledge commented.

"There's that as well," Norman answered. "Still, it doesn't mean that this trouble didn't stem from the war. I expect Anthony Pierce kept an eye out for the Eastfield men. If there was something to hide, he'd have known it. Or someone thought he did. Otherwise, why put an ordinary soldier's identity disc in an officer's mouth?"

Which was a very good point.

Norman prepared to take his leave. "Just keep this bottled up in Eastfield," he said. "And if there's anything I can do, let me know."

With a nod, he walked past Rutledge and was gone.

Rutledge found himself thinking that Norman had wasted no time in coming here to look over the competition. He hadn't been in Eastfield more than a few hours. It occurred to him to wonder who had alerted Inspector Norman to his arrival.

Hamish said unexpectedly, "Someone who doesna' like yon Mr. Pierce's intervention."

Rutledge spent the next hour reading through the statements he'd been given, and they were all consistent with what he'd learned during the morning. Apparently no one had left the pub within half an hour of the time Jeffers walked out of it to his death. And no one in the Roper household had heard anything that would have indicated that someone had been prowling around the barn the night Roper was killed. The old dog on the floor by the bedside of the dead man's father had slept as soundly as his master, his hearing diminished by age.

"Going deaf as a post," the woman who cleaned and cooked for the two men had told Walker. "Both of them." But she herself had heard nothing.

As for the foreman who had discovered Anthony Pierce's body the next morning, he had written that he'd found the outer door shut and hadn't seen Pierce until he had come in and turned toward the stairs.

"Mr. Anthony had gone there to see to a broken gauge, because I found my tools had been moved when finally I went up the stairs to have a look at it again myself."

Which indicated, Rutledge thought, that Pierce had been killed on his way out of the brewery rather than on his way in. No one had been lying in wait for him, but it was likely that someone had followed him there and, finding the door unlocked, stepped inside.

He went out after finishing the statements and walked first to the place on the Hastings Road where the van driver had come upon the body of William Jeffers.

There was nothing to be seen here, but Rutledge had no trouble finding the spot from the description given by the driver.

Standing there on the quiet stretch of road, Rutledge looked around. There was a farmhouse some hundred yards away, but Walker—very thorough in his thinking—had interviewed the family living there. Unfortunately their bedroom windows were on the far side of the farmhouse, and they had not seen or heard anything. Except for tending to a child with a fever who had cried at half past three in the morning, they had slept soundly.

There were shrubs along the side of the road that marched toward the farmhouse lane, and pastures on the far side. The Jeffers house was beyond these, tall, spare, and jutting from the fields like a sore tooth.

"A perfect place for an ambush," Hamish remarked as Rutledge scanned the surrounding landscape.

Next he went to the Roper farm, walking down the lane past the house and to the barn where the murder had taken place. There was no one about, although clothes hung on the line, drying in the warm afternoon sun, and so Rutledge went inside the barn. There were bloodstains on the floor where Jimmy Roper had died, but any footprints that might have been there at the time of the murder had long since been lost as first the maid and then the elder Roper had walked round the body, and then the constable himself, followed by the doctor, not to mention whoever had led away the cow that had been in the now empty stall.

His next stop was the brewery, but before going there Rutledge paused at the hotel to ask where the nearest telephone was to be found.

He was told there was only one telephone in Eastfield, and that was in the office of Tyrell Pierce.

Making his way there again, Rutledge stopped briefly at the door that led into the two-story building where the great wooden kettles were housed, and opened it. The stairs were not ten feet from the door, leading upward into the richly scented heart of the building. Someone had conscientiously swabbed up Anthony Pierce's blood, but the location was marked by the very clean spot on the floorboards where abrasives had been necessary to reach deep into the stained wood.

Standing outside again, Rutledge considered the three murder scenes. All they had in common was their solitude at the time of the killings. But someone had followed each man to his death, and that meant someone had been in Eastfield on each occasion—whether he had been noticed by anyone or not.

Hamish said, "Aye, but he canna' materialize out of thin air. Where does he keep himsel' when he's no' prowling about in the dark?"

It would lead someone to believe that the killer lived in Eastfield . . .

Rutledge left the thought there and walked briskly toward the door leading to the brewery's office.

It was a busy room, bright and cluttered with paperwork, with some half dozen clerks dealing with orders for Arrow beers or placing orders for everything from hops to bottle labels, and there was no privacy at all.

The senior clerk, a man named Starret, led him to the telephone on his desk, then stepped away to let Rutledge use it.

He put through a call to London, and after a time was connected to the Yard. It was another five minutes before Sergeant Gibson was found.

"Yes, sir?" he answered warily.

"I'd like to find out what became of the following men after the war, and I'd like to know if there was anything particular in their records that might have an impact on the murders here in Sussex. Did their paths cross that of the Eastfield Company or of any individual in that company?"

He had written the three names, their ranks and regiments, in his notebook, taken from the discs that Dr. Gooding had retrieved during his examinations.

Gibson repeated them, and then said, "It will be a day or two. Shall I ring you at this number when I've learned anything?"

Rutledge told Gibson how to reach him, and then was on the point of hanging up when Gibson said, "There's been a complaint to the Chief Constable in regard to the Yard taking over this case."

"Indeed?" Rutledge asked in surprise.

"A Mrs. Farrell-Smith, sir."

He remembered the name. She was the woman Anthony Pierce had been seeing recently. But why would she complain to the Chief Constable? He asked Gibson that, careful to phrase his question in a fashion that half a dozen listening ears couldn't interpret and gossip about.

"I can't say, sir. Except that she appears to feel it was unnecessarily complicating matters."

Rutledge thanked him and hung up.

He thanked the clerk as well, and went out the way he'd come in. There was a private staircase to Pierce's office as well as a door leading into it from the clerks' room, and for a moment Rutledge debated speaking to Pierce. He changed his mind and went out into the street.

Constable Walker was surprised when Rutledge walked into the police station and asked directions to Mrs. Farrell-Smith's house.

"I didn't interview her—" he began in apology, but Rutledge cut him short

"She might know something that Anthony Pierce didn't tell his father. It's a long shot, but worth exploring."

"Shall I go with you, sir?" Walker asked, half rising from his chair.

"No. I don't want this to appear to be an official visit. Merely a matter of being thorough."

"I see," Walker said, but Rutledge thought he didn't.

The Misses Tate Latin School was at the head of Spencer Street. Two houses had been connected by an addition that closed the gap between them, apparently by someone who knew what he was about, because the results were pleasing, rather than haphazard. A central door had been let into the addition, but Walker had said that Mrs. Farrell-Smith had chosen to live in the smaller house to one side of the school, and that she could usually be found there at this hour of the day.

He went up the pair of steps leading to the walk and the door, and was let in by a young girl in a school uniform, her hair hanging down her back and held away from her face by a blue ribbon. She was quite pretty, and meticulously polite, asking him to wait in the hall while she inquired if Mrs. Farrell-Smith would receive him.

She disappeared through a door to the left of the staircase and returned with a smile, asking him to come in. He had wondered if Mrs. Farrell-Smith would speak to him, given her complaint to the Chief Constable.

The girl announced him, then went away, closing the door softly behind her.

The room had been turned into a private office, with bookshelves and chairs set in front of a lovely old desk of well-polished walnut. At the moment, it was cluttered with papers and folders, some of them held in place by a large, chipped glass paperweight, as if she had been recording marks or sorting files before the start of a new term.

The woman behind it rose as he came in. She was tall for a woman, and far prettier than she allowed herself to be. Her hair, pulled back into a bun at the nape of her neck, was fair and determined to wave in spite of attempts to keep it straight and tidy. Her eyes were a very dark blue, and her nose was straight above firm lips. He put her age at thirty.

"Inspector Rutledge," she said in acknowledgment of his presence, then waited for him to speak.

"I've come to ask you a few questions about Anthony Pierce," he said, and she seemed to find that surprising, because her eyebrows flew up in spite of her self-control.

"Please, be seated," she replied, and when he had taken one of the two chairs before the desk, she said, "What sort of questions?"

"I expect there were things he wouldn't have discussed with his father. But I was told he'd grown fond of you, and I thought perhaps he might have said something to you that could help the police find his killer."

"I don't think Anthony confided in me anything he couldn't have told his father." After a pause, when he didn't speak, she went on, as if unwilling to allow the silence to go on too long. "Are you saying he had secrets?"

"That's what I've come to ask."

"You believe that he knew where to find his brother. If he did, he never told me."

Rutledge was surprised in his turn. "Daniel?"

"Yes, Daniel. His father is too stubborn to try, but I expect he'd like to know where his other son is."

"I take it you don't care for Daniel."

"Not particularly. He's the sort of person who leaves responsibility to others. I believe in responsibility and self-discipline. I try to make certain that my students understand that these are virtues to cultivate. They will lead happier lives if they do."

It was an interesting perspective on duty.

Hamish interjected, "Aye, but is it the reason she's so set against yon brother?"

Rutledge said only, "How long have you been in charge of the school?"

"Since before the war," she answered, without giving a date. And then she added reluctantly, "It was after my husband died that I came here."

"You must have been very young to take over a school. It would have been a grave undertaking at any age."

She lifted her chin, as if in denial. "I didn't have any choice. And I have made every effort to live up to what my family established. I don't think I've given them any reason to regret their decision to entrust this school to my keeping."

He changed the subject. "Did your husband know Daniel Pierce?" It had been a general question, looking for an explanation for her dislike of the younger Pierce. But much to his surprise, it had struck home.

"I don't see that that's any of your business," she replied curtly.

"Which tells me that he did. Was it before you married him? Or after?"

"He was an older boy at the school where both Anthony and Daniel were sent."

"Then you didn't know them."

"No." Crisp and unconditional.

Rutledge considered her for a moment. She had married a man with a hyphenated name. As a schoolboy would he have despised the upstart—but well-to-do—Pierce brothers? Trade and old money often clashed. Or perhaps there had been very little old money. And the widowed Mrs. Farrell-Smith was now headmistress at a small school in a Sussex village where there was almost nothing that could be termed Society. It would explain why she was willing to accept Anthony Pierce's attentions. Trade or not, there was a comfortable life in store for the brewery heir's wife.

Again, he changed the direction of the conversation. "Did Anthony Pierce have any enemies? From the war, most particularly."

"Why the war years?" she asked, her mind nearly as quick as his to spot anomaly. "Did something happen there that might have had to do with his death?"

In his mind's eye he could see again the identity discs found in the mouths of the dead men. "We have some reason to believe it could have a connection. Yes."

"If there was anything untoward that happened in France, Anthony never confided in me. I don't believe he would have, if you want the truth. He knew I didn't care for unpleasantness." She must have realized how selfish that sounded and added in spite of herself, "We had a number of students over those four years who marched away to war and never came back. There's a list of their names on a board in the school parlor, for all to see and remember. Anthony knew how much this had saddened me."

He thought her self-control remarkable for a woman who had just lost a man she cared for. For that matter, her eyes showed no signs of crying herself to sleep, even though it was only two days ago that Pierce's body had been discovered.

And as if she had read his thought, tears welled in her eyes. "If there's nothing more, Inspector? I find this a very painful subject."

Hamish said, "She's afraid yon brother killed him."

It would explain her very first question to him: not about Anthony's death but in regard to Daniel's whereabouts.

But he left it there. "If anything occurs to you, Mrs. Farrell-Smith, will you speak to Constable Walker? He'll see that the message reaches me."

"Yes, of course." Her voice was husky. "You can find your own way out, I think?"

He thanked her and rose to leave.

The image he took away from the interview that stayed with him as he walked back to the hotel was of her face as he glanced back at her just before closing the door.

Desolation was writ large there. But for herself, he thought, not for the dead.

The long day was drawing to a close when Rutledge went back to the police station, intending to return the sheaf of statements.

Walker was standing by a window, looking out at the last shafts of light that touched the rooftops on the opposite side of the street, and he turned to greet Rutledge as the man from London stepped through the door.

"Any progress?" he asked.

"Not much that's helpful. Tomorrow, I'd like to speak to some of the other men from Eastfield's contingent. Can you arrange it?"

"That's easily done," Walker said, but his mind was clearly on something else.

"What is it?" Rutledge asked, suddenly alert. "What's happened?"

"That's just it. Nothing has happened. So far. But tonight's the third night after Pierce was murdered. I'm wondering if that will change, once darkness falls."

"I see your point. The problem is, our friend out there has the advantage. He has a better knowledge of where and when to strike, because he's obviously laid his plans well. Otherwise you and Inspector Norman would have caught him without my help. All you can expect to do is get in his way and force him to alter those plans. That means patrolling not the village itself but back gardens, barnyards, the brewery precincts, the lanes, anywhere a man might be outside alone. Meanwhile, I'd ask everyone to stay in after dark."

"I don't know if he'll alter his plans, or just wait until we've passed by," Walker said, clearly still worried. "It depends, doesn't it, on what's driving the man?"

"Yes, I grant you that. Garroting is a very physical way to kill. More so even than a knife. Whoever it is may not be able to stop, now that he's started. Unless he only intended to kill those three men. No one else."

"There's that," Walker answered, considering the matter. "Although for the life of me I can't see how they're connected."

"It may only be in the murderer's mind," Rutledge said.

Walker turned to him in surprise. "I hadn't considered that."

"It's possible that whoever it is uses a garrote because the face of the victim isn't important," Rutledge said.

But that would indicate random killings.

7

In the morning, Inspector Norman in Hastings sent a man to Eastfield with the message. He was held up first by the heavy rain and then having to wait for Walker.

Constable Petty, standing in the window of the police station, finally saw his fellow constable coming down the street. Walker, just returning from another round of the village, in an effort to reassure himself that indeed nothing had happened in the night, came through the doorway, nodded, and began to strip off his rain gear.

"A cup of tea, Petty?"

"Much as I could use one, I don't think there's time," the man replied, and he said what he'd been told to say, refusing to answer any of Walker's questions.

Walker, growling in frustration, pulled on his gear again and set out for the hotel.

When he began his rounds the night before, he had had no way of knowing that Rutledge, awake at two and again at three o'clock, had also gone quietly out of the hotel and with only Hamish for company, had also walked through the darkness, pausing now and again to listen to the night sounds around him. It was amazing, he thought as he moved through the silent streets, that a habitation with so little history to scar it could seem so ominous in the broken moonlight. If there had been rape and pillage and fire and sword here at some time in the distant past, it had not left its mark. Except perhaps during those hours between midnight and dawn.

Hamish observed, "Where there are people, there's death."

And it was true. Hopelessness, starvation, plague, disease among the animals, all of these brought death as surely as armies.

As his footsteps echoed on the hard-packed surface of the road then vanished in the soft earth of the churchyard, Rutledge had wondered if he were being watched. He had no feeling on that score, but he considered what he would do in a murderer's shoes. Would he choose one of the taller buildings along the main street, with a wide sweep of views in either direction?

The church tower, tall enough to allow an overview of the village and the surrounding farms? Or the shadows of a dense stand of lilac he'd noticed where the road curved just beyond the brewery buildings on its way out of Eastfield? How had the murderer found his victims, if he hadn't followed them or watched them walk by themselves in a direction in which he could expect to find his killing ground?

Hamish said into the silence, "Ye ken how Donald MacRae found the snipers?"

Rutledge did remember. They had been plagued for nearly a week by a well-hidden sniper, and no one had caught the muzzle flash, because he chose a time when the British line was too busy. Private MacRae had been detailed to watch for it, and instead, he had scavenged old hay from the horse lines and a few ragged planks from a repaired section of trench wall. That night he had piled the bits and pieces just outside the trench. It sat there for two days, the Germans across No Man's Land at first amusing themselves by firing into the debris, testing their skills. And then they ignored it. On the third night, MacRae had poked the tip of a rifle under the edge of the hay, barely visible. And early the next morning he had jiggled a helmet on a bayonet just behind the planking, for all the world like a man sighting down the barrel of his weapon. MacRae had set two spotters to watch as the German sniper took his shot at what he believed to be his opposite number, giving himself away in the process. It had been too tempting, and it had been his last. They had caught two other snipers with the same trick, over the span of six months or so.

It could well be the case here, that someone waited under cover until his quarry had walked into his sights.

But that meant he *could* wait for his opportunity. Coldly, precisely, unemotionally. In no hurry to complete whatever task he'd set himself.

Satisfied at last that there was no one else abroad, Rutledge had returned to his room, slept lightly, and when the clock in the church tower struck the next hour, he had arisen and done it all over again. Just as he reached the hotel, the clouds that had been gathering for the past hour or more consolidated over southern Sussex and Kent, and a steady rain began to fall.

Walker had just come through the door of the hotel and was crossing the lobby intent on climbing the stairs in search of Rutledge's room when his quarry walked out of the dining room after an early breakfast.

The constable passed on the message from Norman, keeping his voice low so that it wouldn't carry to the man at Reception watching them with interest.

Rutledge was very still for a moment. Then he said, "Damn."

The fox had outwitted the hounds. While Rutledge had been scouring Eastfield, the killer had moved on.

"I'm afraid, sir, that Inspector Norman isn't the least bit pleased," Walker said in some satisfaction. "But I'm not denying I'm pleased it wasn't someone from my patch."

"Collect Petty and bring the motorcar around, will you? I'll be five minutes."

It was not a long drive. Suddenly the road came to a cleft in the cliffs and then wended down the hillside. Scattered buildings and cottages gave way to a tumble of houses perched above the shoreline. To the left were rows of tall black wooden net shops—drying sheds—and the fishing fleet, already drawn up on the strand. The rain beat against the motorcar as they reached the bottom of the cleft, and they tasted salt on their lips. To the right, the town itself opened up, streets winding into a maze of other streets, and beyond, the increasingly popular waterfront, empty now of holidaymakers. Waves were coming in as gray as the sky, and their froth looked dingy as they crashed into the shale of the strand.

Hastings had once been a tiny fishing village at the mouth of a valley that had spilled down from the cliffs to the narrow strand below. With time, the village had grown east toward the headland, but it never really flourished as a port even in William of Normandy's day, although later it had been one of the English Cinque Ports, with a castle that overlooked the sea and protected the mouth of the valley. Sea bathing had finally made the coast prosperous, and Hastings had then expanded westward toward St. Leonards. The Old Town, with its sand fishing boats, the tall tarred structures where the nets were dried, and a crowded street of houses and shops reclaimed from the sea, were left as an anachronism as the town built anew for the carriage trade, with prospects, circles, and promenades taking pride of place. This had waned with the war, although sea bathing was picking up again.

Rutledge drove directly to the police station, following Walker's directions, only to be told that Inspector Norman was still out on the headland above the fishing fleet. They went back the way they had come, and as they reached the strand, through the rain they could just see the top of the cliff where it jutted out into the water. Silhouetted against the gray sky were a dozen or so men, tiny figures at this distance, moving about near the edge just above where part of the cliff face had broken away in the past and tumbled down into the sea. Watching them, Rutledge realized that there was a climber making his way back up to them, struggling against the pull of the wind as he worked ropes that were invisible from this angle.

"I don't envy that poor bastard," Walker was saying, watching him. It would have been a dangerous business even in good weather. "What possessed him even to try such a thing?"

Rutledge was silent as he made his way to the funicular that ran up the cliff face just beyond the black net shops.

For a wonder it was working. The two men waited impatiently for the next car to take them to the top. Rutledge could already see a policeman moving toward the upper station, as if coming to meet them.

It was a quick run to the top, and then they were stepping out onto the wet grass, facing the full force of the wind. The policeman, a constable, said to Rutledge, "Inspector? This way, please, sir." He turned to lead the way toward the rounded knob of the headland, where most of the policemen and several civilians were still busy.

Even in the downpour, Rutledge could see that there was something on the ground where they were standing, although most of their attention was riveted on the climber still inching his way up the cliff face. Rutledge realized that what had appeared to be two bodies actually were two men stretched out on the wet grass anchoring the climber's ropes, their heads hanging over the precipice. Two more men held their ankles, to keep them from being dragged over. Rutledge could see that the grass was bruised and slippery as hell, and the wind in this unprotected spot was whipping in off the sea, rushing upward to buffet the knot of figures.

He pulled off his hat to keep it from blowing away, and felt the rain driven against his face.

The men didn't turn as Rutledge came to join the group. He saw that Walker stopped a little to one side, trying to speak to the constable who had come to the funicular to fetch them. He had to shout in the man's ear to be heard.

Everyone looked thoroughly miserable, but they were intent on the drama unfolding at their very feet. Rutledge heard a shout of pain as the wind slammed the climber into the wall he was trying to ascend, and one of the men on the ropes cried, "Are you all right, Ben?"

If he answered, Rutledge couldn't hear him. Others, aware now that someone else had come out here, looked up to stare briefly at Rutledge, but Norman waited without turning as more and more rope was hauled up. And still the climber hadn't crested the top.

Looking out to sea, Rutledge was hard-pressed to tell where the horizon ended and the water began, and he could see heavier clouds forming a line that darkened the sea and sky as it headed his way. He knew without being told that the men here were racing that line.

All at once the men stretched out on the ground scrambled back, and the teams heaved on the ropes with all the strength they could muster. Then, like a jack-in-the-box, a man's head and shoulders popped up, followed by his torso and legs, and he made it to the bruised grass at the edge.

The climber flopped down where he was, flat out, exhausted. His hair was dripping rainwater, his clothes wet through. Someone came forward and draped a tarpaulin over him, but he was sweating from exertion and asked them to pull it away again.

Only then did Inspector Norman turn, as if he'd known Rutledge was there all along. His hair was also plastered to his skull, his face red and raw from the rain and the wind. He shouted to Rutledge, pointing down the cliff face, "One of yours?"

Rutledge made his way to the brink, gripping the shoulder of one of the men who had been pulling in the climber, to keep himself from being blown over.

Below, crumpled on the rocks that were being lashed by the sea, was a body.

The climber had been down there, attaching a sling of sorts to it, with ropes he brought back to the top tied to his belt.

It had been one hell of a climb down there, and even worse conditions trying to work with the body on such a narrow ledge, barely big enough for one man. And then the climb back had been even more hazardous.

Norman, somewhere behind Rutledge, called, "Look out," and he turned to see four men pulling hard on ropes.

He stepped back from the edge and watched as the men—he learned later that they were from the lifeboat station below—began to haul the dead man to the top.

"What makes you think he's one of mine?" Rutledge shouted.

Norman grinned at him, his long thin face seeming to split in two, but there was no humor in it. "When the climber got down there, he said the man's throat had been cut. Took him forever to get those ropes down and attached properly. We didn't want to drag the body against the rocky face. The sling should offer a little protection. But I have a feeling his throat wasn't cut. I have a feeling he's been garroted. That's when I sent for you."

"Why?" Rutledge demanded, feeling a surge of anger at the man's gloating. "Why should it be one of ours? If the killer has moved on, that's a Hastings man lying down there."

"Call it instinct," Norman told him and then turned back to watch the men straining against the dead weight on their ropes. "And these." He drew a pair of field glasses from his pocket. "We had to know if he was dead or alive. I can tell you, the doctor didn't relish going down after him. You could almost see him praying it was a corpse."

He gestured to a middle-aged, balding man with a growing paunch, standing to one side, waiting.

Someone crawled to the end of the cliff and then called over his shoulder, "Easy, lads, easy." The men on the ropes slacked off, caught their breath, and when the signal was given, this time they brought the body up to the top of the cliff and then with a last effort, pulled it over the edge onto the grassy slope. For an instant, it appeared to be on the point of sliding into the abyss again, teetering there until it was finally pulled to safety. Rutledge heard Norman swear.

Two other men ran forward, caught the rope handles on the sling, and gently urged it back to higher ground while the lines were kept taut. When all was secure, the rescuers squatted where they were, heads down, almost overwhelmed with exhaustion.

Rutledge and Norman reached the body in three long strides, kneeling in the rain to slip the sling back and examine the man. The doctor hurried forward to join them.

"He's dead," he said after a cursory examination. "As we thought. I'll tell you more when I can examine him further. This isn't the place for it."

Constable Walker had come up behind them, hands on his knees as he leaned forward to see over Rutledge's shoulder. Rain had soaked Rutledge's dark hair, and rainwater was nearly blinding him as it ran down his face. He wiped it with his hands then considered the body.

The victim lay on his stomach, his clothing dripping water. It was clear to everyone who could see the back of his neck that he'd been garroted, as Inspector Norman had suspected. The deep line of the wound was black in the gloomy light of the stormy day.

The rocks had also taken their toll, his trousers muddy and ripped, a tear in his shirt, signs on the exposed skin of his hands of scrapes and cuts. Still, it was evident to Rutledge that he hadn't used them to protect himself when the wire had come around his throat.

With a glance at Rutledge, Norman reached out and turned the body over, and behind him Walker's sharp intake of breath was audible.

Norman looked up. "Know him?"

Walker said, "Yes, sir—it's Theo Hartle. He and his father work in the furniture-making firm in Eastfield."

"Are you sure? His face is rather battered."

"There's no doubt in my mind," Walker told him. "I've seen him every day of his life, near enough."

"Well, then," Inspector Norman said. "He is in fact one of yours. And on my patch."

The doctor, conducting a swift inventory of visible injuries, said, "No other wounds apparent, just those consistent with his fall and with the attempt to bring him back from the ledge. And it was damned lucky he struck that ledge, or he'd have been taken out to sea and we'd never have found him."

"It wasn't a matter of luck," Inspector Norman told him. "If you know these cliffs, this was the only place along the rim where it was sure that he would be stopped before he went into the sea."

Hamish spoke, startling Rutledge. "Aye, and did yon murderer ken the ledge was there?"

Rutledge looked down at the dead face. Hartle appeared to be in his middle twenties like the other three victims, fair, taller than most, and of heavy build, which had made the task of bringing him up from the rocks even harder.

The doctor was turning away.

Norman gestured to his men. "All right. Get him to the doctor's surgery." He went over to thank the men of the Life Boat Service for their help, giving them a handful of coins as he spoke. "Get yourselves something to warm you. I'll have a statement later, when you're off duty."

Norman had brought a motorcar to the top of the headland, and as they walked through the rain toward it, he said, "It was sheer chance that he was spotted. The fishing boats coming in reported seeing something on the ledge, a leaper they thought, and when we came up to look, I had a bad feeling about it. We got the lifeboat men up here, and began rescue operations, but the ledge wasn't wide enough for more than one man to climb down to it. The way the sea was crashing over those rocks, it's a wonder they weren't both swept away."

They had reached the motorcar, and Norman used his hands to wipe the rain from his face before getting in. Rutledge hesitated, his thoughts as always racing to Hamish, and then pushing them aside, he joined Walker in the rear seat.

Norman said as they crested a slight rise to reach the road and his tires fought for a grip, "A damnable day for this. I told you I didn't want your murders spilling over into Hastings."

Rutledge had pulled out his handkerchief, cold and damp despite his trench coat. He could feel the heaviness of the cloth weighing across his shoulders, and water inside his shoes. "The question is, what brought Hartle here?"

They wound their way down to the town and headed toward the police station. Norman was saying grimly, "That's your lookout, isn't it? But I don't like this business. Not one whit."

The interior of the motorcar smelled of wet wool, unpleasant and heavy in the dampness. As they pulled up in front of the police station, Norman turned to ask, "Where did you leave your own vehicle? By the net shops?"

"At the foot of the funicular."

"I'll send one of my men back to fetch it. Come inside."

They got out and went into the station. It seemed dreadfully cold, without the sun to warm it, and Norman spoke to the sergeant at the desk, asking him to see that they were brought tea from the small canteen.

It was a far larger station than the one in Eastfield, and Norman's office was down a short passage to the left. From the cells to the right, they could hear a man singing in a monotone, at the top of his lungs.

"He's half mad," Norman said in explanation as he shut his door against the sound. "We bring him in from time to time for his own sake. His sister can't control him." He took the chair behind the desk, thought better of it, wet as he was, and searched in one of the drawers for a sheaf of paper. "Here, use these," he said, passing them across the desk. "Or you'll stick to the wood. God, I don't know when I've been this wet." Opening a cupboard door, he found a towel and began to dry his face and hair. "All right, Walker, tell us what you know about this man Hartle."

"He was in the war, with the others. A likeable man. Never any trouble before or after the war. He went to work at Kenton Chairs carving scrollwork for chair backs and desk fronts. His father always claimed he had a natural talent."

Norman looked across the desk at Rutledge. "Factory is a misnomer. The furniture-making concern turns out desks, chairs, tables, bookcases, and bedsteads using a variety of machines, and then finishing them by hand. There's a market in these new hotels springing up along the south coast for quality furnishings that are durable enough to take the rough handling of holidaymakers. It employs a dozen men, I should think?" He looked at Walker, who nodded. "Fifteen at the most. But they're all skilled men, and for the most part, their fathers worked there before them. A man name of Kenton owns it, and Kenton Chairs have been well known for decades, even though they've expanded their line. There's a cottage industry as well, caning the seats."

"Mr. Kenton's grandfather began the business in a shed on his property," Walker added. "The Hartles have worked there for three generations, at a guess."

"So what brought our man to Hastings?" Inspector Norman wanted to know. "If he's employed at Kenton's?"

"I've no idea," Rutledge answered him. "I'd like a copy of the doctor's report as soon as may be."

"We all know the cause of death. You could see the man's throat. But was he killed out there on the headland? Or taken there after he was dead? What do you think? With this rain, any blood or signs of a struggle have been washed away hours ago."

"The only hope is to backtrack him. If he was here in Hastings for some purpose, why didn't he return to Eastfield the same day—or evening, as may be? What was he doing here late at night? And where was he staying?"

"I'll have my men ask questions in the lodging houses and the pubs."

The door opened and a constable entered, in his hands a painted wooden tray that had seen better days. The edges were worn, and the garland of roses that decorated the center was chipped and scratched. But the china teapot, cups, jug of milk, and bowl of sugar resting on it were spotlessly clean and probably a decade newer. Norman stood up, took it from the man, and proceeded to pour three cups. It was blessedly hot, and there was a silence as they drank a little.

Rutledge could feel the warmth spreading through him and was grateful. Setting his empty cup aside, he said, "We'll exchange what information we've found."

"Ah, but is this my inquiry now—or yours?" Norman asked, smiling.

Rutledge was in no mood to argue jurisdictions. "The Chief Constable handed the inquiry over to the Yard. I believe he would agree that Hartle's death falls into the same case I've been pursuing since I arrived in Sussex."

"If I have any say in the matter, the inquest will be held here."

Rutledge said, "He died here. It will be held here. But you said yourself, he's one of ours."

Norman didn't answer. Finishing his tea, he said, "We'll see about that in due course. For the moment, leave me to my work and I'll not interfere with yours. We'll see if we can trace his movements in Hastings.

If you learn anything in Eastfield that will help with that—why he was here in the first place—I'll thank you to make life easier for us."

"I'll speak to his employer." Rutledge rose. "My motorcar should have been brought in by now. Thank you for the tea. I'll be in touch."

Walker hastily swallowed the contents of his cup and rose to follow Rutledge from Norman's office.

Norman let them go without saying anything more, and Rutledge was glad to see that his motorcar was in truth waiting in front of the police station.

He and Walker stepped out in the rain, and Walker said, "Back to Eastfield?"

Rutledge answered, "I'd like to go back to that headland."

Walker's groan was almost audible. Rutledge turned to him. "You needn't get out."

There, Rutledge crisscrossed the headland, looking for clues. It was nearly hopeless, given the conditions, but his eyes were good, and he knew that there was only this one chance to find anything at all.

Hamish said, against the wail of the wind, "Give it up."

He was right. The search turned up nothing more than a halfpenny, which could have been lying in the grass for months, if not years. The bearded face of

Edward VII stared back at Rutledge as he turned it over.

Retracing his steps to the motorcar, he got in and said to Walker, "Do you know the doctor who was out here this morning?"

"Not well. He's Dr. Thompson. His surgery is somewhere in Hill Street."

"Then let's find it." Rutledge drove back the way he had come, and after some trouble, they finally saw the small shingle that hung by the doctor's door.

The doctor's nurse, a tall, spare woman with a sweet face, answered their knock and showed them into the surgery.

A body lay on a long table, covered now with a sheet. Clothing and other belongings had been set aside in a shallow bin to finish dripping.

Dr. Thompson was just washing his hands, and he turned to greet them. Recognizing them, he said, "You were on the headland, with Inspector Norman. Did he send you? I was just about to ask him to step around."

Rutledge identified himself and Constable Walker. "I've been sent by London to take over the inquiry. Hartle isn't the first victim of this killer. The others were in Eastfield."

"Ah, yes, I remember something being said about jurisdiction. I'll tell you what I've learned and confer with Inspector Norman later." He added, after a moment, "As a courtesy."

"What do you know so far?"

"That my initial conclusions were correct. There's the throat, of course. Not manual strangulation but the use of a garrote. Abrasions from the fall over the cliff's edge, but these occurred shortly after death, not before. He wasn't alive when he hit the rocky ledge below. How long he'd been dead, I can't tell you at the moment, but I would make an educated guess of sometime before midnight. Perhaps as early as ten or eleven o'clock. The cold rain hampers any more definitive conclusion. Have a look." He pointed to the sheet where Hartle lay, and Rutledge walked over to lift it.

He could see the wound very clearly, now, and the cuts and scrapes Dr. Thompson had mentioned. "Any thoughts on what sort of garrote it is?"

"Wire, most likely, to cut that deep. More efficient than a silk cord or even knotted rope." He pointed to a long jagged wound in the dead man's abdomen. It had healed, but the scar was still prominent. "Bayonet, I'd say. A miracle he survived the infection that must have followed, never mind the damage done by the blade itself. As you can see, he's a big man. He would have taken some killing. I daresay your murderer has a few bruises to show for it." Lifting one of Hartle's hands, he pointed to the fingers. "Initially I thought this was damage from the fall or the recovery. But I'm of the opinion he tried to pull whatever it was away from his throat. See the broken nails, and there's some indication of dried blood under the others. I'd put his age at about twenty-eight. From the lines around his mouth, he must have been in some pain from his wound. And large as he is, strong as he no doubt was, he isn't as filled out as he should be."

Walker spoke for the first time. "Twenty-eight his last birthday." He was about to ask a question, but Rutledge forestalled him

"Did you find anything else of interest?" he asked.

Dr. Thompson said, "I was just coming to that. Nothing to do with the cause of death or the state of the body, you understand. Inside the man's mouth was an identity disc. From the war, you know. I didn't quite— I was told this victim was Theo Hartle—I believe it was you, Constable, who identified him? From East-field. But the disc would say that this was a man named French from Herefordshire. I don't quite understand why the disc was there—the war has been over for two years, after all—or why there is some question about the name of the victim."

He passed the disc to Rutledge. It was clear that he was curious and wanted an answer to his question.

It was also apparent that the police hadn't made such details public, and Dr. Gooding had examined the other three victims, not Dr. Thompson.

Rutledge said, looking at the name on the disc, "Please treat what I'm about to tell you as confidential. Only a handful of people know that this appears to be the—shall I call it the signature?—or the hallmark of this murderer? Identity discs from another man and another regiment left in the corpse's mouth. If Walker tells us that this man is Theo Hartle, I believe him. Why the disc of one Corporal French should be there we haven't yet determined. Which is why we aren't making this information public."

Dr. Thompson stared at him. "Your murderer must be a little mad to do such a thing."

"We don't know," Rutledge answered, "whether he's mad or clever or just vengeful. Not yet."

Thompson shook his head. "At a guess, there's something buried so deep in him—whoever he is— that he uses unnecessary force to kill with the garrote. The wound in Hartle's throat is obscenely deep. The sea washed away most of the blood, but it must have been a ghastly sight to begin with. And it's personal satisfaction he's after, your murderer, not simply the man's death. He could accomplish that far more easily."

A fascinating point. Rutledge looked at Thompson, reassessing this portly, backwater doctor who had such insight into a killer's mind.

Thompson, who must have guessed what Rutledge was thinking, smiled grimly. "I was in the war myself. I know what men are capable of doing to each other. I have no illusions on that score. I also discovered that some of them enjoyed it. That may be what you're facing here, someone who misses the thrill of stalking and killing. Someone who has discovered he can't live without it. Blood lust, Inspector, isn't something only the lower animals experience."

8

It was nearly one o'clock. Rutledge and Walker went in search of lunch and found themselves in a small corner shop that catered to workingmen. It was situated on a street where buildings backed up to the shelving land. The lower portion of the room was mainly a counter filled with various cooked meats, cheeses, and an array of sandwiches. On the upper level, reached by a half dozen steps, were bare tables and chairs, set out in front of a bar that dispensed tea, coffee, and cider as well as beer and ale.

They ordered from the smiling young woman who came up to their table and presented a handwritten menu listing what was available.

She was just bringing their sandwiches and glasses of cider when the sun came out. The streets and rooftops began to steam as the air warmed, and the neighboring houses gleamed wetly, giving them a just-washed look. The young woman glanced over her shoulder and said, "There. And about time too." Turning back to the two men and noting that one was a policeman with rain-darkened shoulders, she added, "Were you there on the headland when they brought that poor soul in?"

"Just caught in the downpour," Rutledge answered for both of them.

"It's brave they were, going out to the edge of the headland that way, and in such a storm. Bits crumble, and it's easy to lose one's footing and go over. Every summer someone ventures too near the edge and goes over. Never fails. You'd think they'd mind the signs that are put up each year, but they never do. And some of them let their children romp and play up there, as if it were the back garden and safe as houses. Last May it was a little boy flying a kite who fell. I hope this wasn't a child. It's a crime the way some parents haven't the sense they were born with. Even the smugglers knew better!"

And she moved on to another table. Walker said, "There are smugglers' caves all about Hastings. It was a lucrative enterprise when French goods were banned. And there's some who say that it goes on still, when nobody is looking." He bit off the end of his sandwich and added around it, "Do you think Dr. Thompson was right? About our murderer liking the feeling of killing?"

"It's one other solution. It may even explain the discs—that in his mind these keep the war alive. But where did he come by these? That's what I need to find out. Whether or not they have any particular significance."

"Odd that Inspector Norman never mentioned the disc in Hartle's mouth. Or had the doctor told him?"

"There hadn't been time." Rutledge finished his cider and beckoned to the woman who had waited on them. He paid the accounting and waited for Walker to retrieve his helmet and cape from the other chair.

"I've put it off as long as I can," he was saying. "But there's his sister to tell. She'll be broken up about this. I doubt her husband will. They never got on together, he and Theo."

Rutledge stopped on his way to the door. "Do you think he could have done this?"

"His legs are in braces. Poliomyelitis."

As Walker cranked the motorcar, Rutledge looked out to sea. The heavy gray clouds were far out along the horizon now, making their way to France.

Ahead lay the duty he disliked the most. Breaking news to an anxious family. He could have left it to Walker, but that was not his way.

"How did anyone lure Hartle out onto the head-land?" Walker asked as he joined Rutledge in the motorcar. "And after dark. Hartle was a canny man, he wouldn't have gone there without a plausible reason."

They drove in silence back to Eastfield, and Constable Walker pointed out where the dead man's sister lived.

It was a simple bungalow in a street of similar houses, single story, squat roof, and a small garden behind.

Constable Walker broke the silence as they got out of the motorcar. "I've done this three times now. Pray God it's the last."

Together they went up the walk. A curtain twitched in the room to the left of the door.

Even as they reached for the knocker, a woman was opening the door to them, her face anxious, her fair brows drawn together in a frown of uncertainty.

"Constable Walker," she said, her glance flicking to Rutledge's face.

She was very unlike her brother, Rutledge noted. Smaller boned, fair hair where his was the color of wheat, her face softer and her eyes a pretty brown. Behind her, just visible in the shadows over her shoulder, was a man in a wheeled chair, his face pinched and sour.

"Mrs. Winslow, this is Inspector Rutledge from London—"

Her face crumpled. "It's Theo, isn't it? Oh, my God, I knew it—I knew it when he didn't stop by last evening—"

"I'm afraid so, Mrs. Winslow. He was found early this morning in Hastings."

She put her hands to her face and began to cry.

Behind her, her husband put out his hand, as if to offer comfort, and then dropped it.

Rutledge gently led her from the door and into a small sitting room, where he'd seen the curtain twitch earlier, settling her on the stiff horsehair sofa. The man in the invalid chair followed them into the room, saying, "What happened to him then? Tell me what happened?"

Rutledge turned slightly toward him and said, "In due course. Constable, perhaps Mr. Winslow will show you where you could make some tea. I think his wife will be grateful for it."

At first he thought Walker would refuse, but then the constable realized that getting the husband out of the room was important at this stage. He turned to Winslow and said, "Where's the kitchen, then?" as if in such a small house it would be hard to find.

Winslow cast a glance at his wife, then looked at Rutledge and saw that the suggestion was, in fact, a command that brooked no argument. He spun his invalid chair and with poor grace led the constable away.

Rutledge found a clean, dry handkerchief in an inner pocket and gave it to the weeping woman. She took it gratefully. He said, his voice pitched not to carry beyond this room, "Was your brother in the war?" It was an attempt to distract her from her immediate grief.

She nodded.

"With the rest of the Eastfield volunteers?"

A muffled yes came from behind the handkerchief. And then she raised her eyes to meet his gaze, a slow and awful truth dawning. "He—was he—like the others?"

"I'm sorry. Yes."

"I thought—I thought perhaps there had been an accident on the road. He wasn't feeling well, but he went to Hastings anyway yesterday, taking the van. The shipment of varnish from London hadn't come. Mr. Kenton asked him to see if he could find a few tins to tide them over. He shouldn't have been driving at all, but he wouldn't tell Mr. Kenton that. I thought—I thought he might have taken his own life. Trying not to shame us."

Her voice failed, and Rutledge found himself thinking of Rosemary Hume. Murder was sometimes not the worst news to reach a household.

"Why did you fear he might do himself a harm?" he asked, after giving her a moment to collect herself. In another room he could hear the rattle of cups and low voices as the two banished men talked quietly.

"His stomach. It hasn't been the same. He was always one to like his food, but now he had to watch what he ate. No cheese or rich sauces, not even an occasional curry. Nothing with spices. And he did like his mulled cider of an evening when it was cold. He had to give it all up. Only the plainest of boiled meats and potatoes and vegetables. His favorite dish was parsnips roasted in goose drippings, but he couldn't have it. Everything was tasteless, he said, and still his stomach would reject everything sometimes, and he'd be violently ill, you could hear him all over the house. Virgil said it kept *him* half nauseated as well, but I felt for Theo, and lay there in bed listening to him, and praying he wouldn't begin those terrible dry heaves that went on for hours."

"Your brother lived with you?"

"When he first came out of hospital. There was no one else. Mum and Dad were gone, and Mary and the baby died of the Spanish influenza before ever he was wounded. That must have broken his heart, but he never mentioned them when he came home. He went to the churchyard by himself, not even asking me to come and show him where they were. And as soon as he could, he went back to the farm and lived there alone. It wasn't a working farm anymore, but it was our home. He felt comfortable with his memories. That's what he said. Comfortable. As if he could talk to them somehow. Mum and Dad, Mary and the baby."

"How was the relationship between your brother and your husband?"

"Not very good," she told him with resignation in her voice. "Theo didn't want me to marry Virgil, you see. He thought it was pity I felt, and not love." She hesitated, and then asked, "Was it quick? How my brother died?" She waited, braced for his answer.

"Quickly enough," Rutledge said. "You know about the other deaths?"

"Oh, yes, it's all over Eastfield, that's all anyone talks about. I expect they'll be gossiping about poor Theo now. I feel guilty, I've done my share of the gossiping, and now I see it wasn't right."

"Did your brother have enemies? Did anything that happened in the war seem to worry him?"

"He never talked about the war. Not to me. He just came home, put away his uniform, and got on with his life. I asked him once if it was very bad, being wounded, and all he said was, it was the ticket out."

"Was he closer to someone in particular? A friend in the Army, someone here in Eastfield?"

"There's no one I know of who would harm Theo. Why should they? He was a good man, he never was any trouble growing up. He helped his father at Kenton's and never complained. They liked him there. They did from the beginning . . ." Her voice trailed off as she stared into space, reliving another time and place. "I can't see any point to killing him. I mean, there's no money to speak of, although he was never in debt."

"When he came back from France, was he on good terms with the men he'd served with? Did he have any problems with Anthony Pierce?"

"I don't know. I mean, he never spoke of trouble. He never went looking for it, for that matter. They'd all changed—they didn't sit about talking over what they'd done in the trenches. It was as if it hadn't happened, in a way. But of course it had, hadn't it?" She frowned. "Theo was given a medal. He must have been brave. But I don't know what he did."

It was something Rutledge had heard often enough since his own return to England. Censorship, of course, meant that letters home could say very little about where men were or what they were doing. And many of those at home in England had no means of knowing what war in the trenches—or on board ships for that matter—was really like. The images they had were often so far off the mark in many instances that no one would recognize in them the reality of France. He had spoken to a woman who had told him quite proudly that her dead son had had a good bed and clean sheets every night he was away from home. He'd told her so himself. Rutledge hadn't disabused her of the notion—one her son had no doubt cultivated for her sake. And to her question about his own situation on the Somme, he had assured her that he too had slept well. He'd been rewarded by a smile and a nod, as if she had been happy for him. Of course many families had known the truth of the savagery their loved ones were caught up in, but even they had sometimes preferred lies.

Hamish said, "What we did was to die. For naught."

Rutledge flinched.

Mrs. Winslow misconstrued it. "Should I have asked him about the fighting? Was it important?"

"No," he answered her. "It doesn't matter at all."

And then Constable Walker came in carrying the tea tray, and Mrs. Winslow turned to it as if it were a lifeline. Her husband, following him into the room, looked quickly from Rutledge's face to his wife's, as if he could read in the air between them something of what had been said.

They took their leave shortly afterward, and Walker said harshly as the two men reached the motorcar, "I hope to God we find out who is committing these murders."

Dropping Walker off at the police station, Rutledge changed into dry clothes, then went to find the rector of St. Mary's Church.

The signboard at the gate into the churchyard gave the priest's name as Ottley. As Rutledge was about to decide whether to try the rectory or the church first, he saw the man he was after just closing the rectory door and striding down the walk toward him.

"You're the man from London," the rector said, squinting at his face as Rutledge met him on the flagstone walk. He pulled out his spectacles for a better look. "Yes. Do you want me? I was on my way to see Mrs. Winslow, to offer what comfort I could. The constable left word to look in on her."

"My name is Rutledge. Scotland Yard. I'd like five minutes of your time first. Is there somewhere we can speak privately?"

The rector gestured vaguely in the direction of a bench set under an apple tree growing between the church and the rectory, its gnarled, spreading branches offering good shade as the watery sun strengthened. "Will that do? My housekeeper is mopping floors. I doubt she'd care to have me tracking back inside."

Rutledge led the way, and the vicar dusted the bench with a handkerchief before settling himself in one corner. Rutledge took the other.

"Sad circumstances we're in," the rector said with a sigh. "I can't quite bring my mind around it, you know. Four murders! It's unspeakable. I never dreamed of such a thing here in Eastfield."

Rutledge could hear bees buzzing about over his head, where the tight knots of young green apples were nestled. "I'd like to ask you about Eastfield. You've been rector here for some time?"

"Nearly thirty years, now," he answered. "Twenty of them without the support of my dear wife. But one copes, somehow."

"Indeed. You knew these four men who have been killed. What can you tell me about them? I'm not asking for secrets of the confessional, but for observations you must have made as you watched them grow into manhood."

"They were boys. In and out of scrapes, but no harm done for the most part. A rowdy bunch, excepting of course for Anthony Pierce, who played with them only occasionally. Still, there were one or two more serious incidents, as you'd expect. And then they were strong enough to help out at home, and their childhoods changed. No longer collecting eggs before school or bringing in the cows afterward, they were set to heavier work, mucking out the cowshed or the barn, helping with the planting and the harvest, whatever was needed. Some were able to stay with their school-ing, others weren't so fortunate. Hartle, of course, was apprenticed to his father at Kenton's. The Pierce brothers went away to public school. And the nonsense stopped."

It was a common picture of life on farms: girls working under their mothers' eye, sons learning first-hand the trade of their fathers. Large families helped eke out the needs that slender purses couldn't meet, though they meant more mouths to feed. As a rule on small holdings, food was more plentiful than money for wages, and the system worked.

"Did anything happen in the Army—before they left—after they were in France—that might lead to this sort of killing?"

The rector shook his head. "I never heard of it, if anything did. But they wouldn't have told me, would they? They'd have confessed to a chaplain. And what-ever it was would have stayed in France."

Hamish said, "You'll never uncover the truth, then."

But he had to. He made one last effort, saying to the rector, "Is there a place to look? I don't ask you to reveal any secrets. But it will save time—and lives—if I am given a direction to follow."

"It's not a conspiracy of silence," the rector told him. "At least not on my part. It's just that we don't recognize whatever it is as the problem. We may be looking in the wrong places. On the other hand, what places ought we to be searching? I don't know."

Rutledge found himself suddenly remembering the case that Chief Inspector Cummins had failed to solve. Was this of the same ilk? He refused to believe it. Somewhere—somewhere—there was a grain of truth to pursue, and one way or another, he would find it.

Hamish said, "Start with the most obvious."

It was good advice. But not very helpful.

He thanked the rector and went back to find Constable Walker.

Striding into the police station, he said, "Every victim so far fought in the war. Either in the village company or as in Pierce's case, in another. I need that list of their names, every single one of them."

Walker frowned. He'd been up most of the night, Rutledge remembered, and had had little time to work on anything else.

"I've started it, sir. Do you want the Navy as well?"

Rutledge took a deep breath. "Everyone. If he wore a uniform, I want his name on that list."

Walker pulled a sheet of paper from the side drawer of his desk and picked up his pen.

Mumbling to himself, he went through the village in his mind, house by house,

At length he looked up. Rutledge had waited patiently, watching the list grow.

"Seven," Walker said. He turned the sheet around so that Rutledge could read the names he'd written and their branch of service.

"Very good," Rutledge said. "How many of these were in school together as boys?"

"All but this one," he said, pointing to Alistair Nelson. "He came here when his father was brought in to work at the brewery. He was sixteen, at a guess, and he went off to join the Navy as soon as war was declared."

"Then withdraw his name, if you will. That leaves us with six men. Find them for me, and bring them here to the station. And tell them to be prepared to be away from home for three nights. I may need longer than that, but we'll begin with three."

"Here, some of these men have families—duties— they can't just walk away."

"Tell them they have this afternoon to find someone to help them with their work. But I want them here an hour before nightfall."

"What are you planning on doing with them?" Walker asked. "They'll want to know that as well."

"They don't need to know. But I intend to lock them up here and hold them without visitors."

"Incarcerate them? But what have they done? That's a bit harsh—"

"Murder is harsher. I want them under your eye until I return. And I shall hold you responsible if they're set free for any reason at all."

"And where will you be?" Walker asked, goaded.

"I'm going to track down some of the men whose identity discs we have. If I can't find answers here in Eastfield, I can at least make certain no one dies while I'm in another part of the country. I'll leave written orders. You won't be held accountable for my actions."

Walker studied him for a moment. "You believe the men whose names are on this list may be the next victims? Sir? One of them is my nephew!"

"All the more reason to keep him safe," Rutledge replied. "One man has already died on my watch. I won't see another killed while I'm away. We can't protect all six of them all of the time, Walker, we don't have the manpower, and I don't think Hastings will agree to lending us men. But if this killer keeps to his schedule, there will in fact be another murder before I return. The solution is to put his victims beyond his reach. It will be inconvenient, I grant you. But the risk is not acceptable."

It was easier said than done. Walker sought out each of the six men, sent them grumbling to the police station, and even after Rutledge had explained why he was taking this step, there was strong opposition to his plan.

"I can't be away for three nights," Hector Marshall exclaimed. "I've got cows to milk, vegetables to hoe, chickens to feed."

Another man added that his wife was pregnant and likely to deliver at any time.

Two more told Rutledge they could look after themselves and didn't need his help doing it.

He answered only, "I'm sure Theo Hartle would have said the same. He was a bigger man than any of you. And still he was murdered."

Walker's nephew, Billy Tuttle, said, "With all due respect, sir, what if it's one of us? The killer, I mean. And we're shut in together?" He looked at the others defiantly. "I'm not saying it is, not by any means, but it bears thinking about."

The last two to come in asked why they should be punished when they'd done nothing wrong, refusing outright to stay in a cell.

Rutledge listened patiently to their protests and then said, "Very well. Let's make it simple. We needn't draw straws. Tell me, which of you will volunteer to become the fifth victim? Step forward. I'll release you as a stalking horse, to see if you're on the killer's list.

Or not. And if the murderer should be one of you, he will most certainly have to wait until he's free before killing again. He's not a fool, whatever else he may be. He won't kill here."

They stared at him.

"It won't work," Marshall told him point-blank. He was a small, compact man with a broken nose and an obvious dislike of authority. "You can't be sure that madman is after one of us. Why not the greengrocer? Or the foreman at the brewery? The rector, or the clerk at the hotel?"

"Are you volunteering?" Rutledge asked.

"I'm not volunteering—" Marshall began.

Rutledge cut him short. "I remind you, each victim was alone after dark. No one saw the killer arrive, no one saw him leave. Think of a better plan, and I'll consider it."

Marshall objected again. "Look, we don't know why those four died. I'm not saying it's something they did. Or didn't do. But my conscience is clear. Why should I run with my tail between my legs, like?"

There was a silence.

"Step forward. Who among you feels safe enough to take such a risk? You survived the war, the lot of you. Are you feeling lucky?"

They talked amongst themselves and then turned back to him.

"Three days," Walker's nephew said. "Not an hour more."

"Thank you. But I warn you, if you give Constable Walker here any reason for complaint, I'll have the lot of you in charge for obstructing the police. Is that clear?"

The man called Henderson said, "Where will you be?"

"Tracking down connections between the living and the dead. Unless you can tell me what you believe this is all about? Unless you know something that I don't—and Constable Walker doesn't. What happened in France?"

"Nothing," Henderson replied. "Nothing that would lead to murder, then or now. We served with honor. All of us." There was the ring of truth in his voice.

But he hadn't been in the company that left Eastfield together. Three years younger than the rest, according to Walker, he'd volunteered on his seventeenth birthday and had served with the new tank corps. Like Anthony Pierce, he was an outsider. Still, Pierce had been murdered anyway.

No one else spoke up. Rutledge waited, looking each man in the eye, and they dropped their gaze first, even Marshall.

Hamish said into the silence, "Ye ken, it might not be what they did, but what they failed to do. And they wouldna' remember that."

Rutledge answered him in his mind. This killer could have moved on to Hastings or Rye or even London. But he hasn't. Because his quarry is still here.

Half an hour later, he left Eastfield behind.

Walker's parting words were, "I hope you find something that makes this incarceration worthwhile." There was an undercurrent of doubt in his voice.

Rutledge's first stop was in Hastings to see if any progress had been made in tracing Hartle's movements before he was killed.

Inspector Norman said testily, "It's early days. But he was seen in a shop that carries varnish at half past ten in the morning. They didn't have what he needed, and he went to another place of business and found it closed. He came back half an hour later and bought four tins of the varnish. He was to pick them up at two o'clock. At that point, it appears he had lunch in a small pub that fishermen frequent. Apparently he knew the pub's cook in France. He visits the man whenever he's in Hastings. Yesterday the man wasn't there. His wife's mother was being taken to hospital in Eastbourne for suspected appendicitis. We checked, and she was admitted for surgery. Hartle waited for him at the pub, and the cook returned to Hastings at three-fifteen. The two men sat down together for a good twenty minutes, and Hartle asked if the family was able to pay for the mother-in-law's care. Then a little before four o'clock, Hartle left to retrieve his tins, ostensibly on his way home to Eastfield, or so the cook says. He could think of no reason why Hartle would delay returning—he'd got what he'd come for. We know for certain our man left the pub close on to four. Half a dozen people can vouch for that. After that, we lose him."

"Then that must be when he encountered the killer."

"You can't be sure of it. It's possible my men will turn up something more by the end of the day."

"Where is the van he was driving when he arrived in Hastings?"

"We haven't found it yet. It doesn't mean we won't. I don't fancy the idea that this man, whoever he is, is setting up shop in Hastings. I want him to go back to Eastfield. At least until you've made a little progress toward identifying him."

"This fellow soldier Hartle visits when he's here in Hastings—is the man in the clear?"

"Oh yes, he couldn't overpower Hartle if he tried. Consumptive, if you ask me. Thin as a rail."

Rutledge drew a breath in frustration. "Keep looking. I'm on my way to London to investigate these discs. Call the Yard and ask for Sergeant Gibson, if you need to reach me."

But he wasn't ready to leave Hastings just yet. He went in search of the pub, The Fisherman's Catch, and saw that it was a small establishment that catered to men who ate hearty in the morning and were in bed well before nine in the evening, to sail with the sand fleet before the sun rose.

Hamish said, "He wouldna' stay o'er long, if he was to reach home at a reasonable hour."

"He must have done this time. Was someone following him? Or did the killer know he was being sent to Hastings yesterday? It's uncanny how well someone understood the habits of the first three victims and where to find them alone at night. If he's watching them, he lives in Eastfield. That's one of the reasons I penned those men in the police station."

The cook, one Bill Mason, was in the middle of preparing a roast for the evening meal, and Rutledge agreed to interview him in the kitchen.

It was small, crowded, noisy, and almost unbearably hot. Claustrophobic, Rutledge felt the beginnings of a cold sweat.

"I've already talked to Inspector Norman's men," Mason said, busy basting the roast and then preparing potatoes and onions to add to the pan. Inspector Norman had called him thin, but he was cadaverous, his hands shaking, his cheeks sunken, a nervous tic by one eye.

Rutledge recognized the symptoms. Shell shock, not consumption. He swallowed hard, to keep his own voice from cracking as he said, "They must have asked you about when Hartle came here, and when he left. I want to know if he was afraid of anyone?"

The sunken gray eyes turned to gaze for a moment at Rutledge's face.

"Afraid?"

"Yes. Of anything. Anyone. Did you serve with him in France?"

"We met in hospital. We never fought together." Mason turned back to his work, as someone from the bar shouted a request for a ham sandwich with pickle. A helper, who had been listening in to the conversation, reluctantly turned away to fill the order. Mason watched him for a moment, then said quietly, "I don't know that Theo Hartle was afraid. Not exactly. But he saw someone here in Hastings. Yesterday morning, while he was looking to buy the varnish. He couldn't put a name to the face, and that worried him. He caught just a glimpse, mind you, but he couldn't get it out of his head. When I came back from Eastbourne, he was waiting for me here. He wanted me to help him search, and see if I recognized the man. I told him to leave well enough alone."

"Why did he think you might know this man?"

"When he was in hospital, there were days when Theo was barely conscious. He thought I might be able to put a name to the face. He said it was important to know." He finished peeling the potatoes and set them aside.

Rutledge said, "He was hoping it was someone from the hospital? Or not?"

"He was hoping it was. He said he'd feel better if it was."

"Did the man seem to recognize Hartle?"

"I don't know. Theo didn't say anything about that. He just didn't want it to be the father."

"Whose father?"

The cook's hands were shaking. He put aside the carrot he was trying to scrape and clutched the edge of the table with taut fingers, his head down. "Just go away. Now. I can't—you're pushing too hard. Please."

Rutledge could hear his own voice saying, "Lives depend on this. Whose father?" But he was watching the color drain from Mason's face, and the way his eyes were blinking, as if he couldn't focus them properly.

Hamish's voice was loud between them, warning Rutledge to stop. And Rutledge could feel himself losing control, blackness sweeping through his mind, the sound of the guns so loud he wanted to press his hands over his ears and hide from it.

But he was here for a reason, and he gripped that the way most men would grip sanity, and said again, "Whose?"

He could hardly hear the reply. It was a whisper lost in the roar of guns that wouldn't stop.

"He wouldn't tell me. For God's sake, he wouldn't tell me. And I let him go hunting for that man alone, because I'm a coward."

Rutledge reached out and clapped Mason on the shoulder, a comradely gesture, but the man shrunk from him, cringing until he was lying on the floor in a tight knot, protecting his body.

"He wouldn't tell me. For God's sake, he wouldn't tell me. And I let him go looking for the man alone."

Ashamed, Rutledge stumbled out of the kitchen, somehow found his way to the door and into the street. He leaned against the wing of the motorcar, sick. The sounds slowly receded, and after a time, the darkness also withdrew. He straightened up, ignoring Hamish still raving in his mind.

9

Leaving the motorcar where it was, Rutledge began walking, heading nowhere, one street after another, left and then right and then left again.

After a while, he found he was standing in front of a small shop, its black-and-white-striped awning affording a little shade from the now warm sun. Gradually he noticed that he was staring at a display of porcelain figures, jeweled fans, small dolls in colorful costumes, enameled silver snuffboxes, and ornate black lacquerware with scenes from fairy tales fancifully painted across the tops.

He had no idea where he was. Looking up at the scrolled letters on the shop window, he realized that this was where Russian émigrés had put their personal belongings up for sale.

Turning away, he tried to get his bearings. There was the distant headland, green now in the sunlight, where Hartle's body had been found. Using that as his guide, he walked in an easterly direction until he realized that he was coming out of a side street that ended near the water.

The pub was several streets over. Glancing at his watch, he realized that he'd been walking for more than an hour. He swore and was about to turn up toward the pub and his motorcar when another shop window caught his eye.

The display was of all things military. Gold braided tricorns, an assortment of swords, and a polished table where tiny lead soldiers fought pitched battles. There was a rusty halberd, books on military tactics from wars long past, a pistol with a split barrel, and even a well-used Kaiser Wilhelm helmet with its pointed spike, and a long spear that appeared to be East African.

On the spur of the moment, he went inside. The proprietor was an elderly man with streaks of gray in his fair hair, and bright blue eyes. He glanced up from a sock he was mending as the bell over the door jingled, and smiled at Rutledge. "Looking for anything in particular?" he asked in a deep, gruff voice.

"Identity discs from the war. Do you ever see them? Or have them for sale?"

The crinkles around the blue eyes deepened. "There's no market for that sort of thing. They were rather flimsily made, as a rule. Buttons, now, and uniforms—they turn up. I have a button hook, from the Grenadier Guards. Any number of shell casings, some of them with trench art, others plain. An officer's whistle, well-polished riding boots with gilt spurs—even several pairs of field glasses."

Hamish had subsided in his mind, and Rutledge was about to turn away when something caught his eye in the glass display case where he was standing. It contained smaller and more expensive objects kept under lock and key. There were an ivory pipe, a cigarette case made from what appeared to be tortoiseshell, a flint knife, a few American Civil War lead soldiers, and assorted buttons, watches, rings, and other pieces of jewelry inscribed with military insignia.

He pointed to the knife. "What can you tell me about that?"

"It's said to be quite old. Struck from a single large flint. The gentleman who brought it in told me his grandfather had turned it up while working in his garden. It set him off on a search for an ancient burial site, thinking there might be funeral goods. But to no end." The proprietor took the object out of the case. "You can see how the blows were struck to shape the blade. Careful," he added as he passed it to Rutledge. "It's sharp enough to cut hide."

Rutledge took the blade. "How was it used?"

"According to a Dr. Butler who comes in from time to time, it would have had a handle, a length of wood with a fork at one end, into which the blade would have been inserted." He pointed to the blunt end. "See how it's notched? Rawhide would be wrapped tightly around wood and blade, and perhaps soaked, for a tight fit. If you knew what you were about, you could flense a hide just with the blade, but if you were of a mind to stab a woolly mammoth, you'd need the handle for a sure grip. Short handle for jabbing, longer piece of wood for throwing. Of course, if this is as old as it's said to be, the wood and the rawhide have long since rotted away. A pity, but there you are."

"Yes, I see." Rutledge gingerly tested an edge, and could see that it was quite remarkably sharp still. "Where did you say it was found?"

"I didn't. But from what I was told, the old grandfather lived in East Anglia. There's flint there, along the north coast." He reached into the case again and drew out two or three unprepossessing round gray stones, and with them half of a stone, showing the shiny black surface of the flint inside. Rutledge was well aware of what flint looked like. But he let the proprietor continue his explanation of how flint tools could be made. "Stone Age or not, but whoever discovered how to do this sort of work must have had a monopoly in his day. Everyone came to him for their blades. Until someone else learned how to do it a little better or a little faster. Striking the blow in the right place to make a sharp edge rather than break the edge off—that's the skill right there."

Rutledge said after a moment, "A long way to come, to sell you this find."

"I was of the same opinion." The man shrugged. "But it's a fine piece of its kind. Only it never sold. There's not much call for something this old. I've kept it more as a curiosity than anything else. What's a military shop without what must have been one of the first tools of war?"

"How do you remember who brought you each item?" Rutledge asked.

"I've kept a record over the years. I read it sometimes. There was a gilded sword that had belonged to one of Napoleon's generals. Inscribed as well. I was reluctant to sell it, but money is money."

He pulled a dog-eared ledger from beneath his counter and opened it at random. Rutledge could see that he had listed each object he'd bought, the date, and the price paid. He'd also drawn a fine sketch of it as well.

"Let's see." He thumbed through the pages until he'd found what he wanted. "There it is: 1908. Flint knife blade." He pointed to the clever sketch, filled in with black ink. "Sold to me for fifteen pounds by a Charles Henry. No provenance that it is as old as it appears to be, but it is a fine example of flint workmanship, and I rather liked it. But it never brought in the profit I had anticipated." He turned more pages, and then pointed out that he had sold a button hook to a man from Kent on holiday in Hastings. "This is the half of the ledger where I keep my sales listed."

Rutledge thanked the man and was on the point of leaving when he changed his mind and asked the price of the flint knife.

"Sixteen pounds, I'm afraid. Necessary to turn a profit even after all this time."

Rutledge bought it, and then asked if it could be wrapped and put into a box for mailing.

Ten minutes later, he walked out of the shop and went to find the post office. There he sent the small parcel to Chief Inspector Cummins.

He'd added a brief message:

I found this in a shop in Hastings, Sussex. It is said to be old, but I should think anyone who knew how to work flint could make one just like it. Add a handle, wrap it well with rawhide, and it would make a formidable weapon. It would most certainly explain the bit of flint found in your victim's wound. And it could explain, in some measure, why he was a sacrifice. This may not be as old as Stonehenge, but it could most certainly have been used to kill men as well as animals. What do you think?

At the Yard, Sergeant Gibson had the direction of the three men whose discs had been found before Rutledge had arrived in Sussex.

He had had time, on the long drive, to consider which of the men to call on first. And he'd chosen the man whose name was connected with Anthony Pierce. Pierce the officer, the anomaly.

Corporal Trayner lived in Belton, Yorkshire, and Rutledge drove on late into the night to make up for lost time, finally stopping in Stafford, in a hotel near the railway station. This was industrial country, and the town's buildings were black from coal smoke. Stafford's narrow streets and tall church tower had always reminded him of etchings he'd seen of German villages.

Late the next morning he arrived in the little town of Belton and asked at the local police station for directions to the Trayner house. It proved to be one of six

Victorian cottages down a lane just past the churchyard: solid houses of no particular distinction except for the gardens that grew rampant in the small space between the gate along the road and the door. Hollyhocks stood tall in the back of the gardens, holding pride of place at this time of year. A rose climbed to the small porch of the fifth house, and a small sign by the walk identified this as SPRING COTTAGE.

Rutledge went to the door and lifted the knocker, a brass dolphin.

A young woman answered the summons, and asked his business.

Rutledge identified himself and asked to speak to Corporal Trayner.

She invited him in, saying over her shoulder, "Dear, there's a Mr. Rutledge to see you. From Scotland Yard."

She led the way into the front room. Although the curtains stood open, the room felt dark, closed in, despite its eastern exposure and the brightness of the morning sun. A man sat in one of the chairs, a cushion at his back and a white cane at his side. He rose as Rutledge entered and held out his hand. But his eyes were scarred and blind, and he waited for his visitor to come to him.

Rutledge took the extended hand, and then the chair that Trayner indicated. He was fair, with broad shoulders and a ruddy complexion. He said, "What brings you here, Inspector?" There was only curiosity in his voice, not strain. If he had a guilty conscience, it was well concealed.

Rutledge briefly explained his reason for driving to Belton, and added, "Can you tell me if you are still in possession of your identity discs?"

"I don't think I ever had any. Not of the sort you describe. I know what they are. I just sewed labels in my uniforms, mostly in the pockets, and that was that."

It was an unexpected response.

Rutledge said, "You're quite sure about this? It's rather important."

"Yes, I'm sure. To tell you the truth, most of the men in my company were not impressed with the fiberboard discs. We were regular Army, you see. Or I was, until this." He gestured in the direction of his eyes.

"Did you know an officer by the name of Pierce? Anthony Pierce?"

Trayner shook his head. "No, the name means nothing to me. Should it?"

"Does Eastfield, Sussex, mean anything to you? Or these names: William Jeffers, James Roper? Theo Hartle?"

Trayner frowned but said only, "I'm afraid I can't help. You must be mistaken."

"Your name was on the disc I saw. I can't be wrong on that."

"And you say that this must have something to do with me? But what?"

"I don't know," Rutledge said slowly, feeling his fatigue as he spoke. It had been a long drive for nothing. And time was short. He had three days. Not enough time to go elsewhere. And yet now he felt compelled to try.

Finally he asked, "Was there anything that happened in France—anything at all—that might make someone feel he had to avenge your blindness?"

"Revenge is a very strong term. But if any of my men felt that I had been wronged, they'd have taken their anger out on the Germans. Not the British. It was a German shell that did this."

Rutledge had to leave it there. He asked them to contact the Yard if they could remember any detail that might have been overlooked, and they agreed.

Mrs. Trayner saw Rutledge to the door. He apologized for disturbing them, and she smiled wryly. "I've never seen anyone questioned in a murder case before. It breaks the tedium of our days. But my husband is telling the truth, Inspector. He always does."

Rutledge thanked her and turned away. But Trayner's voice called to him from inside the house, and Rutledge heard him stumble as he hurried toward the door. Mrs. Trayner went quickly to help him, but her husband brushed her aside impatiently.

"No harm done, Lucy! Don't fuss." He came out into the passage and asked, "Are you still there, Inspector Rutledge?"

"Yes, I'm here. What is it?"

"I was right when I told you I didn't remember your Anthony Pierce. But there was another Pierce—David, I think it was. A lieutenant in the sappers. He was attached to our division for two or three weeks. I don't think I met him, but I knew of him. Is that any use to you?"

"David?" Rutledge queried.

"No, David isn't right." Trayner's sightless eyes squinted in the direction of the sky as he pondered. "Daniel. That was it, Daniel Pierce." His eyes came back to where he thought Rutledge was standing. "He had a reputation for being difficult, as I recall. That's how I came to hear of him. But damned good at his job, from all reports."

Trayner was pleased with himself, as if this was a small victory over his sightlessness, proving to Scotland Yard that he was a reliable witness, even if he couldn't see as other men did.

"That's very helpful," Rutledge answered, thanking him and moving on to the motorcar.

Just as he was about to drive away, Hamish said, "Is he still there?"

And Rutledge looked back. Trayner was standing in the open door, as if savoring the world beyond his doorstep. His wife hovered in the background, fearful that he might take it into his head to do something that would harm him.

There was a severe thunderstorm as he crossed into Wales, and Rutledge took shelter in a small hotel that was miles short of his destination. The Welsh border had once been as turbulent as the Scottish border, but this hotel catered to day-trippers coming across from Worcester, and the dining room was crowded with those caught out by the weather on their way back to England.

He sat in the bar, looking out at the lightning, and wondered what he would learn from J. A. S. Jones, Welsh sapper. He turned as the man behind the bar asked what he'd have, and gave his order. Noting the man's limp and a ragged scar down his arm, he asked, "In the war, were you?"

The man smiled grimly. "I was that. And you?"

Rutledge gave his regiment, but not his rank.

"At the Somme, were you? Lost my brother there, I did."

"Bloody shambles," Rutledge answered, agreeing with the unspoken condemnation he heard in the Welshman's voice.

"It was, and all."

He brought Rutledge's ale, and said, "I've found it hard to settle again. I don't know if it's because of my brother or because I can't see any sense in anything now. We were close."

"What about your family?"

"That's what my da asks, over and over again. What about my wife and children. I don't know the answer. I think I've changed. And they haven't."

He went away to serve another storm-bound driver, and then came back to where Rutledge was still standing.

"How've you managed, then?"

"I was wise enough not to marry before I went away to fight. Just as well, as it happened." He regarded the man. "What did you do with your identity discs, when you came back?"

The man gave a bark of laughter. But it was bitter. "Burned them, I did. In the grate. As if I could burn away all that went with them. Sadly, it made no difference."

More people were coming in, and he was busy. Rutledge took his glass and went to an empty table by the window. He'd hardly finished his ale when the storm moved on almost as suddenly as it had appeared, and the rain changed from downpour to a light drizzle that barely concealed the sun.

Moving on, Rutledge discovered that J. A. S. Jones lived in a town so small it hardly took up space on the map he'd used to bring him this far. The small slate-roofed houses huddled together against a hillside, and the road seemed to help pin them there, preventing them from sliding down into the brisk little stream on the far side.

J. A. S. Jones lived above his father's greengrocer's shop. A stair to one side of the shop door led up to another door at the top, and here Rutledge knocked several times before anyone came to answer the summons.

Jones was a small, dark man, with thinning hair and a short beard. He looked at Rutledge quizzically and said, "If you're wanting your money, I don't have it. Not this week."

"My name is Rutledge. From Scotland Yard in London—"

"Good God, I know I'm overdawn at the bank. They needn't have sent the Yard!"

"I know nothing about your banking arrangements," Rutledge said. "I'm here to ask a question about the war, to do with a murder inquiry in Sussex."

"Sussex? I don't think I've ever been there." His frown appeared to be genuine. "What is it you want of me?"

"Can you tell me what became of your identity discs?"

Jones stared at him. "I—I don't really know. Is it important?"

"Very. If they are here, will you look for them, please?"

"Come inside, then." Jones stepped back from the door. "I'm a bachelor. There's nothing tidy about the place."

It was true. Half-eaten meals littered the tabletop in the long single room, and clothes had been dropped helter-skelter on the floor, the two or three chairs, and the posts of a bed. Rutledge could see the tiny kitchen at the far end opposite the door.

"I'm out of work at present," Jones told him, dragging a small battered trunk out from under the high, old-fashioned bed. "My family does what it can to keep me out of the poorhouse, but it's been a close-run thing." Unlocking and then lifting the lid, he considered the contents, mostly the uniforms. "Why would you want my discs? I served out my time, there's been no problem with the Army." He began to delve into a corner, fingers poking here and there.

Rutledge said, "There have been several murders in a village where all the men served together. In each case, a disc was found in the dead man's mouth. The names on the discs appeared to be random—Yorkshire,

Cheshire, Wales. We're trying to find out what connection the discs could have with events in the war."

Jones looked up from his search. "You're saying one of these men had my disc in his mouth? But that's not possible, I have my discs here. There must be some mistake."

"If you have your own discs, then I shall have to agree with you there," Rutledge responded.

Jones went back to searching and finally brought out a thin strand of rope, from which two fiberboard discs dangled. "Here they are, then," he said triumphantly.

Rutledge took the rope and examined the discs. Both were there, the name on each one worn but still legible. The only difference between the two he held now and the one that had been found in Sussex was a small nick in the edge of the one owned by Jones.

"You're right," he said slowly. "You have both." After a moment he passed them back to Jones. "Did you ever serve with men from the vicinity of Hastings? Anyone named Theo Hartle, Jim Roper, Anthony Pierce, or William Jeffers?" He deliberately put no rank to the names.

An army in the field was seldom made up of one homogenous regiment. To bring a regiment up to strength, the army took what it needed from whatever troops were available. And so a company from Hastings might for a time serve with a company from Glasgow, only to see it replaced by a company from Cornwall if it suffered heavy casualties.

But Jones shook his head. "I don't think so."

"You were a sapper. Did you ever serve under a Lieutenant Daniel Pierce?"

"Never served with him, but we knew about him. There were stories of his going back into a tunnel to see why a charge hadn't blown. Or going back after men caught in the tunnel when it collapsed. One such story claimed he broke through into a German countertunnel, and the two men shook hands, then shot each other. I don't know how much of it was true, but we were always willing to believe the tales. It gave us a glamour, you might say. They claimed he dug a hole down to hell one night, and dined with the devil. There was always something being whispered behind the backs of our officers. It was their opinion such tales encouraged recklessness. It was dangerous duty at the best of times."

"What else was whispered about Lieutenant Pierce?"

"Oh, I dunno. That he was unlucky in love, that sort of thing." He set the discs back in the trunk, straightened the contents where he'd been digging around, and added over his shoulder, "He wasn't the only one unlucky in love. I came home to find that the girl I was to marry had eloped with a bo'sun from a frigate. An Englishman at that."

Hamish was saying something in the back of his mind, but Rutledge was already posing the question. "How did you know that Pierce was unlucky in love?"

"One story said the girl he was to marry had died. Another said that she'd chosen another man. Either way, she was lost to him, wasn't she? And where there's smoke, there must be fire." He shoved the trunk back under the bed and got up, dusting off his hands. "Will there be anything else, Inspector?" he asked warily, as if the discs had been a trick to get Rutledge in the door and the truth was to come out now.

Preoccupied, Rutledge said, "No. Thank you. I'm satisfied that all is as it should be."

But when he left, Jones was standing in the doorway, watching him go, as if to make sure Rutledge wasn't playing some sort of game.

Rutledge could feel his gaze on the back of his neck and wondered what Jones had done that made the man so suspicious of a policeman's visit. On the whole, Rutledge thought, his answers had appeared to be truthful.

It wasn't his inquiry, and he let it go.

Hamish, in the back of his mind, said as the motorcar turned around and Rutledge headed for England, "He was verra' careful of yon trunk. He brought back souvenirs he shouldna' have had."

And Jones wouldn't have been the first to do that.

Coming through Gloucester, Rutledge realized he would pass not twenty miles from where Rosemary Hume lived. She had told him to go away, but that was in the heat of anger and heartbreak over her husband's death. He debated, and then decided to stop and speak to her. She could have changed her mind, and he owed it to Max, he thought, to do what he could.

When he reached Chaswell, the first person he recognized was Max's cousin Reginald, sitting in a motorcar outside a greengrocer's.

He pulled alongside and Reginald looked up, greeting him with the warmth of a man doomed to boredom for a good half hour more.

"Inspector. What brings you back to Chaswell? You're the last person I expected to see this afternoon."

"I've been to Wales to interview a witness. I'm on my way back to London and thence to Sussex. How is Rosemary?"

"She's taken it hard—but you know that. She hasn't forgiven poor Max. And nothing I can say will change her mind. So I've given up trying. I'm surprised she wants me here. But she does. And in time that should help the healing." He made a deprecating gesture. "Or possibly she's afraid the journey back to Scotland will kill me, and she doesn't want my death on her hands."

Rutledge smiled, ignoring a lorry driver sounding his horn as he edged past the two motorcars half blocking the road. "Anything I can do?"

"No. Just—stay in touch." His gaze went to the shop door as two women emerged, baskets in their hands, chatting together. Then he turned back to Rutledge. "I haven't got much longer. I know that, and so does Rosemary. I expect that's why she hasn't sent me away." He paused, staring down the road, as if he knew where it was leading. He didn't look at Rutledge as he asked, "Will you come and see me, if I send for you? For Max's sake?"

Rutledge thought he knew what Reginald was saying, that with Max gone, he felt the need of someone to be there at the end. For it was not a death he could ask Rosemary to watch.

"I give you my word I'll try."

Reginald nodded. "It's no more than I expected. Thank you, Ian." It was the only time he'd used Rutledge's given name.

And then Rosemary Hume stepped out of the shop, and looked up to see Rutledge speaking to her houseguest. For an instant he thought she was about to turn away. Instead she gave him a cool greeting, and Rutledge asked how she was coping.

"I've had time to understand what happened to us, to Max and me," she said. "If he didn't care enough to go on living, if he couldn't face me with the truth of his feelings, then our marriage was over." She held out one hand, stripping off its glove. Her finger was bare of rings. "I intend to take him at his word, and go on with my own life as I see fit." But as she turned to pass the basket filled with her purchases to Reginald, Rutledge caught the reflection of unshed tears in her eyes. Recovering, she said, "I thought you had pressing Yard business in Sussex."

"It's what took me to Wales. I'm returning to Sussex now." He hesitated. "Rosemary—"

"Ian, no! Don't make excuses for him." She turned to Reginald, but before he could step out of the motorcar to turn the crank, Rutledge forestalled him.

"I'll see to it."

He did, and moved to one side. With a nod, she drove away.

Hamish said, "Ye canna' talk to her. No' until she's at peace."

"Yes," Rutledge answered, returning to his own vehicle. "That's true. At least Reginald has stayed with her. In the end, that may help her more than anything I could do or say."

He didn't stop in London. The three days were up at sundown. He paused in Hampshire and tried to put a telephone call through to the brewery, but there was no answer. He realized that Tyrell Pierce's office must already be closed. And there was no way now to reach Constable Walker, to tell him to keep the six men under lock and key until he could arrive in Eastfield sometime in the early hours of the morning.

He tried next to telephone Inspector Norman in Hastings, in the hope that he could get word to Eastfield. But Inspector Norman was out on another case, he was told, and Rutledge would have to wait for his return.

He attempted to explain the situation, but the man on the other end of the line said firmly, "I'm sorry, sir, you'll have to speak to the inspector."

Swearing to himself, Rutledge grimly set out again, making the best time he could.

He hoped that Walker would have the good sense to wait. But with each mile he was more and more convinced that the objections of the incarcerated men would prevail, and Walker would let them go. After all, he had to live in Eastfield, long after Rutledge had returned to London.

And there was nothing to be done about it but to pray that the waiting killer failed to find one of his targets alone and vulnerable.

10

It was closer to five in the morning when Rutledge drove into Eastfield and drew to a halt outside the police station.

He had had to stop for an hour's rest somewhere in the New Forest, pulling to the side of the road in an effort to rest his eyes. The night sounds around him were soothing, and he had slept instead. For a wonder Hamish was quiet. He had been busy ever since Rutledge had left Chaswell, taking advantage as he so often did of the stress that was already filling Rutledge's mind.

It was becoming increasingly apparent that something more than an event in the war lay behind these murders. For one thing, there was the face that Hartle couldn't place, a face that worried him, on the day he was killed.

Who was it he'd seen, and had he not only tried to find that man again, but encountered him in the dark on the headland? And why the headland? For another, the connection between those identity discs and the murders was less clear than it had first appeared.

And there was Daniel Pierce as well, whose name kept cropping up.

Were these pointers toward the truth, or was he still missing something that would bring the disparate pieces of the puzzle together?

But even Hamish was silenced by sleep, brief though it was—no more than twenty minutes, but twenty precious minutes if a man's life was hanging in the balance. The day had broken now. Whatever was going to happen had already happened.

He sat for a moment in the motorcar, fighting his fatigue and staring at the closed and silent police station.

It was one of the hazards of police work, making the wrong judgment. He had done his best to protect the six potential victims of this killer, rather than taking the chance that the murderer wouldn't strike again while he was away. But at the same time, he'd accepted a risk of a different sort—by denying the killer his opportunity, he could have changed whatever plan there was to these murders and caused it to take on different, possibly more personal overtones. He wasn't interested in finding out whether he could outwit the murderer or not. He was only intent on stopping him.

He got out of the motorcar and stretched, his muscles tight and cramped from the drive from Wales. And then he walked to the door of the police station and put out his hand to lift the latch.

The door was firmly locked.

He stood there for a moment, his tired mind trying to grasp what that meant. A police station was always open. If the constable wasn't there, he left a message on the desk telling whoever needed him where he could be found.

Foreboding gripped him. He knocked firmly, using his knuckles. And there was no answer.

He had no idea where Walker was. At home? At the scene of another death? And there was no one about at this hour, the street quiet and shuttered.

And then Rutledge remembered Mrs. Sanders, who had seen the lorry driver come through Hastings and then return again for the police after he'd spotted the first body on the road. Rutledge had read her statement.

He turned and looked across the way. Where was she? Not in the shops—or even above them. Then he saw the tall, narrow house wedged between a milliner's and an apothecary's. It looked to be one of the oldest buildings in Eastfield, brick and timber, the upper story leaning slightly to one side, as if the foundation had begun to subside when the newer apothecary's had been built.

Crossing the street, he walked up to the front of the house and looked up at the double windows of the first floor.

One window was open to the slight morning breeze, the lacy white curtain billowing into the dark room behind, and Hamish said, "'Ware!"

Rutledge peered intently at the window and then realized that behind the panel of white curtain was a tiny, wizened face, looking to be as old as the house itself.

He called to the woman staring down at him, pitching his voice so that it carried to her but didn't rouse neighbors on either side.

"I'm looking for Constable Walker."

"Come in," Mrs. Sanders called after a moment. "I never lock my door."

He turned and lifted the latch. The door swung open easily, and he stepped into a narrow dark passage. To one side, stairs climbed to the first floor. To the other, shut doors led into two rooms, and then a third door closed off the passage at the far end.

He took the stairs two at a time, and rounded the railing toward the open door of the room that overlooked the street.

A chair stood by the window, and in it sat the woman he'd glimpsed from below, cushioned and pillowed and covered with a quilted comforter.

She turned her head to smile at him, the wrinkles in her face smoothing across her withered cheeks. But the eyes in that face were neither clouded nor dim. They were the color of pansies, almost a purple they were so dark a blue. Her well-brushed white hair, drawn back into a smooth braid that lay over one shoulder, looked like a pale halo in the shadow of the curtain.

"Come in, young man. You must be the policeman from London. I've seen you come and go from the station with Constable Walker."

"Yes, I'm Inspector Rutledge. Mrs. Sanders?"

"Indeed I am. There's a chair behind you. Do sit down."

He sat. "I'm trying to find the constable. Unaccountably, the station is locked."

"So it is. He came out shortly after midnight and walked away. I think he locked the door as a precaution."

"A precaution?"

"He was afraid those who were inside would try to leave."

Rutledge felt a surge of sheer relief. "He's kept the six men locked up inside?"

"Oh, yes, but it wasn't an easy task. I could hear the yelling last night. My guess is, that's why Constable Walker left. There's nothing wrong with my eyes or my ears. Only my limbs have given out."

"I believe you. Do you sit at that window every night?"

"And every day, except when I take my meals. I'm nosey, you see. And I have the world spread out before me here. I don't need much sleep. I doze when I feel like it, and the rest of the time, I watch. It can be quite entertaining. Eventually the whole town passes beneath my window or across the street from me."

"You gave Constable Walker a statement regarding the lorry driver—" He had been about to say, the driver who found the first body, but broke off.

"Don't be shy, young man. There have been four murders in this town, if you count poor Theo Hartle. I have a woman who comes and cleans for me, and another who brings my evening meal. We gossip."

He was sure they did.

"Have you seen anything else from your window? Strangers who come to Eastfield in the night but who aren't to be found during the day?"

"There was a man, before the killings began— perhaps a week before. It was dark when he came walking up the Hastings Road. I couldn't see him clearly enough to identify him. He was moving without haste, like a sightseer taking in the view. I thought it was odd, even so, but I decided he was looking for work and trying to determine whether he stood a better chance here or in Hastings. I expect he chose Hastings, because I never saw him again."

He said, taking a chance, "Did you know Daniel Pierce well enough to say with any certainty that the man wasn't Pierce?"

Her eyebrows rose. "Danny Pierce? Do you think he's come home? Or considered it?"

"I don't know. You must tell me."

She gave that some thought. "I can't see Danny slinking through Eastfield in the dark. He'd come striding in. There are those who would be happy to see him, if he did."

"Then who else could that man have been?"

"If I come up with a name, I'll tell you," she promised. "Meanwhile, there's Constable Walker standing by your motorcar, wondering where you might have got to."

Rutledge rose and glanced out the window. And he had a perfectly clear view of the constable, framed as neatly as a photograph for Mrs. Sanders's pleasure.

He thanked her and left, closing the house door behind him. As he started across the street, Constable

Walker called testily, "I wondered where you went. I was about to try the hotel." He waited until Rutledge had reached him and added, "What did you learn about those discs? I hope it was worthwhile. I've had to put up with enough abuse while you were away."

"The Yorkshire corporal had never had discs. The Welsh sapper found that his were still in his trunk, where he expected them to be. There was no time to move on to Cheshire, but I'm beginning to think we need to take a closer look at those discs we have."

"You're saying there's no feud between companies?"

"The two men I questioned had never heard of our victims. But they knew Daniel Pierce by hearsay. He was a colorful man, apparently."

Walker frowned. "Mr. Pierce—his father—won't be pleased with that news."

"And you are not to tell him. This is a Yard matter. We'll leave him out of it until we need to question him again. Meanwhile, I was very glad to see you'd kept your charges."

"Actually, I let one of them go in the middle of the night. His wife had her baby, there were complications, and Dr. Gooding sent to ask if he could come home. I locked the door to the police station and took him there myself. As it turned out, mother and child are fine, but they could have lost the baby."

"Well done. Let's see how the rest of our charges are faring."

Walker unlocked the door to total silence. He glanced at Rutledge, and crossed to the cabinet behind his desk to retrieve the lantern he kept there. Then he led the way to the large holding cells where he'd incarcerated the six men. When he opened the second door into that passage, his eyes had to adjust to the gloom before he saw his five remaining prisoners. They were standing, backed up against the cell wall, faces pale and eyes squinting against the sudden glare of the lantern, trying to see who was behind it. And then they recognized their jailer, their gaze traveling on to the tall figure behind him.

There was an outburst of protest, vociferous and heated.

Rutledge had expected their anger to be directed at him, since he'd insisted on locking them up here. He wasn't disappointed. As he sorted through the words tripping over one another as the men demanded to know why Walker had abandoned them for the remainder of the night, he realized that they had come to agree with him about the danger they were in.

After a moment, Rutledge raised his own voice, accustomed to being heard on a battlefield, and stopped them in midsentence.

They glared at him but fell silent. He turned first to Walker's nephew.

"Now. One at a time. What's happened?"

"There was someone outside. Not fifteen minutes after my uncle had left with Tom. And here we were locked tight in here, like fish in a barrel," Tuttle told him.

"What do you mean, someone outside?" Walker demanded. "In front?"

"No, *there*," Tuttle said, pointing to a side door.

Walker said to Rutledge, "There's an alley outside. It led down to the stables and outbuildings. They were torn down at the turn of the century, and a warehouse for Kenton Chairs built in their place, facing the street that runs behind the station." He strode down the short passage and shook the latch, but it was still secure. As he came back, someone else took up the story.

"At first it sounded as if he was trying to force the lock. And then for a time there was nothing. We were just settling down when we could hear him again. I swear it sounded as if he was sliding something under the door. Marshall thought he might be blocking it, but after a bit it smelled as if he was trying to burn his way through. The passage filled with smoke. You can still smell it!"

Walker sniffed the air, then turned to Rutledge. "Do you?"

Rutledge nodded. It was faint, but enough smoke lingered to pick it out, now that it had been brought to his attention. Walker went again to the door and this time opened it. "Inspector? Sir?" he said after a moment, and Rutledge went to see what he'd found.

Charred rags were jammed against the bottom of the door, and Rutledge bent down to touch them. They were still damp, as if they had been lit and then nearly doused, to create a maximum of smoke with a minimum of fire. Rutledge looked up the alley toward the main road, but he couldn't see Mrs. Sanders's window. Which meant she couldn't have seen whoever was at work here.

"He could have set the building on fire," Walker declared, kicking the rags away from the door, and then squatting beside them to sift through them. But they were torn cloths, something that could have been found in a dustbin or a tip, Rutledge thought, used for cleaning and then discarded.

"I doubt the station would have caught. The outside of the door is blackened but not heavily charred. I think he was intending to stampede your charges."

Walker got to his feet. "If that's what he was after, he succeeded. There must have been pandemonium. Nobody relishes the thought of being burned alive."

"He must have seen you leave with Tom. He knew he was safe."

Walker looked at Rutledge. "I don't like the sound of that. That he was watching." He took a deep breath. "I was of two minds when you wanted these men clapped up. But now they'll be released, and the two of us can't watch six of them."

"But fright may have sharpened their memories. Let's find out."

They went back inside and told the anxious men in the holding cell what they'd discovered.

Tuttle, Walker's nephew, said, "Be damned to him, then. He's a coward."

But Marshall disagreed. "My uncle was out in India for a time. He told me that old tigers got a taste for man, when they couldn't kill larger prey. And they were more dangerous because of that. Their brethren in the jungle would slip away if they got the scent of a person. But not these."

"He's not a tiger," one of the other men said. "He's mad, that's what he is."

"I don't think so," Rutledge answered him. "And I ask you again. Is there anything in your pasts that could have come back to haunt you? Is there anyone who has ever held a grudge? In the war, here in Eastfield, in any place for that matter."

But they shook their heads.

Hamish said, "It was something loomed large in the killer's mind. But ye ken, not in theirs."

"How well do any of you know Daniel Pierce?" Rutledge asked. Out of the corner of his eye, he could see Walker's gesture intended to stop him from asking these men about the younger Pierce. But this was a murder inquiry, and Tyrell Pierce couldn't set limits on the directions it took.

"We knew him as a boy. But not as a man," Tuttle said after a glance at his companions. "He went away to school, you must know that, and even when he was home during holidays, he didn't have anything to do with us. Then after the war, he was hardly here in Eastfield before he was gone again. It was 'Mr. Daniel' then, and touching your cap to him."

"Did you resent his going away to school? Or was there something between you before then, while he was still Daniel? An old hurt, a misunderstanding, a case where no harm was meant, but he took it hard? Or perhaps you did?" His eyes swept the half circle of men, and he read nothing there that would help him.

"He gave as good as he got," Marshall answered, his glance sliding toward Walker and then away again. "We avoided him if we could manage it. He was Anthony's—Mr. Pierce's—little brother, and no one cared to have him tag along after us. What's more, he was a tattletale if we weren't careful, and on purpose he never got it right. Often as not, we were in trouble for something we hadn't done. I was that glad when he and his brother went off to that school. We'd had enough of both of them."

Rutledge considered the man, wondering what he had to hide. Because his voice and his shifting gaze betrayed him.

Hamish said, "He didna' care to be caught."

And that was very likely it—Marshall had been a ringleader in whatever mischief was afoot, and Daniel Pierce was a thorn in his side.

"The only reason we was allowed to play together was Mr. Pierce was busy at the brewery and couldn't always keep an eye on Anthony. And who else was there, I ask you, his age? The rector's son was older, and Dr. Gooding only had girls," Henderson added.

"Anthony was all right," one of the other men put in. "He never caused any trouble."

Which was an odd way to put it.

Still, they were getting nowhere. Burning down an empty mill and frightening lovers in a churchyard hardly led to murder. On the whole, he thought Hamish was right, the killer saw injury where others did not. If, in fact, it was the past that had led to these deaths.

He said, "When you leave here, don't take what happened last night lightly. Don't go out alone after dark. Not even on your own property. Take someone you trust with you. Between nine at night and early morning, lock your doors. If someone summons you, ignore it unless there's another person to go with you. And don't turn your back on a stranger. It could cost you your life. The four men who were killed had no chance to cry for help. Remember that. They were dead before they quite knew what was happening to them. It's not a risk worth taking."

And he let them go home. There was nothing else he could do.

Walker watched the five men gather their belongings and walk out the door of the police station without looking back. Even Tuttle, his nephew had nothing to say as they left.

"Do you think they'll heed your warning?" Walker asked.

Rutledge shook his head. "We'll know when the next victim is found."

Rutledge left the constable at the police station and went to The Fishermen's Arms to shave and change.

After an early breakfast, he went to the brewery and waited patiently in the office until Tyrell Pierce had finished overseeing the work on a new gauge for their primary vat.

He came in, brisk and busy, the distinctive aroma of roasted hops following him in the door. He ushered Rutledge into his office and said immediately, "Is there any news? Have you found this killer?"

"Not yet." Rutledge took the chair Pierce indicated and watched the man round his desk and sit down.

Hamish was saying, "Do ye reckon there's a reason his son canna' come back to Eastfield? And the father knows what it was he did, and who is to blame for it?"

Pierce was fit enough, Rutledge found himself thinking, but it was difficult to see what Daniel Pierce was afraid of—or was ashamed of. No one else seemed to remember. Unless of course the smoking rags under the police station door was a red herring, and the four men who might have told the police the truth were already dead. It was hard to believe that Pierce had murdered his elder son to protect the younger.

He recalled Tyrell Pierce's barely concealed fear on his first visit, fear that Daniel was somehow involved. Or at least that the police would suspect him.

Rutledge said, "Several differing possibilities are emerging in this case. I had thought initially that the war was at the bottom of these murders. The identity discs most certainly pointed in that direction. But the more I learn, the more questionable that assumption may be. Which brings me to another line of inquiry. Your son Daniel."

For an instant Rutledge thought Pierce was going to come across the desk after him. The man's face suffused with blood and there was such a deep anger in his eyes that Rutledge wondered if he'd taken Hamish's suggestion too lightly.

And then Pierce got control of himself and said tightly, "Are you like all the rest? At a loss to find the truth, and eager to lay these crimes at the door of a man who hasn't lived in Eastfield—really lived here—since well before the war?"

"I'm not interested in crucifying your son, Mr. Pierce. The best way to clear his name is to confront reality, not hide from it. Did your sons get on well together?"

"Of course they did," Pierce snapped.

"Were they both in love with the same girl?"

That caught the older man by surprise. "What are you talking about?"

"I spoke to a sapper in Wales. A man by the name of Jones. He told me that Daniel Pierce had quite a reputation during the war. Tales of his exploits were popular fare amongst sappers. There was even the story that he'd dug his way to hell and supped with the devil."

Pierce forced a laugh. "Hardly surprising. Daniel was nothing if not brave. And he had a cool head. Always did. He said it made him an ideal sapper."

And the murderer of four men also had a cool head, Hamish was reminding Rutledge, but he said only, "Your son was a man who preferred to work alone in the tunnels, when he was setting the charges. I imagine he must have had trouble with authority. He wanted to do things his way, including how to mine tunnels properly."

"All right, yes," Pierce said, goaded. "He wrote something in a letter. Something about the fact that if he was going to die, it would be his own mistake, not that of anyone else."

"They also said he appeared to live a charmed life. But that he was unlucky in love. The girl he wanted to marry died. If memory serves, before Anthony took an interest in Mrs. Farrell-Smith, he was engaged to a girl who died young."

"That's true. As far as it goes—"

"Is it possible that his brother Daniel was in love with the same woman?"

"I've never heard anyone even suggest that he might have been."

"Was there another girl, then?"

"I was unaware that my son fancied anyone, much less had formed an attachment. He'd always said that he never wanted to settle down to an ordinary life. As a boy he was forever reading about explorers and lamenting that there was nothing left to discover."

"Perhaps his brother was already set to inherit the only life Daniel wanted to live."

"Nonsense!"

"Men will also say such things when they've been disappointed in love."

"You never knew my son," Pierce told Rutledge, his voice harsh.

"On the other hand, I believe that Mrs. Farrell-Smith's late husband did in fact know Daniel. At school, perhaps?"

That surprised Pierce. "I don't know anything about that."

"When I called on her, Mrs. Farrell-Smith believed at first that I'd come to her because we knew where your son was."

"What are you driving at, man?"

"It makes me wonder how attached she was to Anthony Pierce. Or if she was fond of him because he was your heir."

That left the older man speechless.

"This is a small town," Rutledge continued, "hardly more than a village that has outgrown itself. It's difficult to keep secrets when people have known each other most of their lives. Men here went to the same school as children, they served in France—what else connects them? I don't know. Yet. You can't ignore the fact that when this killer has finished his work here, he could begin to search for Daniel next. Does your son know the danger in which he stands? Or will he be caught off guard like the first victims? You may feel that obstructing the police protects your son, but it could have just the opposite effect. Because he could possess the missing piece of information that could save other lives, including his own."

Tyrell Pierce's face was as pale as the shirt he was wearing.

"I've lost one child to this killer. I don't want to lose another. The truth is, I don't know why Daniel won't return to Eastfield. Or where he is. I write to him in care of a tobacconist shop in St. Ives, Cornwall. I have reason to believe he doesn't live there, that his mail is forwarded to him by the friend or acquaintance who owns the shop. Or whoever comes to collect it. It's a fragile link, but it's all I have, and I will preserve it at any cost. I want you to understand that. If you do anything to interrupt this line of communication—send policemen to question that shop owner or have my son's mail watched, or interfere in any way—I will see to it that your career at Scotland

Yard is over. I have the power to break you, and I will break you."

Rutledge believed every word of that warning.

"You can try," he said. "But if I were you, I'd do everything in my power to keep my son safe." He stood up, and for a moment regarded the frightened man on the other side of the desk. "Including asking the police to help me. As it is, if Daniel is killed, it will be no one's fault but your own."

He turned and walked out the door, not waiting for a reply. Behind him he heard Pierce clear his throat, as if on the point of calling him back, but in the end, he did not.

Rutledge went from the brewery to the school begun by an émigré Frenchman and now run by Mrs. Farrell-Smith.

She was just finishing a report when the girl on duty that morning led Rutledge to her office. She frowned when she saw who was standing in the doorway, but signed her name to the report, put it in a folder, and set it to one side before acknowledging her visitor with a nod.

Rutledge suppressed a smile. She would, he thought, have been quite happy to live in the era when a policeman was relegated to the servants' entrance and was shown to the family's quarters by a housemaid stiff with disapproval.

He stood there in silence, and finally, she was irritated enough to offer him a chair and ask him what brought him to the school this morning.

"Daniel Pierce," he said, and waited.

It took her a moment to compute this, clearly having expected him to begin with the murders.

"Daniel Pierce?" she repeated, trying to recover control of the conversation. "And what have I to do with Anthony's brother?"

"I'm waiting for you to tell me."

A slow flush crept up her fair skin. "Nothing," she snapped. "I have nothing to do with him."

"I'd wondered why you had been willing to take this position with the Misses Tate Latin School. I thought perhaps you were in straitened circumstances after your husband's death. Or that you felt a strong family tie to your aunts. Now I'm coming around to the possibility that you chose to accept this position because Daniel Pierce lived in Eastfield, and you expected him to return to the village when the war was over. Which he did. But he hardly spent a fortnight here. Was it because of you?"

"I shall have you recalled for incompetence and rudeness—"

"Rudeness to my betters? I'm sure you'll try. Meanwhile, I'll leave you with a problem that has been on my mind since Theo Hartle's murder. He recognized a passerby while he was in Hastings, the day of his death. He couldn't place the face he'd seen, but it disturbed him enough that he could well have gone in search of that person when he should have been returning to Eastfield. And that could very easily have cost him his life. Who did he see? Was it Daniel Pierce?"

He stood, and walked to the door. "I don't know why you feel I'm your enemy, Mrs. Farrell-Smith. Why you should feel more comfortable with Inspector Norman conducting this inquiry. I have no wish to probe into your personal life or your secrets. But I have four dead men to whom I owe a duty. And six living men I'm here to protect. If you can put your antipathy aside long enough to help me do what I came to do, we might save Daniel Pierce's life. It could well be that his name is on this murderer's list. Like his brother, he served in the war, and like his brother, he went to school here as a boy. If someone believed he had a good reason to kill Anthony Pierce, then it's likely that he also has a good reason to kill Daniel Pierce. Please consider that."

He walked out the door without waiting for an answer or looking back to see how Mrs. Farrell-Smith had taken his suggestion.

He was halfway down the passage when he heard her call his name.

But he kept going, and she didn't call a second time.

From the school he went to collect his motorcar, and drove to Hastings.

There was a telephone available in the offices of the Pierce Brothers Brewery, but the favor Rutledge expected to ask of Sergeant Gibson was not something he wanted to be overheard by anyone in Eastfield.

A LONELY DEATH · 183

But he kept going, and she didn't call a second time.

From the school he went to collect his motorcar, and drove to Hastings.

There was a telephone available in the offices of the Pierce Brothers Brewery, but the favor Rutledge expected to ask of Sergeant Gibson was not something he wanted to be overheard by anyone in Eastfield.

11

H amish was vocal as Rutledge drove to Hastings. "Ye've got nowhere," he reminded Rutledge. "And ye've annoyed yon brewer and the woman. They'll have ye recalled. It wasna' the chief superintendant who sent you here. Ye ken, he willna' stand by ye."

"I understand," Rutledge answered him aloud, the wind whipping his words away as he descended into Hastings. "But either Daniel is the danger—or he's in danger. Either way, I've got to find him."

"He's one man. There're six ithers at risk. Six ithers closer to hand."

"I know." He had reached The Stade at Hastings Old Town. The sound of waves rolling in was regular and soothing, with no wind or storm to drive them today. He pulled to one side and watched the sea for a time. The whisper of the water just before it turned to race back into the sea was soft and seductive.

Rutledge had always liked the water. He'd learned to row at an early age but had never had the opportunity to sail. If the war hadn't come when it did, he thought he might have taken the time to learn. His life had stretched before him then in measured decades, and he had been happy. Marriage lay ahead, and with luck, children. He would have grown old with them, and watched their children in turn take their first steps toward a life of their own. It would have been enough. But that had never happened. He wasn't sure whether he missed it, or was glad that it had only been a dream. Broken dreams were easier to walk away from than broken lives.

He watched as sunlight danced across the water, and far out to sea a smudge of smoke marked the passage of a ship. Lines from O. A. Manning's poetry came to mind and he was unaware that he'd spoken them aloud.

"I look now and then at the sea
And the reflection of myself is there.
Restless sometimes
Or calm, or angry,
Or even uncaring.

But never happy.
I remember then I came from the sea,
And someday must go home."

Oddly enough, he had never liked the idea of drowning. The revolver was swifter and the darkness came faster. Max Hume had known what he was about.

Hamish said, "Aye, but first ye must write a letter to your sister."

That jarred him. What would he tell Frances that she would understand?

And that had been Max's dilemma and why he had not written to Rosemary.

Rutledge put the motorcar in gear again and drove west into Hastings New Town until he found a sizeable hotel. "There ought to be a telephone here," he said under his breath and found a place to leave his vehicle.

The White Swans was built with a wide balustraded terrace across the main front, warmed by the sun and sheltered by a projecting wing on either side. A great deal of architectural detail, reminiscent of a wedding cake, gave the three-story hotel an elegant air, and judging from the handsomely dressed families sitting under broad pastel umbrellas as they finished late breakfasts, it was expensive as well.

Rutledge took the shallow stairs that led up from the road two at a time, crossed the terrace, and entered the high-ceilinged lobby filled with chairs and potted plants and an air of style and grace. Reception was to one side of the ornate staircase, and he asked for a telephone. He was directed down a passage to a glass door. Inside was a leather chair and a small table with a telephone, a lamp, and an enameled tray holding a pen and hotel stationery.

He put through a call to Scotland Yard and was relieved when Sergeant Gibson came to the telephone almost at once.

"Sir? Any news?" Gibson asked. In the background, two men carried on a conversation, low-voiced, the words indistinguishable. Rutledge thought they were standing in Gibson's doorway or just outside.

"Not yet. I need information on a Farrell-Smith who died before the war, leaving a widow who is now in charge of the Misses Tate School in Eastfield. He went to public school in Surrey and was there at the same time as Anthony Pierce and his brother, Daniel. That's all I can tell you. But you should be able to trace him through the school."

"Do you know which school it was?"

"No, but you might try Whitefriars first."

"Indeed, I will. Where am I to find you, sir?"

"Send your reply by post to The Fishermen's Arms in Eastfield. I don't want to be overheard taking this call in the brewery office."

There was a moment of silence. Rutledge had assumed that Gibson was writing down the particulars of his request and also where he could be found.

Instead the sergeant had been waiting for the men outside his door to walk on down the passage, for as the voices in the background faded, Gibson said rapidly, "There's been a complaint. The Chief Constable spoke to the Chief Superintendent not half an hour ago. Rudeness and unprofessional conduct."

Rutledge said grimly, "The woman, Mrs. Farrell-Smith. She has not wanted the Yard to take this case away from the Hastings police. Is Bowles viewing this seriously?"

"Early days, sir. But is it wise to be looking into her family's background, under the circumstances?"

"She's a suspect. I can't give her special consideration just because she complains about me. And the best way to protect myself is to find out what it is she's afraid of and either strike her from the list of suspects or charge her. Go ahead with the queries. I'll accept the consequences. Just be as discreet as possible."

He rang off, sitting there in thought for several minutes before opening the door and stepping out into the passage.

As he did, he realized that a man was standing at Reception, waiting for the clerk behind the desk to return. And the man was staring at Rutledge with concentrated interest. Their eyes met.

"He kens who you are," Hamish warned. Rutledge was already striding toward Reception.

The man quickly turned his back and hurried out of Rutledge's line of sight. By the time Rutledge reached the lobby, the man had disappeared. Rapidly scanning first the staircase and then the lounge, Rutledge realized that the only direction the man could have taken was through the hotel door and out to the terrace.

He hastily surveyed the terrace, but the families and couples who were sitting beneath their pastel umbrellas seemed not to have noticed anything amiss. And on the street below the broad steps there was only a woman walking with a small child.

He went down the steps and stopped her, asking, "I just missed my friend. He came out of the hotel and I didn't see which way he was going."

Startled, she looked up at him. "A man? Um, I think he went that way," she told Rutledge, gesturing east. "No one has come by me going in the other direction." She inclined her head toward the west, the way she had come.

He thanked her with a smile that brought an answering smile, and then he was walking east along the Hastings Road.

But it was hopeless, there were more people on the walk now, and one man could easily have disappeared among them or popped into one of the small shops that catered to holidaymakers. He would need half a dozen policemen to help him search them all.

Standing to one side so as not to obstruct pedestrians coming toward him, he waited, on the off chance that the man, thinking himself safe, might reappear.

But his quarry was far too canny. And even though Rutledge returned to The White Swans and sat for a time in the quiet lounge, facing Reception, he never returned. Rutledge even spoke to the desk clerk, but he had been busy putting a jewelry box into one of the hotel guest safes, and never noticed the man waiting at Reception for him.

Rutledge drove back to Hastings Old Town and stopped where he had before, near the net shops. Even this space was more crowded than it had been, but he closed his eyes and tried to recall his brief glimpse of the man's face before he had turned away.

What had he seen? What could he be sure of?

How many times had he asked witnesses to describe someone?

The man was of a little above medium height, broad shouldered, hair a medium shade of brown, eyes indeterminate, but Rutledge thought they must be light rather than dark. Gray, possibly, or a pale blue.

Hamish said into the silence in the motorcar, "Gray eyes. Ye ken, he was wearing a gray suit."

It was true.

"What else?"

"He moved well."

That was true. That swift turn, almost on the thought, so that Rutledge could no longer see his face. And he was able to leave the hotel and cross the terrace without creating a stir, even when he was hurrying.

And he had fit in, at The White Swans. Clothing and appearance in keeping with the clientele. Nothing to make him stand out or seem memorable in a crowd. Even the woman with the child, when questioned, had paid him little heed, because he attracted no attention.

Rutledge gave it another few minutes, but there was nothing else.

He got out and started the motorcar and then for a moment debated where to turn. Not to Inspector Norman. Constable Walker, then.

He set out for Eastfield, his mind busy.

He would like to believe that the man was Daniel Pierce. But how could Pierce recognize him on sight? Rutledge was aware that he too had fit into the hotel scene, comfortable in his surroundings and in no way attracting attention to himself. No one had walked past the telephone room while he was making his call. He was certain of that, for he could see clearly through the glass doors. The man couldn't have overheard part of his conversation, then. Their first contact came as he was stepping out of the telephone closet and starting down the passage. The man must have looked up, seen him, and in that same instant known who he was.

Hamish said, "Unless he followed you into the hotel. And wanted a better look."

"That's unlikely."

But was it? Where had the contact begun? In Eastfield, for instance? Had someone stalked Rutledge just as he'd stalked his victims, to take the measure of his opponent? There were enough dark corners and darker alleys, someone standing silently in the shadows could have escaped Rutledge's notice. But could he escape Hamish's?

There was no way of knowing. Before, when he had walked half blind out of the Hastings police station, he might well have attracted the notice of someone during that hour of helpless wandering. Still, he wanted to believe that it was unlikely. He didn't care for the feeling of vulnerability that being followed at such a time gave him.

Reaching Eastfield, he left the motorcar at The Fishermen's Arms and went on foot to the police station.

Constable Walker was just leaving to eat his midday meal.

He saw Rutledge's face as he came through the door, and said immediately, "Something's happened."

Rutledge answered, "I'm not sure. Describe Daniel Pierce for me."

Walker said, "Pierce? Let me see. Not as tall as you. Dark hair, light blue eyes. Slim. At least he was the last time I saw him. He'd just come home from France. He may have filled out since then. Why?" He frowned. "Don't tell me you've found him!"

Was it Pierce?

Hamish said, "The sun could ha' lightened his hair."

That was true. But was it Pierce?

Or had he caught a glimpse of the murderer, who would have every reason by now to know what the man from London looked like.

Better to let it go. Rutledge said, "I was probably mistaken."

"Or wishful thinking," Walker replied with a grin. Then it vanished as he added, "Despite what his father says, I don't know of any reason for Daniel to be living in Hastings, within a stone's throw, you might say, and not keeping in touch with his family. If you want my opinion, for what it's worth, Daniel Pierce is living in London, where he's his own man. It's what I'd do, in his shoes."

Rutledge was sorely tempted to ask Tyrell Pierce if he kept a photograph of his sons at the brewery, but better judgment prevailed. It was not yet the time to let the man at The White Swans—if he was indeed Daniel Pierce—know that he'd been identified.

On the other hand, there was a question he wished to put to Theo Hartle's sister.

He went to the Winslow house and knocked at the door. He was almost certain someone was inside, and he waited. Eventually, Winslow himself opened the door, his face sour.

"I'm not up to visitors today," he said plaintively. "You must come back another time."

"I'm sorry to have disturbed you. It was your wife I wished to see."

That brought a grunt from the man in the chair. "She's not here."

Rutledge thanked him and left.

As he walked back to the Hastings Road, which formed the main street of Eastfield, he asked himself where Mrs. Winslow could be found at this hour of the day. The greengrocer's, the butcher's, the bakery?

He stepped into each shop, but didn't see her. Not doing her marketing, then. He paused outside the police station and thought about it.

Her brother was dead. The rectory. He turned and walked toward the churchyard.

Hamish said, "Aye, she wouldna' wish to have her husband with her."

And Rutledge saw that she was indeed standing in the churchyard, pointing to a space next to two stones. Hartle's wife and child?

The rector and Mrs. Winslow looked up as he approached across the freshly mown grass of the churchyard.

"Not more bad news?" the rector asked anxiously.

"No. I've come for a word with Mrs. Winslow, when she's finished her business here."

She pointed to the markers at her feet. He saw he'd been right: here lay her brother's wife and child. "I was just asking Rector if there was room here beside Mary. He says there is. I don't know quite what sort of service to have." She frowned. "My husband feels it ought to be brief, without much ceremony. But Theo didn't kill himself, did he? It doesn't seem right."

"A proper one," Rutledge answered her without reservations. "The fact that his life ended abruptly makes no difference. The service should be the same as he'd have been given as an old man, with all honor due him."

She smiled, tears filling her eyes. "Yes. Thank you. That would be fitting." She turned to the rector. "There we are, then. I'll think of what hymns he'd have liked, and any favorite scriptures." She bit her lip.

Rutledge knew what was on her mind.

"Your brother's body," he said gently, "will be released very soon."

She nodded, unable to trust her voice. The rector took her arm and walked with her a little way until they were out of the churchyard and standing in the drive up to the rectory.

Rutledge gave them a chance to finish their private discussion, but as the rector turned and nodded to him, he caught them up.

"Now," Mrs. Winslow asked brightly, as if to affirm that she was in control of her feelings again, "you wanted to speak to me?"

He thanked the rector, and then said to her, "There's a tearoom next to the bakery, I believe. Would you like a cup?"

She hesitated. "Yes, I would," she admitted frankly, "but there's my husband. I ought to see if he's all right."

"He will manage very well," Rutledge told her, and gestured toward the road. She went with him, the two of them walking in silence until they were halfway to the tea shop.

"I wonder," Rutledge began, "how well Theo Hartle knew Daniel Pierce?"

"Daniel? The Pierces didn't have much in common with the rest of us, once they'd been sent away to school. They were home on holidays, of course, but you didn't walk up to the Pierce house and ask if Daniel or Anthony were in, did you? Their lives had changed more than ours. But on the whole, I think Theo liked Anthony better. Myself, I liked Daniel. He was always nice to me. Nicer sometimes than Theo." She looked away, her mind elsewhere. Finally she added, "Theo was my brother, and I shouldn't speak ill of the dead, but he could sometimes be very selfish at that age. I'd like to think it was the influence of those he ran with, back then. What one couldn't think of, the others could. I was glad when Theo outgrew them. I think that's why my parents agreed to let him be apprenticed so soon at Kenton Chairs, and they were right, it was best for him in many ways."

"If your brother saw Daniel Pierce on the street— let's say in Hastings, or somewhere like that—would they stop to chat?"

"Well, it would depend, wouldn't it, on the occasion. If Daniel was alone, and Theo as well, they might speak. If Daniel was with a lady or friends, they'd nod in passing, I'd think. But Theo would let Daniel take the first step. It would be proper, you see."

It would be proper, Rutledge thought, for the workingman to defer to the brewery owner's son, in the matter of recognition in a public arena. Old habits died hard, even after the upheaval of the war.

"There was nothing between the two men that might make your brother uncomfortable, encountering him again after all this time?"

She considered that as Rutledge opened the door of the tea shop for them. Silence fell in the busy room, and every eye turned their way.

Mrs. Winslow hesitated, as if she'd been caught fraternizing with the enemy, her face turning pink.

Rutledge took her gently by the arm and said in a voice intended to carry but apparently for her ears alone, "I think a cup of tea will make you feel much better." He summoned the woman waiting on tables, and asked for tea and a selection of pastries. Then he guided Mrs. Winslow to a seat by the window. She turned to him with anxious eyes, and he said only, "The rector will never forgive me if I don't keep my promise. You shouldn't have had to make such a visit alone."

"My husband—" she began.

"Yes, it would have been difficult for him. But a friend, perhaps?"

He could see from her expression that she had few friends. He could understand why.

Their tea came, and the pastries. She let him pour her cup, and pass her the pastries, and as the occupants of the shop realized that there was to be no arrest or harsh interrogation to report to their friends, they lost interest. Mrs. Winslow nibbled a pastry, and then shyly reached for another. He realized it was a treat for her, that such outings had stopped long ago.

It was not until they had left the shop and he was walking toward her home that she answered the question he'd asked earlier.

"Daniel and Theo had a falling-out. Oh, it was years ago, Theo couldn't have been more than nine or ten. Daniel was seven at the most. I don't know what they fought about, but it couldn't have been very serious, at that age, could it? Still, Theo gave Daniel a bloody nose, and afterward he came home terrified that the police would be sent for and take him up, that Tyrell Pierce would see that he was sent to Borstal. But nothing came of it, and Anthony told Theo later that Daniel claimed he'd fallen off Will Jeffers's stallion, trying to ride him bareback." She smiled at the memory. "I expect he was ashamed of being bested by Theo, but he was only seven, after all."

"When was the last time your brother saw Daniel?"

"It was before the war. I'm sure of it. That fortnight when Daniel came back from France, Theo was still in hospital."

"Did you see Daniel then?"

"Only once, and not to speak to." She hesitated. "He'd just left the Misses Tate School, and it appeared that someone had hit him in the face, because there was a big red mark on his cheekbone. And he was angry. I did wonder how he came by it."

They were at the corner of her street now, and she put out a hand. "If you won't mind, I'd rather go the rest of the way alone. My husband keeps watch—"

He stopped, and she thanked him profusely for the tea and the pastries, then hurried on toward her door, as if acutely aware of how long she'd been away from home.

Hamish said, "A bluidy nose doesna' lead to murder."

"No," Rutledge answered him silently. "If that was all there was to it. Theo Hartle may not have told his little sister the whole story."

Still, it lent credence to the possibility that someone was erasing the worst memories of Daniel Pierce's childhood. But what was more interesting was how Daniel had got that mark on his face.

He went back to the hotel for lunch, and found a letter waiting for him.

It was from Chief Inspector Cummins. Rutledge took it to his room and opened it.

Ian.

Thank you for the surprising contents of your parcel. It had not occurred to any of us to look for a flint knife. We were told that the wound was oddly shaped, and so we developed a list of foreign knives— African, Southeast Asian, Middle Eastern—and the theory was that in his travels, Wheeler had lived in a port where such souvenirs were available to buy or steal. Portsmouth, Southampton, Dover, London, and so on. We had one promising lead, an Oxford don, retired to Dartmouth, whose home was broken into while he was abroad and several objects from his Near Eastern collection were stolen. Alas, when he returned and inventoried what was missing, a selection of Yemeni knives, they didn't match the dimensions of the wound. Your flint knife is a far more likely candidate. What more can you discover about its origins? Meanwhile, I shall ask a friend who is interested in such topics if he can detect traces of human blood on your find. His home laboratory must surely be useful for something other than mystifying his wife, family, and friends.

I must say, this is encouraging. But I absolutely refuse to let my hopes be raised again, lest they be dashed as so many others have been.

I must have intrigued you with my account of this unsolved mystery. I should have warned you that it was bound to cause sleepless nights and over-work one's imagination.

And it was signed simply *Cummins*.

Smiling, Rutledge returned the letter to its envelope and put it in his valise.

Now if he could only have equal success in solving his own mystery.

Mr. Kenton, who owned the furniture works where Theo Hartle had been employed, came into the dining room of the hotel as Rutledge was finishing his luncheon.

He was a tall, stooped man with graying hair and spectacles. He stood in the doorway, looking around, and as the woman who served meals approached him, he asked her a question.

Rutledge looked up from his plate of cheeses just as she was pointing to him.

The man came over, introduced himself, and asked if he could join Rutledge for a few minutes, or if

Rutledge would prefer to meet him in the hotel lobby after his meal.

"Yes, of course, sit down," Rutledge answered, and signaled the woman to ask for a fresh pot of tea.

Kenton thanked him and said, "This business with Theo has been heavy on my mind. I come here reluctantly, you understand, because what I'm about to tell you is something I refuse to believe. Still, I'm no policeman, and if there is any possibility that I am right, then I have a duty to those who have died to talk to you."

He broke off as the fresh pot of tea and a dish of biscuits was set before them. When the woman had gone away again, Rutledge said, "I appreciate your sense of duty. I shall look into the matter. I can't promise anything, but I will respect your confidence as far as I'm able."

Kenton appeared to be relieved. That was clearly what he had come to ask.

"Theo was a good man," Kenton went on. "I don't know how we're to replace him. Steady, dependable. Amazingly gifted when it comes to working with wood. Well liked by the others in the firm. Such a loss. I've been asked to say a few words at his funeral."

He paused, stirring his tea, as if it were the most important task of the day.

Rutledge said, watching his face, "I don't think that's what you've come here to tell me."

Kenton met his gaze. "No. No, it isn't. I don't know where to begin, I suppose."

"What had Hartle done that could be of interest to the police?"

He turned to the window, ignoring the question. "My mother had a companion for many years. She had an arthritic condition and was a regular visitor to the spas of Europe, looking for a cure for the pain if not the disease. When she fell ill at Würzburg, a young woman named Hilda Lentz nursed her back to health. When my mother recovered, she asked Hilda to come back to England with her. The idea of travel must have appealed to her, because she agreed. But instead of returning to Germany, she married the son of one of our friends, a man named Peter Hopkins, and they had three children. She continued to work with my mother until her death. And Hilda died of appendicitis a year or so later. She'd lost a child, a daughter, in childbirth, but her sons were treated more or less as members of our family. Carl Hopkins in fact came to work for me, because he has a way with machinery that's invaluable."

"What does he have to do with Theo Hartle?"

"Nothing. Everything. I don't know." He shook his head vigorously. "Carl was torn about the war, you see. His eyesight was damaged by a case of the measles, and there was no doubt that he couldn't serve, when the war came. But his younger brother George joined the Army with the Eastfield Company. And Carl's favorite German cousin—Hilda's sister's boy— hurried to join the German army. Carl considers himself English, but he was worried about his brother and his cousin. Neither of them survived. It wasn't long after we heard about George that someone sent Carl an anonymous letter saying that George had been shot in the back while crossing No Man's Land. The Army refused to confirm or deny the story, but the letter claimed that George had been shot because he had a German mother, spoke fluent German, and wasn't to be trusted."

George Hopkins. Rutledge remembered the name. He'd been one of the two Eastfield soldiers who died in the war.

"Go on."

"When the Eastfield soldiers began to come home from France, Carl asked them how his brother had died, and in Carl's view they were evasive. Well, apparently it was a night attack just as George's commanding officer had told us in his letter. No one really knew how he died. Were you in the war? I can't imagine that it's a tidy business, attacking at night. I suspect the letter—which was posted from London—was meant to be hurtful, not true. Unfortunately, about this same time, Carl's aunt wrote to him to say that his cousin had died of his wounds as an English prisoner, and she believed he hadn't been given proper attention. It was understandable, she was upset, looking for someone to blame, but she told Carl that he ought to be ashamed of his English heritage, because the English had killed both George and his cousin. Carl withdrew into himself. Dr. Gooding gave him something to help him, because he walked for hours every night, unable to sleep. Thank God, early last year he got over whatever it was, came back to work, and seemed to be himself again. I can't tell you how relieved I was."

"Then why are you telling me about him now?"

Taking a deep breath, Kenton met Rutledge's gaze. "Several weeks ago, he received a letter from someone in Germany. His aunt had hanged herself. Despondent still over the death of her son, according to her priest, and enclosed was a copy of the letter from her doctor, documenting her ill health. An effort, I should think, to convince the church that she was not an intentional suicide, but it made sad reading. Carl showed it to me, asking what to do. I suggested making a small gift to the church, in her name. And that was the end of it for all I knew. Now . . . now I'm betraying a trust."

He stopped, his face drawn, his eyes reflecting his discomfort and anxiety.

Rutledge said, "I'll speak to him. Quietly, without making it obvious. Thank you."

"I'm not saying—I'm not pointing a finger, you understand. But my God, four men are dead, and if I don't speak up, there may be others. I love Carl like a son, I'll do anything to help him. But I was fond of Theo as well. I can't believe Carl could have harmed him. Not Theo."

"It took a great deal of courage to come here. But you did the right thing."

Kenton rose from the table. "Have I? He could have been my son, you know. But my mother persuaded me not to marry Hilda. And she was right, in the long term we were much happier with our respective spouses. All the same, I still remember how I felt at the time."

As he walked away, Rutledge wondered if that last was true. Or if over the years Kenton had convinced himself that it must be true, that his mother had been wise.

He went directly to the police station and found Constable Walker reading a message from Inspector Norman.

He looked up as Rutledge came in.

"There's a woman in Hastings who saw Theo Hartle at seven o'clock, speaking to a man. The Inspector wants to know if you'll be interested in interviewing her with him. I told Constable Petty that we'd come as soon as I tracked you down."

"Let's go," Rutledge said, and turned toward the inn to collect his motorcar. He told himself that Carl Hopkins could wait.

But he was wrong.

12

Inspector Norman was waiting for them, impatient and short tempered. He greeted Rutledge with a sharp, "I was about to go on without you. I've got a murder inquiry of my own, two women killed in a house on Brent Street. They walked in on a man ransacking it. There's an intensive search in progress. I don't appreciate the distraction of your inquiry."

"We'll talk to this person ourselves, Constable Walker and I."

"This is my patch. I told you." He reached for his hat and led the way back to the street. "We'll use your motorcar, if you please."

And so Rutledge had no choice but to accommodate Inspector Norman, Constable Petty, and Walker, with no space left for Hamish where he usually rode.

However, the distance wasn't too great, and in a matter of minutes they were walking into a shop that catered to newborns and small children. There were caps and blankets, gowns and christening robes, finely woven blankets and the dresses that children of both sexes still wore when very young, rich with embroidery and ruching and tucks. There was also a small selection of prams, rocking horses, and the Teddy bears that the American president had made so popular, as well as a tray of silver rattles, spoons, cups, and teething rings.

The woman waiting on a customer was large and motherly, with a low-pitched voice and a warm manner. She glanced up as she saw the four men enter the shop, but her discussion of cap ribbons never faltered. And so the four policemen were forced to stand idly waiting until the customer was satisfied and had left with a small parcel done up in silver paper.

"Mrs. Griffith?" Inspector Norman asked, coming forward.

"Yes. How may I help you? I doubt you've come for christening robes or china kittens."

Inspector Norman gave their names, and then said, "You spoke to one of my men. About Theo Hartle."

"Oh, yes. I heard that the police were trying to find out where he was before he was killed. I saw him where the main road divides just at the foot of Marine Street.

He was speaking to a man. A friendly conversation, as far as I could tell, but rather serious as well. I was walking with a friend, and we weren't going in that direction, and so I didn't have an opportunity to ask after his sister."

"You know the family?" Rutledge asked, surprised.

"His mother and I went to school together. And then we were married and went our separate ways. But we stayed in touch. Peggy Winslow is my goddaughter, and I have tried to keep an eye on her for her mother's sake. But that worthless complainer she's tied to keeps her on a short rein. A pity, but there you are. She always enjoyed the little treats I planned for her visits. But she doesn't come to Hastings these days."

Rutledge remembered how Mrs. Winslow had seemed to enjoy the pastries at the tea shop in Eastfield.

"Did you know the man Hartle was speaking with?"

"I don't think I do, although I may have seen him about from time to time."

"And Hartle didn't appear to be afraid of him, or uncomfortable in his presence?"

"No, not as far as I could tell."

"What time of day was this?" Inspector Norman asked.

"Closer to seven than six, at a guess," she said. "I wasn't exactly keeping track of the time."

"And they were still there talking when you last saw them?"

"Still there, on the corner. I couldn't have said where either of them went after that. I find it so hard to believe that Theo is gone. He survived the war. The Germans couldn't kill him, and then some murdering maniac takes his life. I shall go to the funeral, no matter what that husband of Peggy's has to say. And I'll bring her here as well," she ended vigorously, and Rutledge had no doubt that she would do just that.

"Can you describe the other man?" he asked.

She pursed her lips, thinking. "Not as tall as you. Brown hair, slim. I had no particular reason to take note of him."

All the same, it sounded like the man Rutledge had encountered at The White Swans Hotel. No certainty, of course, but still, very likely.

Hamish said, "Ye ken, it doesna' mean he didna' follow his victim and kill him when it was finally dark."

And that was true as well.

"You were never near enough to hear any of their conversation?" Rutledge asked. "You couldn't judge the other man's accent, for instance?"

"No, not close enough by a long chalk," Mrs. Griffith replied. "Are you thinking he might have been a foreigner, then?"

"Actually I wondered what class of man he might have been."

"I can tell you, he was dressed more like a gentleman."

Inspector Norman had turned to stare at Rutledge. "Are you suggesting what I think you are?"

He was a sharp man, and Rutledge had forgotten that.

"No one—that is to say, no one alive—has heard the killer speak. He could be a Scot as far as we know. Or from the Midlands. It would be helpful if we could place him."

Norman grunted, then turned to Constable Petty. "If you'll take Mrs. Griffith's statement?" And to the woman, he added, "When the shop is closed, we'd like you to come in and read it over before signing it."

"I don't know that I've been any help," she said doubtfully. "But yes, I shall come in and sign the paper."

They left her, then, and on the street once more, Inspector Norman stopped by the motorcar, instead of getting in. "You think it was Daniel Pierce, don't you?"

"I've been given no reason to suspect Pierce," he said, keeping to the literal truth. There was only circumstance and conjecture so far, hardly evidence. "But

I'm told you wouldn't mind seeing him taken up for this crime or any other."

"And you have a reason for thinking as much," Norman went on relentlessly, ignoring the denial. "Don't hold out on me, Rutledge!"

"I'm not holding out," he retorted. "So far there's no clear motive for these murders. And as long as there isn't, I have no more reason to suspect Pierce than I do any other person."

"I'm told you went away for several days. What was that in aid of?"

Rutledge wondered who had told him that? Walker? Or someone else? "I went to see two of the men whose names were on the identity discs we've found. One man swears he never had them—and that's likely. He was a career soldier and sewed his name into his uniform. The other man I spoke with found his discs in the trunk where he kept his uniform and souvenirs. I saw them for myself. I didn't pursue the question any further. There wasn't time. But if two of the discs are false, then the others are likely to be."

"If these are false, then where did the killer get real names to put on them?"

"From transport manifests, burial details, payroll accounts, censoring letters—or merely sitting in a pub and keeping his ears open."

"And so where does that leave us?" Inspector Norman demanded.

"I'm not sure. The discs we've found in the mouths of victims appear to be real, but that means someone has learned how to counterfeit them well enough to pass for authentic discs. It would be easy enough, I should think. But why should anyone go to that much trouble? And if he did, why not simply make up the names on them? Or use the victim's name? If I'm any judge, the two men I spoke with hadn't heard of or met anyone from the Eastfield Company. Nor did they know Anthony Pierce. Instead the killer used real people. The point, then, seems to have been the confusion these discs have created."

"There's only one reason I can think of to use the wrong names," Inspector Norman said, opening the door to the motorcar. "If he'd used the names of the real soldiers involved, then we'd be able to trace *them* and learn precisely whatever it is that's behind these murders." He got in and waited until Constable Walker had turned the crank and stepped into the rear seat. "What if the Eastfield men fired on another company by mistake, and killed a number of them?"

Constable Walker spoke up for the first time. "That's not likely. My nephew is one of the Eastfield Company. And he'd never cover up something of that sort. And I knew each man in that company. If they'd done wrong, he'd be the first to try to take responsibility and make amends."

"That may well be. But there were other things going on at the Front. Like shooting an unpopular officer in the back during an attack."

"You weren't there," Constable Walker persisted.

"Neither were you," Inspector Norman retorted. They had reached the police station, and he got out as the motorcar pulled in by the main door. "Well. I don't know if Mrs. Griffith clarified or clouded the issue. But for what it's worth, I'll see you get a copy of her statement, when it's drawn up and signed."

And then he was gone, striding into the police station with the intensity of a man who knew he had long hours ahead of him, his mind already busy with the two women killed by the intruder.

As they drove away, Constable Walker said, "He's wrong," as if that settled the matter.

Rutledge let it go. Inspector Norman's remarks had distracted everyone from the subject of Daniel Pierce. And Rutledge was not ready for a witch hunt that muddled the case prematurely.

He said to Walker, "I have a stop to make before we leave Hastings. You can wait in the car, if you will."

"Yes, sir," Walker replied, his mind still on Inspector Norman's charges.

Rutledge found the military shop again and leaving his motorcar just out of sight, walked in to collect more information about the man who had brought in the flint knife.

The proprietor was going through the pockets of an officer's greatcoat as Rutledge came through the door.

"Hallo. Looking for more flint knives?"

Surprised, Rutledge said, "Do you have any others?"

Smiling, the proprietor hung up the greatcoat and shook his head. "No, more's the pity. That's to say if you were looking to buy another one."

"I'm after information this time. I'm curious about the man who brought them in. I'd like to know whatever you learned from him. Perhaps he kept one or two more such knives, better made than this one."

The man shrugged. "I doubt he has any more. He'd probably have sold them with the original one. Would you like me to contact him for you?"

"Thanks, but I'd rather write to him myself." He could feel the man's reluctance, and added, "I don't mind paying a finder's fee, if he's got other examples." This was not his inquiry, and Rutledge had no authority to invoke the power of Scotland Yard to ask for the shopkeeper's cooperation.

The proprietor smiled. "You're a man after my own heart, Mr. . . ."

He let his voice trail away, hinting.

"My name is Rutledge. I'm from London. I'm here in Hastings on a matter of business."

"Then, Mr. Rutledge, if you'll give me five minutes, I'll look in my books and see what I have that will help you track down the former owner of a fine flint knife. Meanwhile, is there anything else you'd care to see?"

"Not at the moment."

It took fewer than five minutes for the man to find the proper entry, and he wrote the name on a sheet of paper in a bold, clear hand. Even upside down, Rutledge could read the name: Charles Henry. It was what he'd remembered from the first visit.

Below were the rest of the details. 21 June 1908. Grandfather East Anglia, dug up in garden. Not definite when found.

1908. Three years after the murder of the man found at Stonehenge, Rutledge thought. But—on the summer solstice. Coincidence?

Rutledge thanked him, and after an exchange about the greatcoat that the proprietor had been preparing for sale, he left.

Walker said as he came through the shop door, "Were you buying identity discs?"

Rutledge realized that the constable was quite serious, and answered him in the same vein. "I'd asked if there were any for sale. I was told that he didn't carry any because there was no call for them."

"Too bad. It would have made our work easier." Walker sighed. "We've not made much progress, on the whole. It's mostly finding out what isn't there, like looking for trouble and finding none. And then trouble turns up on the doorstep."

It was true. But so far, there hadn't been any other deaths. And that in itself was progress of a sort.

When they drove into Eastfield half an hour later, Walker said, "Who, pray, is that?"

A man was standing in front of the police station, a grim expression on his face.

Rutledge took one look, and swore.

"You know him?" the constable asked, surprised.

"Yes. And I have a feeling I know why he's here."

Instead of leaving his motorcar in the hotel yard, he drove the short distance to the police station and drew up there.

Rutledge got out but stood by the motorcar's door.

"Inspector Mickelson," he said in greeting.

Mickelson made no effort to return the greeting. "I've come to relieve you," he said coldly. "Officially. There have been complaints about your conduct. Chief Superintendent Bowles assured the Chief Constable that these would be taken seriously, and you'd be withdrawn before the day is out. That was this morning. And as you can see, I am here." He turned to Constable Walker. "And you are?"

Walker gave his name, and looked from one man to the other. "I don't quite understand why Inspector Rutledge has been replaced. Misconduct, sir? Of what sort?"

"That's a matter between the Chief Constable and Scotland Yard." Turning to Rutledge, he added, "Your orders are to return to London immediately."

Rutledge said, "I've several matters that need my attention first."

"Not anymore. You have been relieved." Mickelson turned again to Walker and said, "I'd like to see the statements you've taken from witnesses and the medical reports on the dead men. I'd also like to meet Mr. Pierce as soon as possible, and also Inspector Norman." He opened the door of the police station, and Constable Walker hesitated.

"You needn't look to Mr. Rutledge for instructions, man. I've told you, I'm here now." And he strode into the station without waiting for Walker or saying anything more to Rutledge.

Walker, behind his back, began, "Sir—"

But Rutledge said only, "I'm leaving for London. Keep an eye on things until I'm able to return."

He got back into the motorcar, and Walker had no choice but to step inside the station after Inspector Mickelson.

Furious, Rutledge drove first to the school and asked to see Mrs. Farrell-Smith. The girl who opened the door said nervously, "She's not in, sir."

"She should not ask you to lie for her," he replied quietly, and took the stairs two at a time.

Mrs. Farrell-Smith looked up as Rutledge opened her office door without knocking. Then her gaze went to the girl at his back. "I thought I told you—" she began, but Rutledge cut her short.

"She told your lie for you. I didn't believe her." He turned to the girl, still standing in the doorway, her cheeks pink with uncertainty. "Thank you," he said gently. "Please close the door as you go."

She hesitated, and then did as he asked.

Mrs. Farrell-Smith said, "I have nothing to say to you."

"But I have something to say to you. You've made a serious mistake, and it could easily get someone else killed. Will you rescind your complaint?"

"Why should I? I never wanted the Yard to handle this business in the first place. Inspector Norman is quite capable of clearing up these murders promptly and efficiently."

"No doubt he could. He's a good man. But you haven't got Inspector Norman. Instead you still have the Yard, Mrs. Farrell-Smith, and I think you'll find Inspector Mickelson is cut from a very different cloth."

She stared at him. "But I expressly told them—"

He didn't wait for her to finish. "I'm sure you did. But Mr. Pierce insisted earlier on bringing in the Yard, and I expect the Chief Constable understands that it is Mr. Pierce's son who is among the murder victims, not yours. If you want to call off the Yard, then I suggest you find someone with more authority than a brewery owner to do your work for you."

He didn't wait for an answer. He turned and went out the door.

This time, she didn't call after him.

He packed his belongings quickly, left the hotel, and drove to London in a cloud of anger and bitter frustration. Hamish, reacting to the tension in his mind, reminded him that he had admitted that he had not come to any conclusions himself about the identity of the killer loose in Eastfield.

"And that," Hamish added as the motorcar finally reached the city, "is the only way ye'll find yoursel' reinstated."

But Rutledge didn't respond. He found a place to leave his motorcar, and once inside the Yard, took the stairs two at a time, in search of Sergeant Gibson.

He found the sergeant in the canteen, having what passed for his dinner, a plateful of sandwiches and a cup of tea. Gibson looked up, saw Rutledge, and said, "Not here."

Carrying the plate of sandwiches with him and balancing the cup of tea, Gibson followed Rutledge to his office, and as Rutledge took the chair behind his desk, Gibson carefully set down first the cup and then the plate on the corner of a box of files.

"Sir, Superintendent Bowles never liked the fact that he wasn't here to choose who was to go to Eastfield. And you gave him the excuse he needed to change inspectors."

"I didn't give him any such thing," Rutledge retorted. "Mrs. Farrell-Smith has her own agenda. I don't know what she expects to gain from it, but at a guess, I don't think it's the murders that are worrying her. It's an earlier run-in with the Yard."

Gibson stared at him. "How did you know?"

"I didn't. It was the only explanation I could come up with on the long drive back to London."

"There was an inquiry into her husband's death. He died of a fall while walking in Derbyshire. The police felt that the circumstances didn't quite match the version of his fall that Mrs. Farrell-Smith had given them. She was present, you see, but had sat down on a rock to catch her breath, and her husband went on alone for some distance because he wanted to take a photograph from the overlook. He fell just after she caught him up. She said. She admitted to having witnessed it."

"What was the outcome?"

"The inquest brought in death by misadventure, but Mrs. Farrell-Smith was still under a cloud as far as the police were concerned. They couldn't find a motive for her to kill the man, and without that, they couldn't manage to charge her. It would have been easy enough, according to the sergeant I spoke with, for her to tip him over the edge if he was busy with his camera. The footing is uncertain at best at that spot."

Rutledge was reminded of the drop from East Hill in Hastings, the headland where Theo Hartle was killed.

"Was that because the Derbyshire police couldn't come up with a reason that satisfied the Crown, or was it because they didn't care for her on general principles?"

"I couldn't say. But there was no medical evidence that her husband had been struck or tripped. No bruises and the like. She claimed he'd experienced a bit of vertigo, that she put out a hand to him, and he turned the wrong way." He paused. "She had scratches on her hands from where he clawed at her as he went over. But no one could tell whether they occurred as she tried to save him or whether it was as he tried to save himself and she let go."

"Either way, she would have to move house, and live where she wasn't known." Rutledge nodded. "Very selfish of her to want the Yard out of the picture, but it's understandable. I need to speak to Chief Superintendent Bowles."

"He's not here, he's on his way to testify in a trial in Lincoln. Remember that one? He had to examine the firm's books himself."

"Damn. It could be days before that's finished." He debated following the Chief Superintendent north, and then thought better of it. "All right, I'll go back to Sussex and have a word with the Chief Constable."

"I'd be cautious on that score, sir. The Chief Constable wasn't best pleased by Mrs. Farrell-Smith's complaint. Apparently he'd wanted the inquiry to be left in the hands of the local police, but Mr. Pierce had been very persuasive. He said as much to me, and then when I'd brought the Chief Superintendent to the telephone, he was still angry. I couldn't help but overhear the Chief Superintendent blaming you for the lack of progress in the inquiry, and he apologized for your conduct and your incompetence. Something was said about the fourth murder, because I heard Old Bowels reply that if you'd spent less time annoying people and more in finding the killer, someone would have been in custody by now."

Rutledge said only, "I'll be careful."

It was late evening before he left the Yard. He had used the time to put in two telephone calls of his own. He had managed to speak to the corporal in Cheshire whose name had been on one of the other identity discs—the inspector there had been more than willing to find and bring the man to the telephone. The corporal had never possessed identity discs, and he knew nothing about the men of the Eastfield Company The inspector had come back on the line and vouched for the man. That avenue had led nowhere, just as Rutledge had expected.

The second telephone call elicited the fact that the name on the fourth set had died of his wounds in England after a valiant fight against the odds.

Hamish said as Rutledge put up the telephone after the last conversation, "Ye ken, it was a trick. And a verra' good one. But is the war a trick as well?"

"Early days," Rutledge answered absently, thinking that someone had gone to a great deal of trouble to draw the police into a lie. If that was true, then what secret had the discs been used to conceal? Was it a member of the company itself who was behind these murders?

When he left the Yard, the shadows were long and the heat of the sun already dissipating. He started the motorcar and drove with only half of his mind on what he was doing, still considering the case that was no longer his to think about.

Hamish was silent, and it was several minutes before Rutledge realized that he knew the motorcar just in front of his. It belonged to Meredith Channing.

13

At the next intersection, as Mrs. Channing was preparing to turn left, Rutledge pulled up beside her vehicle.

"It's good to see you," he called.

In truth. The last time he'd spoken to her, he'd asked her not to go away on the extended trip she was planning to take. She had hinted at a year or more abroad, in order to put her own life back together. She had even admitted that there was someone she cared for, and that that had been a factor in her decision. All he could think of, in the face of her sudden, unforeseen decision, was to say what he felt.

And then he'd walked away, refusing to look at what had motivated his words. Afterward, he had avoided her—her house, mutual friends, and any place in London where he had encountered her in the past.

Now, he searched her eyes for something to guide his next words, prepared to drive on.

And then on the spur of the moment, he added, "It's late, but would you care for a coffee?"

She smiled. "Yes. Yes, I would, actually."

He tried to think of a restaurant that was open. "The Marlborough Hotel?" he suggested. Neutral ground.

"I'll follow you." She pulled back into the line of traffic just behind him. He reached the hotel first, and she quickly found a space for her motorcar as she caught up with him. They entered the hotel Reception together, and she saw a small table in the lounge, set in an alcove with a long window. Several other couples were having tea or coffee in the room, and the atmosphere was quiet, pleasant.

"There?"

He nodded. They sat down, and he ordered two coffees.

Into the silence that followed, Rutledge said, "You're out late."

"I went to a lovely dinner party." She smiled, reminiscing.

They had met at a dinner party. He had been afraid that she saw into his mind, her eyes seeming to read his thoughts. It was his own fear, he realized later. But she had a way of understanding people that was unexpected in one so young. And he had been drawn to her against his will.

Their coffee came. Rutledge waited until the young man serving them was out of earshot. Then he said as she passed the sugar bowl to him, "Why did you stay?"

He'd intended to keep his voice level, but it had taken an effort to achieve that. Hamish had set up a deafening roar in his head from the moment he'd recognized her motorcar.

She was playing with the silver spoon in her fingers, paying excessive attention to it, twisting it so that it caught the light and then went dark. Bright again in the lamplight. Dark again. He watched it too, thinking that it was very like their relationship, fragmented by too many shadows.

"Ian," she said finally, not looking at him. It was a warning not to open that door.

He drank a little of his coffee. It was bitter in his mouth. "I've been in Sussex," he went on. "Do you know Hastings? The water there is worth seeing." He swore to himself. It was hardly an exciting conversational opening, but it was the best he could do in the circumstances.

"Is it? No, I've never been there." After a moment, as if she too was struggling to find common ground, she added, "I've always liked the sea. But I've never been fond of sea bathing. I'm content to sit and watch the tides."

He searched for something else to say. "How is your shoulder?" It had been dislocated a few weeks earlier when a train traveling north to Scotland had derailed on a curve, killing or injuring more than a score of passengers. He had been among the first on the harrowing scene.

"Quite well, actually. I thought at first—but the doctors were very good. And I stayed with friends in order to be near their surgery. I quite fell in love with Dr. Anderson. He must be sixty-five, at the very least. He has a way with patients. I wished many times that he'd been with us out in France. I trusted him, and did the exercises he prescribed to please him. But I missed London. I always come back here." Her voice changed on the last words.

Rutledge took a deep breath, toying with his cup, shutting out Hamish's warning. "Do you know what shell shock is?" he asked.

She met his gaze. "I've seen it," she answered. Warily, he thought.

He couldn't go on after all. He couldn't tell her. He finished lamely, "My sister knows a doctor who treats it in much the same way. By gaining the trust of his patients."

"A rare gift," she agreed, setting her cup aside. "Tell me more about Sussex."

There wasn't much to tell without bringing up the murders that had taken him there. But he scoured his memory. "There's a shop that sells all things military. From lead soldiers to a noon gun. Including a flint knife."

She was interested. "You mean worked from flint? How unusual. Is it very old?"

"Very. Or so I was assured. I bought it and sent it to a friend who was—intrigued by it. He has just retired from the Yard."

What had promised to be a pleasant hour had devolved into stilted conversation. Her coffee was half finished now. She took a deep breath. "Ian. You know I served as a nurse in France?"

He froze, certain he could guess where this subject was heading. That he would find out, finally, what she had seen when he was brought in to the aid station after nearly being buried alive. He had been shell-shocked, barely aware of where he was or what he was saying. He hadn't been aware of her, hadn't even known she was there until he'd met her last year at a New Year's Eve dinner they'd both attended. "Yes." It was all he could manage.

He was wrong. There was something else on her mind.

"I went into nursing for a very selfish reason. My husband was reported missing early on, in the fighting near Mons. I thought, if I could get to France myself—if I could be there—I could find him. Or hear something useful. Anything was better than sitting at home, with no news. But I was in France for nearly three years, and no one could tell me if he was alive and a prisoner—or dead."

She had never mentioned her husband before this.

"I'm sorry," Rutledge said, and meant it.

Meredith Channing looked at him, smiled briefly. "Thank you." And then her gaze moved on to the window, watching the passing traffic on the street.

"I call myself a widow," she went on. "It's more—convenient—in society. But am I?"

Rutledge asked, "Do you want to be a widow?"

She pushed her cup away. "It's late. I really must go. Thank you so much, Ian."

He stayed where he was. "Do you want to be a widow? Meredith?"

She turned to face him. "I go to concerts held every year on the anniversary of his birthday. I honor his memory in every way I can. I'm close to his family and visit them often." Her eyes filled with tears and she looked away. "But it's you I dream about, Ian. And I can't go on living with that guilt."

Before he could respond or stop her, she had risen and was walking swiftly toward the hotel doors, head down so that no one could see her face. He started to follow, and realized at once that it was the wrong thing to do. A public hotel was not the place for a scene.

The waiter came to the table to ask if there was anything else that Rutledge wanted.

Watching Meredith pass by the window on her way to her motorcar, Rutledge answered without looking up.

"A whisky," he said. "If you have it."

Hamish said, "It doesna' matter if she's a widow or no'. You couldna' tell her the truth."

And those words were to follow him home, echoing in his head.

He realized that it didn't matter how he'd come to feel about Meredith Channing. Or how she felt about her own circumstances. In the end, there was nothing for either one of them.

The next morning, he stared at the paperwork on his desk awaiting his attention and decided he couldn't face it. Instead he drew out of his pocket the information he had collected about the flint knife and considered it.

Charles Henry. That was the name of the man who had claimed his grandfather had found the knife in his back garden in East Anglia, miles away. If it was true, what had decided Charles Henry to sell it to a shop in Hastings? Why not offer it to a museum, or if it was money he was after, there must be a dozen other places that would be interested in the knife. In London, for one. Why a small shop on a back street in Hastings? Unless Charles Henry lived nearby.

Cummins had been right, it was hard to put the case out of his mind, and the more Rutledge seemed to learn, the more the puzzle pulled at him. And how to go about finding this man? After so much time had passed, he could have died, gone to war, or immigrated to Australia.

The odd thing was, Charles Henry sounded as if someone had given his Christian names, not his surname. Charles Henry Blake, Charles Henry Browning, Charles Henry Tennyson. Or perhaps it was, simply, Charles Henry.

And what—if anything at all—did Charles Henry's grandfather have to do with Harvey Wheeler, the man who was found dead at Stonehenge?

Probably nothing at all.

Rutledge drew pen and paper toward him and wrote a note to Chief Inspector Cummins, giving him the details that the proprietor of the military shop had provided.

He added,

This will provide enough information to lead you to no possible conclusions, but should keep your mind busy for a few days, guessing at answers.

He signed it, put it in an envelope, stamped it, and set it aside for mail collection.

But he was unsatisfied, and went down into the bowels of the Yard to find the file that was stored there.

There was nothing more of interest in the folder—during their conversation, Cummins had given him a thorough summary of all the details. All the same, Rutledge sat there, studying the face of Harvey Wheeler in the photograph attached to the file.

What sort of person had he been in life? The dead eyes told Rutledge very little beyond their color, and there was nothing in the face to indicate greed or kindness, passion or cruelty, honesty or slyness. All expression had been smoothed away.

And yet there were details, if one looked closely. The eyes were wide set, the jawline firm, the nose straight, the ears well shaped. A pleasing face, structurally.

Hamish said, "Ye canna' be sure, but dress him well, and he'd pass for a gentleman."

And that would be useful, if the man had set out to swindle women of their life savings. The appearance of trustworthiness, at least, if nothing else.

The police in Kirkwall and in Edinburgh had identified the likeness as Wheeler's. But what if they were wrong? They hadn't seen the man for several years, after all.

Hamish said, "Ye ken, two constabularies canna' be wrong."

Yes, and that was the assumption that everyone had made: they couldn't be wrong.

What if Wheeler, after his second brush with the police in Edinburgh, had turned himself around and lived an exemplary life thereafter? It was not likely, given his predilection for finding himself in trouble. But stranger things had happened. Men sometimes married a woman for whom they were willing and even eager to change. Or had a child, for whom a man would rethink his past and decide that being a proper father was worth the effort it entailed to transform himself into a hardworking, honest citizen. Even an encounter with the church could make a difference sometimes.

Or quite simply, Harvey Wheeler might have fallen under the wheels of a lorry or taken ill of pneumonia and died in a charity ward, an unknown consigned to a pauper's grave.

"Aye, but he died on yon Sacrifice Stone."

But what if he hadn't?

Still, Chief Inspector Cummins was a seasoned and clever policeman. If he had found no trace of Wheeler, then possibly there was none to be found.

"Verra' like yon inquiry in Hastings."

Rutledge tried to ignore the comment.

If the dead man wasn't Wheeler, it would mean starting the inquiry at the very beginning—so many years after the fact. With witness memories uncertain, with evidence tainted or lost, with no assurance that any resulting conviction would be any more correct than the initial one, person or persons unknown.

Cummins had been obsessed because the answers were out of his reach. It was the blot on his copybook, a personal failure that he couldn't quite accept.

But by the same token, Rutledge reminded himself, a man had died violently, and the person or persons unknown who had killed him had escaped the workings of the law.

He closed the folder and put it aside to be returned to the files where old cases were kept.

Setting his teeth, he reached for the first of the reports awaiting his attention, refusing to think about what was happening in Sussex.

But Hamish's remark about the murders in Hastings still rankled. And there was nothing he could do about it.

A trial in which Rutledge was to give evidence was unexpectedly returned to the court docket after a long postponement, and he was summoned to Winchester the next morning. Sergeant Gibson brought him word shortly after two o'clock in the afternoon. He left at once to pack and drove through the golden light of late evening to the hotel room reserved for him. There was time after breakfast before he was scheduled to begin his testimony, and he walked in the cathedral precincts for half an hour.

The constable who was sent to fetch him was an older man, gray and stout.

As they walked back to the courts, Rutledge said, "Do you recall the man who was found murdered at Stonehenge in 1905? The case was never solved."

Constable Gregg frowned. "My good lord, sir, I haven't thought of it these dozen years or more. How did you come to know about it?"

"I knew the inspector who headed the inquiry. He retired recently."

"He was a good man. If anyone could have found an answer it was him."

"The Salisbury police were first on the scene, were they not?" It was a question designed to draw out his companion.

"It was a Winchester man. Constable Dutton. He was on his way back from giving evidence in a trial. On his bicycle, mind you, and he had a flat. By the time he'd walked to the next village and managed to get the tire mended, it was after dawn. The people celebrating the summer solstice had sent someone to walk to the nearest village—they happened to be one and the same. This man's name was Taylor. Clerk in a bank. He'd been sick at least twice, and nearly fell flat on his face when he saw Dutton coming toward him. All he could manage to say was, 'A body. At Stonehenge.' So Dutton pedaled off, and there it was, hanging on that stone at the end of the avenue. And a group of would-be Druids were sitting on the grass, looking like they wished they were back at home in their beds. Dutton didn't know whether to stay at the stones and send someone out on his bicycle, or go himself. In the end, he sent the schoolmaster for help. That's when it was turned over to Salisbury. All the witnesses were interviewed two and three times, but they never saw anything of any use."

Gregg shook his head, marveling. "There's usually something, you know. You find the slimmest bit of evidence, a piece of paper, a pencil stub, a footprint. And it opens the inquiry right up. I kept up with the case, you see."

"And someone looked into the background of each of the latter-day Druids?"

"Oh, indeed, sir. They were all what they appeared to be."

They had reached the courts and were climbing the stairs to the room where Rutledge's case was being tried.

As he stood there waiting to be called, Rutledge said, "Was there a Charles Henry among the Druids?"

"Charles Henry? Not precisely among the Druids," Constable Gregg replied. "I believe that was the name of the solicitor the schoolmaster sent for. Yes, Charles Henry. He was—"

He turned as the door opened and the summons came. Rutledge was still looking toward Gregg, but he was moving away, nodding, as if to wish him well. He had no choice but to walk on, seeing the sea of faces turned his way in the crowded courtroom, the judge in crimson and the KC in black, their wigs properly appended to their heads, and the prisoner in the dock, his expression taut with concern. Rutledge moved to the witness box, fighting to clear his mind of Cummins's obsession, which was fast becoming his own, and to dredge up the facts in this case. As he was taking the oath, he felt the calm of duty settle over him, and as he stated his name and rank as he'd done so many times in this box, he was ready for the first question.

Half an hour later, cross-examined and finally dismissed, Rutledge left the courtroom and went in search of Constable Gregg.

But he was told the man had been sent for and was on his way to take down a witness's statement in another case.

The trial dragged on into the second day, as the Crown rested its case and the defense presented its view of events. At long last the jury was sequestered and Rutledge was free to go.

He could spare the time, the days were long, and so he drove on to Salisbury, in search of Charles Henry, solicitor, but it was as he'd expected. If the solicitor had been there in 1905, he was not there now. Rutledge asked at chambers he passed as he went up and down several streets, and even stopped in the main police station. The answer was the same. No one recalled the name or the man himself. It had been fifteen years, and Henry had played only a minor role in the case.

Hamish said, "Did he sell yon knife in Hastings?"

"How did he come to have it?" Rutledge countered. "No, there's something else at work here, I think."

He should have been on his way to London an hour or more ago, but it had been important to track down

Charles Henry, if he could. He walked back to where he'd left his motorcar, feeling unsatisfied. But it hadn't been his case, it had been someone else's.

Still, Charles Henry rankled.

He arrived in London later than anticipated, held up by an overturned lorry blocking the trunk road, and stopped by the Yard to leave his notes on the case in which he'd given evidence. There was a message on the blotter, waiting for him.

Chief Inspector Hubbard wished to see him. The note had been amended at the bottom, indicating he'd come looking for Rutledge a second time.

My office, please, eight o'clock in the morning.

Rutledge knew Hubbard, had spoken to him from time to time, but had never worked with him on an inquiry. He had a reputation for strict adherence to rules, a strong sense of fairness, and a razor-sharp mind.

It would be a refreshing change from Chief Superintendent Bowles.

The next morning he arrived at the Yard fifteen minutes before time, and as it happened, met Chief Inspector Hubbard on the stairs. He was a man in his late forties, what he called the sunny side of fifty, still very fit, his manner brisk.

"You're prompt," Hubbard said. "Come with me, we'll get started. How was the case in Winchester?"

"The jury was still out when I left. But at a guess, the Crown expects them to see matters its way. The evidence was clear, solid."

"That's what I like to hear. I daresay the results will be in today." They had reached Hubbard's office, and Rutledge was offered a chair. Hubbard set his hat on the top of the taller file cabinet, and sat down at his desk. He took a deep breath and said, "I hear that inquiry in Sussex is a sticky one."

"Whoever the killer is, he's clever. Nothing is what you expect it to be. But I'd started ruling out possibilities when I was sent for. Constable Walker is a sound man, he'll bring my replacement up to speed very quickly."

Hubbard nodded, then picked up a folder he'd put to one side on his desk. He opened it, read the contents, as if to familiarize himself with them, and then set it down.

"I've been informed that Inspector Mickelson is preparing to make an arrest in these murders. Possibly as we speak."

His comment, casually spoken, caught Rutledge completely off guard. "I'm glad to hear that," he said sincerely. "It was touch and go, whether we'd find the killer before he struck again. Can you tell me who it is?"

"Yes, one Carl Hopkins. A German sympathizer, I believe."

If he'd been surprised before, Rutledge was stunned now. "Hopkins? I was about to interview him when I was taken off the case. Hardly a German sympathizer— I was led to believe he was distraught because of what had happened during the war to his younger brother and his cousin."

"Yes, well, according to Inspector Mickelson, he's good with his hands and obviously was able to counterfeit those identity discs to throw the police off."

"How did Inspector Mickelson come to suspect him?"

"Apparently Mickelson drew up a list with Walker's help of all the people you'd spoken with, and went back to interview them. Someone at the hotel remembered the owner of the chair firm calling on you. Mr. Kenton was very reluctant to discuss the conversation he'd had with you—he's related to Hopkins, I believe—but in the end Inspector Mickelson threatened him with a night in gaol to rethink his reluctance, and he gave a brief explanation of what had brought him to you in the first place."

Rutledge didn't argue the matter. He hadn't been there—he hadn't spoken to Carl Hopkins. Nevertheless, the man's motive was plausible, and it made sense that someone known to the victims could walk up to them in the dark without arousing suspicion or fear.

He wished he could put a face to Hopkins, to weigh what he'd seen for himself against Mickelson's certainty. After all, it had begun as his inquiry. He still felt a responsibility for its outcome.

"Thank you for telling me, sir. Inspector Mickelson is to be congratulated."

Hubbard said, "Yes."

After a moment Rutledge said, "I should like to have a day or two of leave. For personal business. Would you have any objection to that?"

"Not at all. You're between cases. I see no harm in taking a little time."

"Thank you, sir." He started to rise, but Hubbard motioned him to sit where he was.

"We haven't discussed the matter about which I'd summoned you."

Rutledge sat down again, his hat on his knee, and waited.

"The woman who reported you for misconduct. A Mrs. Farrell-Smith, I believe?"

"Yes, sir," Rutledge replied.

He'd had no warning. Not from Sergeant Gibson, not from curious stares or people turning away as he passed. Not even from his usually acute intuition. But of course he'd seen no one last night when he came into the Yard. Only a skeleton night staff was on duty, since there was no major London case on the docket that required every available man.

Hubbard's voice was chilly as he said, "I understand from Sergeant Gibson that you were interested in learning more details concerning her background. Was that a personal issue, Rutledge?"

"Personal?" he repeated, staring at Hubbard. "Hardly. Her late husband had known one of the possible suspects in the murders. This was before the war. I was curious about the suspect's background, and I'd hoped that she could tell me something about him. Even secondhand, it could have been useful. She refused, got angry with me, and I wondered why. When I first met Mrs. Farrell-Smith, she seemed to believe I'd come to see her about that suspect, but I hadn't. What's more, she had objected to the Yard being brought into the inquiry to start with. Any good policeman would begin to consider what if anything was behind her attitude. Three men were already dead, the fourth victim would be found shortly. Most people would be eager to help us find that killer."

"Sergeant Gibson tells me he warned you that she was complaining of your conduct, but you still insisted that he find out what he could about Mrs. Farrell-Smith's husband."

"Her complaints were, in my opinion, a matter for the Yard to deal with. I needed information that I could use to pursue a killer."

"Not to coerce her into dropping her complaint?"

Rutledge opened his mouth and shut it again. Finally he said, "That's absurd."

"Is it? Sergeant Gibson came to me—and rightly so—when he discovered that Mrs. Farrell-Smith's husband had died under suspicious circumstances. She was cleared in the matter."

"I was told he died in a fall."

"I don't think that's any of your concern. The point I'm trying to make is that it smacks of impropriety for you to be investigating the woman who filed the complaint about your behavior. You also brought Sergeant Gibson's conduct into question by asking him to do something that he felt was unwise."

"It wasn't my conduct," Rutledge said tightly. "She wanted me off the case. And she was right. The new man sent to Eastfield has found the murderer in a very short time, and this German, Hopkins, has nothing to do with Mrs. Farrell-Smith. Or her late husband."

"Are you impugning Inspector Mickelson's ability to conduct this inquiry?" There was anger in Chief

Inspector Hubbard's blue eyes and his tone was decidedly cold now. "Perhaps if you'd kept your objectivity, none of this would have happened."

Rutledge regarded him for a moment. And then he said quietly, "We are getting nowhere. What do you intend to do?"

Chief Inspector Hubbard realized that he'd made a mistake. He grimly got his temper in check, then said, "You should take that day or two of leave coming to you. While this is sorted out."

Rutledge said nothing.

"Ian. You asked for it yourself. This is for your own good. I quite take your point that you weren't aware of Mrs. Farrell-Smith's complaint when you telephoned Sergeant Gibson and asked to know more about her background. It's the perception of impropriety here."

But Hamish was reminding him that Gibson had warned him about the complaint, and he hadn't listened. He had not, in fact, expected the Yard to take it seriously.

Then who had? And why?

"If you take a short leave of your own accord, there will be nothing on your record. After all, this inquiry has come to a successful conclusion, there was simply an unfortunate coincidence in timing in regard to the situation with Mrs. Farrell-Smith, no harm intended nor done by your request. She has been satisfied that you were withdrawn from the case and is unlikely to pursue the matter further."

Suddenly he knew.

It was as clear as if the words had been spoken aloud. But he thought Hubbard did not know, and that explained why *he* was dressing Rutledge down, not Chief Superintendent Bowles. Hubbard had been chosen because he could be trusted to handle the matter with circumspection and convince Rutledge to put the matter to rest, nothing on his record, just whispers that would never go away. And it would not be seen as Superintendent Bowles playing favorites. But it would clear the way for Inspector Mickelson to be promoted to fill Chief Inspector Cummins's shoes.

He rose, and this time Chief Inspector Hubbard didn't stop him. "I'll notify Sergeant Mitchell that I've asked for leave and will be away from the Yard for the next two days on personal business." Mitchell was the man in charge of Yard personnel records.

"Yes, do that, Ian," Hubbard said cordially, relieved to find Rutledge so cooperative. "This will all blow over, mark my words."

Rutledge left, strode down the hall to find Sergeant Mitchell, and said as soon as he saw him, "I'm taking a few days of personal leave. I've cleared it with Chief Inspector Hubbard."

Mitchell's face gave no indication that he had been expecting this. He simply took Rutledge at his word. The whispers hadn't started. But it was too early for that. In time they would.

"Very good, sir, I'll make a note of it. Will you be staying in London, sir? In the event you're needed?"

But he wouldn't be needed. That was certain. Still he answered civilly, "No, I'm visiting a friend. In Kent."

That had popped into his head. But the more he thought about it, the more he knew it was the answer. Melinda Crawford lived in Kent. And she would ask no questions, she would accept his visit as one long overdue. There he could come to terms with what had happened, and by the time he returned to the Yard, the molten anger possessing him would have cooled.

"Have a safe journey, sir," Mitchell told him, as if Kent were in the wilds of Africa, and it would require days if not weeks of travel to get there. But Mitchell was a Londoner and felt lost outside the crowded metropolis.

It would have been amusing in any other circumstance. But not now. Rutledge thanked him and went down the stairs and out the door, grateful not to meet anyone.

When he reached his motorcar, he swore, sitting there with clenched fists on the steering wheel.

Chief Inspector Cummins had no doubt suggested Rutledge as a suitable choice for his replacement. Cummins was well respected, and his suggestion would carry some weight. And so the Chief Superintendent had jumped at the chance to use Mrs. Farrell-Smith's complaint to put a stop to that possibility. A charge of improper conduct was a serious matter. It could follow a man for the rest of his career at the Yard. But Hubbard had given him a way out, a way to keep it out of the official record. He had thought he was protecting Rutledge's future. What he had unwittingly done was to ensure that everyone would eventually know why Rutledge was being passed over for Cummins's position. Rumor would begin soon enough, quietly fed from above, and most people would come to believe that Chief Superintendent Bowles had, in fact, looked after his own, shielding Rutledge from public disgrace.

It was an adroit move.

14

Rutledge drove to his flat, packed his valise, and shut the door just as the post arrived. He paused on his doorstep to sort through the handful of letters, and found one there from Chief Inspector Cummins.

He put that into his pocket and set the rest of the post inside on the table where he habitually kept it, then turned the key in the lock and walked out to his motorcar.

Hamish had been busy in the back of his mind for some time, and he tried to ignore the voice. But it followed him out of London and most of the way to Kent.

"Ye ken," Hamish was pointing out, "yon inspector kept his eye on the main chance from the start. He was canny enough to study where you'd been before him, to appear he finished what you werena' there to do. And so he got full marks for your work. All because ye let yon headstrong woman draw ye into a personal challenge."

Mickelson had indeed done just that and would receive the coveted promotion. Aside from any personal feelings toward the man, Rutledge knew all too well that he was vindictive and shallow. Chief Inspector Cummins had been neither, and he was respected for leading by example, bringing out the best in the men under him. All the same, Chief Superintendent Bowles would cover any mistakes, if for no other reason than to make certain Mickelson's failings didn't reflect on his own judgment.

As for Mrs. Farrell-Smith, Rutledge hadn't challenged her so much as he'd threatened her in some fashion. What was she so afraid of? Something she didn't want him to know? Or something that she didn't want to become public knowledge?

He couldn't stop dwelling on events in London, and he knew that was because he was still very angry indeed. It was a lovely summer's day in what many called the Garden of England, the road unwinding at what felt like a hideously slow pace, even though he was making good time. He had not telephoned Melinda Crawford. He had intended to surprise her. Now he realized that he should have been more courteous. Too late now. He'd have to rely on her joy at seeing him again. When his sister had gone there for a visit recently, along with his godfather, Rutledge had had his own reasons for not joining them.

The truth was, Melinda, like Meredith Channing, saw too much. Many years and a vast difference in experience separated the two women, but in their own way, they had much in common. Both had lost their husbands at a young age and had had to make peace with that loss.

Was that why he had come here? Because Melinda reminded him of Meredith?

Nonsense, he told himself sharply. Melinda had been friends with his own parents, and he'd known her most of his life. Hers was a story that had appealed to a boy's sense of adventure. As a child she'd survived the Great Indian Mutiny and the bloody, vicious siege of Lucknow. She had married her cousin against all advice, and then after her husband's death she had not led a retiring life. She had visited friends all over India, traveling on her own. Finally she had journeyed back to England by a circuitous route that had been of her own choosing, a shockingly forward thing for a well-brought-up woman to do, disappointing those who had expected her to be murdered in her bed for disregarding their dire warnings. Now she lived with her Indian staff in a house that had been in her family for many years, amidst a collection of treasures that she had readily shared with an inquisitive little boy.

At length he found himself at the foot of her drive, the summer borders rampant with color. Melinda loved color and often said that she had lived too long in the desert stretches of India, where the few trees offered only fragile shade and the land was barely fit for camels and goats.

When the door opened, the Indian woman standing there stared at him in disbelief, and then said, "You are a ghost. Come to bring us terrible tidings." But the smile in her eyes belied her words.

He returned the smile. "I've come to beg a room for a day or two. Do you think Melinda will spare one for me?"

"She will be happy indeed. It's been too long." Leading him into the cool shadows of the hall, she added, "I think you haven't forgotten your way? Or must I come and announce you?"

He said, "I know my way."

"But still I will come with you, if only to see the Memsahib's face when she finds you in the doorway."

He tapped lightly on the first door in the passage across from the broad staircase and heard a voice call testily, "It's about time. I saw you come up the drive. Let me look at you and then give me a kiss."

Laughing, Rutledge did as he was told, crossing the room to kiss the wrinkled cheek of a woman who had kept her youthful beauty into old age, her iron gray hair still framing her face and dark eyes as it had done for as long as he could remember, and giving her a presence that few women possessed.

She held his hand for a long moment and then said, "What's happened?"

"Nothing has happened. I missed you."

"Your eyes are angry. Well, you'll tell me when you're ready. I'm just grateful you are here, and I'll make the most of it. Go on, your room is ready for you—it always is—and then come back and tell me about London."

Rutledge did as he was commanded, and brought down with him a book he'd been keeping to give her. She thanked him and set it aside. "I'll read it when you've gone. I've missed your company. Tell me all the news and gossip."

The next two days flew by. Rutledge soon realized that Melinda was making it her business to keep him entertained in an effort to counteract the seething anger that he'd brought to her door.

She knew something about men, and so she asked him no questions. Although she never spoke of it, he thought she'd guessed that he had turned from France with a wound that couldn't be seen or touched or healed. What he didn't know was how much she knew. Certainly not about Hamish, thank God, but possibly about his shell shock. For she had worried about him for the past year or more, and when he had survived and then found a way to live rather than die, she had quietly applauded his courage.

He found himself telling her about the murder that had taken place in 1905, and she had listened attentively, saying only, "On what was his last day at the Yard, why did this man Cummins tell you about such a long-ago crime?"

"I think, to get it off his chest. He isn't the sort of man who accepts failure lightly."

"No, I expect there was another reason. You've told him of your own discoveries? What has he had to say about them?"

"In fact, there was a letter from him in the post before I left London." He patted his pockets, found it, and drew it out.

It was very brief. A matter of a few lines. He read them aloud.

*My grandfather was Charles Henry Cummins. I
visited his home as a child. In East Anglia. His
garden was his pride and joy. What the hell is this
all about?*

"Well, well," Melinda said after a moment. "I
wonder why this man chose Hastings to sell his murder
weapon?"

Rutledge said slowly, "I don't know. I've asked
myself that same question."

"It was deliberate, you must see that." Melinda
frowned. "If he went to so much trouble to make sure
the knife was carefully documented, then he had a
reason. Perhaps it was his name—the murderer's. Or
the name of the victim."

He thought, fleetingly, of the Salisbury solicitor who
was nowhere to be found. Was it that connection—or
Cummins's?

"That's a fascinating idea. I'll have to give it some
thought. But why, three years later, would a man who
had successfully eluded the police and had nothing to
fear, leave clues that could lead to his arrest?"

"A guilty conscience?"

"Murderers seldom have guilty consciences," he told
her wryly.

"But if this was a sacrifice, perhaps he did?"

Rutledge smiled. "You should have become a police-man, Melinda. The Yard would have benefitted from your cleverness."

"Oh, no, my dear, the Yard doesn't want women underfoot. We could prove to be too much competition for men set in their ways." Her dark eyes sparkled. "As my late husband could have told you, I have no ambitions."

He left the next morning, reconciled to what lay ahead. Melinda Crawford had kept him too busy to dwell on the Yard—he had an uncomfortable suspicion that it was intentional—that she had seen the tension in him and even without understanding it, she had dealt with it by distracting him. He wished he could have said something to her about Meredith Channing, to hear her opinion there. But if he had, he'd have had to tell Melinda more about his time in France than he could bear to put into words.

Her house was in the most western edge of Kent, and he had just crossed into Surrey when a Kent police vehicle quickly overtook him and waved him to one side.

Rutledge pulled over, assuming that the Yard was searching for him. He waited for the constable sitting beside the driver to get out and come to speak to him.

"Inspector Rutledge?" the constable said, bending his frame a little so as to see Rutledge's face more clearly. He was a tall, angular man with a scar across his chin.

"Yes, I'm Rutledge. What is it?"

Hamish, from the rear seat, said, "'Ware!"

"You're wanted in Hastings, sir. Straightaway. I've been sent by London to find you and bring you to Sussex as quickly as possible."

Surprised, Rutledge said, "I'm no longer involved with the inquiry there. Didn't London tell you that?"

"Their instructions were to take you directly to Hastings. If you don't object, sir, I'll ride with you to your destination."

Rutledge said, "You aren't a Hastings man. No need to waste your time there."

"No, sir, I'm from Rochester. And we have our instructions, sir."

Rutledge was silent for a moment, weighing that, and then said to the constable, "Get in."

The man nodded and walked around the bonnet to open the passenger door.

Rutledge had expected the other vehicle to turn back, but when he drove on, it followed him at a distance. It was still there when he headed south to Sussex at the next crossroads. The constable was staring straight ahead with nothing to say for himself.

"What's this about? Do you know?"

"Sir, I'm not at liberty to discuss the matter."

Giving it up, Rutledge fell silent, an uneasy feeling beginning to build in his mind. This was how a suspect was arrested if found on the road. Except that he would be asked to step into the police car, leaving the constable to drive his.

There was the charge of improper conduct against him, but Chief Inspector Hubbard had all but told him that if he took a few days leave voluntarily, it would be ignored.

What else had Mrs. Farrell-Smith found to say about him? He'd have thought she would have been satisfied to see him withdrawn from the case.

Or had she learned that he had uncovered the facts surrounding her husband's death? That was an old case, not something that he had permission to reopen. But did she know that?

It was another hour before Rutledge drove through Eastfield and down the Old London Road into the Old Town. He hadn't expected to return here, now that the inquiry had been successfully concluded.

The morning sun sparkled on the water, touching the tips of the choppy waves with gold and catching the sail of a small private craft tacking down the coast, a white triangle against the blue of the sky.

He reached the police station and pulled in behind another vehicle standing there, and the constable accompanying him got out.

"Thank you for cooperating, sir. It's much appreciated." He gestured to the door. "This way, if you please."

Rutledge led the way inside, and the sergeant on the desk recognized him.

"If you'll wait here, sir, I'll send someone to fetch Inspector Norman."

"I know the way to his office—" Rutledge began, but the sergeant shook his head.

"If you'll wait here," he repeated.

"Yes, all right," Rutledge said, irritated now.

Five minutes later, Inspector Norman strode briskly into the room and said without any greeting of any sort, "Inspector Ian Rutledge, I am arresting you on the charge of attempted murder."

Rutledge stood there, speechless. And then he was being led away, and the constable from Rochester was turning to leave.

"What the devil is this all about, Norman?"

Hamish was warning him not to lose his temper, and he held on to that advice with a tight grip.

Inspector Norman had nothing to say to him, and Rutledge had no choice but to go with the constables, who escorted him to a room in the back of the station.

They asked him to empty his pockets, give them his belt and his tie and his watch, and then they wrote out a careful receipt for him. There were holding cells in the back of the police station, and as he was escorted there, Rutledge had the impression they'd been dug out of the bedrock, because they were windowless, and he could feel the dampness emanating from them. There were four of them, and they looked, in fact, more like a dungeon than prison cells. There was no natural light, no fresh air, and they were too small to contemplate. And before he was quite ready to face it, the iron-barred door was swinging shut behind him, and the two constables were walking away, leaving him there.

He tried to think why he should have been arrested on a charge of attempted murder, and then realized that if anything had happened to Mrs. Farrell-Smith, the Hastings police might wish to question him. But an arrest?

It would have required the approval of the Yard to send the Kent police looking for him. Had they been to Melinda Crawford's house, asking for him? Or had they been scouring the county for him, and had just had the good fortune to spot him on his way to London?

He refused to consider where he was, he refused to look at the dimensions of the cell, the walls, the furnishings. He hated confinement, and this was the ultimate of that. He kept his eyes on the floor, and wished for his watch. It wouldn't be long before someone came for him. He couldn't remain here for very long. He could already feel panic rising.

He waited what he estimated to be half an hour, his temper nearly getting the best of him, before Inspector Norman came back to the holding cells and said, "I'll not handcuff you. Call it professional courtesy, one officer to another. But you'll have to give me your word that you'll not cause me any trouble while I take you to my office for questioning. They're sending someone down from the Yard, but this is my patch, and I'll do my own questioning, thank you very much."

"I give you my word," Rutledge said through clenched teeth, and the cell door was opened. Without looking back, he followed Inspector Norman to his office and took the chair indicated. "What are the charges against me? I've a right to hear them."

Norman walked around to his own chair, sat down, and considered Rutledge. "I've told you. Attempted murder. Very likely murder—it's going to be touch and go on that. Dr. Gooding holds out little hope. When we put in a call to London with word of what had happened,

Chief Superintendent Bowles ordered us to bring you in. He himself spoke to the Chief Constable in Kent, where you were said to be staying. And the Kent police went looking for you. Now London is sending someone down. Hubbard, I think the name was."

"And who is it I'm said to have attempted to kill?"

Inspector Norman said, "Where were you these past two nights?"

"I was staying with a friend in Kent. Mrs. Crawford." He gave directions for finding her house, and then said again, "Who is it I'm said to have attempted to kill?"

Norman finished his notes and set them aside. "Inspector Mickelson was struck on the head night before last. And as we have one Carl Hopkins in custody for the other murders, we couldn't look in that direction. The finger of guilt seems to be pointing directly at you. I was told there was bad blood between the two of you."

Rutledge stared at him, stunned.

"Why should I wish to kill Inspector Mickelson?" he asked finally.

"I understand he was being considered for a promotion that you wanted."

Rutledge stopped himself from swearing. "That's hardly a reason to commit murder. It defeats the purpose, in fact."

"I told you. When I spoke to London, Chief Super-intendent Bowles informed me that you and Inspector Mickelson had had trouble before this. He also said you'd agreed to a short leave after disciplinary action, and walked out of the Yard in something of a temper, telling Sergeant Mitchell to look for you in Kent if he needed to find you. That's to say, practically on our doorstep. And then you dropped out of sight. This wasn't a garroting, mind you. The case is very strong, Rutledge."

It was indeed. "When was he attacked? Where?"

"I can't discuss the murder with you. Those are the instructions I received from Scotland Yard."

"This is nonsense and you know it. Let me drive to London. I'll speak to Chief Superintendent Bowles myself and clear it up." He was angry enough to face the man down.

"You know I'd be in trouble if I allowed you to leave." Norman sat there, studying Rutledge.

The two of them had had their own disagreements.

Was he gloating? Rutledge couldn't tell. Did he agree with the Yard? It was impossible to be sure.

He said after a moment, "What were your views on the arrest of Carl Hopkins? Did you find the garrote when you searched his residence?"

It was Inspector Norman's turn to be caught off guard.

"Hopkins?" he repeated, as if he'd never heard the name before. "I don't know enough about the facts of the case to make a judgment."

"Don't tell me you haven't kept up with events in Eastfield. Especially after one of the victims died right here in Hastings. You know as much about the murders as London does."

Inspector Norman flushed slightly, caught in a lie and handed an uncomfortable truth.

Rutledge went on. "I'd have done the same in your place. I'd consider one death on my patch reason enough."

He sidestepped the question. "There is the fact that the killing stopped after Hopkins was taken into custody."

"Hardly stopped. If you count Inspector Mickelson. And I do. He got in the way, if you think about it. Whoever has been killing these men could well have been afraid that Mickelson was about to change his mind. Blaming Hopkins would have been very convenient if our murderer had finished whatever it is that he'd started." Rutledge didn't believe it was finished. But he wasn't about to weaken his own arguments by adding that.

"Mickelson wasn't garroted. What's more, why didn't our murderer kill *you*? You thwarted him by locking up those village men—" He broke off. It was an admission that he'd kept up with the inquiry.

Rutledge ignored the opening. At the moment, he wanted Norman on his side. "I hadn't made an arrest. I was useful as long as I didn't—my very presence promoted fear of more deaths, and he got to Hartle. But Mickelson did take Hopkins into custody, and if that's the wrong man in your cell, then we haven't finished with these murders. What we don't know—unless Mickelson took Constable Walker into his confidence— is whether he stumbled on something that either clears Hopkins or brings up serious doubt about his guilt. Either way, Mickelson had to be stopped before he reported that to the Yard. If the killer had used the garrote, we'd have had proof we'd gotten the wrong man. Don't you see?"

"There were no discs in Mickelson's mouth."

And that was interesting.

"I'm not surprised," Rutledge told him, considering the comment. "It means he wasn't one of the chosen."

"Or you didn't have any of them to put there."

"True." He didn't argue. After a moment he went on, "I have witnesses, you know, that I never left Kent until this morning. Very reliable ones, in fact. Someone should have asked about that before having me stopped and brought here. It smacks of leaping to conclusions."

"Unless your witnesses were sleeping in the same room with you, it doesn't preclude leaving in the middle of the night. You could have slipped out and back in again, with no one the wiser," Inspector Norman countered.

Rutledge said only, "We'll see. Can Mickelson be questioned yet?"

"I don't think he's regained his senses. You'd better pray he doesn't die." Norman rose, preparing to take Rutledge to his cell when there was a flurry of voices from the sergeant's desk in the front of the police station.

They paused where they were, Norman undoubtedly believing that Chief Inspector Hubbard had arrived.

But it was not Hubbard.

The flustered sergeant on the desk came to the door, saying, "I tried to stop her, sir. But she insists she has information on Inspector Mickelson's murderer."

And they looked beyond him to see Mrs. Farrell-Smith coming through the doorway behind him. She took in Rutledge standing there in the passage with Inspector Norman and said, "That's the man I saw in Eastfield the night Inspector Mickelson was attacked. I saw him drive up, speak to that poor man, and then drive away with him. They were in front of the church, and my bedroom window looks out toward the gate to the rectory." For emphasis, she pointed directly at Rutledge, as if she were already in the witness box.

Rutledge's mouth tightened. And then he said, "Are you so certain that Daniel Pierce is the man we're after, that you are willing to lie to shield him?"

She retorted, "I know nothing about Daniel Pierce."

Rutledge turned to Inspector Norman. "This is Mrs. Farrell-Smith, headmistress at the Misses Tate Latin School. If she really wanted to protect someone, she could have looked back into the school's records to see if anything happened in the past that could have some bearing on these murders. All the victims were together there for at least two or three years. If it isn't the war, and it isn't the present that caused someone to start killing, it could very likely lie in the distant past. I'd prefer to be escorted to my cell now."

She opened her mouth, and then shut it again.

Inspector Norman nodded to the sergeant, and Rutledge went with him, already regretting his impatient request.

He said to the sergeant, trying to delay entering his cell, "Am I the only prisoner here?"

"No, sir. There's another man at the end of the row. We were preparing for the inquest to be held this very week, but it must wait now for the Inspector to recover."

This must be where Carl Hopkins was also being kept, as he'd thought, and he said under his breath, "Poor devil."

He went into his cell and watched the door swing shut with a clang and the large key turn in the ancient lock. It sounded like a death knell.

This time he couldn't ignore his surroundings. He had no idea how long it would be before Hubbard arrived, and he was faced with the possibility that he would remain in this place for several days, at least until it was certain whether the charge was going to be attempted murder or murder. He wasn't sure he could manage it.

The cell contained a narrow cot, a bucket, and a basin on a shelf with a pitcher standing in it. Near the flat, ugly pillow, a tin cup lay on the blanket that covered the cot. What little light there was came through the barred square in the door. The walls were painted a dreary dun color that had faded into a shade like cream gone off. Although the cell was clean enough, and the water in the pitcher fresh, there was a lingering odor of urine that rose from the floor, and the smell of fear that seemed to cling to the walls. He hadn't noticed it before. He'd been too intent on matters being set straight in a hurry. Now—now, his fate lay in the hands of Inspector Mickelson.

Hamish said derisively, "Ye've been inside a cell before this."

But always knowing that he wasn't the occupant, that when he was ready to leave, the door would open and there would be a reprieve from the panic. Now Rutledge was battling his claustrophobia, fighting the urge to promise anything if they would leave that door unlocked. He thought about the night to come and shuddered, then began to pace. In the dark, the walls would begin to close in.

Hamish cautioned, "There's no help for it, ye ken. Sit doon and close your eyes. Ye willna' see the door, then."

I'm going to make a fool of myself, he thought, when I start screaming. And then they'll know. But after a time, he sat down and shut his eyes, as Hamish had counseled, imagining the room to be as long as the drawing room in Melinda Crawford's house, counting first one and then another of the furnishings and trea-sured objects that filled the space. It helped, but only a little against the rising tide of dread.

A constable brought him a meal later, as well as fresh water, and he realized it must be noon, or possi-bly one o'clock. The food was hot, plentiful—fried fish, roasted potatoes, fresh bread and peas. He wondered if

Inspector Norman was hedging his bets by treating his thorny prisoner with some care in the event the Yard had to eat its words.

The afternoon dragged by, and Rutledge set himself the puzzle of why there was murder being done in Eastfield.

If Inspector Mickelson had taken the wrong man into custody, the murderer had only to bide his time, and then kill again. It would have made Mickelson look a fool. Why then had he targeted Mickelson?

What had the man done that had angered the killer? From the time that Scotland Yard had arrived in the village, whoever was behind these murders knew he was risking being unmasked. He must also have known that dispatching one inspector would only bring another in his place, someone even more determined to search him out.

What had made it necessary to rid himself of Mickelson before the inquest? Rutledge had told Norman that it was what Mickelson knew—or was about to do. But was that true?

Or had Kenton, trying to persuade Mickelson he was wrong about Hopkins, lost his temper and acted rashly? Something as simple as that?

He went to the door and raised his voice, but only loud enough to reach to the last cell down the passage. He had heard the door being unlocked and a lunch tray passed to the prisoner there. But the man had been quiet. If he had spoken at all, it was so softly that the words hadn't carried.

"Carl Hopkins?"

There was no answer.

Rutledge tried again. "Mr. Hopkins. I'm a policeman. I was in Eastfield before Inspector Mickelson."

"I remember." There was a pause. "Why are you in a cell?"

"Inspector Mickelson was attacked. For lack of a better idea, they think I'm involved. I didn't like the man. The feeling was mutual. Meanwhile, I'm waiting for my movements to be cleared up." He hoped that was true.

"It's a trick of some sort. Well, it won't do you much good. I didn't kill anyone. I have nothing to confess."

"It's no trick."

But Hopkins wouldn't say anything else and Rutledge let it go.

I didn't kill anyone . . .

Rutledge sat down on the cot, staring at the walls, hearing in the back of his mind the distant French guns, and then the artillery from the English lines. Before very long, he knew he'd begin shouting commands to his men, and then he would be lost.

He wasn't sure how much time had passed. He had even lost track of where he was, the tramp of men's boots as they formed a line in the trench, waiting their turn to go up the ladder and follow their offi- cers into battle, had seemed so real he could smell the stench of the water in the bottom of their trench and hear the whispered prayers of men who knew they could die in the next five minutes. He was preparing to blow his whistle for the charge when the present intruded.

The sound of voices drifted down the passage and then grew louder. After a moment the constable ap- peared to unlock Rutledge's door. The relief that swept over him as the door swung wide was almost physical, and for a moment he had to struggle with the images fading into the back of his mind.

"You're wanted in Inspector Norman's office," the man said and stepped aside.

Rutledge got up from the cot and walked out the door. He knew that Hubbard must have arrived, and when he stepped into Inspector Norman's office, the first person he saw was the Chief Inspector.

"A mistake has been made," the Chief Inspector was saying to him. "I'm sorry."

Rutledge stood by the doorway, waiting.

Inspector Norman said to Rutledge, "Come in." He pointed to the other chair.

Rutledge joined them. But still he said nothing.

Chief Inspector Hubbard turned to Inspector Norman. "Chief Superintendent Bowles was misinformed. Inspector Rutledge was visiting friends in Kent when the murder occurred. We've spoken to Mrs. Crawford. She was quite clear. Inspector Rutledge couldn't have left her house, driven to Eastfield, and returned without the staff or she herself being aware of his absence. What's more, his leave had been requested before the subject of Mrs. Farrell-Smith's complaint had been brought up with him."

It was an outright lie, blandly told.

"She's made a second statement this morning. She claims she saw Rutledge speaking to Mickelson and then taking him up in his motorcar the night before the attack was discovered. How do you answer that?"

Hubbard was clearly unprepared for this information. He recovered quickly. "She reported this to Constable Walker?"

Norman hesitated. "Not straightaway. No."

"Had you sent your men to look for Rutledge in Eastfield, after you spoke to the Yard?"

"I saw no harm in sending Constable Petty to keep an eye on things. Until someone arrived from London." He shot a glance in Rutledge's direction, then returned his attention to Hubbard.

"And Mrs. Farrell-Smith didn't speak to Constable Petty about what she'd seen?"

"He's still in Eastfield," Norman said, grudgingly. "I don't know. She didn't mention having spoken to him."

Chief Inspector Hubbard said, "I must wonder why she felt it necessary to leave the school and come directly here to you, when there were other avenues in Eastfield open to her. Mrs. Farrell-Smith, it appears, prefers not to deal with underlings."

Norman said, "You haven't read her statement. But you're convinced her evidence is flawed."

Hubbard took a deep breath. "Inspector, I shall be speaking with Mrs. Farrell-Smith myself in due course. But understand this. If Mrs. Crawford swears that Rutledge did not leave her house, as a witness she is more reliable than Mrs. Farrell-Smith."

"And who is Mrs. Crawford, when she's at home? I know nothing about her."

"Mrs. Crawford's veracity is vouched for by Neville FitzThornton at the Home Office. On the other hand, it's possible that Mrs. Farrell-Smith has lied to the police before this."

Rutledge smiled to himself. The police and the Yard answered to the Home Office. He wondered how Melinda had come to know FitzThornton. But the fact that she did cheered him. The thought of returning to the confinement of that cell left him feeling cold.

Inspector Norman said, "My advice is to leave matters the way they are until someone is able to question Mickelson. Then the veracity of witnesses won't come into it."

"And very good advice it is. But I'm told that the Inspector is on the point of undergoing surgery to relieve the pressure of the swelling on his brain. He may not be able to speak to us at all."

In the end, Hubbard got his way, by rank if not by persuasion. Rutledge's belongings were accounted for and returned to him. As he signed the receipt, Inspector Norman asked, "What am I to do with Carl Hopkins?"

It was a question designed to irritate Hubbard. It failed.

Hubbard said blandly, "He stays where he is until the inquest. And at the moment, that must wait on Mickelson's recovery."

"I'd like five minutes with Hopkins," Rutledge interjected, speaking for the first time as he accepted his watch and his keys from the constable.

Hubbard hesitated. "I don't think that would be wise."

"It isn't a matter of wisdom. Come with me, if you prefer. But if I'm to take over this inquiry again, I need to know where Hopkins stands."

"Take over—it was understood that I should carry out Inspector Mickelson's brief."

Rutledge turned to him. "You know why I was removed from this case. You know why I found myself in these straits today. You owe me a chance to redeem my character."

"This is not the time nor the place to decide this. Propriety—"

"Propriety be damned." He turned and walked to the door, continuing down the passage toward the cells at the rear of the police station, listening for the order to stop. And none came.

He found Carl Hopkins lying on his cot, one arm over his eyes. Rutledge wished he had had the forethought to ask the constable for the cell keys. But it was too late to go back. He looked at Hopkins's cell. It was a mirror of his, and he could feel that frantic sense of being closed in sweeping over him again.

He had been buried alive on the Somme, when their salient had been blown up by a shell falling short of the German lines. The miracle was he had lived through it, but lying in the suffocating darkness, pinned there by the weight of the body under which he lay and the heavier earth above them both, he had known no one could reach him in time. He could hardly breathe, as the minutes turned into what seemed like hours, and then just as the small pocket of air that had sustained him was used up and his mind was beginning to struggle to keep track of where he was in that cold black void, help had finally come. Hands dug frantically, the weight lifted, and as he was pulled out, loose earth cascading from his hair and uniform like water, he had seen the face of the man who had saved him. It was Hamish MacLeod's dead body, and the pocket of air that had been a gift of life had been created by Hamish's clothing. The shock had left him unable to speak, and his rescuers had put that down to near suffocation.

It was not until he'd reached the aid station and was given a few hours of rest that he'd heard Hamish MacLeod's voice in his ear, taunting, reminding him that his men were dead, and he had no excuse for being alive.

Getting a grip on the memory now, Rutledge called Hopkins's name, and the man dropped his arm, swung his legs to the floor, and looked toward the barred window of his cell. He hadn't been asleep. That was obvious. "What do you want? Is this another trick?"

He was a tall man, slim and very fair, Nordic fair rather than English, with dark blue eyes. But he had broad shoulders and was at second glance a great deal stronger than he first appeared. Deceptively so, Rutledge thought.

"We're keeping you here for a few more days," Rutledge told him. "For your own safety. But I need to know. What was your relationship with the four Eastfield men who have died? Did you go to school with them?"

"I was apprenticed at the furniture works when I was young. We were in school together for perhaps three years. And then my mother taught me in the evening, when I came home with Mr. Kenton at the end of the workday."

"What do you remember most about them?"

Hopkins didn't need to think about his answer. "They were all of an age. Except for the Pierce brothers. And good at sports. Less so in the classroom. I was far better in mathematics, I remember. And better at spelling as well."

"Were they troublemakers?"

"No more so than most boys."

He changed the subject. "I'm told you hated the English for what happened to your family during the war."

Hopkins got up from the cot and crossed to where Rutledge was standing at the door. "It made me ill for a time. I hadn't been able to serve, you see. I wasn't there to help them. I'd try to sleep at night and I'd wonder what their last thoughts were, if they'd called to me and were hurt that I didn't come. I didn't even know when they died until weeks afterward. I'd been living my life, talking with friends or working—even sleeping—as they were struggling for their last breath. When I'd see a British soldier, I'd want to ask, were you there? Did you try to save them? Did you even care? Some would boast of the Germans they had killed. Callous bastards. I wanted to hit them, make them suffer too." He shrugged. "It was stupid of me, but there was so much pain I couldn't think straight. I even considered suicide. But when I spoke to Rector about what comes after, he didn't know. All the words he preached, and he didn't know what was on the other side. What use was it to kill myself, if I couldn't be with them again? The happiest days of my life were spent with those two. My English brother and my German cousin. And when people called my cousin a butcher, a Hun, and hoped he'd gone to hell, I hated them with all my heart."

He stood there, not crying, not cursing, his shoulders slumped.

Rutledge said after a moment, "Did you hate them enough to kill them?"

"I thought about it. If I'd known where to find a gun, I might have tried. But I didn't. I could only curse them all." He looked away. "That takes courage, acting on what you believe. I didn't have it."

Hamish said, "He wouldna' creep up behind a man and garrote him."

But Rutledge silently answered him, Not in the cold light of day. But after a sleepless night?

His intent on coming back here to the cells had been to hear Hopkins defend himself face-to-face. He'd almost believed the man earlier. Now, he was not so sure.

Hamish argued, "Ye were in yon cell yoursel' and no' thinking clearly."

Rutledge considered the prisoner. He looked older than his years, a defeated, sallow figure with nothing to buoy him up and carry him through the loss that was eating him alive. It was possible that Carl had taken his own sense of worth from that brother and the cousin, and was unable to find his way alone. Would killing alleviate some of the pain? Or would it only add to the distressing burden of guilt that Hopkins already shouldered?

"Who do you think attacked Inspector Mickelson?" Rutledge asked.

"The man from Scotland Yard? He badgered Mrs. Winslow, and made old Mr. Roper half ill. Mrs. Jeffers came into Eastfield and told Constable Walker that the Inspector had made her cry, wanting to know about the war. Then he discovered from someone at the hotel that Mr. Kenton had come to speak to you there, and soon enough he badgered me too. I live alone, I didn't have any proof I hadn't killed those men. He was a policeman, and that's what policemen do, when they've got the upper hand. They badger." He looked Rutledge in the eye for the first time. "I didn't like him well enough to mourn when I was told he'd nearly been killed, and I hadn't cared for what I saw of him when he was alive. Maybe I wasn't the only one."

With that he turned his back on Rutledge and went to sit again on his cot, his head in his hands. Rutledge stood there watching him, then walked away.

15

When Rutledge came back again to Inspector Norman's office, it was clear that the two men had been having words. He could almost feel the tension, and their faces were flushed.

"I didn't learn anything of interest," he said. And with a nod to Inspector Norman, he walked out to where he had left his motorcar. After a moment Chief Inspector Hubbard joined him.

"Is there somewhere we can talk privately?" he asked.

Rutledge said, "By the water."

They drove toward The Stade, pulling over where they could. The fishing boats were in, and the air smelled of salt, tar, and fish. The tall net shops were black against the sun, almost sinister, and the headland above them was a deep, rich green.

"That's where they found Mickelson. In one of those sheds, hanging from a hook," Chief Inspector Hubbard told Rutledge.

"Good God!" After a moment Rutledge said, "I assumed he'd been found in Eastfield. Small wonder Inspector Norman was unwilling to step aside. As it is, he'll keep probing. That man of his, Petty, is very good."

"The fleet goes out very early," Hubbard went on. "That means he must have been put there while it was still dark. The killer brought a length of rope from somewhere, to pass over the hook. Or he found it in one of the sheds."

Hubbard turned to face Rutledge. "If Carl Hopkins hadn't been in custody—and if Mickelson had been garroted—I might find myself wondering if you hadn't been very very clever. He very nearly got you killed. Twice over, if I remember."

Rutledge laughed grimly. "You know damned well I didn't touch him. You also know what Chief Superintendent Bowles was playing at, calling me to book for misconduct. He must have panicked when he heard about Mickelson. He must have thought he was next."

Hubbard said only, "I wouldn't joke about that, if I were you."

"He was protected by Bowles. If I'd been tempted to kill the man, I'd have done it in London and put his body into the river somewhere east of The Poole. By the time they'd fished him out, there would be no way of knowing how he died, where he died, or by whose hand. They would be lucky to know who he was. I might as well have hung a placard around his neck with my initials on it, leaving him in that net shop. I'm not that much of a fool. And I have no wish to hang."

"Then who met him outside the churchyard and lured him into a motorcar? Assuming, that is, Mrs. Farrell-Smith is remotely telling the truth."

"Who found the body?"

"Fishermen coming for their nets. Must have scared them out of ten years' growth, I should think. Why the hell are they so tall and narrow, these net shops?"

"A blow to the tax man, I'm told. When the town tried to levy new taxes on building footage here, the fishermen looked at their long drying sheds and thought, why not build them vertically? They did, the taxes were eventually revoked, but the sheds stayed. They must burn from time to time or fall over in a gale, but the fishermen thumbed their noses at the authorities."

"You haven't answered my question about the motorcar," Hubbard pointed out.

"If it's true, if Mickelson was met by someone, then the killer came looking for him." He gestured toward the dark red bonnet of his motorcar. "In the dark that could be red. Or green. Or even blue or black. She saw the shape of a touring car, not the color. Or possibly she saw the two men talking, and invented the motorcar to throw suspicion in another direction."

"Why should she do that?"

"She could have thought it was Daniel Pierce. She's been waiting here for him to return since before the war. And he did come home, to stay in Eastfield only a matter of a few weeks."

"She's in love with him?" Hubbard asked.

"I don't know," Rutledge said, "whether she wants to have him or kill him. It depends on whether or not she killed her husband for him."

"Quite," Hubbard said as Rutledge turned the motorcar and drove out of Hastings. As they climbed toward Eastfield, he added, "But Mrs. Farrell-Smith is not our business at the moment. Are you certain these killings aren't war related?"

"I'm sure of nothing. Someone knows the answer— but that someone may not realize the importance of it. Whatever happened, it appears not to have made a deep impression on the victims of these murders. That makes it all the more personal to the murderer."

"Then I should think this man Hopkins fits the bill very well indeed. From what I was told he held a grudge that no one else knew about."

They were silent for the rest of the drive, but as they were coming down the Hastings Road into Eastfield, Hubbard said, "I'm not comfortable, leaving you to cope alone."

"Then you still believe I struck Mickelson."

"Be reasonable, man. It was a misunderstanding."

But Rutledge remembered the feel of that cell and the walls closing in on him, and the miasma of fear and hopelessness embedded in the very paint. He stopped the motorcar at the hotel and said, "I'll find someone to drive you to the nearest railway station after you finish your business here." As he got out of the motorcar, he added, "I've lost the promotion. I understand that, even if Mickelson lives to clear me. You can tell Chief Superintendent Bowles—"

He left the sentence unfinished, and walked away.

Chief Inspector Hubbard had the good sense not to follow him.

Of all the people he could think of who would talk to him, Theo Hartle's sister seemed to be the best choice.

He found her just clearing away the tea things, and she said as she came to her door, "We've just finished—would you care for some tea?"

"Thank you, no. I need to talk to you, Mrs. Winslow. It's a pleasant afternoon. Will you walk a little way with me?"

She cast a glance over her shoulder. "I think my husband has nodded off in his chair. I ought to be here, if he wanted anything when he wakes up."

"He's just had his tea. I shouldn't think he'll need you straightaway."

She came reluctantly. "Where's the other man, then? If you're back again?"

"Didn't you hear?" But he could see she hadn't.

"We're not often in the village," she explained. "I only go when I really need something."

"He was nearly killed."

"Like those other men?" She stared at him, horrified.

"No. Someone fractured his skull."

"He's a *policeman*," she said, as if that made it all the worse, that authority itself had been flouted and threatened with chaos. "I didn't care for him, but still and all—" She looked over her shoulder, as if there was someone following them. "We're all that afraid of going out at night. Hardly anyone stops by the pub, they say."

"That's not why I'm here. Tell me about your brother's life."

"He was a bouncing baby. That's what Mum always said. Full of vinegar from the start." She smiled, tears welling in her eyes. "But he was never in any trouble. Just mischief, that sort of thing. I didn't like it when he was teasing me about my freckles. But he meant no harm." She shook her head.

"Teasing can hurt," he said.

"It did sometimes," she admitted. "He called them my spots, and told Mum to wash my face in buttermilk. And he tried it once, but they didn't go away. 'You've got spots,' he'd say, and sometimes I'd cry. Mum said he was just being a boy. They went away when I was older, my freckles, I mean, and I was glad of it."

Boys will be boys . . .

Where else had he heard that? Was it Constable Walker who had said it?

Rutledge stopped, turning to face her. "Did he tease anyone else? Or were you his favorite target, because you were his sister?"

"Oh, they were always teasing one another," she said. "It could be cruel, sometimes, you know. But they didn't mean it to be. It's just that children see things that adults try to pretend don't exist. Jimmy Roper's ears stuck out when he was small, and they told him he looked like a jug. And Mary, Will's sister, stuttered. They'd mimic her something fierce, which only made it worse. This was in the school yard, when the school-

mistress wasn't in hearing. Or on the way home, sometimes. Miss Tate helped her overcome her stutter, but it
must have been hard to do. And there was another boy,
I forget his name. But they tormented him too, when no
one was about. We never told. We didn't dare, although
I said to Theo more than once that it was unkind." She
shaded her eyes to look up into Rutledge's face. "Boys
don't always think, do they? That words can hurt?"

"And the other boys—Jimmy Roper, Will Jeffers,
even Anthony Pierce—went along with tormenting
other children?"

"Anthony didn't like it, but he was too afraid to
speak up. He was a little younger, and not as big then
as the other boys. Could we turn back now? I really
shouldn't have walked this far."

They had reached the churchyard. Rutledge said as
they reversed their direction, "You've been very helpful, Mrs. Winslow. If you think of anything else, will
you leave word for me at the police station?"

"Yes. I will."

She walked back into her house and closed the door
on the narrow world that encompassed her life now. He
thought how pity, mistaken for love, could ruin lives. It
was what he hadn't wanted from Jean.

Which reminded him of Meredith Channing, but
he shut his mind to that memory and went to find the
constable.

Walker was glad to see him. "Speaking no ill of a man unable to speak for himself," he said after greeting Rutledge and asking if he was taking over the inquiry, "but Inspector Mickelson was not pleasant to work with. I can't think why the Yard would replace you."

"Mrs. Farrell-Smith complained of my conduct. She also believes I tried to murder Inspector Mickelson."

Walker smiled. "How would she think that? You weren't in Eastfield that night."

Had Walker said as much to Hubbard? Rutledge wondered.

"She claims she saw someone in a motorcar meet Mickelson by the churchyard and then take him up. If she's right, then that someone owns a motorcar very much like mine."

"Now that's odd," Walker said, the smile vanished. "As I remember, that's what Daniel Pierce drives. Only it's dark green. I didn't know he'd come back to this part of the world."

"It's not an unusual motorcar," Rutledge pointed out. "But I rather think Mrs. Farrell-Smith is afraid it did belong to Pierce."

"I didn't think she knew him."

"How well do you remember Daniel as a child? Was he bullied by the older boys? Or was he spared because he was Pierce's son?"

"If they did bully him, it never came to my ears. I do remember a time or two when Daniel came home from school bloodied, and his father was angry with Anthony for not protecting him. Anthony told his father that Daniel had deliberately started the fight."

Daniel as the aggressor didn't make sense. Rutledge said, "Did Pierce come to you?"

"I was young and green. I talked to Daniel, but he was stubborn even then. I got nowhere. But I told his father I thought he'd learned his lesson."

"I want you to bring in two or three of the men we incarcerated. I'll talk to them, see what they can tell me."

"Now?"

"Before dark. I'll see that they reach home safely afterward."

He left Walker and went to the hotel, where he was given a room. He asked if Inspector Mickelson's room was on the same floor, and the young woman behind the desk said, "He's—he was—in number seventeen. Constable Petty and then a man named Hubbard were here, asking about it."

"I'd expected as much," he said, smiling. He took his key and went up the stairs two at a time. It didn't take him long to discover that his key also fit number seventeen, after a little jiggling. He opened the door and stepped inside.

The bedclothes were turned down, but the bed hadn't been slept in. Mickelson's clothes were hung tidily in the wardrobe, and his razor, toothbrush, and soap were on the washstand. The towels on the side rack appeared to be fresh, untouched.

Where had Mickelson gone between his evening meal and that appointment at the rectory gates?

Rutledge opened the desk drawer. There was stationery inside, and a few sheets had been used to jot down notes. Rutledge read through them.

For the most part they consisted of brief references to what he, Rutledge, had done while in Eastfield: *R to Pierce, R to rectory, R to F-S, K to R,* as Mickelson retraced his predecessor's steps.

In London, Chief Inspector Hubbard had mentioned that Mickelson's method had been to revisit Rutledge's progress—or lack thereof—and draw new conclusions.

Under the list he'd already scanned there was a question mark, and then the comment, *Kenton says Hopkins is obsessed. Lives alone, no witnesses to his comings or goings. Motive strong enough? Talk to him again.*

And a later notation: *Gave his permission to search premises. Not surprising, no garrote. Denies making discs. But good with tools. Could have stamped them out after hours, when other employees had left.*

On a separate sheet were listed the names of the murder victims, and below that, another of potential victims—all of them the men Rutledge had kept in gaol while he was trying to locate the ex-soldiers whose names had been imprinted on the identity discs shoved into their mouths after death.

Near the bottom of the page was a larger question mark, drawn in heavy strokes.

Doesn't feel right, Mickelson has scrawled just below it. *What if I'm wrong and the killing begins again after we've all gone away?*

The final line was ambiguous.

Why Hastings? Ask R.

Rutledge set the sheets back inside the drawer and closed it.

Did the second sheet represent uncertainty on Mickelson's part before or after he'd arrested Carl Hopskins? They weren't numbered.

Why Hastings? Ask R.

Standing there, looking down at the street below, Rutledge considered that *R.*

He found it hard to believe that Mickelson would have contacted him about Hastings. Who, then, was the *R?* The rector?

Opening the door a crack, he listened, but the passage was quiet, and he stepped out of the room, shutting the door again. Glancing at his watch, he could see that he just had time to call on the rector before dinner.

But the rector wasn't at home, and his housekeeper, an elderly woman with a plain face, informed Rutledge that he was with the elder Roper, the second victim's father.

"He's been feeling rather down, since Jimmy's death. Rector takes a book and goes to sit with him from time to time. Poor soul!"

"Can you tell me if Inspector Mickelson called here at the rectory two nights ago? It may have been rather late."

"He's the one they just found in Hastings," she said, and shook her head. "I don't know what the world's coming to. Has he died, then?"

"He's still unconscious. Was he here, do you know?"

"I leave after setting out Rector's dinner," she said. "Unless he's ill. I live with my sister, and we sew of an evening. So I wouldn't know who comes to call later than seven."

He thanked her and left, walking through the churchyard as the sun's heat dissipated. Looking up at the church tower, and the weather vane swinging slightly west in the light breeze, it occurred to him that the rectory housekeeper often knew more about events in a village than anyone else—sometimes including the rector himself.

Retracing his steps, he knocked again. When the housekeeper answered a second time, Rutledge said, "I wonder if you could help me, since Mr. Ottley isn't here. Have you lived in Eastfield most of your life?"

"All my life," she told him complacently, "save when Mr. Newcomb and I went to Cornwall on our wedding trip."

She invited him inside, leading him to the parlor and offering him a chair with the simplicity of someone accustomed to receiving the rector's visitors and making them comfortable until he returned. But when it came to sitting with him, she was clearly ill at ease, perching on the edge of her own chair.

"How well did you know the murder victims? I wonder if you could tell me what they were like as schoolboys. Were they often in trouble, or were they generally good youngsters?"

"Not troublesome, precisely," she answered, considering the matter. "Lively, I'd say. Thoughtless, sometimes, as when they set fire to the old mill. The fire could have spread, you see, but it didn't. Except for Mr. Anthony, his brother Daniel, and Theo Hartle, they were farmers' sons, and eager to be outside, not shut up learning history and Latin and the like. Not that some of them weren't good students. The elder Miss Tate told me once that Jimmy Roper could have made something of himself if he hadn't been the only son and expected to inherit the farm. Theo was very good at numbers, and if he hadn't had such a gift for working with wood, I think Mr. Kenton would have made him bookkeeper."

Here finally was the information that Mrs. Farrell-Smith could—should—have found for him in the school records.

"I've heard," he said, choosing his words carefully, "that there was some problem with young Daniel Pierce."

"He got his nose bloodied a time or two," she said, nodding. "But he was a sweet boy, nevertheless. He just never wanted to be a brewer. That was Mr. Anthony's life, he was always underfoot there. The foreman's wife told me once that Mr. Anthony wanted to go hop picking, to learn more about them." She smiled at the memory. "His mother put a stop to that. 'When you're older,' she told him."

"Were the brothers on good terms with each other?"

"They got on well enough together. They were just different. Mr. Daniel was always adventuresome, and Mr. Anthony more bookish. In 1910 when there was all this talk about going out to Africa to grow coffee, I told Mr. Newcomb it was a shame Mr. Daniel wasn't old enough to give it a try, but he said if the boy didn't care for the brewery, then he wouldn't be one for growing the coffee beans."

Rutledge brought her back to the subject at hand. "Who bloodied Mr. Daniel's nose, if it wasn't his brother?"

"It was the other boys, if you ask me. They'd band together sometimes and tease Mr. Anthony or Mr. Daniel about their clothes or their accent or their manners. Mr. Anthony would ignore them, but Mr. Daniel was not one to turn the other cheek. I remember Rector had a word with him about that."

"Was there much teasing or taunting, do you think? If they turned on the Pierce brothers, who did the other boys harass? People tell me boys will be boys, but sometimes it's cruelty, well beyond the bounds of teasing."

"Yes, sometimes it did get out of hand. I remember that poor Summers lad. He was overweight to begin with, and afraid of his shadow. Not good at sports, his face all blotched, clothes never together properly. Mr. Newcomb worked on the wormwood at the school one September, and he told me the boy was the butt of all manner of jokes and pranks and never stood up for himself. Mr. Newcomb wanted to say something to the elder Miss Tate, but it wasn't his place. Mr. Newcomb did speak to Constable Walker, when Mr. Daniel got into trouble about fighting, defending him, like, but nothing came of it."

Rutledge had heard some part of this story before. From Mrs. Winslow? Yes, as she talked about her brother Theo tormenting her about her freckles. He asked, "What became of the Summers boy? Does he still live in Eastfield?"

"Oh, heavens no. His father was a clerk at Kenton Chairs, and he was made a better offer by a firm elsewhere. Lincolnshire? Staffordshire? I can't remember just where, but he packed up and left. There was just the two of them, a boy and a girl. Their mother died when they was very young. She's buried in the churchyard here."

Walker—speaking about the near-drowning of a boy—had said the family moved away.

"Do you remember the child's first name?"

"I believe it was Tommy. Tommy Summers. I haven't thought about him in years. I hope things worked out better for him, wherever he went."

Yet sometimes a child was marked, and other children sensed it, like wolves turning on the weakest member of the pack. It was a poor analogy, perhaps, but it served.

"I wonder if Inspector Mickelson came here to ask Mr. Ottley about the Summers boy?"

"Where would he hear about him?" Mrs. Newcomb countered. "I daresay half the people in Eastfield have forgot about him by this time. I had, myself."

But Tommy Summers may not have forgot Eastfield or the wretched years he'd spent here.

They talked for ten minutes or so longer, but Mrs. Newcomb had very little to add to what she'd already told him or he'd learned elsewhere. And so he took his leave.

Walking back down the rectory drive, Rutledge asked himself if Tommy Summers, a grown man now, could be slowly wreaking revenge on his erstwhile playmates. But then what about Carl Hopkins?

16

Rutledge encountered Constable Petty on the High Street as he was walking back to the hotel. Petty stopped, saying, "I was about to report to Inspector Norman."

"Did you take anything from Inspector Mickelson's room when you searched it earlier today?"

"No, sir, I did not. I made an inventory of his personal belongings. Inspector Norman was waiting for instructions from Scotland Yard regarding their disposition."

"Is Mickelson in hospital in Hastings?"

"I was told he had been transferred to Chichester. There's a man there who knows a good deal about head injuries. It wasn't considered wise to try to move him to London."

"No, I understand. I want a daily report on his condition. If you're here to keep an eye on things for Inspector Norman, then you might as well serve me too."

"Sir, I—"

"Yes, yes, I understand. You're Hastings police. But I'll have that report each day. I think you'll find that Inspector Norman will raise no objections."

"Yes, sir."

"Did Chief Inspector Hubbard leave?"

"He found someone from the hotel willing to take him to the station. Or so I was told."

"How did you get here, Petty?"

"Bicycle, sir."

"There's something else you can do. Keep an eye out for motorcars similar to mine, but the color scheme may not be the same. I'd like to know where they're going and who is driving them. If there's one in Hastings Old Town that doesn't belong there, I want to hear about that as well."

"I'll do my best, sir."

Rutledge nodded and walked on.

Petty had only one loyalty. But Rutledge needed his eyes.

He brought back to mind the man he'd seen at The White Swans. Most likely Daniel Pierce, not Tommy Summers. The descriptions differed.

Hamish said, "Aye, but ye canna' judge how the Summers lad looks now."

And that was an important point.

As agreed, Constable Walker had collected his nephew, Billy Tuttle, Hector Marshall, and Alex Bullock, and they were waiting for Rutledge in the Eastfield police station.

They sat on the bench, stony faced, as if expecting Rutledge to lock them up again, already resisting what he was about to say.

But there was new information since he had summoned them, and so he asked, "Do you recall a village child called Summers? He and his sister attended school with you."

They stared at him.

"His father moved north when the boy was about ten, I should think—not all that many years ago. Tommy Summers."

Tuttle turned to Bullock. "I don't think there was a Summers lad, do you?" Looking back to Rutledge, he added, "He must have been younger. Or older, even."

Marshall said, "Summers. There was a girl by that name. My sister's age. Long blond plaits down her back."

"Was she the Summers girl? I thought she was dark."

They argued amongst themselves, but the upshot was, they had no recollection of Tommy Summers at all.

Rutledge said, "You tried once to drown him as a witch."

Something stirred in Marshall's eyes, but he shook his head.

Tuttle shrugged. Bullock looked at the far wall, as if expecting more to follow, and this was somehow a trick to lull them. They were more interested in the present than the past.

Rutledge said, "Someone fought with Daniel Pierce for defending the boy."

Walker said, "I remember that. Was Summers his name?" He pulled out his watch and added, "It's growing late."

"Yes, all right. Take them home, Constable." There was no use pushing the issue. He watched them go, grumbling amongst themselves at the waste of time. As Hamish was pointing out, it was high summer and their busiest months.

And as if he'd overheard the remark, Marshall said in a voice intended to carry to Rutledge's ears, "He hasn't volunteered to milk the bloody cows, now has he? Londoner." But there was bravado in the words.

Walker admonished him and followed the men into the street.

They had gone no more than twenty yards when Tuttle turned and glanced at Rutledge, as if of half a mind to call to him or go back, but Walker said, "Come along, then, it's getting dark," as if he were all too aware of Inspector Mickelson's fate. The sanctity and authority of a policeman had been shattered. He was taking no chances being out in the night alone.

Rutledge waited until he'd returned, reluctant to leave the police station until he was sure Walker was all right.

The constable came in after Rutledge had lit the lamps, and shut the door with undue haste, as if he were shutting out the shadows waiting in the street.

"You're still here, then."

"I waited to ask you the same question I'd asked the others. You told me once, I think, about a boy being bullied. Do you remember any other details?"

"Not bullied, exactly. He was just one who never quite fit in. I'd have intervened if they'd done any real harm," he said dismissively. "They were young lads. It happens."

But words could hurt as much as blows.

"Where did the father go, to take up his new position?"

"Did I tell you that?" Walker was surprised. "North, I think. Staffordshire?"

"Has Constable Petty left for Hastings?"

"Half an hour ago." He hesitated, and after a moment asked, "Is the killing over, do you think? We assumed, after Hopkins was taken into custody, that it was. Then Inspector Mickelson—it doesn't make sense, does it?"

Which was precisely why the police had come for Rutledge, but he said nothing.

Walker added, "I did tell the others to take the same precautions as before. To be on the safe side." He grinned. "Marshall called me an old woman. But his wife told me once it's dark, he's under her feet."

"We'll patrol the streets until Inspector Mickelson regains consciousness and can tell the police what happened. Did he call on the rector that night, before he was attacked? Or was it a coincidence that he encountered someone near the rectory?"

Walker shook his head. "Rector never mentioned it. I think he would have, under the circumstances."

'I'll take the first four hours, as soon as it's full dark." It was the most dangerous time, based on the earlier killings. "I'll come for you, shall I, when it's your turn?"

Walker opened his mouth and then shut it again. "I'll be awake. Good evening, sir," he called finally as Rutledge was about to close the police station door behind him.

Hamish said as Rutledge was on his way to the hotel, "It would ha' been best to give yon constable first watch. Or to share it. Ye're no' a trustworthy witness, ye ken that. The ithers will believe what he tells them, but no' you."

He's older. Rutledge almost said the words aloud, stopping himself just in time. *And not as fit.*

"And what if there's no trouble atall?"

I've wasted four hours of sleep.

He recalled his impression of Carl Hopkins. Whatever anger the man harbored, Rutledge couldn't quite imagine him using a garrote. Physically, he could probably have managed it, but was there the strength of mind needed to kill four men with it?

"But ye havna' seen him in a frenzy. Only despondent in yon cell."

Which was a very good point. There had been three days between each of the murders, three days in which a man could whip himself into another killing temper.

"It willna' be easy returning to the Yard," Hamish warned, "if Mickelson doesna' recover, and Hopkins is convicted."

As he put out his hand to open the hotel door, Rutledge heard someone call his name. Turning, he saw that Tyrell Pierce was coming toward him. He paused and waited for the older man to catch him up.

"I'd expected you to call today," Pierce said without greeting him. "Sad business about Inspector Mickelson. But I would be lying if I said that I wasn't glad to have you back in charge. What happened, anyway? You were here, and then you weren't. Walker wouldn't tell me anything, so I had to assume he knew nothing to tell."

Rutledge didn't answer him directly. "Who do you think attacked the inspector?"

"I daresay it was the killer. I'm not particularly happy to be out at this time of evening myself." As he reached Rutledge, light spilling from the windows was reflected in his face. There was tension around his eyes, a grimness to the set of his mouth.

"Then why didn't he use the garrote?" Rutledge asked him.

"Yes, I wondered about that myself. I decided he must not have had it with him. Well, I shouldn't care to be walking around with the damned thing in my pocket, in the event I was stopped because I was a stranger in town. Walker stopped someone just yesterday. Did he tell you? A man on his way to Hastings, as it happened. That's what my foreman told me—he'd witnessed the incident. According to him, the man might have been able to handle a garrote, but he'd have been hard-pressed to use it on Theo Hartle." He gestured toward the door. "Have you had your dinner? I was just going to the hotel hoping to find you."

They walked in together, and as they paused on the threshold of the dining room, they saw Mr. Kenton sitting by one of the windows. He looked up at the same time, and beckoned to them. They joined him, and as Rutledge sat down, Kenton said, "I didn't expect Carl to be taken into custody. I merely told you about him out of a sense of duty."

He had ordered his dinner but it hadn't arrived. The woman serving meals that evening brought over a menu, and Rutledge, after scanning it, made his selection.

While Pierce was considering his choice, Rutledge turned to Kenton. "I never passed on that information to Inspector Mickelson. Nor to Walker. Someone else saw you with me."

He could tell that Kenton didn't believe him.

"I should have thought that what happened to Mickelson proved beyond a doubt that Carl isn't guilty."

"We don't know if that attack and these murders are connected—"

"Any fool will tell you that there aren't two murderers running loose in a village the size of Eastfield! Carl is one of my best workers. I'm going to have to find a replacement soon. And I don't want to do that. I wish I'd never come to you. I expected you to ask him a few questions, clear the air." But that wasn't the impression Rutledge had got when Kenton first approached him.

Hamish said, "Second thoughts."

Pierce turned to them and said, "What's this about Carl?"

"I was just saying he was one of my best workers. I've known him all his life, I can't see him committing murder."

Rutledge thought that when Kenton was speaking to him about Hopkins earlier, he had been driven by his own uncertainty, perhaps even the fear that if the killer was shown to be an employee as well as a personal connection of the owner of Kenton Chairs, it might seem that Kenton had protected him.

Pierce said, "I'm of two minds there. Anthony would have trusted him, if he'd come into the brewery looking for him."

It was to Pierce's advantage, Rutledge knew, to distract the police from any interest in his son Daniel. But would the man go as far as letting another person take the blame? He reminded himself that Pierce might have attacked Mickelson if he had been on the verge of finding new evidence that pointed in Daniel Pierce's direction.

Kenton scowled. "And why, pray, would Carl need to find your son, in the brewery or out of it?"

"I'm only saying—" He broke off as their soup arrived, and then added, "How is Inspector Mickelson? Any news in that direction?"

"Just that he's alive and holding his own," Rutledge told them. He hoped that it was still true.

Pierce said, "Nasty business. I suppose he hasn't spoken yet?" The question wasn't as casual as it seemed. Rutledge understood now why Pierce had sought him out when he'd failed to come to the brewery.

"He was found in Hastings, I'm told. Just as young Hartle was," Kenton put in. "I don't see why that shouldn't clear Carl."

They argued through the first course and well into the second. Rutledge was heartily sick of it. And then Kenton asked, "When is Daniel coming back to take his brother's place? He'll require some training, I should think. He was never as interested in the business as his brother was, although I wondered if that was only a facade. He said to me once, before the war, that there was no room for him at the brewery and it was all he knew. What has he been doing since the Armistice? New interests of some sort?"

Pierce said shortly, "When he's ready, he'll take his place at Pierce's."

"You're not growing any younger," Kenton pointed out. "I'd considered leaving Kenton Chairs to Carl, before all this happened. Now I'm not so sure if it's the right thing to do. Last thing I heard about Daniel, he was going into business with someone. Mrs. Farrell-Smith's husband, as I remember. But then the man died rather suddenly, and nothing came of it. Race horses, was it?"

He was goading Pierce, using Rutledge's presence to keep the moment civil.

Rutledge thought, Kenton has heard rumors about Daniel Pierce, and the father's smugness has irritated him.

Pierce was outraged. "Race horses? Good God, where did you hear that nonsense? I grant you they were at school together—Anthony was there as well. As for any business venture, they were hardly of an age before the war to be thinking about such matters. In fact, as Mrs. Farrell-Smith can attest, she and her husband were only just married, and Daniel was considering the law as a profession."

"My mistake," Kenton answered, smiling. "Shall we take our tea in the lounge?"

Pierce signaled to the woman who had served them. "It's late, and I really must look in at the brewery." He rose and said good night.

Kenton watched him go. "He's in trade as well as I am. But you'd think the brewery set him up higher than the rest of us. I never could abide self-importance."

"You rode him hard," Rutledge said. "His son is one of the victims."

"He was prepared to believe that Carl had been to the brewery the night Anthony was murdered," Kenton retorted. "Anthony moved in such exalted circles he probably wouldn't have recognized Carl on the street. Ironic, isn't it? Pierce wanted the Yard here in Eastfield. And I trusted the Yard, to my sorrow."

Rutledge left shortly thereafter. It was nearly time to start his patrol of the streets, and he went first to his motorcar to fetch his torch.

The shops had closed hours before, and the sun had vanished behind a bank of clouds. Shadows had deepened along the High Street, and beneath trees there were already pools of blackness. A gray cat trotting past a stationer's shop disappeared around the corner, leaving him alone as he left the hotel behind and turned toward the brewery. He turned again to walk down the side street by the Misses Tate School, and doubled back toward the Hastings Road before moving on in the direction of the rectory. It was a random pattern, his ears attuned to the silence around him, his faculties alert.

Hamish said, "It's an uneasy quiet."

It was. A warm evening usually drew couples out to walk, holding hands in the darkness, or men talking together and laughing as they headed to the pub or sat on the bench outside the baker's, having a last smoke. Instead, doors were shut, closing the sound of voices and laughter in, rather than letting it spill out into the night. Occasionally he'd seen a curtain twitch as someone looked out, then quickly pulled it across the window again.

The gate to the rectory was just ahead. He looked up at the long window that marked the staircase to the first floor, a hanging lamp glowing softly through the glass. As he did, out of the corner of his eye, he thought he saw movement in the churchyard beyond, and he turned his head for a better look.

It was that time of night when objects lost their color. Beneath the trees in the churchyard were patches that seemed impenetrable they were so thick with shadow, gravestones irregular splotches of gray, the church itself a stark silhouette beyond.

He stepped through the rectory gates, crossed the lawn to the wicket into the churchyard that rectors time out of mind had used to reach the church. The gate hinges squeaked a little, betraying his movements, but he walked on, wishing he could turn on his torch to prevent himself from stumbling over the settling ground and the footstones nearly hidden in summer grass. But to do so would mark his progress and take away his night vision.

It was near that tree, he thought, using a beech to keep himself oriented. He couldn't tell whether someone was still near the thick trunk or if the figure had moved on. After a moment, he stopped, trying to listen.

Hamish said, "There. By the corner of the kirk."

His eyes were adjusting to the gloom, and he could almost swear there was a figure disappearing toward the south porch, used sometimes for funerals when it was raining. He changed direction and followed, nearly sprawling headlong as the toe of his boot caught in something, tripping him up. Swearing silently, he reached the corner of the church and paused, one hand on the cooling stone.

It was very dark here, the grass and wildflowers heavier under foot. He could barely pick out the thicker blackness of the church porch, against a patch of sky.

The hair on the back of his neck seemed to rise.

Someone was there, he was sure of it. But in the porch, or in the darkness on this side of it?

Hamish muttered, "'Ware!" but Rutledge was already debating the wisdom of going forward.

Was he being lured? As the first victim, William Jeffers, could have been? Or was the unseen figure as eager to see him turn away as he himself was to go?

He moved on, keeping one hand on the church wall as he walked. He was halfway to the porch when he heard the slight grating of the door into the church, as if someone had gone inside.

But he wasn't convinced. He thought the man must still be inside the porch, waiting for him.

"I know you're there," he called softly into the shadows. "Come out and let me see you."

Silence followed.

And then movement again, as if someone had slipped out of the porch and was going east, toward the apse.

But then a footfall on pavement, a shoe scraping in the gritty entrance as someone turned back to the porch, came to him.

A trap, then. Set with care. For him? For Walker? Did the figure ahead of him know who was following?

Forewarned, he kept his eyes on the porch, one hand still brushing the stone wall of the church, his feet thrusting through the thick summer grass with care. Sinners and saints alike wished to be buried as near to the church wall as possible. And on that thought, his felt his foot strike the edge of a gravestone.

His quarry must have heard it as well, and this time the figure ahead of him slipped out of the porch and disappeared.

Rutledge continued until he'd reached the porch himself. He kept one hand on the wall as it jutted out to form the porch, guided himself to the opening into the porch, and with one hand out before him, made certain that the small space was empty.

He stepped out of it, again using its shape to judge where he was going, and moved on toward the apse.

But he sensed now that there was no one ahead of him. While he had been investigating the porch, the fox had eluded the hounds, slipping around the apse and up the far side.

Rutledge rounded the church himself, and moved quickly up the north side and on toward the gate in the churchyard wall.

He had left it half open, but it was standing wide now.

Stepping through it, he closed it and crossed the rectory lawn again, fairly certain that he had lost whoever it was. But where had he gone? Up the Hastings Road or down it? There was no way of guessing which he'd chosen. And his head start had allowed him to vanish up a side street or into the shadows of a doorway.

Why was he out in the night? His movements had been furtive, and that boded trouble.

Rutledge turned back toward The Fishermen's Arms, trying to recall any detail about the figure that would help identify him. Tallish, he was sure of that, and quick as a cat on his feet, because he had either known the churchyard well or had eyes better adjusted to the night.

And then in the distance behind him, he heard a motor turn over. He whirled but could see nothing, not even the flash of headlamps. No vehicle came his way, and after a moment, he was fairly certain that it had disappeared in the direction of Hastings.

There was no way he could catch it up. By the time he had reached his own motorcar, this one would have too great a head start, disappearing into the busy streets of the town.

Rutledge went to find Constable Walker. Wearing shirt and trousers, his mouth wide in a yawn, he came to the stairs in the police station as Rutledge called his name. "I'm up here. What's happened? I was just dozing off."

"Someone was in the churchyard." Rutledge gave him a swift account of what he'd seen, and by that time, Walker was wide awake.

"I'll just fetch my tunic," he said, and disappeared. A lamp was turned up, and when Walker came back to the stairs and started down them, he had his torch in his hand. Rutledge was already out the station door, ahead of him.

They searched the churchyard carefully, and even went into the church. There their torch beams were lost in the high ceiling arching over head, and the pews were dark shapes that cast long shadows, the spaces between them stretches of pitch blackness. Their footsteps echoed on the bare paving stones as they moved forward in concert. The pulpit looked like the prow of a ghost ship, and the choir stalls could have concealed half a dozen bodies. But there was no sign the intruder had ever been inside. Even the choir loft was empty.

What's more, there was no body tumbled into the high grass or hidden behind a buttress or a gravestone.

It took them a good forty-five minutes to be sure. As they were on their way back to the High Street, Walker said, "He saw you. That probably saved someone's life. But what's this, if Carl Hopkins is in gaol in Hastings?"

"We don't know why he was here." He looked up at the rectory as they passed. "That light in the rectory stairwell. It's been burning for some time. Is that usual?"

"No, it's not." Walker turned to Rutledge, alarm on the pale oval that was all Rutledge could see of his face. "You don't suppose it's Rector he's after? My God!"

They reached the gate between the churchyard and the rectory in long strides, going through it to the house door.

Walker was there first, his fist pounding on the wood panels.

Rutledge, staring up at the long window, watched the stairs, but no one came. He said, "Try the latch."

The door was unlocked. Rutledge swore. Mr. Ottley had far too much trust in the sanctity of his office—or too much faith in the goodness in human beings.

They went in. Rutledge took the stairs two at a time, calling Ottley's name while Walker went through the ground floor, searching each room. He was soon at the bottom of the staircase calling, "Any luck? He's not down here."

"Nor in his bedroom. Or in the other rooms. I'm going to the attics."

But in spite of his torch, that took longer than he'd anticipated. He came back to where Walker was waiting. "He's not here. Where would he be at this hour?"

"At Mr. Roper's? Jimmy's father. He's taken the loss of his boy hard."

To save time they went back to the hotel for Rutledge's motorcar and drove out to the Roper farm.

The house was dark, not even a light in an upstairs room.

"Do we knock at the door?" Walker asked in a low voice, staring up at the bedroom windows.

"If Ottley were here, there would be a light showing. No, let's not frighten the old man. The rector must have gone elsewhere."

He backed carefully down the drive until they had reached the lane.

"I don't know where else to look," Walker said. "Unless we start a search of the village. Is he dead, do you think?"

Rutledge said, "Why would someone kill the rector?"

"I don't know. That motorcar—you said it was driving toward Hastings. Do you suppose the rector was in it? That he was destined for those net shops? Or the cliffs?"

"It doesn't make sense." Rutledge turned back toward Eastfield.

"Mrs. Farrell-Smith saw that motorcar just outside the rectory gates. She saw Inspector Mickelson talking to the driver, and then leaving with him. The rector could know something about that," Walker argued.

"If he had, he'd have told you."

"There's that," Walker agreed. The rectory was just coming into view. Walker, peering through the windscreen, said, "Who is that?"

Rutledge could see the man some twenty yards from the rectory gate. He pointed the motorcar's bonnet in that direction so that the headlamps pinned the man in their great twin beams.

Walker exclaimed, "Look, it's Rector! Is he all right?"

Rutledge slowed as they reached the man standing staring into the light, as if mesmerized by it.

"I was just looking for you," he said as he recognized Rutledge and the constable in the vehicle. "But they told me at The Fishermen's Arms that you'd gone out. I've remembered something. I think it may be important."

17

Rutledge said sharply, "You shouldn't be walking out alone at this hour of the night."

Mr. Ottley said, "I can't neglect my duties, Inspector. Not if there were six murderers in Eastfield. God walks with me."

Exasperated, Rutledge felt like telling the man that God helps those who help themselves. He bit his tongue instead.

Beside him, Constable Walker said, "I'll walk you up the path to your door, Rector, and Mr. Rutledge here will drive his motorcar back to The Arms. Then he'll join us. I'd give much for a cup of tea."

"Yes, I could do with one myself." He waited for Walker to join him, and Rutledge watched the two men safely inside the house before driving on.

Ten minutes later, he was standing in the rectory study. There were not many feminine touches here, and he remembered that the rector had been a widower for many years. What softness there was, he put down to the good offices of Mrs. Newcomb. There was even a slender vase of roses just opening out of the bud, and the silver tea service shone.

The rector poured and Constable Walker passed the first cup to Rutledge. They had chosen to sit in the half circle of chairs facing the cold hearth, but the brass fan that concealed the grate was polished to a high sheen.

Rutledge said, after the rector had handed them slices of cake that Mrs. Newcomb had baked for his dinner, "Where were you, tonight, Rector?"

"I'd gone to see Theo Hartle's sister and her husband. You'd think that being paralyzed also meant being free of pain. But it's not true. And she must bathe him in warm water and manipulate his limbs to keep the muscles from atrophy. Sister Kenny was a strong proponent of exercising wasted muscles."

Sister Kenny was the Australian nurse who had made advances in the treatment of polio cases that upset many established medical opinions. There were many reasons given for her successes, none of which included credit to her methods. Rutledge had seen newspaper accounts suggesting that a nursing sister did not have the qualifications required to make strides in the field.

"Peggy works hard," Constable Walker agreed. "Theo was often there to help. Lifting Winslow is no easy task."

Rutledge, trying to bring them back to the subject at hand, said, "And this pastoral visit was what brought back the memory you spoke of in the road?"

"Well, it was something Virgil was saying. That when he was first struck down by poliomyelitis, he had prayed to die. That he couldn't contemplate living if he couldn't use his legs for the rest of his life. And he admitted to me that when I came to visit, he was afraid to tell me what it was he was praying so hard for. He thought I might use my powers as a man of the cloth to intercede with God and prevent his dying. Later, when he was older, he was ashamed to confess his prayers in that moment of crisis."

Constable Walker set down his cup. "I daresay it was normal for an active lad to think his world had come to an end."

"What inspired him to tell you now?" Rutledge asked.

"We were talking about Theo, and Virgil wanted to know if Theo had ever confessed to me that he'd nearly done something unforgiveable. Mrs. Winslow was very upset. I told him that he was mistaken, that Theo had had nothing to confess. And Virgil answered that he was only curious, having just told of his own secret guilt. You see, Virgil sometimes likes to shock. It's his way of making people notice him, to say horrible things. And then they pity him, and he manages to escape being brought to book for being abrasively outspoken. I know there were times when I myself was unwilling to add to his burdens, and let small transgressions go. And of course as a result, he's never been held to ordinary standards. I feel responsible for the way he uses his wife. She doesn't deserve it."

"Did Hartle ever confess to you? Do you know what it was that he'd nearly done?" Rutledge asked.

"That was what I remembered just as I was leaving. It was as if a light had gone on in my head, illuminating the incident. It was before Hartle went to France with the Eastfield Company. He came to see me because he had something on his mind. He said that he didn't want to die unshriven."

"What did he confess? Can you tell us?"

"I thought about that all the way back to the rectory. It was a confession, though not in the strictest sense. And I'm not sure I was told the whole story. But my own conscience was clear on that issue by the time I saw your motorcar coming toward me tonight." He looked up at the clock on the shelf above the hearth. "Well, it's nearly tomorrow isn't it? I hadn't realized it was so late."

Rutledge said, "Are you certain you are comfortable telling us what Hartle said?" For it appeared that Mr. Ottley was postponing the moment of revelation as long as he could, almost as if he regretted making any mention of it to them at all.

"As certain as I can be. But you must promise me that this will not be made public. That if it helps you in any way, you won't use what I told you in a courtroom. I won't have Peggy Winslow suffer on my account. And I have a feeling that's why Virgil brought it up. I think he was tired of seeing her mourn. He wanted her full attention, and if he had to ruin Theo's memory to do it, he was willing."

Rutledge said nothing, waiting.

Constable Walker said, "For my part, I give you my word. Peggy won't learn of it through me."

The rector put his own teacup down and walked to the windows. The wind had picked up as the clouds moved nearer, and the first rumble of thunder rolled through the darkness.

"Theo came to me because when he was about ten, he'd frightened another boy to the point that the child almost leaped to his death to get away from him. The story was that Theo had played truant one day, and cadged a ride to Hastings on the back of a hay wain. He'd intended to explore some of the so-called smugglers' caves, to see if he could find any treasure. This child wanted to go too, and Theo couldn't get rid of him. He called him an ugly little toad, pushing in where he wasn't wanted, and still the child clung to him. Theo, who was large for his age, had expected to pass as an older boy, but now he thought that with the other child in tow, someone would take more notice of them and send them home with a flea in their ears. He lured the other boy far out on East Hill, and told him that there was smugglers' gold below, and if he'd go down and look for it, he'd be given half of all he discovered."

Ottley walked aimlessly about the room, not looking at the two men listening to his story, and found his way back to the window. "But of course," he went on, "he lied, there was no pirate gold to divide, the cliff face was extraordinarily dangerous, and Hartle was hoping the other child would walk too close to the edge, and then his weight and gravity would carry him over. I don't think—I don't believe—that Hartle understood the consequences. He was frantic to enjoy his day of freedom, and he just wanted the other boy to go away. At any rate, the child found himself out on the very edge, became frightened, and froze. He started to cry, begging Theo to give him a hand to hold so that he could make his way back. But Theo walked away and left him there. The child finally made it to safety by crawling out of danger, and then he was late for his dinner, and his worried father disciplined him to teach him a lesson. He too was a truant, remember."

"Gentle God. Who was the child?"

Closing the window finally and turning back into the room, the rector said, "Theo Hartle wouldn't tell me. He said that there was no making amends, and the other boy would probably have begged him to keep his mouth shut. Perhaps he would have. Perhaps not."

Rutledge said, "And so Hartle, for his sins, was killed there on the headland and his body rolled over the edge."

The rector said, "I know. It—the circumstances— are too close to Hartle's death for comfort. I didn't remember, you see. I don't think I wanted to remember."

"Are you certain," Constable Walker asked, "that the child wasn't Virgil himself?"

"I think that's very unlikely. If it had been, then I think he'd have said so."

"Then how did Virgil Winslow come to know about this story?" Rutledge asked. "I can't imagine Hartle bragging to anyone about what he'd done. I mean to say, if Hartle had gone back to that headland and found it empty, found that the other boy wasn't there, it must have given him an appalling shock. He couldn't have known where his victim had gone—over the edge or if he had pulled himself out of his paralysis of fear and found his way back to safety. And surely, when Theo reached Eastfield and discovered that the child was alive, he must have expected the police on his doorstep at any moment. That the boy had told someone. A teacher, his parents, even other children."

"I asked him just that question," Ottley replied. "Hartle told me that he expected retribution at any moment, but the longer it was delayed, the more he'd thought that the child was afraid to tell what had happened that day. Hartle felt enormous relief, he said, and swore he would never again do anything he'd be ashamed of. Besides, he had had his own irate father to face when the school wanted to know why he'd played truant."

"And you're sure he said nothing that would tell you who this other child was?"

"Just the phrase, 'he was an ugly little toad.' As if that explained everything."

Constable Walker spoke up. "Do you think it was the Summers boy?"

He had spoken to Rutledge, but the rector said, "Was he still in Eastfield? I did ask—Theo told me Summers had already left to take up his new position."

"Hartle must have lied to you. He probably knew that's why Summers left here. The boy must have told his father something about what had happened. He'd been terrified, after all. Hartle didn't want to take the blame for that as well. His confession had its limits."

The rector said, "He was the butt of much teasing, I'm sure. A very unpopular child, never could put a foot right. But do you think he really was Hartle's victim?" There was lingering doubt in his voice. "Still, there's the problem of how Virgil Winslow knew."

"I don't think Winslow knew—not this story, at least. I think tonight he may have been whistling in the dark. We'd asked his wife if her brother had any secrets. Winslow must have assumed that he had—because he'd been murdered." Rutledge added, "Thank you, Rector, for telling us this. We'll use the knowledge to look into the matter. If nothing comes of it, then I think perhaps Hartle exaggerated what happened. That with time he'd blown it out of proportion, and it seemed more ominous than it was."

The rector's face brightened. "To tell you the truth, I found it hard to believe that young Hartle could be so—vicious. He was a good man, he would have made a good father."

But there were dark places in many a child's life. Temptation was hard to resist when it was something that a child very badly wanted. The ability to know right from wrong wavered in the face of longing. The lemon drop at eye level in the greengrocer's shop, the toy that another child played with, the larger biscuit on the plate, the biggest apple in the bowl. These seldom led to attempted murder, but a child who had planned his truancy carefully, was already half frightened by his audacity but intent on finding smugglers' gold, would be desperate to rid himself of what he perceived as an intruder, someone who was about to ruin everything he'd longed to do in this one glorious escape from authority. Consequences never entered his head. Only being caught before he could find treasure. Would he have gone as far as murder? Or would he have considered it murder, if the boy fell over the cliff without his help?

Who could say?

They thanked the rector and left, warning him to lock his doors.

Walker said as they were out of earshot, "You let me lie to him. The story will have to come out."

"Perhaps. Perhaps not. Meanwhile, what good would the truth have done, do you think?"

The first drops of rain struck them in the face, blown by the wind, great wet drops that promised a downpour. Lightning illuminated the rectory gate, and thunder followed almost on its heels.

"We'll have to speak to Roper's father. To see if Jimmy knew this story. And Mrs. Jeffers. I don't know if we'll get much joy from Tyrell Pierce. Anthony could do no wrong. The heir and hope," Walker said as they dashed through the gate and ran for The Fishermen's Arms. There was another flash of lightning, and then the rain came down in earnest. They arrived damp and breathless.

"I'll borrow an umbrella." Walker cast a glance at the sky. "Are we still patrolling the streets?"

"No. I think he's gone, whoever he was."

"Then I'll say good night." He went into Reception, where there was a porcelain stand filled with umbrellas for the use of guests, chose one, and with a nod to Rutledge trotted out into the rain.

Hamish said, "Yon priest. He didna' want to remember. Ye ken, these were lads."

"And it was a very long time ago," Rutledge said.

"Aye. Now they must judge the men the lads became."

And that was true. The men had turned out well. They'd served their country with honor and distinction, they had respectable lives ahead of them, and the foibles of the past were forgiven.

Rutledge said, "It's late. There's nothing more I can do tonight."

"Are ye forgetting The White Swans?"

He stopped in his tracks, halfway up the stairs. He had forgot.

Without a second thought, he went pelting down the steps and out to the motorcar. The drive to Hastings in the heavy rain was not pleasant, and he felt his tires slip several times as he ran down the twisting road into the Old Town.

The White Swans was quiet, most of the guests in their beds. He walked into the lounge and beckoned to the sleepy attendant at the far end.

"Whisky," he said and chose a table that was secluded enough that his presence wasn't obvious. As he sat down, he remembered another hotel, the Marlborough in London, and Meredith Channing's last remark.

He took a deep breath, trying to put it out of his mind. But he couldn't. He'd tried for days, but it was there, underlying everything he did during the day and his last thought as he fell asleep at night.

He couldn't imagine a future with her. He couldn't imagine a future without her. That was the dilemma. There was something about her, the poise that was so unusual in one so young, the quiet understanding that had seen him through a rough afternoon, the willingness to help even when she didn't particularly care for the fact that he dealt with murder and violence. Her voice, low and soothing. He'd fallen in love with Jean because she was pretty, she was of his own social class, and she was amusing. He had slowly fallen in love with Meredith Channing because she was herself.

What sort of man had her husband been? The war was over. Had been for two years. If Channing had been missing for four—five—years, it was more than likely he was dead. But she refused to accept it. Had she loved him so much? And was her guilt the growing realization that she must admit he was dead?

Rutledge didn't know. But he was a policeman, and solving riddles was bread and butter to him.

A good many men had gone missing. Blown up, their bodies mutilated beyond recognition by shells and gunfire, rotting in No Man's Land under the summer sun until the black, bloated body held no resemblance to the living.

Had she loved him so much?

The attendant brought his whisky and Rutledge paid for it on the spot. The harsh swirl of his first taste seemed to burn down his throat, and he set the glass aside.

This had been a wild goose chase. If the man from St. Mary's churchyard had come to Hastings, he wasn't here, or if he was, he was in bed and asleep, where he himself ought to be now.

But he waited all the same.

And just before dawn, after he'd finished his whisky and was fighting the fatigue that was slowly dulling his senses, he heard footsteps, brisk and male, crossing the marble floor of the lobby.

He turned his chair very slightly, so that he could see the elevator. But the man didn't use it, he took the broad, carpeted stairs two at a time.

Rutledge reached the lobby about a dozen steps behind him, and setting his hat on his head at an angle that shadowed his face, he went up after the man.

He reached the first floor in time to see his quarry disappearing into the fifth door on the seaward side. Rutledge followed, leaning lightly toward the door to listen.

A warm female voice said, "You're late, my dear."

And a man answered, "But I'm here now."

She laughed, a silvery sound, pleasant. "Come to bed, then."

Rutledge looked at the number on the door.

He moved silently away from it and then walked back the way he had come, down the stairs to Reception, where he rang the bell for the night clerk. The man limped as he stepped out of an inner office, his face slack with sleep.

"May I assist you, sir?"

Rutledge said, "Scotland Yard. You can verify that by contacting Inspector Norman, if you like. I just need information at the moment. And my request will not fuel the morning gossip. Is that understood?" He set his identity card on the mahogany counter. "Who are the guests in number eight?"

He repeated it, as if trying to take it in, then he opened the book and scanned the entries. "Number eight. The guests in that room are a Mr. and Mrs. Pierce. Is there any problem, sir?"

The last thing Rutledge wanted was for this man to wonder about the occupants of number eight. And so he said, "Someone in London must have made a mistake. They aren't the guests I was expecting to find in that room."

"They've been here for several nights. Newlyweds, I'm told."

Surprised, Rutledge said, "Indeed? I wish them happiness." He turned and walked out to the terrace and down the broad steps to the street. The rain had stopped, but the waves, invisible in the darkness, were rolling in with the wind still behind them. He could smell the sea, and feel the spray on his face.

He turned in the street and looked up at the hotel facade, counting windows and focusing on what must be number eight.

And as he watched, the lights went out, and someone drew the curtain wide, letting in the sound of the sea. Rutledge turned away, wondering if he'd been seen. He walked on to his motorcar without looking back.

Daniel Pierce was in Hastings New Town. And with a wife. A new wife, according to the clerk at Reception.

That hardly sounded like a murderer. And yet—and yet the man had been out very late. Alone.

Hamish said drily, "This willna' sit well with Mrs. Farrell-Smith."

When Rutledge awoke in the morning, the sun was well up. As he'd crested the ridge coming out of Hastings, he had seen the first hint of dawn struggling for a foothold among the clouds scudding east. The sun, apparently, had finally won, although there was no strength to it, as if it held on by a thread.

He ate a hasty breakfast and drove first to the home of Jimmy Roper. It was early for a social call, but not for the police to knock at the farmhouse door.

The housekeeper opened it a crack and peered out. "If you're wishing to see Mr. Roper, he's not himself this morning. Call again, if you will, later in the day."

"Scotland Yard. It's important that I speak to him."

Grudgingly, she opened the door to allow him to come inside. The passage was furnished simply, one narrow table with cut flowers in a black glass vase, a portrait above them, and across the way, by the stairs, another portrait facing it.

Looking at that one, a man and a woman in wedding clothes, he thought this must be the elder Roper himself and his wife. Young and happy and unaware of what the future might bring.

The housekeeper led Rutledge to a small parlor, opening the door to usher him in. It faced west, and on this dreary morning was still filled with shadows.

Rutledge thought he was expected to wait here, but as he turned he saw that Roper was seated in a chair by the window, a rug across his knees, his head tilted at an angle that indicated he was dozing.

"Mr. Roper?" the woman said, crossing the room to nudge him gently. "There's an inspector from Scotland Yard to see you."

The man lifted his head and looked up at the woman bending over him. "What did you say, Sadie?" The words were slurred.

"Scotland Yard to see you."

"I thought the bastard was dead," he replied in clearer tones.

"As far as I know, he's still alive," Rutledge answered, coming forward so that Roper could see him in what light there was. "I spoke to you in the village, shortly after your son was killed."

Roper turned to stare at him. "So you did. What brings you here?"

"I'd like to talk to you about your son. Do you feel like answering a few questions?"

"My son is dead," he said flatly. "What's the use of talking about him? It won't bring him back, will it?"

"It won't," Rutledge agreed. "But in remembering, you may find a little solace."

Roper was quiet for some time, and Rutledge had almost despaired of an answer when the man said, "He was a beautiful baby. My wife said so, and even I could see that he was. A good one too, never any trouble. Well, that changed when he started walking. Nothing was safe, he'd clamber on anything, and never cry when he brought it all down with him. More surprised than afraid, as if he'd expected it to hold." A flicker of a smile touched his mouth, pride in his son. "He was a good student. He wanted to go on to university, but of course there was no money for that. He said that farming was changing, and we had to change with it or be left behind. And then there was the war. When he marched away, it was the blackest day of my life. But he came back, like he said he would. Though it changed him, I could see that. I thought he might marry and settle down, but he said he needed to forget first. He didn't say what he needed to forget, but I expect it was the horrors."

"Did the Misses Tate feel that he should go to university?"

"They spoke of him as promising. He never had to study long hours, he just listened to his lessons and remembered what he'd heard. He took after my dear wife, there. She was a great reader, and read to him of an evening in winter. I liked listening to her voice. She could make you believe the story was real."

"Did he get on well with his fellow students?" Rutledge probed patiently.

"Oh, yes. He rose to corporal in the war, did you know? But he didn't like soldiering very much."

Rutledge had no choice but to bring up names. "Was he friends with Theo Hartle? Or William Jeffers? Or young Tuttle? Did he get on well with Virgil Winslow or Tommy Summers? Or the Pierce brothers?"

Roper turned to look at him. "Imagine you knowing all their names! I'd not say friends, so much as they grew up together. Still there's a bond in that. He didn't care much for Winslow, he said he traded too much on his illness. Some do, you know. Others never let it change them."

And Summers's name was conspicuous by its absence in his recollections.

Rutledge said, "What about the Summers boy?"

"As I remember, he left Eastfield early on. I doubt I could put a face to him now. I don't think Jimmy much cared for him. It was sad, you know, the girl was such a pretty little thing, took after her mother. And the boy was plain as a fence post, with a nature to match. I don't think I've ever met such a disagreeable child. Jimmy told me he could never keep up and was always whining. What's more, he could never see when he wasn't wanted."

"Was there ever any particular trouble between Tommy Summers and your son?"

Roper shook his head. "Jimmy was never a troublesome child. Well, there was the fair in Battle. As I remember, Tommy's father had given him a pony for his birthday, and Tommy was to show it at the fair. For a lark, Jimmy and the other boys painted the pony's hooves purple the night before the fair. They thought it would wash right off, Jimmy said, but of course it didn't, and they were sorry for that. It wasn't meant to keep the pony from being shown. They just wanted to see Tommy's face when he walked out of the barn that morning."

"What did Tommy's father have to say about this prank?"

"He was that upset, of course, but I said to him, they are only lads, they didn't know the paint would stain the way it did. Even blackening the hooves didn't help, when the sun struck them, the purple showed. I sent Jimmy over to apologize to Tommy, and that was that."

But of course "that was that" may have satisfied the father, but what about the boy?

And Roper answered as if Rutledge had spoken aloud. "Tommy was the butt of more than one prank, now that I think about it. But it's all part of learning to get on together, in my book. The lad just seemed to have the knack for making a nuisance of himself."

Rutledge found himself wondering how Roper would have felt if the shoe had been on the other foot. But he said only, "Was Jeffers one of the youngsters who painted the hooves?"

"I believe he was. It was such a long time ago, and my memory isn't what it used to be. I do recall sending Jimmy to apologize. To his credit, I don't believe he was as thoughtless after that. It was a good lesson learned."

"What about Anthony Pierce? Did he take part in these pranks?"

"Jimmy said he didn't care to join in, but he never told on any of them, either. When one of the Misses Tate asked him about some difficulty Tommy was having with his books and belongings disappearing, Jimmy told me that Anthony professed ignorance of the whole episode, and of course Miss Tate believed him. He was a good sort, Jimmy said, never ratting them out."

And that had been Anthony's sin. He'd wanted to belong as well, and he stood by while the torment went on, rather than trying to protect the Summers boy or telling the Misses Tate what was happening. Many a bullied child suffered in silence, afraid to ask for help, enduring what couldn't be stopped. Rutledge was beginning to see why Tyrell Pierce had sent his sons off to public school in Surrey. The sons of brewery workers and farmers and the like were not his sons' peers. Farrell-Smith must have been more to his liking.

Mr. Roper was tiring, and Rutledge rose to leave, thanking him for his time.

The man said, his dry, thin hand shaking Rutledge's, "He's still dead. It didn't help."

Rutledge said, "Sadly."

Driving back to Eastfield, Hamish said, "This was in the past. Ye canna' crusade for justice for Tommy Summers. It's too late."

"I don't want to crusade for him. I need to find out now if he's turned to murder to settle old scores."

"If it's old scores, why did he put yon discs in the mouths of the dead?"

"To put us off the track? And if it was, he nearly succeeded. But there could still be a connection we've overlooked."

18

Rutledge went next to Hastings New Town. He arrived at The White Swans to find that the clerk at Reception was not the same man he'd spoken to the night before. He asked for Mr. Daniel Pierce, but he was told that Mr. and Mrs. Pierce had gone out. He waited for an hour, but they didn't return. Rutledge went back to Reception.

"Could you tell me, please, how long the Pierces intend to stay at The White Swans?"

The clerk consulted the register. "The rest of the week at least," he said. "Would you care to leave a message?"

"I think not. I'd like to surprise them."

The clerk smiled. "They should be dining in the hotel this evening."

Rutledge thanked him and then left.

He stopped next at the police station, to ask after Inspector Mickelson.

The latest report confirmed that he was holding his own, but only just. He had come to his senses very briefly during the night, but had had no idea where he was or why. That, Hamish pointed out, boded ill for clearing Rutledge's name.

Inspector Norman was in, and Rutledge asked to speak to him.

Norman received him with ill-concealed distaste. "If you've come for Carl Hopkins, you're wasting your time."

"I need your help," Rutledge told him. "I want the loan of Constable Petty. We need to patrol Eastfield at night, and Constable Walker can't do it alone. If you want Petty to spy for you, you can spare him for my purposes as well. I'll see that he's put up at The Fishermen's Arms."

After a moment, Inspector Norman said with evident reluctance, "He has a cousin there. Works in the brewery. He can stay with him. I don't want him beholden to you."

Which, Hamish was pointing out, went a long way toward explaining how Inspector Norman had been keeping an eye on Eastfield.

Rutledge answered, "That's fair enough. I'll expect him there tonight."

"It won't stop your murderer. If that's what's in your mind. Even with three of you, you can't be everywhere at once. It takes no time at all to garrote a man and then walk away."

"It's better than nothing," Rutledge answered shortly. "There was someone in St. Mary's church-yard last night. I followed him around the church itself, where I lost him, and then I heard a motorcar leaving without its headlamps turned on."

Norman's manner changed. "Is that the truth? Where was it heading? Which direction, did you see?"

"Toward Hastings. There were lights on in the rectory as well, but the house was empty. We searched for Mr. Ottley, and finally met him walking toward us as we came back into Eastfield from the Roper farm. He sometimes goes there to sit with the second victim's father. But for a time, we were afraid he might have been the next target."

"Ottley is a good man," he said, defending the rector, "but sometimes he puts duty before common sense. He nursed the Spanish flu victims in Eastfield, day and night, without thought for his own safety. Before that, one evening when he was in Old Town, we had a ship in trouble off the East Hill. He went to the lifeboat station and offered his services if they needed another man. He'd kept a sailboat here in his youth. He'd have gone out with them."

"He may be at risk, all the same. If Carl Hopkins is innocent. I'm not convinced that these murders are connected with the war. They may have to do with someone with a long memory for the past."

"That's the trouble with educating a policeman," Inspector Norman said. "You're easily distracted by ideas."

Rutledge laughed. "Carl Hopkins is your war connection. But you haven't found the garrote and you haven't found where or how he managed to create those identity discs. It shouldn't have been hard to do, mind you, but he'd need the same type of fiberboard and the same type of rope, as well as the names of men in other units. Show me those, and I'll go back to London."

Inspector Norman's mouth twisted sourly. "Early days," he said as Rutledge took his leave.

He went back to The White Swans to look for Daniel Pierce, but he still hadn't returned.

Using the telephone, Rutledge put in a call to London.

Sergeant Gibson was wary, and Rutledge could almost hear the man trying to work out whether the inspector was back in good odor or not.

Rutledge told him what he wanted.

"It's a needle in a haystack," Gibson complained.

"His father went north to work when he was nine or ten years of age. Start with the War Office. If he was in uniform, they should know where he lived in 1914. And unless he has married, Somerset House won't help us."

"I'll do what I can," Gibson told him and asked how to reach him.

"Leave a message at Reception here in The White Swans."

But he was not destined to be there when it came through. As he was driving to The Stade, a police constable spotted him and hailed him.

Rutledge drew to the verge. "Constable?"

"Inspector Rutledge? Inspector Norman asked us to be on the lookout for you. Someone telephoned Hastings Police from the Pierce Brothers Brewery office. They've found another body."

Rutledge swore. "All right, thank you, Constable. I'm on my way."

He drove out of Hastings and made good time to Eastfield. Constable Walker, his face marked by sleeplessness and strain, was waiting for him at the police station.

"It's Hector Marshall," he said as Rutledge walked through the door. "He was garroted, like the others, and a disc was found in his mouth. We've taken the body to Dr. Gooding's surgery. He says there's no doubt. The wounds are much the same. Very little struggle. Left where he was killed, as far as we can tell."

"Where was he found?"

"He raises pigs out on the road to Battle. He goes about Eastfield with his cart, collecting scraps people save for him, and he takes milk from the dairy herds that they can't sell. He was on his rounds before first light, and stopped in a copse of trees just north of the turning for Hastings. It appeared his horse was lame, or he thought it was, and he drew up out of the road. Or someone hailed him, we'll never know. But the horse is indeed lame, a stone in its shoe. We found that out when we tried to turn the cart for a better look at Marshall's body."

"My motorcar is still outside. Show me."

The copse was some hundred yards past the turning to Hastings, just as Constable Walker had described it. On the far side, where the trees began, there was a small grassy opening among the trunks, and Walker pointed to it.

"Just there. The body was still warm. And if you look hard enough, you can see the roof of Marshall's barn beyond the treetops in that direction. He died within sight of his own farm."

Rutledge turned. There was indeed a barn roof, nearly hidden by the leaves of a stand of trees.

"Have you notified his family?"

"Not yet. Do you want to deal with that and afterward see the body?"

"They'll be wondering where he went. We'll go there first. What sort of family did he have?"

"A mother who lives there with him, his wife, and three small children. He always claimed he made up for the war years as soon as he got home. He was wounded early in 1918, and by the time he was fit to return to active service, the war was over."

They could smell the pigs as they approached the farm, but the house was tidy and there were flowers along the track that led to the door.

An elderly woman opened the door to their knock, fear in her eyes. And then she clapped a hand to her mouth as she read their faces.

"He's dead." It wasn't a question. "When he didn't come home with the cart, I knew something must have happened." Her voice was low, almost a whisper. Ushering them into a front room, she added, "My daughter-in-law is upstairs nursing the little one. Let her finish." She glanced up the stairs and then shut both doors quietly.

Rutledge identified himself. "I'm afraid we've come to confirm your fears, Mrs. Marshall. Your son was found this morning in the copse down the road. He was murdered."

"Like the rest of them. I told him. I said, you mustn't leave so early." She pressed her knuckles against her mouth, as if to stifle the scream rising in her throat. A low moan escaped, and she sat down suddenly. And then with an effort of will, she raised her head and said, "Where is he now? My son?"

"At Dr. Gooding's surgery," Constable Walker answered her.

"He lived through that awful war. And now this." It was an echo of what Mrs. Winslow had said. "I want to see him."

"I think—" Constable Walker began,

But she cut him short. "I brought him into the world. I'll see him out of it." Again she looked upward, as if she could see through the ceiling to the room above. "How am I going to tell her?"

In the silence that followed, Rutledge could hear the faint, rhythmic sound of a rocking chair moving back and forth, and a low hum, as if someone was singing softly.

Mrs. Marshall stood up. "I'll just call up to her, and then we'll go. The rest can wait. I want to see my son now."

They couldn't dissuade her. In the end, she did as she'd said she would. She called to her daughter-in-law,

"I'm just stepping out, Rosie, I'll be back shortly. Mind the soup on the fire."

Then she led Rutledge and Constable Walker to the motorcar and sat beside Rutledge as Walker turned the crank. Rutledge had a moment's panic as the constable turned and opened the rear door, but he couldn't look to see where Hamish was. He felt the motorcar shift as the man settled in his seat. And then he had no choice but to drive on, pointing the bonnet back to Eastfield.

Mrs. Marshall sat in stoic silence, her eyes straight ahead. Neither Rutledge nor Walker could find words of comfort. None seemed adequate.

People on the street turned to stare as they passed. Rumor had already run ahead of them, and villagers knew who was in the motorcar as well as where they were going.

Rutledge pulled into the drive in front of Dr. Gooding's house, and before he could step out and open her door, Mrs. Marhsall was already out of the motorcar and striding toward the surgery.

She was a tall, rawboned woman in a faded apron over a blue dress patterned with small white sprigs of flowers, her graying hair drawn back into a bun. But she moved with the dignity of a Spartan woman preparing to receive and bury her dead. Rutledge watched her and was moved.

Dr. Gooding was surprised to see her, looking over her head at Rutledge and the constable.

"She wished to see her son," Rutledge said, and Gooding said, "Er—give me a moment, and I'll take you back."

He disappeared, and Mrs. Marshall showed no sign that her resolve was weakening. Dr. Gooding's nurse came out of an adjoining office and asked Mrs. Marshall if she would like a cup of tea before her ordeal.

"No, thank you, Mrs. Davis, I'll be all right. Rosie is waiting at home for me."

The doctor came back just then and escorted them to the room where the body had been examined. It was tidy, and Hector Marshall lay under a sheet drawn up to cover the ravaged throat.

Ignoring the others, Mrs. Marshall walked straight across the room without faltering and looked down at her son's face. After a moment she touched his hair, which Dr. Gooding had combed. Then she bent to kiss him. Her voice was audible, but not the words as she addressed him. She stared at him a moment longer, and before the onlookers could stop her, she stripped back the sheet. Nodding at the body as if she understood something, she gently pulled the sheet back into place.

"I'd thank you to take me home, now."

Rutledge moved to her side, but she walked out of the room without help, down the passage, and out to the motorcar, thanking the doctor for taking care of her son.

Walker was there to open her door, and she got in without another word. When they had delivered her again to her home, Rutledge said, "Would you like us to help you break the news to your daughter-in-law?"

"Thank you, no, she'll be able to cry if we're alone." She turned to Constable Walker. "Could you send someone to feed the pigs today? They will be hungry by now."

He promised, and with a nod she disappeared inside, shutting the door quietly.

Rutledge said, "Will she be all right? Should we send someone to look in on her later?"

"Best to let them mourn," Walker said.

Rutledge turned the motorcar, hearing Hamish's voice like thunder in his head. And as he started off down the track, he heard a woman's scream, so full of pain he winced.

They went back to the surgery, but Dr. Gooding could tell them very little more.

"When was he killed?" Rutledge asked.

Gooding said, "Later than the others by a good four hours. After the rain ended, I think. Marshall was on his back, and his clothing was wet from lying in the leaves. His chest was dry. Of course the killer had to wait for him to start his rounds, that may account for a change in timing."

Or the killer had been thwarted, unable to reach the victim he had been waiting for.

"I was driving back from Hastings close to that time," Rutledge said slowly. "I'm surprised I didn't meet anyone on the road." But Daniel Pierce had walked into The White Swans just before dawn broke. Where had he been?

"It's a tragedy," the doctor finished, after showing Rutledge the identity disc from Marshall's mouth. "I can't believe there's no way to stop this madman. And what about Carl Hopkins? I thought he was the killer. Is he still in jail? Surely the police will have to let him go, after this."

"He's still there," Rutledge said. "Our murderer would have been smarter to let well enough alone, and let Hopkins take the blame."

"Pierce won't like it. He was so certain his son's killer was in custody. I ran into him just after Inspector Mickelson had taken Hopkins to Hastings. You could almost see the relief in Pierce's face. As if a burden had been lifted." Gooding covered the body again. "My nurse wondered if perhaps he'd been worried about Daniel having some role in this business. She asked if Daniel would be coming for Anthony's funeral, and he all but snapped at her. Where is Daniel? Does anyone know? I haven't seen him since just after the war."

Walker said, "Mr. Pierce hasn't said."

"Do you remember Tommy Summers?" Rutledge asked the doctor.

"Summers?" Dr. Gooding frowned. "Oh yes, I do remember him. He was a clumsy child, and his father brought him to me to see if there was anything to be done. Some children are just naturally poorly coordinated. He wasn't a very prepossessing boy. Sadly, such children are seldom popular at that age. And they seldom grow into swans, do they? Nature is often unkind."

"What did he look like, do you recall?"

"Rather pudgy, and short for his age. Sandy hair, I think."

"He couldn't have been mistaken for either of the Pierce boys, then?"

Gooding smiled. "No, of course not. Far from it. What are you driving at?"

Rutledge said, "How would you describe Daniel Pierce, the last time you saw him?"

"Daniel? He'd just come home from France, and he was quite thin. He couldn't settle to anything, apparently, because he was away again soon afterward. He's a little above medium height, brown hair."

The description would have fit a dozen men Rutledge had seen on the streets of Hastings. Except for the thinness, it fit the man he'd seen at The White Swans.

"I don't understand why you should be asking about Pierce?"

"I'm curious about anyone who lived in Eastfield at one time and who isn't here now," Rutledge answered easily. "There was someone in the churchyard last night. Before Marshall was killed. I never got a good look at him, but he didn't move like a heavy man."

"Yes, I see," Gooding replied, but Rutledge didn't think he did.

They left the surgery and went back to the police station.

Constable Walker said, "You've asked a good many questions about this Summers boy. And now you're asking about Daniel Pierce. Have you made up your mind that the killer isn't someone in Eastfield?"

"I haven't made up my mind about anything," Rutledge countered. "But if Carl Hopkins isn't our killer, who is?"

"There are the other survivors of the Eastfield Company. I asked my nephew just last night if he could make head nor tail of this business, and he refused even to consider anyone from the war. Unthinkable, he said. He'd served with them, they'd gone through too much together in France. Besides, if one of them believed he was still in France killing Germans, he'd have used a shotgun."

"That's probably true. And I understand what Tuttle is telling you. Battle is a man's testing ground."

Walker nodded. "Well, then I asked him about Tommy Summers, and he laughed. Summers wouldn't have been able to overpower Theo or Hector. Or even Jeffers."

"People change," Rutledge reminded him. But Walker shook his head.

"Inside sometimes, outside seldom."

Rutledge didn't argue. "I'll collect Kenton, and we'll go to Hastings to bring back Carl Hopkins."

"I'd leave him there a little longer," Constable Walker said. "He's safer."

But Rutledge remembered the bleak cells, and shook his head.

"Where does our murderer go, between killings?" he went on. "We need to find out. He can hardly be staying in Eastfield. Under the circumstances, a stranger would have caused considerable comment."

"I've wondered about that," Constable Walker agreed. "There's no derelict building he could hide in. No castle ruins or such. For that matter, no rough land. He must come up from Hastings. Or over from Battle. There you can wander the abbey grounds at will, you know. Still, someone hiding there would attract notice."

"What about these smugglers' caves in the Old Town?"

"Well, that's possible. Not all of them have been explored. Although boys must have poked about in them long before this and never said anything. Caves and treasure—irresistible. My own father told me the caves were still in use when he was a lad. I wasn't sure whether to believe him or not—he might have been making certain I never ventured into them."

"It might be wise to have a look, if Inspector Norman can spare the men. By the way, he's letting us have Constable Petty for the duration. On his terms, of course. But we need an extra pair of eyes."

"It didn't do a hell of a lot of good last night, did it? Our watch. The devil's determined, and he finds a way."

"The question is, why was he in the churchyard, if he'd already set his sights on Marshall?" Rutledge looked at his watch. "I must go back to Hastings. I'm expecting a telephone message from the Yard—"

Mr. Kenton came down the street, hurrying in their direction. "I say. There you are, Rutledge!" he hailed them.

Rutledge turned to him. "Just the man I wanted to see. You had a clerk some years ago, by the name of Summers. He left for another position. Do you recall where he went?"

Caught unprepared, Kenton said, "What? Summers? My God, that was fifteen or more years ago. Somewhere in Staffordshire, I think. Or was it Shropshire? Yes, it must have been Shropshire. A firm of wardrobe makers. The name escapes me. Never mind Summers! I've come about a far more important matter. I've just been told about Hector Marshall. I want Carl out of that jail, do you hear me? I won't take no for an answer."

"I was just going down to Hastings. Follow me in your own motorcar and you can bring Carl back to Eastfield."

Kenton spun on his heel and went back the way he'd come.

Watching him go, Walker said, "He's happy. Mr. Pierce won't be."

Carl Hopkins was almost dazed with relief when he was brought to Inspector Norman's office.

"They say I'm free to go. Has there been another murder, then?"

"Hector Marshall," Kenton said.

"Dear God." Hopkins shook his head. "When is it going to stop?"

Inspector Norman said, "Yes, it's a good question, Rutledge."

He ignored the taunt.

After the formalities were complete, Rutledge walked with Hopkins out of the station, followed by Kenton.

"I didn't think I could manage another night in that cell," Hopkins was saying. "I'd started to imagine things. Is there any news on Inspector Mickelson?"

"Nothing new," Kenton said from behind them.

Hopkins sighed, looking up at the blue sky. And then his jaw tightened, and he said, "Do I still have a place at Kenton Chairs?"

Kenton had the grace to look ashamed. But he said, "I never doubted you, my boy. You must believe me."

"Then why didn't you come to see me? Why didn't you bring me books—some writing paper?"

Rutledge walked away, leaving them to sort out the changes in their relationship. He drove to The White Swans and asked at the desk for any messages. There were none.

After a brief hesitation, he went up the stairs to the room belonging to Mr. and Mrs. Pierce.

The maid was just closing the door after cleaning the room, and Rutledge said to her, "I just wish to leave a message."

She looked uncertain, but he handed her a few coins, and she pocketed them almost before her fingers had closed over them. "I'll just be across the way, then," and she gave the door a little shove to open it again.

Rutledge walked in. The room had been serviced, and there wasn't much to see. It was well appointed, in a French Provincial style that was suited to a bridal suite. Long windows overlooked the street, and beyond that, the strand, and he remembered someone opening the curtains last evening. He walked over and looked out.

It was indeed a beautiful view, far out to sea. Sunlight glistened on the water, sparkling as the waves rolled inland, and the salt-tinged air blew the lacy curtains against his face.

Turning back to the room, he considered it. A wardrobe. A desk. Tables on each side of the bed, drawers below. One could hardly hide a garrote and a supply of identity discs here, and risk having a maid or one's bride stumbling over them.

Crossing to the desk, he picked up the scrolled silver frame that stood there and looked at the man and woman standing by the white swans that guarded the terrace. They looked happy, carefree, holding hands and smiling for the camera.

He recognized the man at once. A high brow, strong straight nose, firm chin. He'd seen him before, only not as clearly as here in the photograph. The first time, he'd been standing at Reception, staring, when Rutledge had stepped out of the telephone closet. And he was the man Rutledge had followed to this room only last night—or early this morning to be more precise. Had he also been in the churchyard last evening? Hard to say. Yes, possibly.

Daniel Pierce looked nothing like his brother. A good face but not attractive, as Anthony had been even in death.

Hamish said, "The second son."

Second in all things.

The woman beside him was fair and very pretty, dimpling into a smile that made her seem almost beautiful.

He recalled hearing his sister Frances saying something about all brides being beautiful, and here it was certainly true.

At her feet was a little dog, tongue out as he panted in the warmth of the summer's day. Of indeterminate breed, fur overhung his dark eyes in a fringe that was almost frivolous, and he looked up adoringly at his mistress. Her dog, then.

Rutledge walked to the wardrobe and looked inside. There was a pair of suitcases, without monograms, her clothes and his, side by side, shoes below, hats on the shelf above.

Shutting the wardrobe doors, he saw the small dog basket next to this side of the bed, and in it, folded into a square, was a blanket hand-embroidered with the name *Muffin*.

Leaving everything as he'd found it, he walked out of the room and shut the door. The hotel maid smiled at him as he passed, and he thanked her again.

Outside in the bright sunlight, he decided to put in a call to Sergeant Gibson and turned back into the hotel. But the sergeant was not at his desk. Rutledge didn't leave a message. He'd learned his lesson.

He went back to The Stade, and looked again at the strange black towers that held the drying fish nets.

How long would it be before Gibson found his man? The sergeant was very good at what he did, always thorough. Rutledge debated going to London to see what he could learn for himself. But he knew that would get him nowhere. And he wasn't prepared yet to deal with Chief Superintendent Bowles or face the curious glances of everyone at the Yard. The story had got out, it was bound to, and he knew any shouting match with the Chief Superintendent was sure to feed the rumor mill. He was still furious about the charges brought against him, and even if he could rein in his temper, he would be hard-pressed to pretend that he didn't know why they had been brought: because Bowles was suddenly afraid that his machinations had led to murder.

And Meredith Channing was in London as well. He didn't want to know the answers to the questions that wouldn't go away. Not now.

Inspector Norman came up, looking with him at the odd black structures. "You're no closer to the truth than you were when you left. And men continue to die."

"Are you saying that Inspector Mickelson didn't make it?"

"As far as I know, he's not out of danger. Nothing has changed. Look, if it wasn't Carl Hopkins—and it appears that he isn't our man—then bring the rest of that Eastfield Company in, and keep them there until someone admits the truth. They work for their living, every one of them. They can't afford to stay cooped up in a cell indefinitely."

Rutledge thought about Mrs. Marshall asking for help to feed the pigs. Every one of these deaths had created a hardship of some sort. "It's tempting. But I think they're as much in the dark as we are."

"I can't believe that. If you've fought side by side with a man for four years, you learn very quickly what he's made of." It was an echo of Constable Walker's words.

"Why would the survivors keep their mouths shut, when one name would make the rest of them safe? These murders are as deadly as sniper fire. Men are picked off at will."

"Because there's something none of them wants to come out. What's the worst crime a soldier can commit?"

Thinking about Hamish, Rutledge said, "Desertion under fire."

"They'd hardly cover that up. Shooting prisoners? Shooting one of their officers in the back?"

"Then why did Anthony Pierce die? He wasn't in their company."

"Point taken. I'm glad you were sent back here. I won't have to face the blame for coming up empty-handed on this one. That's in your future, not mine."

Would this become the case he couldn't solve? Like Cummins and the murder at Stonehenge? He'd already considered that possibility.

"I'll let you know. You'll be happy to come and gloat."

Inspector Norman laughed. "If we weren't so much alike, we could be friends." He turned and walked away.

Rutledge watched him for several minutes, then went back to the motorcar. The leather seats were hot from the sun, and there were holidaymakers strolling along the promenade and The Stade. The lush grassy slope of the East Hill spoke of peace and plenty. He watched three young girls flirting with a young man their own age. Carefree, pretty faces shaded by parasols. They were dressed to suit the fine weather in white or lavender or palest green. If he squinted his eyes, he thought, he could almost pretend it was 1914, and the war was only a shadow to come.

And then Hamish said something, and the image was shattered.

He went to see Mrs. Jeffers, and found her in her kitchen, bottling plums.

The child who had answered the door and conveyed him there went skipping out into the kitchen garden, chasing butterflies.

"They can forget, for a time. I wish I could," she said, her gaze following her daughter. She had auburn hair that had been pulled back out of her way, and her hands were red from working with the boiling water and hot jars. "I have to keep at this, or they'll spoil," she told him. "To tell the truth, I don't know what good talking to me will do. I wasn't there when Will was killed. And I can't think he had any enemies. How could he have? He hadn't done anything to be ashamed of. He was a good man. I don't know how we're to get on without him." Her eyes filled, and she wiped at them with the cloth in her hand. "I tell myself I can't possibly cry any more, and the next thing I know, I'm crying again."

"Did your husband know Tommy Summers well?"

"Tommy? I doubt anyone did. He was not easy to know. I think his feelings had been hurt so many times that he just locked himself deep inside and let nobody else in. It was a crying shame how the boys treated him, Will among them. I sometimes thought, if he dropped off the face of the earth tomorrow, who would care? His father, or maybe his sister. But that's all." She sealed two jars and turned to fill a third. "Now his sister I liked. A pretty girl, and sweet natured. She was younger than most of us. Her mother was dead, and I was sometimes paid to keep an eye on her after school. I'd have done it for free, if it hadn't been for Tommy, always lurking about, as if he was spying on us. I wrote to her for a time after the family moved away. I thought it a shame she had such a wretch of a brother, but then I was a child myself and hardly knew better. Now, thinking back on it after such a long time, I can see that he wasn't nearly as bad as we liked to make out. He had this look about him of having bitten into something bitter. Sour, that's what it was. I didn't trust him."

"Do you still have those letters?" Rutledge asked, realizing that he might find the sister faster than Sergeant Gibson would.

"Oh, I never kept them after I got married. I didn't see any point in it, did I? We hadn't seen each other in so many years we'd have been like strangers when we met, with nothing to talk about but the weather and our children. But I did think about inviting her to my wedding. It wouldn't have worked out, but when you're happy, you want everybody to know it, don't you?"

"Do you remember how to get in touch with her?"

"Oh yes, it was such an odd name. Regina Summers, Old Well House, Iris Lane, Minton, Shropshire. I couldn't think what an old well house must look like, and my sister said it must be a hole in the ground because Tommy the slug would live in a hole. She thought it was funny, but I didn't."

"Was your husband friendly with Daniel Pierce?"

"Mr. Daniel? Whoever told you such a thing? Will knew him of course, we all did. But Mr. Daniel's father had money, and our fathers didn't. That's a great barrier to friendship, even when you're young. Not that Mr. Anthony or Mr. Daniel put on airs, it was *understood*.

They were different, even when they were doing what we were doing."

As he thanked her for her time, Mrs. Jeffers said, "Finding Will's murderer is the only thanks I need."

Leaving a brief message on Constable Walker's desk with a schedule for the nightly patrols, he packed his valise, left The Fishermen's Arms, and set out for Shropshire.

He had fewer than three days to find an answer.

Rutledge stopped in London for clean clothing, and found a letter waiting for him from Reginald Hume.

I'm still with Rosemary. The thought of this empty house filled with Max's ghost was too much for her, I think, and caring for me has given her something to do. I'm no trouble, and I stay out of her way as much as possible. The doctors here are trying to persuade me to go to America and a place called Arizona. They believe the dry air there may help, but I don't believe I could survive the journey at this stage. And I have something to do before I die. Just wanted you to know that Rosemary is beginning to accept. But there's a long road ahead.

And then he was on the road north and west, to find Minton, Shropshire.

19

It was late when he neared his destination. Rutledge had had to stop and ask for Minton half a dozen times before he finally learned that it was the next village over but one.

He stayed in a small inn that boasted no more than five rooms, and the next morning drove on to Minton.

He'd always liked Shropshire, sitting on the Welsh Borders. The River Severn divided the rolling land to the north from the southern plains, and just below Buildwas was the tiny village of Minton. It looked down on the tree-lined river and huddled together, as if half afraid of disappearing if it spread out.

Iris Lane was just that, a short track edged its entire length with beds of iris, the broad green swords of their leaves unmistakable, although there were no blooms now. Old Well House was a pretty cottage, windows open wide to the morning air and a line of wash already hung out at the side of the kitchen garden.

Rutledge tapped lightly at the door, and a young woman came to open it. Her face was flushed, as if she'd hurried down the stairs.

"Oh," she said, encountering a stranger on her step. Looking over his shoulder she saw the motorcar. "I thought you might be—well, never mind, you aren't. Have you got yourself lost?"

She was of middle height, with soft fair hair done up in a knot, and she wore a damp apron. He wondered if he'd caught her at the washtub.

"I'm Inspector Rutledge, from London. Scotland Yard," he began.

"Dear heaven, they've found Tommy!"

"Was he missing?" Rutledge asked, surprised by her shock.

"He never came home from the war. Well, not really. He was in hospital for a time, but then went back to France in October of 1918. I had a letter or two from him, and after that, nothing." She realized she was chattering on the doorstep and said, "I'm so sorry, please do come in." She led him to the front room. "You're from London, you said? That's a long way to come to bring me word of my brother."

"As a matter of truth," he said, "I've come to ask you about your brother. You lived in Sussex, when you were young?"

"Yes, and I cried for days when we left, I was so sad. My father had a better position, but I sometimes thought he'd left because of something else. My mother is buried in St. Mary's churchyard, you see. I thought perhaps he wanted to leave his memories behind."

"How did your brother like moving across England?"

"He was so excited. I thought, it will be the same, he'll annoy the other lads, and they'll play tricks, and then he'll be unhappy again, and nothing will change."

"It was his fault that he didn't get along with the boys in Eastfield?"

She frowned. "He didn't try. I'm sure he didn't. Other boys managed it, didn't they? That one—what was his name?—whose legs were crippled. He was the same way, never trying. A smile would have helped, or a willingness to be friendly. But Tommy surprised all of us, didn't he? He lost several stone of weight, his face cleared up, and he got along just fine. And I told him, it's wonderful how you've changed. He said the oddest thing then—he said, 'I had to change. And I hated it.' You would have thought he'd been forced to do something awful."

"How did he fare in the war?"

"He was a good soldier. He did everything that was asked of him. He told me he had learned that others wanted to make him over in their image, and so he did it for them, only it was merely on the surface, and they were too stupid to see."

"And after the war?"

"He was wounded in late spring of 1918, and he went to a clinic in Bedfordshire. I saw him there, and he seemed to be excited about what he'd done in the war. He was eager to go back. He admired the Ghurkas. Those dark little men from Nepal. He wrote that they were the best at what they did, which was killing people. He would have liked to be a Ghurka officer. They had English officers, didn't they? He stayed in France for six months after the Armistice. When he did come back it wasn't to Minton. He was searching for his nurse from the Bedfordshire clinic. It was closed, of course, the remaining men sent elsewhere, and no one knew just where she was. Such a pretty girl. I was happy for him, I hoped he would find her. That was in 1919. And after that, there has been nothing. It was as if he'd vanished. I reported it to the police in Buildwas. They asked me if I suspected foul play, but of course I had no reason to think any such thing. He was just missing. They were polite and kind, but they did nothing."

"Perhaps he found his nurse and together they left England."

"He'd have told me, wouldn't he? He'd have wanted me to be happy for him." Her eyes filled. "I was beginning to think he could be dead. People sometimes aren't identified straightaway, are they?"

Rutledge said gently, "We make every effort to find a name. Do you have a photograph of him? It would help."

"He didn't like being photographed. There's one with my mother, but he was only a year old." She smiled shakily. "You wouldn't be able to tell what he was like as a man, would you? And I'd rather not part with it anyway, I don't have many photographs of her."

Rutledge cast about for a better way to broach his next question, but there was no way to soften it.

"I'm curious. Did your brother harbor any hard feelings toward his schoolmates in Eastfield? Did he talk about them or wish he could—um—punish them for the way he'd been treated? Or didn't it matter, after he'd grown used to another life?"

"I asked him that, once. He told me it was all right, that he'd cursed them. I suppose it made him feel better, but of course that's all it did. Their lives went on, and I doubt they've given him a thought in all these years. He didn't matter as much to them as they did to him, you see. You'll keep looking for him, won't you? I'm to be married soon. My father's dead. It would be lovely if my brother could give me away."

He promised to do his best, and left.

She went with him to the door and watched as he reversed down the track.

Regina Summers was serene in her certainty that her brother bore no ill will for whatever had gone wrong in his childhood. And perhaps he didn't. But men's lives were in the balance.

Rutledge stopped the motorcar, got out, and walked back to the cottage door.

"Your father," he said. "Do you think he saw how wretched his son was, and decided to take him away from Eastfield?"

Her eyes widened in surprise. "That never occurred to me. For Tommy's sake? Oh, no, Tommy never told him about the things that went on at school. He never told the Misses Tate, either. He thought they would see. And they never did."

"Why not? Surely, someone recognized the situation? After he nearly fell off the cliff at East Hill."

"My father was so busy mourning my mother he saw very little. And as for the school staff, no one liked Tommy. He didn't fit in. The Misses Tate saw him as a troublemaker."

"And you did nothing?"

She smiled sadly. "I was too young to understand. I just knew that people liked me and they didn't like my brother. I was glad they liked me, and I didn't want to lose that."

"Did Daniel Pierce take your brother's part when he was being bullied?"

"Sometimes he did. I think it was to be contrary, not because he liked Tommy. My brother saw Mr. Daniel after the war. He told me in his last letter. He expected Mr. Daniel to remember him, and his feelings were hurt when Mr. Daniel didn't. But he said Mr. Daniel had changed, that he was thin and not himself. He thought he'd been ill."

"Do you know when this was? Or where?"

"May or June of 1919. In London, I should think."

He thanked her and walked back to the motorcar.

Hamish said, "This is a verra' fine cottage, with yon flowers, and a' just as she likes it. She only needs her brother to walk her doon the aisle, no' here."

But if that brother was the killer, what, after all these years had set him on this road?

His route south and east took him within striking distance of Chaswell, and Rutledge decided he could afford half an hour out of his way to call on Rosemary

Hume. Although he'd received Reginald's letter, his duty to Maxwell was personal.

As Reginald had noted, some of the sharp edges of the anger that had made her bitter had been blunted, and when Rutledge was shown into her sitting room, he could just see the telltale redness around her eyes from tears shed in the night.

Still, she greeted him with cool civility. He hadn't been forgiven.

"You find extraordinary excuses to come by Chaswell. I thought you had been sent to Sussex. That's a fair distance, if I recall my *Baedeker*.

He didn't take offense. "I think you'll find that Wales and Shropshire are in your vicinity. But yes, it was Sussex business that took me there."

She had never been comfortable with the fact that he was a policeman and not a solicitor or even a barrister if he chose to deal with crime at all. It had seemed to be a step out of character and out of class.

Relenting, she smiled and asked if he cared for tea. It was too early, she suggested, to offer him a drink.

"Thank you, but no. I must be on my way. Is Reginald still with you?"

"If you stopped in London to retrieve your mail, you will know that he is. I posted a letter for him not three days ago."

"I'm glad. He seemed in great distress at the funeral. I think Maxwell's death is partly to blame, and his lungs the rest."

"Stupid war," she said with some heat. "And where did it get us? Poorer than we were, and the world changed beyond our wildest expectations."

"It isn't Reginald's fault that he was gassed," he reminded her. But he knew what was in her mind: that her husband's cousin should have been the one to kill himself, not Max. Anyone but Max, anything but this drastic alteration in her world. "Do you think he would wish to see me, while I'm here?"

"He's in the garden. You know the way. You'll forgive me, won't you, for not walking out with you." She rose and held out her hand. "It was good to see you, Ian. Thank you for coming by."

He took her hand, held it for a moment. "When Reginald is—gone, if you need me, I'll come."

"I—thank you."

He turned away before she could know that he'd seen the tears welling in her eyes.

Reginald was sitting in a deck chair in the shade of a large maple. He appeared to be asleep, but the painful rise and fall of his chest told Rutledge he was not.

"You've become quite the man of leisure," Rutledge said as he came nearer, so as not to startle the ill man.

"This is a surprise! Hallo, Ian, it's good of you to come. Have you seen Rosemary?"

"Yes, just now. She thinks I've mistaken my *Baedeker*—Chaswell is nowhere near Sussex."

Reginald began to laugh, and it was cut short by a spasm of gasping for breath that was painful to watch.

When he had control of his breathing again, he said, "I'm glad you will be looking in on her. I'm not doing as well as the doctors had expected."

"Nonsense," Rutledge began in a rallying tone.

"I saw the doctor this morning. Doctor Bones, I call him. He is forever telling me that I shan't make old bones. But he's right. It's more and more of a struggle. And one day, it will be over. I could be at peace with that save for two things. Rosemary is one of them."

"And the other?"

"I don't want to be alone. But I don't want Rosemary to have to face it with me."

"I've already promised—"

"I know. But there's the Yard. Your time isn't your own. I've left instructions in a letter my solicitor keeps for me. And if you aren't here, there's another letter meant for you. For old time's sake."

"I'm glad you told me. I shall be here, if it's at all possible."

He rose and took Reginald's hand. "Would you prefer to be at home?"

"No, no. I think the decision to stay on here was a good one. Whether she wants to admit it or not, sometimes when I rattle about the place, she can pretend that Max is just in the other room, or upstairs, or sitting out here in his favorite chair. He'd taken to smoking a pipe out here, every afternoon, did you know? Smelled like the very devil, but he thought it might steady his nerves."

Rutledge said, "Then you've done the right thing."

He left soon afterward, wondering if he was likely to see Reginald alive again. But he'd meant his promise, and he would try to keep it.

Hamish was his companion on the rest of the drive back to Sussex, and they debated the whereabouts of Tommy Summers and Daniel Pierce, before the discussion moved on to Reginald and the war. Rutledge could feel the tension mounting as the voice grew louder in his ears, and he could feel himself slipping back into the waking nightmare of the trenches. He couldn't remember much about the last one hundred miles, but it was late when he rolled into Battle, passing the great gatehouse of the abbey ruins. Eastfield was not far away. He dreaded to hear that there had been another killing. Tuttle or one of the others.

Where the bloody hell was Tommy Summers? He knew where to lay hands on Pierce.

No one had died in his absence.

And Constable Walker was relieved to see him.

"There's no better news of Inspector Mickelson," he told Rutledge, "but Inspector Norman has asked to set up the inquest without him. Now that Carl Hopkins has been released. Waiting for the inspector to recover doesn't serve any purpose now."

"Yes, all right. And send word by Constable Petty that Hartle's body can be released. Perhaps we can tempt our murderer to attend the funeral service."

He had said it wryly, but Constable Walker asked, "Do you think that's likely?"

"That depends. Is there anyone in Eastfield who isn't well known to you? A distant cousin come to visit? A mate from the war—someone we could have overlooked?"

"Nobody. I've been thinking about it. I'd recognize Tommy Summers if I saw him."

"I doubt it." Rutledge told him of the visit to Regina Summers's cottage. "You're remembering the child, not the man. He could be someone we see every day but never think twice about."

"Constable Petty?" Walker asked with dry humor. "He's a great help, I don't doubt that, but the man gets on my nerves. Always creeping about. It's as if he knows where he's not wanted, and pops up there on purpose."

"If there are no strangers, what about someone who has lived quietly here for the past year or less? A new worker at the brewery? A laborer on one of the farms? Someone at Kenton Chairs? Above suspicion, because he's been accepted?"

"There's the groundskeeper at the school," Constable Walker said, suddenly galvanized. "I hadn't thought about him."

"What is his name? Where does he come from?"

"He called himself Ned Browning. Ex-soldier looking for work, never any trouble, kept himself to himself. I saw him once or twice in The Conqueror, but he wasn't a drinking man, as far as I could tell. When I asked Mrs. Farrell-Smith how he was getting on, she told me he knew something about gardening and pruning, and did what he was told without complaint. Deferential, she said, knew his place. He was allowed to live in that tiny cottage behind the stables, where the coachman lived in the Misses Tates' day."

Rutledge could see another cottage, Old Well House, with its long beds of iris and other plantings. He had assumed that Regina was the gardener. Or had she just kept up the work that her brother had begun?

He hadn't thought to ask. Landscaping was landscaping, except to admire the results.

"What does he look like?"

Constable Walker said with a shrug, "Not as tall as you are, as I remember. Brown hair, shaggy, falling into his face. Looked like it had been trimmed with his own secateurs. Ordinary features. If he was on the street or at the pub, he'd wet it down and slick it back, making it appear much darker. Rarely looked you in the eye, but not hangdog. More like the life had been sucked out of him. I doubt I heard him speak a dozen words."

"An ex-soldier? But not with the Eastfield Company?"

"No, from the north, I was told. My nephew wondered if he'd been shell-shocked, but I didn't see any signs of that. You'd know, wouldn't you?"

Rutledge felt a frisson of panic at the words *shell shock*. As if the constable could see in his own eyes the shame that haunted him.

He managed to say, "Where is he now? You used the past tense."

"That's the devil of it. He only stayed a few months and left in late winter, giving Mrs. Farrell-Smith the opportunity to hire someone else before spring. She said it was very considerate of him, and gave him an excellent reference."

"That reference. Where was he going with it?"

"He said he had an offer from one of the large estates in Staffordshire. I didn't know of any, but that's neither here nor there."

Staffordshire. Kenton had had trouble remembering where the elder Summers had taken up his new position. He had dithered between Staffordshire and Shropshire.

Another connection. They had been plain to see, if one had just known where to look.

Rutledge said, "There's Moseley Old Hall at Bushby—Wolseley Hall at Colwich—Pillaton Hall near Penkridge. It's possible. But is it likely?"

"We must speak to Mrs. Farrell-Smith, then."

"There are two tasks I must see to first."

He left directly for Hastings and The White Swans. When he got there, he learned that Sergeant Gibson had returned his telephone call as expected, but he had left no messages.

"And your guests, Mr. and Mrs. Pierce. Are they still here?"

"I'm afraid they left yesterday morning, unexpectedly. The housekeeper told me they were unhappy with their room."

Unhappy with it—or had they learned of Rutledge's intrusion? The maid could have said something.

Hamish was an angry buzz in the back of his mind.

"Never mind," he said far more pleasantly than he felt. "Do you know where they were intending to travel next?"

"He left a message for anyone who asked after him. Mr. Pierce said he was intending to travel to Brighton."

Rutledge thanked the clerk and went to the telephone closet, where he put in a call to the Yard.

Sergeant Gibson was away from his desk.

Rutledge rang off.

He went next to the police station. "Did you know," he asked as he walked through to Inspector Norman's office, "that Daniel Pierce was staying at The White Swans with his bride?"

"Was he, indeed. Well, I'll be damned. Does his father know?"

"I doubt it. The happy couple never came to Eastfield. But that isn't to say that Pierce didn't come here to see them."

"How is he connected with this business? I'd find it easy to believe that he had some part in it."

"Evidence is slowly but inexorably pointing to one Thomas Summers. The problem is, he doesn't appear to be in Sussex. And Pierce is. But in his case, there's the question of motive. Why would Pierce turn to murder?"

"To rid himself of his brother," Norman said unequivocally.

"Then why does he continue to kill?"

Norman shrugged. "The excitement. He couldn't have expected that, could he? The hunt for victims—avoiding the police. He was a sapper, wasn't he? That's perilous work. A man can miss danger."

It was possible. It was also possible that he'd come to his senses, finally, and walked away from temptation. "No word on Mickelson?"

"He appeared to be awake for a quarter of an hour this morning. The doctors sent the constable charged with keeping an eye on the sickroom to alert the local police, but by the time they reached the hospital, Mickelson had slipped into unconsciousness again. Damned incompetence, if you ask me."

"I'm glad to hear there's been some improvement."

"Because you care about the man, or because whatever he can tell the police stands to clear your good name?"

"I'll let you decide." Rutledge hadn't taken a chair. Now he turned to leave the room.

"What are we to do about this Summers person?"

"We must find him first. Constable Walker wonders if your man Petty could be Summers."

Shutting the door behind him, he strode out of the building and to his motorcar. Even the five minutes he'd spent there had forcibly reminded him of his cell. If he never saw the police station again for the remainder of his life, it would still not wipe away the memory.

Back in Eastfield, he went to call on Tyrell Pierce.

"Do you bring me news?" he asked as his clerk showed Rutledge into his office.

"Not at present. I would like to ask you several questions. The first is about your son Anthony's connection with Mrs. Farrell-Smith."

"I had hoped he would look in that direction. I won't lie to you. She comes from an excellent background, and she has money of her own, from her late husband's estate. There was no fear she was after Anthony's inheritance. And she's very attractive. I could see that for myself. Pleasant, well educated, good company at dinner, a fine hostess. She would have been a very good match for Anthony."

Hamish said, "He's verra' attracted to her himsel'."

And it was true. Rutledge, considering him, realized that he was still young enough to marry again and have a second family. Rutledge wondered if Pierce knew anything about the shadow hanging over the late Farrell-Smith's death. Probing, he asked, "What happened to her husband?"

"Yes, a pity he died so young. She told me privately that he drank too much. Anthony mentioned that he'd been at loose ends after he left school. Moody, his temper uncertain. He felt that Farrell-Smith had married before he really knew his own mind about what he was going to do with his life. But young men in love are often impulsive."

Rutledge could see that Mrs. Farrell-Smith had cleverly sown seeds of doubt about her husband's state of mind. If it came to Pierce's ears that the man had killed himself, he would understand why.

He abruptly changed the subject. "Have you met Daniel's wife?"

"Wife? Where did you hear that Daniel had married?"

"He was in Hastings, with his bride and her little dog."

The elder Pierce's face flushed with anger. "It's not true. I can tell you it's not *true*."

"Why shouldn't he wish to marry? The war is over, he wouldn't be the first man to look for an anchor in his life."

"Because the woman he has been in love with since he was sixteen is already married," Pierce answered, goaded. "And I was glad of that, damn it. She wasn't suitable, and I told him so. I thank God on my knees every night that her husband is still alive. And I pray that he stays amongst the living until whatever passion it is that my son feels for her has burned itself out."

"Who is she?"

"Mrs. Winslow."

Rutledge sat there and digested what he had just been told.

"Does she return his feelings?"

"She did when she was sixteen. But I put a stop to that. And a good thing too, because just before the war she chose to marry Winslow. I'm sure she's regretted it every day since then. Martyrdom is best enjoyed briefly."

A vicious remark, but then Peggy Winslow had threatened this man's view of how his sons would prosper as he had prospered, climbing the social ladder with their looks, their charm, and their money. He'd seen Mrs. Farrell-Smith as eminently suitable for Anthony. He didn't seem to know she preferred the younger brother.

"Where is he now, your son?"

"I don't know. But that's why he left Eastfield again so soon after coming home from France. He couldn't bear to be in the same village with Winslow. He was afraid he'd do him a harm. And if you pass that on to anyone, even Constable Walker, I'll tell the world you lied."

That, Hamish was pointing out, explained why Pierce had been distraught when village men began dying. He'd been terrified that their deaths, even his own son's, had been random, to make Winslow's death, when it happened, seem part of a pattern that had nothing to do with the man's wife.

Rutledge said tightly, "It's not my intention to gossip. Unfortunately, I can't walk away from potential evidence, however odd or unimportant it appears to be."

"Did you see Mrs. Winslow's cat?" Pierce asked.

"Cat? No, I'm afraid not. Should I have done?"

"He gave it to her. A tortoiseshell. Named the damned thing Arrow, after our firm, and told her that as long as she possessed Arrow, she had his heart in her hands. He'd found it as a kitten in a corner of the brewery wall one winter's night. He had a soft spot for cats. I never could understand that. With any luck, Arrow has used up her nine lives and has gone on to whatever heaven God reserves for animals."

Rutledge thanked him and was walking to the door when Pierce added, still fuming over Rutledge's allegations about Daniel, "I know you're lying to me. I can prove it. Daniel can't be in contact with dogs. They make his eyes red, and he wheezes. And so you may tell Inspector Norman that this trick won't wash."

Standing in the doorway, Rutledge said, "I'm sorry?"

"We had him to specialists in London. Daniel. Dogs and chocolates. We were warned that either of them could kill him by choking off his air."

Closing the door, Rutledge stood there, his mind flying.

If that hadn't been Daniel Pierce and his bride with her dog Muffin, who the hell had it been?

20

Rutledge turned on his heel and knocked at the door behind him, opening it almost at once before Pierce could deny him entrance.

"Do you have a photograph of your son?" he asked the man behind the desk. "As recent as may be."

Pierce said warily, "Not here. At my home. Why do you need a photograph? I have told you, Daniel isn't a murderer."

"To eliminate him finally from the queue of suspects."

"I'll bring it to the hotel later in the day, shall I?"

Rutledge had to be satisfied with that.

He asked the clerk, Starret, for the use of the brewery telephone. He thought at first that the man would refuse, for he looked toward Pierce's office uncertainly.

It took some time to reach Gibson at the Yard, and his voice was testy.

"I've not found this Thomas Summers. The Army records show that he enlisted in Buildwas, Shropshire, he was wounded twice in France, he was demobilized in early 1919 because he was attached to the details reburying the dead. His current residence is still in Shropshire. They don't have a more recent one."

"I've been there," Rutledge said, Hamish hammering in the back of his head to the point that he could hardly think. "He's not there. What else?"

"I was at Somerset House, and after looking up Lieutenant Pierce's marriage—there is no record of it—I took the liberty of looking up Corporal Summers's records. I see his birth, right enough, there in Eastfield. He was married in Brighton three weeks ago to one Edna Stallings, spinster, from Bedford. He put down Shropshire again as his residence."

Rutledge swore with feeling. He'd had the man within reach, and he'd lost him.

Hamish said, "He used another man's name."

And how had he convinced his bride to allow that?

My friends will track us down, they'll stand on the terrace and serenade us. It will be shockingly embar-

rassing. Everyone will stare. Daniel is a good friend, he
told me he doesn't mind, as long as we don't leave him
to settle up.

She would laugh and find it exciting to be someone
else.

She had a sweet face, she'd stared up at her husband
adoringly in that wedding photograph. Was she the
nurse he'd gone in search of?

"Did you by any chance look into Edna Stallings?"

"I did that, sir, when I discovered who her father was.
Matthew Edgeworth Stallings. She's a little younger
than Summers, at a guess, and was a nurse in a clinic
in Bedford during the last two years of the war, before
going to live in Hertfordshire with an aunt until she
came of age this past spring."

Matthew Stallings, it seemed, had made his modest
fortune in footwear, and the Army contract for boots
had sealed it. He'd died of a stroke six months after the
Armistice, leaving a large sum to the National Trust
and another to a fund for war widows. The bulk of his
estate went to his only child. His daughter, it appeared,
was an heiress.

"Well done," Rutledge told Sergeant Gibson. It was
praise well earned. There was more he wished to say
to Gibson, but not with half the brewery office staff
listening with one ear.

Putting up the receiver, he thanked Starret and left the brewery.

Constable Walker was not in the police station when Rutledge stopped there. And so he drove on to Hastings with all the speed he could muster.

He caught Inspector Norman just as he was leaving his office and said, "There have been developments. I need to speak to you."

"Not now," Norman told him. "I've just been informed that Inspector Mickelson is showing signs of coming to his senses again. And I'm not letting this opportunity slip through my fingers, I can tell you. Your developments can wait."

And he got into the motorcar waiting for him, one of his constables at the wheel.

Rutledge watched them pull out into the afternoon traffic, then returned to his own vehicle.

For the next six hours, he called at every hotel of any size between The White Swans and the town of Brighton.

And as he searched, he tried to think through this swiftly evolving situation.

So much was explained now. How Summers could afford to live at The Swans as Daniel Pierce. How he had been able to reach Eastfield and disappear at will. How in fact he had managed to learn the details of his victims' lives, where he could find them when he was ready to kill them. And how he had been invisible, because the lowly school groundskeeper who kept to himself roused no interest in the village.

There was always a social hierarchy.

A groundskeeper at the school was in effect a laborer. The farmers and their wives, the tradesmen and their wives, would have nothing in common with him, and people like the brewer and Mr. Kenton, who felt they had risen above both classes, would hardly be aware of his existence, though they would know where he worked. It was that which gave him his place in the village, not his face or his qualities or his hopes and dreams. The rector would be kinder, the doctor would treat the man and whatever family he had, and the Mrs. Farrell-Smiths of this world would see that he was paid but barely know his name.

At each hotel he came to, Rutledge requested the list of guests, scanned them for any name that was familiar—Stallings, Summers, Pierce, Hartle, Jeffers, Roper, Ottley, Gooding, even his own—and each time drew a blank.

But of course Summers could have used his wife's mother's maiden name, or that of his sergeant in France, and Rutledge would have no way of connecting it with the man he was seeking.

Hamish said, "Go back to what ye know. It's the only way."

All right, then.

Summers had left a forwarding address of Brighton. But was he telling the truth? There were still men alive who went to school with him. He couldn't have finished his work. Surely he wouldn't have gone much farther than Brighton. He had too much invested already in his revenge.

Where then?

Rutledge thought about the case that Chief Inspector Cummins had never solved, and how misdirection had served a different purpose there. It had almost seemed that Cummins's murderer had wanted to leave something behind, for the sake of his own conscience if not for the police.

But this Sussex killer had no conscience. If he had, he'd have stopped with William Jeffers's death.

Rutledge looked up at the exotic lines of Brighton's glory, the Prince Regent's Pavilion, almost foreshadowing that his niece would one day be Empress of India.

Why would Summers leave such a message?

The most logical answer: to buy time.

To send Rutledge on a wild-goose chase in the wrong direction while he went in another.

Rutledge was already sprinting toward the hotel he'd just left, oblivious of the stares of strollers along the promenade, his mind keeping pace with his feet.

He'd been outfoxed, and it angered him. Hamish, pointing out his failure, was like a demon at his shoulder.

Could Summers still be in Hastings New Town, in another fine hotel? Or had he turned east instead of west? Or north? It was impossible to guess.

And what was the man telling his bride, how could he explain cutting their wedding journey short—or flying off in an entirely different direction?

Would he suggest that now his friends had caught up with them, they'd play a trick of their own?

Hamish said, "Ye ken, he left her alone at night. He used a false name at yon hotel. Would she no' grow suspicious after a while?"

Rutledge felt a surge of apprehension.

Is that what had happened? Had there been unexpected difficulties over his behavior? What had prompted that marriage in the first place? Was it a love match—or was it the fact that Summers needed his new wife's money? He hadn't held a job in months, and The White Swans was one of the most elegant—and expensive—hotels along this stretch of seaside towns.

Rutledge reached the Regency Hotel and slowed his pace, striding into Reception and waiting impatiently as an elderly couple spoke to the woman behind the desk about the availability of rooms.

Yes, they had a telephone, the woman told him when the couple had left. For the use of their guests. "This is an urgent police matter," he told her curtly, and reluctantly she pointed to a door just past the desk.

He put in a call to the Yard, silently cursing the delay as someone went in search of Sergeant Gibson. While he waited, Rutledge was already scanning the map of Sussex and of Kent in his head.

There was an isolated church, St. Mary's, out in the marshes near Dymchurch. One could hide a body there. But of course in time it would be found, and if it was identified, then the police would begin to look for Summers.

That was true almost anywhere else. Corpses had a way of returning at the most inconvenient of times, whether left in marshes or the sea. Besides, if the man wanted his wife's money, he'd have to keep her alive until he could persuade her to make a will in his favor.

But what if Summers had already worked out a contingency plan? Leave his work unfinished until the hue and cry had died down, disappear into France meanwhile, and return at a later date? The southern parts of France along the Mediterranean Sea had been untouched by war, though strongly affected by the state of the French economy in general. Still, it was warm, lovely, expensive, and increasingly popular. And his wife might find such a suggestion exceptionally attractive.

Dover, then, and the ferry across the Channel. And he, Rutledge, was already six hours too late.

If the Kent police could find Rutledge himself after he'd left Melinda Crawford's house, they might be lucky enough to find Tommy Summers for him.

He told Sergeant Gibson what it was he wanted, and then went in search of his motorcar, several streets away.

The motor almost misfired as he turned the crank, and he had to start again. Once behind the wheel, he made a looping circle through the streets and drove as fast as he dared through the holidaymakers, heading east. Behind him the clouds were gathering and far out to sea, the wind had picked up. He could feel the cloying heat that presaged a storm.

The road ran along the coast for the most part, one seaside community after another, the congestion at its peak at this hour. The storm was catching him up as he drove, bits of paper and little swirls of dust marking its progress, and before very long, the sun was half hidden in the haze. Before he'd reached Hastings, the sky was dark, and the rumble of thunder followed him.

Hamish gave him no peace, seeming to gather strength with the storm.

He paused at Hastings just long enough to leave word with Inspector Norman, and then turned toward Eastfield.

The rain found him just before he got there, huge wind-driven pellets, and the lightning was fierce.

At the police station, Constable Walker listened to what he had to say, then handed him a framed photograph that Tyrell Pierce had left at The Fishermen's Arms.

Rutledge looked at it, and damned the man. The sun was behind the subjects, and he could just recognize Anthony Pierce, smiling beneath his officer's cap, one arm around his brother's shoulders. Daniel's face was harder to make out, and Rutledge had to be satisfied with his general build.

Pierce must have spent an hour or more searching through photographs to find one that was so useless.

He handed it to Walker. "I should have the man arrested for obstruction."

And then he was gone again, driving through the pelting rain and the early darkness.

He stopped for petrol in one village, and to have a tire inspected in another, praying that the Dover police had found their man.

Hamish reminded him, "It's no' certain that he's even there."

Summers might as easily have chosen London or Southampton and taken ship anywhere. But France was closer, and the man knew the country. It made sense.

In the predawn hours when he reached the Dover police, the skies were clearing. The fishing fleet had put out to sea, their sails tiny dots on the horizon, and the first ferry to France was just pulling out.

But Dover had nothing for him.

The inspector he spoke with said, "You realize he could have sailed before you reached us."

"Yes, yes, that's very likely. I was hoping that we'd been in time." He rubbed his face, hearing the scrape of beard on his chin. "All right, keep looking. I'll be at the hotel. Did you reserve a room?"

"Yes. The Nancy Bell. It's run by a retired policeman. We try to give him a little business now and again."

Rutledge found it, a small inn at best, almost at the outskirts of town, but Sergeant Bell greeted him, took one look at him, and said, "Go up, then, top of the stairs, I'll bring hot water and hotter tea."

He was as good as his word. A bluff, graying man, his shoulders still broad and the line of his jaw firm, he carried the tray in one hand and a pitcher in the other, setting them down on the table. "You'll want to sleep," he told Rutledge. "If there's word, they'll send for you here."

But after shaving and drinking his tea, Rutledge was restless, unable to settle, and he left The Nancy Bell and went out to walk.

Dover sat at the foot of chalk cliffs and was divided into two parts. Beneath the towering bulk of the castle was the port with the residential area south of it. The war had not dealt well with the town, for it had seen thousands of men and ships coming and going, expanding almost faster than the town could absorb the dramatically increasing population, and then the war had ended after four hard years, and Dover had had to shrink into itself again, finding the fit difficult.

Eventually he reached the strand and walked down on the shingle hard packed from the heavy rains of the day before. There were others doing much the same, enjoying the morning air, fresh and cool off the water. This was not a bathing center, like the towns along the southern coast, but he, like the others out this morning, enjoyed the smell of the sea, the wind buffeting his face, and the sun just warming his skin. He thought that Darwin had not been too far off the mark—men must remember coming from the sea, whether they realized it or not.

He noticed a dog racing along the strand far ahead, running to greet the handful of hardy souls walking just above the tide line. He watched it for a time, and then it began to strike him as odd that the dog showed no interest in chasing the gulls scavenging for food and starting up in a fluster of wings as humans approached. Instead, the little dog seemed frantic, dashing up to someone, racing around, then moving on to the next walker.

Rutledge started to jog toward it, feeling a growing certainty that he recognized it. And as he grew nearer, and the dog looked his way, he realized that it was trailing a lead.

What was the name on the dog bed he's seen in The White Swans Hotel, in the room occupied by Mr. and Mrs. Daniel Pierce?

Muffin.

He whistled, and the dog stopped, ears pricked, listening. He whistled again and called its name. The dog stared at him uncertainly, and then came bounding toward him, only to stop, puzzled, as he drew close enough to pick up Rutledge's scent on the errant breeze.

Rutledge called to him again, and the dog came forward slowly, warily, as if half afraid. Head down, it begged for assurance and had no reason to feel any.

Rutledge stopped, letting the animal come to him, and when finally it did, whimpering, belly dragging, he bent down to fondle its ears.

It was the same dog he'd seen in the photograph of the bride and groom, nestling among the folds of the woman's skirts. He was prepared to stake his life on it.

After a moment the dog rolled on its back, and Rutledge scratched the animal's chest. And then it leapt up, half afraid again, and looked past him down the beach toward another couple strolling some twenty yards behind.

It had been abandoned here on the strand, he was almost certain of it, and he reached down to pick up the end of the lead.

If this was the same animal, where was Mrs. Summers?

21

The dog refused to leave the shoreline. He struggled against his lead, and even growled as Rutledge lifted him into his arms.

It took half an hour to make any progress with the animal, and even then he thought it was more a reflection of the dog's growing despair than his own blandishments. The fact that Rutledge knew the animal's name seemed to weigh, because when Rutledge made to move back toward the road, the dog stood there whining, torn between waiting and going, and finally he came forward, head down, and let Rutledge pet him again.

Still, it was an uphill battle back to The Nancy Bell, and when Rutledge arrived on Sergeant Bell's doorstep, both he and the dog were out of breath.

Bell, staring at the two of them, said, "And what's this?"

Rutledge explained, and Bell got down on one knee, ruffling the dog's ears, then led it to the kitchen, where there was a little roast beef left from the night before.

But the dog was back at the door after wolfing down the beef, scratching the wood paneling and crying to be let out.

"That's pitiful," Bell said, watching it. "It's known only the one mistress, you can see, and wants none other."

"She may be dead," Rutledge answered. "I don't think he would have left her side otherwise. If she were alive, she'd have fought to keep him with her."

The sergeant scratched his chin. "If they took the boat over to France," he said thoughtfully, "your man could have told her that the dog had to stay below. And she wouldn't know, would she, until she landed and went for him that he was not there."

"Dear God, that's precisely what he did. I need to speak to the port authorities, and ask them to contact France."

He left the dog with Bell and could hear it barking frantically as he drove away.

After three hours at the port, being passed from office to office, he learned that Mr. and Mrs. Summers

had indeed embarked for France on the channel crossing the preceding day. At first he was surprised that
Summers had used their real names, and then it was
clear why: there had to be a record of Mrs. Summers
leaving England for France, for her solicitors to see
later that all was aboveboard, the couple happy and still
enjoying their wedding journey.

The harbormaster said, "It was a rough passage, right in the teeth of the storm." Grinning, he
added, "There'd be decks to swab after that one made
landfall."

"While you're at it, ask the French if there was a
small dog with them. Long haired, black and gray,
with some white," Rutledge added.

The harbormaster got in touch with the French authorities, and was told that Mr. and Mrs. Summers had
landed safely, although both were the worse for wear
from seasickness.

The message ended, "Madame was very ill. Monsieur
had given her something to help the nausea, and it was
not working. We recommended an hotel in Honfleur,
and he told us he felt he could drive there. No dog ac-
companied them."

Rutledge left the office, still worried. The fact that
Mrs. Summers had landed in France surprised him—a
seasick woman leaning over the rail needed only a

small push to send her into the sea as the boat tossed and twisted in the storm.

Something was wrong with the picture painted by the French authorities.

"They didna' see her," Hamish pointed out. "They saw a verra' distressed woman."

And that was true, Rutledge thought as he drove back to The Nancy Bell. She could have been drugged. Or she could have been anyone wearing Mrs. Summers's clothing.

But there was nothing he could do without authority from the Yard to have the couple taken into French custody. They had left the port by now, and were no longer under its jurisdiction. And they had broken no laws. There was not sufficient evidence to hold Summers at all.

Misdirection. Summers was a master at it.

Rutledge went back again to the Dover police and used their telephone to call the Yard. Explaining the situation to Sergeant Gibson, he added, "I want a watch on all ports for someone coming in under the name Summers or Pierce, or any other on this list." And from the sheet of paper he'd made out, he read the names of anyone who was associated with this case. "He may return as a single person or as a couple—it will depend on how safe he thinks he may be with an ill wife."

"That's a tall order," Gibson pointed out. "Something will be said about the number of men required for that."

"Clear it with the Chief Superintendent. This man hasn't finished. He'll kill again."

"I'll do my best," Gibson said, doubt heavy in his voice. He cleared his throat and asked, "Have you heard what Inspector Mickelson had to say? He regained his senses."

"There hasn't been an opportunity to ask anyone," Rutledge responded. "If he got into a motorcar with his killer, he ought to be able to provide a description."

"You'd best ask Inspector Norman," Gibson answered cryptically, and Rutledge had to be satisfied with that.

The problem of the dog was more easily dealt with. Sergeant Bell agreed to keep it until it could be used to identify Summers or reunited with its proper owner. That done, Rutledge turned back toward Hastings.

He had had no sleep to speak of, and he was feeling it. But he drove through Kent back to the Sussex coast. By the time he had reached Eastfield, he knew it was too late to find Inspector Norman in his office. He went to his room at The Fishermen's Arms and slept for seven hours.

Inspector Norman met Rutledge at his office door and said, "Let's walk."

With foreboding, Rutledge turned to follow him. They left the station and had nearly reached The Stade when Norman said, "I was there when Inspector Mickelson was questioned. He could remember most of what happened before he was struck on the head. He said you had sent a message that he should look at the net shops before dawn, that you had a feeling that he'd find the garrote there. And so he went with the man you'd sent to find him, and when he reached the sheds, something hit him."

"That marches with what Mrs. Farrell-Smith claimed. She saw two men talking near the church, and they drove away together."

"Exactly."

"His first mistake," Rutledge said crisply. "I can show I was far away from Sussex at the time. I could have arranged to have him lured to Hastings, but I wasn't there to deliver the blow. It was a trick. And it worked."

"Inspector Mickelson had Carl in custody but hadn't been able to lay hands on the murder weapon. Yes, it worked a treat."

"Was he able to give you a description of the man in the motorcar?"

"A hazy one at best. The reflection from the head-lamps cast shadows. Besides, Mickelson was busy trying to decide how you'd worked it out about the garrote when he hadn't."

The question had to be asked. "Does Mickelson believe I lured him into a trap?"

"My impression was, he is still of two minds about that. His accident, after all, brought you back into the case."

"Yes, it did." Rutledge gave it some thought as they walked along the road above the net shops.

Norman hesitated. "The man in the motorcar told Mickelson his name was Daniel Pierce and that you'd asked him to handle this because his own brother was among the dead. Mickelson had no reason to doubt what he was told. The elder Pierce is an upstanding member of the community, after all."

"And Mickelson wasn't intended to live long enough to tell us that. Have you spoken to Tyrell Pierce about this?"

"Not yet. I wanted to hear what you had to say before going to him. You still maintain that this man you're chasing is not Pierce's son. I went to The White Swans. Whoever had stayed there registered as Pierce. And the description could fit him, with a little stretch of the imagination. He was never the man his brother was, to look at. It was as if Anthony's features had been passed on to his brother, only a little blurred, a little less distinctive."

And Summers had known that. He'd also known that Daniel Pierce hadn't returned to Sussex for two years. It was a safe enough gamble.

Rutledge related what had transpired in Dover, and Inspector Norman whistled.

"Any chance of bringing him back from France?"

"On what evidence?" Rutledge asked. "Whatever I can prove, it isn't strong enough to convince the French police."

"Damn." Norman glanced up at the headland where Theo Hartle had been found and said, "You make a good case for Summers. The question remains, what do we do about the inquests into these deaths? Now that we know Inspector Mickelson will survive, do we wait until he's well enough to present his case, or do we look to you?"

"Adjourn them again if you have to. But keep your eye on Eastfield. That's where our killer will turn up, as soon as he returns to England. Mark my words." They turned back toward the police station.

Rutledge stood there on the street for a moment, after Inspector Norman had gone inside, debating what to do. Waiting in Eastfield would accomplish nothing.

The best course open to him was to return to the Yard and make certain that the watch on the ports was kept in place as long as need be.

When he arrived in London, Rutledge found another letter from Chief Inspector Cummins waiting for him.

Opening it, he lit the lamp and sat down in the chair by the window, although the day had faded into dusk.

Rutledge,

You're a marvel. I've considered everything you'd uncovered, and I decided (having the free time to do so) to drive to East Anglia and visit my grandfather's house. It was sold shortly after his death, but I remember it quite clearly. The present owners have kept it up amazingly well, even to the gardens that were his pride, and I sat for some minutes in my motorcar, remembering a very happy childhood. The man who lives there now happened to see me as he came back from marketing and he asked if I were looking for someone. I explained about my grandfather, and to my surprise, this stranger invited me inside. I must have an honest face!

He allowed me to walk about and reminisce, then to my even greater surprise told me he had something he thought belonged to me. He was gone several minutes while I strolled in the back garden, and then he reappeared with an envelope. He handed it to me, and I was stunned to see my name on the outside. I asked where in hell he'd got this, and he said that in 1908, a young man came to the door. His mother was living at the time, and said he was quite polite, asking if my grandfather still lived here. She told him that he had died. The man explained that he was looking for me, the grandson of the previous owner, and he asked if he might leave a letter here for me, in the event I came back to the house one day. She told the young man that she'd be glad to take the letter, but considered it was unlikely that I would ever return. But he claimed he might miss me in London, and it would be a kindness to know that one day I'd find the letter and know that he cared. And so, being the trusting soul that she was, she took the letter and kept it. Before she died, she mentioned it to her son—this was nearly ten years later, and the letter was still in her possession—and asked what to do about it. The son wondered if I'd been abroad, and felt that someday if I retired from whatever post it was that had taken me away, I might come here looking for it. And so he took on that charge in his mother's stead, and she died a few months later. He and his wife then moved into the house, and the letter waited. I could hardly believe anyone would have been that considerate of a stranger's request, but apparently the mother had been quite taken with him.

At any rate, I left soon afterward, letter in hand, and the man's last comment to me was, he hoped that I would be in England to stay now. I didn't open the letter until I reached London. It was a confession, Ian, a confession to that murder at Stonehenge. But the man wasn't fool enough to give me his name. He wrote that the man who was killed had deserved to die, but in fact, his death had been an accident. Now, Ian, I'd seen the body and that wound. It couldn't have been more accurate, that knife slipping in. How, pray, could it have happened by chance?

But the writer went on to say that the man had done terrible things, and his death had protected others from further cruelty. I found that self-serving. He did explain that the body had never been identified properly because the victim had been on the point of leaving the country, and everyone just assumed he had, without fanfare. He was not liked well enough for people to wonder why he had moved up his departure, and the feeling was he had not expected a send-off, a farewell dinner, that sort of thing. And so he had decided not to put himself in a position where people might assume he wanted a show of regret at his leaving. There was no one in England he cared for, and there had been some quiet speculation that his continued employment might soon be in doubt. Those who could have spoken out about his private life and assured his dismissal were too frightened to do so. "I was one of them" he wrote at the end of his confession. "I killed rather than endure silently as so many did. I took the knife he used as a desk ornament—someone had fashioned a handle for it, to please him, he said—and struck out blindly. I was astonished to see him fall, and thought it a trick. I left him there and went directly to a trusted friend. For my sake, he and one other person helped me dispose of my victim. I write this to ease my own conscience and to leave a legacy for you, since the crime has not been solved. But the clues I have left were obscure, and I wonder if—even to ease my conscience—I really am ready to face the horror of what I did."

Well, then, Ian, my friend, I wonder what you will make of this!

Rutledge put down the letter. What indeed to make of it? He agreed with Cummins that the author of the letter had purposely made the clues difficult to follow. Still, if Cummins had happened on that flint knife in the course of another case, would he have followed the same steps toward finding an answer? Was that the point, that the killer had felt he had done his duty, secure in the knowledge that his role would never come to light?

What's more, were there clues in that letter that might lead to the name of the victim, if not the murderer?

Without the original, he wasn't able to make an educated guess about that. But surely Cummins would examine all the possibilities?

Hamish said, "Ye canna see ye're ain way. You canna' worry oe'r much about the ins and outs of anither man's inquiry."

But Rutledge said, "It's a puzzle. Like this one of Summers's doing. God knows how long he has planned his revenge, but so far he's carried it out without so much a qualm. The men he killed, the woman he took to France, the dog he'd abandoned."

"If ye had never gone to yon hotel room at The White Swans, you wouldna' ha' known about yon dog."

It was true. And the Dover police had been particularly interested in how he had known about the dog and how he had come to learn what it was called.

He'd replied simply that he had been several times to the hotel where the Pierces were staying. True, as far as it went.

Rutledge took a deep breath. "He's coming back. I can feel it," he said aloud into the silence of the room. "And sooner than we expect. And I don't know how to stop him."

Hamish said, "With any luck ata', he'll drown on his way back across yon Channel. I was never sea sick mysel', but ithers were, and dying was a cheering thought."

"But that's the problem. He could come back through a dozen different ports."

And hovering in the back of his mind was the inescapable knowledge that if he hadn't believed the false lead to Brighton, he could have reached Dover in time.

Rutledge let it go. There was nothing he could do this night, and sometimes an answer came more readily if he ignored the problem.

He went out to find his dinner, choosing a restaurant where he wasn't likely to encounter anyone from the Yard. The food there was edible, the clientele older and quiet, and he didn't linger over his meal.

When he came home again, there was someone huddled in the doorway of the flat, only a thicker shadow
among shadows.

His first thought was Summers. Or—his wife?

Bracing himself, he called, "Who is it? Who is
there?"

The shapeless figure turned, taking on the outline of
a woman, and then a voice he knew said, "Ian? Please,
I need your help."

It was Meredith Channing, and he went forward
quickly, taking her arm with one hand, opening the door
of his flat with the other. Thank God, he thought, he'd
left a lamp burning. He put her into a chair, closed the
door, and went to find a handkerchief, for he could see
that she was crying. He gave it to her, and as she pressed
it against her eyes, he said, "What is it? What's wrong?"

"I didn't know where to turn," she answered him
after a moment, her eyes still hidden behind his handkerchief. And then as if she had found the courage
to say what she had come to say, she set the rumpled
white square of cloth aside. He could read the anguish
in her face. "My friends—I could ask any of them, and
they would help me. But then they would know, you
see—once the words are spoken, I can never take them
back. And when they look at me, I'll know that they
remember, and I couldn't bear that."

He took the chair across from hers. "I've never judged you," he said quietly. And waited.

"Shall I tell you a story, Ian?" she said when she was calmer. It seemed like hours later but perhaps no more than ten minutes had passed. She had stopped crying now, resigned. "Much of it may be familiar. It's about a young man marching off to war. He was deeply in love, he said, he wanted to marry because even if the war only lasted until Christmas, he had a feeling he wouldn't come home again. I asked him how he could say such a thing, and he smiled and said, 'I just know.' I begged him not to go. I even promised I would marry him, if he'd refuse to join the Army. But he had to, you see, all his friends had already enlisted, they were excited and buying uniforms and talking about glory, and he was a man, he couldn't bear to be left behind. And I married him, because I thought if I do, he'll have a reason to keep himself safe, a reason to defy that silly superstition, and he'll come back. I didn't love him, Ian. I liked him. Immensely. And so I was willing to do this for his sake, even if it meant spending the rest of my life with him. I thought, it will be worth it. We can be happy. I was young—I thought, if he's killed, I'll never forgive myself."

She leaned her dark head against the back of the chair and stared at the ceiling. "He went missing shortly after the first gas attack at Ypres. I was suddenly neither wife nor widow. And I blamed myself for not caring, for not loving him in the way he loved me. I kept telling myself that he knew, that somehow he'd realized why I had married him, and he'd lost his talisman, so to speak. I couldn't bear the guilt, and so I thought, I'll find him and save him. And so I trained as a nurse, and I worked very hard, I did my best, from mopping ward floors to keeping my nerve in the operating theater, and soon I was shipped to France. But I went for selfish reasons, I see that now. I never found Mark among the unidentified wounded. I could find no one who had seen him die. It was as if he were in a limbo of some sort, and no one had the key."

It was hard to listen to her confession. Rutledge had wondered, time and again, but never asked. He realized now that he hadn't really wanted to know. Her marriage was in the past, let it rest there. But he said nothing.

"I paid for my folly. For not having the courage to tell Mark the truth. For thinking that I could save him. For thinking that I could find him." Her gaze came back to him. "One day in France, I saw someone who had been brought in for superficial wounds. He was dazed, and I was told he'd been buried alive when a shell fell short and exploded in his sector. He was the only survivor. All of his men were killed. But he kept asking for them, he didn't want to be treated until he was sure they were seen to. An orderly took him away to rest for a little while, and I asked someone the officer's name. I looked in on him later, and he was sleeping. I could see the shadows under his eyes, I could see that he'd been in the line through some of the worst fighting. And I knew I could love this man. I wanted to hold him and keep him safe. All I could do was ask that he be given a little longer to recover, but every man was needed. I was told to wake him up and send him back. I couldn't. I asked someone else to do it." She took a deep breath. "I never saw him again after that, though I'd hear some snippets of news from time to time and knew he was safe. I never asked. But I listened for his name. It wasn't until this past New Year's Eve that I found him again. I thought, we could be friends, it would be all right." She added wryly, "I was still lying to myself, you see."

He didn't reply. He knew she didn't want his sympathy or his compassion.

"I kept telling myself that I could always go away, if there were problems. After all, I was still married. And I couldn't—wouldn't—let myself deny that."

This time when she fell silent, he said, "Meredith. Would tea help? Sherry?"

She shook her head.

That poise he'd found so attractive had deserted her now. He could see her hands shaking, even though she clasped them tightly in her lap.

"A little while ago—no, it must have been this afternoon," she went on, frowning. "There was a telephone call. A group that works to find the missing has kept in touch from time to time. They told me they believe they've found Mark. He's in a Belgian hospital, very badly damaged. In fact, for some reason they'd believed he was a Belgian, a Fleming from Bruges. There were a few who fought with the British, you see. But when he improved a little last week, they realized he doesn't seem to understand Flemish. He responded a little to English, and so the hospital called in someone who could speak to him in English. It was necessary, you see, so that his answers could be taken down accurately."

Her voice broke as she added, "I must go to Belgium, Ian. I need to see this man. And I can't go alone. Will you come with me? As a friend?"

He could hear only Hamish in his head, Meredith's words a distant hum, and yet he knew what she was asking. He didn't think he could do it. Not with this inquiry ongoing, he told himself. Not when I care too much, he added, facing the truth.

Someone was saying, "Yes, of course I'll do what I can. If the Yard will allow me to take leave."

A thought flitted through his head: the last time he'd asked for leave of his own accord, it was to attend Max Hume's funeral.

He expected her to cry again, then. Instead, she looked down at her hands and replied quietly, "Thank you, Ian. From the bottom of my heart."

"I'll speak to them tomorrow."

He took her home soon after, touching her only to help her into the motorcar, seeing her to her door, and saying good night when her maid had opened it.

She smiled a little, and went inside.

The next morning he was as good as his word. He went to the Yard, ignoring the stares and the whispers as he passed along the corridors. Chief Superintendent Bowles was in his office and was caught quite by surprise by his inspector's sudden appearance.

Rutledge faced him grimly, knowing Bowles for what he was, giving no ground as the man behind the desk seemed rattled for a moment, then collected himself.

"I thought you were in Sussex," Bowles said gruffly. "Or failing that, in Dover."

"There's nothing I can do in Dover. And as long as Summers is in France, then Sussex is safe. I've come to ask for a few days of leave."

Bowles's face brightened. But he said, "I thought I'd just given you leave."

"It's been some time since then. This is a personal matter."

He could see Bowles mulling it over, vacillating, emotions flitting across his face like shadows. The good fortune of being rid of Rutledge at this impossibly sticky time. The realization that if Summers reappeared in England while Rutledge was away, he could send another man to cope with it. The knowledge that Rutledge was the butt of gossip and speculation which Bowles himself could do without—they were all there. He had even heard one rumor that Rutledge had had his revenge for Mickelson's interference—embarrassing the Chief Superintendent.

"Yes, all right," Bowles declared finally. "Take your leave and report back in four days. By that time, something should have turned up at the ports."

He clearly expected Rutledge to be satisfied, for he picked up the paper he'd been reading when he was interrupted.

But Rutledge stood his ground, and said with something in his voice that made Bowles look up sharply, "About Inspector Mickelson's theory that I was involved in the attack on him. I would suggest that it's an aftereffect of that blow on the head. You know as well as I do that I was not involved. I couldn't have been. I had no reason to be. Whatever my personal feelings may be about Inspector Mickelson."

"A combination of misinformation and mistake," Bowles agreed hastily.

Rutledge left it at that. He would never have an apology from this man, and while he'd been angry enough to beard him in his den and tell him publicly what he thought about him, he had more to lose than Bowles: his position at the Yard, which was still his lifeline to sanity.

He didn't want to call on Meredith Channing. Last night was still too fresh in his mind. But he drove to her house anyway and knocked at the door.

And she had foreseen his difficulty. Her maid answered his knock, and he gave her the message for her mistress.

"Mrs. Channing would like to leave for Dover this afternoon, if that's possible," the maid replied. "Will that be convenient?"

The sooner it was over, the better, he thought, but said only, "I'll be here at one o'clock."

"Thank you, sir." She closed the door. He stood there for a moment, then turned and walked away.

Hamish was giving him no peace, a reflection of the strain he was under. As a precaution when he went home to pack a small valise, he added some things to his clothing and shaving gear.

One o'clock came all too soon, and he was outside the Channing house five minutes early.

And she was ready. The door opened almost at once, and he went to meet her, taking her case and adding it to his own in the boot. She said, "Ian—" and then shook her head, stepping into the motorcar when he opened her door.

They drove through London in silence, and were soon on the Dover Road.

They arrived in good time for their crossing, and Rutledge took a few minutes to call on Sergeant Bell.

"The laddie is still restless," he said. "I took him for a walk along the strand today, and he was searching for scents, wanting to run up to anyone he spotted. There's no word on Mrs. Summers?"

"None."

Bell said, "Well, then. We'll see that he's fed and kept safe."

The boat left on time. Meredith stayed below, while Rutledge stood by the rail, watching the water pass under the hull.

He had sworn, once, that he would never set foot in France again. And here he was, not on police business after all but to support a friend.

Friend.

He ignored that thought and instead considered the letter that had come into Chief Inspector Cummins's possession.

What sort of man would have a flint knife sitting on his desk, what kinds of interests would he have? Historian, schoolmaster, world traveler, expert in ancient weapons, geologist, even a collector of oddities.

It would take hundreds of man-hours to find likely men in those fields and interview them.

Schoolmaster . . . Hadn't it been a schoolmaster who had brought the latter-day Druids to Stonehenge for the summer solstice?

He was above suspicion, Cummins had said when Rutledge asked about him. But where had he taught? And were there other masters in that same school? Had Cummins interviewed any of them? But of course at the time Cummins hadn't had the benefit of Rutledge's find of the flint knife. He had been completely in the dark about the murder weapon.

Hindsight seldom caught murderers.

He walked along the deck, watching the white cliffs of England recede, the castle a gray mass on the top of the highest cliff. France was still a blue smudge on the horizon. The wind striking his face was warm, and sometimes laden with salt spray. Skirting the busy crew coiling ropes, stowing gear, and seeing to the general running of the ferry, he paced for a few minutes, deep in thought.

If the killer considered the victim's murder well deserved, what had the man done to earn it?

Rutledge recalled studying the photograph of the dead face and thinking that the victim looked far more intelligent and of a better class than Harvey Wheeler was said to have been.

There was only a small window of time when the body could have been carried to Stonehenge—or the living man brought there to be dispatched. After all, this was the shortest night of the year. And the situation was complicated by the latter-day Druids celebrating the Summer Solstice.

He could have been there when the Druids arrived, depending on what route they had taken to cross Salisbury Plain to the site. In fact, he must have been put there as soon as it was completely dark. Too much activity by the heel stone after they'd reached the stone ruins, and the killer could have been discovered in the act of tying his victim there. But had the killer and his accomplices known about the celebrants? Or had they left the body there because it was an isolated place and it was unlikely to be discovered for several days?

The letter writer hadn't mentioned the Druids.

But the Druids had been drinking mead and chanting. To distract them from what was happening just out of sight?

He must write to Cummins again and open a new avenue to explore.

Pausing by the railing, he could just make out the coastline of France now.

Someone stepped to the rail beside him, and he turned to see that Meredith Channing had come on deck.

Staring at the landfall in the distance, she said, "I shouldn't have come. I should have listened to my better judgment. This won't be Mark. None of the others were. I shouldn't have brought you into this. But I was afraid this time. I don't know why. Very cowardly of me."

Her shoulder was touching his, her unconscious need for human comfort overcoming her reticence.

"I'm glad you did," he said, and wondered if it were true.

"When it seemed that you weren't at home, I didn't know what to do. I couldn't go to Frances, or to the Yard, and ask where you might be."

"How did you know where to find me?"

"I've known for a very long time where you lived. I'd just never had occasion to go there. Until last night."

They were silent for a time. He could feel her shivering, whether from the wind or from nerves, he didn't know. After a moment, he put his arm around her shoulders, and she leaned into him until the shivering stopped.

When the boat had docked, and they had cleared the formalities, they turned north, on the road to Ypres and Belgium. To make conversation, Rutledge said, "I lost a murderer to France this week." And he told her how the dog had been found, and what the French had had to say about Mr. and Mrs. Summers.

"Do you think she was just ill from the crossing? Or had he given her something to make certain she didn't say anything untoward?"

"She was probably given something. I can't see how she would have let her husband leave the boat without bringing her dog to her. Most certainly she'd have created a scene. And why get rid of the animal, unless he intended to do away with her as well?" He slowed to pass a procession of villagers carrying the small statue of a saint and bouquets of flowers. They appeared to be on their way to the church on a slight rise.

"He needn't, you know. Rid himself of her. There used to be these little convents scattered about, where the nuns took in the ill or the mad, and if there was money to pay for her board, she could stay indefinitely in their care."

It was an interesting thought.

They were driving now on what had been the road where the German Army and the small British Expeditionary Force sent to stop their progress had clashed. Roofless ruins, shattered walls, toppled church towers still marked where the fighting had been most intense, and some fields lay fallow and torn. Villages and towns were striving to rebuild, life was struggling to return to normal, but as Rutledge looked around him, he felt a surge of tension, of memory. This was what he'd lived with for four bloody years and had hoped never to see again. But night was falling, covering what they didn't want to see in blessed darkness.

Rutledge stopped just before the Belgian frontier for dinner and found a small pension that smelled of new mortar and paint, as if it had just been refurbished, where they could spend the night. The food was not up to French standards, but they had very little appetite. Rutledge saw Mrs. Channing to her room, and she wished him a good night. He waited until her door had been locked from the inside before going on down the passage to his to sit by the window instead of going to bed.

They reached Bruges the next day, and found their way to the old city inside its ring of canals. In the southern part, on a side street not far from the Begijnhof, a large house had been turned into a hospital that cared for the human detritus left behind by war.

It was a tall building, and broader than most. Rutledge thought it must have once been the town house of a wealthy merchant family. Even here were the scars of war—bullet holes in the facade, a niche statue of the Virgin by the door decapitated, the hasty repairs of damage from shrapnel still visible. Someone had repainted the door, to hide the nicks and scratches in the wood.

As he reached for the brass knob, Meredith Channing stopped him, putting out her hand. "Ian. I must do the rest myself. Will you wait?"

He agreed, and went to sit in the motorcar. After a moment, she resolutely turned the knob and disappeared inside.

An hour passed, and then the second. He walked for a time but never out of sight of the motorcar. Hamish was his constant companion, the voice dinning in his ear, the war seeming to crowd in on him.

And then she was coming through the door, her face so pale he went to her at once, and took her hands. She had left her pretty hat somewhere. "Was it very bad?" he asked.

"Worse than—oh, Ian, you should see him. He's lying there looking at nothing, his poor face so scarred I hardly knew him."

They were in a very public place, people passing on the street around them, faces turned to stare. He led her to the motorcar and put her inside.

She said as he got behind the wheel, "I was told there was a little church near the Gruuthuse Palace. Could we walk there, do you think?"

He found it for her after going astray near the Begijnhof, where the Benedictine Sisters lived in their little white cottages in a tree-lined courtyard. Two or three were sitting in the sun, warming themselves, a small cushion on their knees, weaving the fine webs of their lace, bobbins flying in nimble fingers. There Meredith bought a small handkerchief to cover her dark hair in the church.

The Church of Our Lady was known for its tall, striking tower. It soared above the surrounding buildings, and Rutledge found himself thinking it was an ideal mark for German artillery firing on the town.

Down a side aisle was a chapel with a small but perfect white marble statue standing on the altar. It was, he realized, Michelangelo's *Madonna and Child*. She was seated, the child at her knee, the smile on her face movingly sweet. Rutledge's godfather, the architect David Trevor, had traveled in Europe on a Grand Tour as a young man, and he had told Rutledge that this face, young, serene, without shadows, was the same as that of the Virgin in the *Pietà* in Rome's St. Peter's, only there it was marked by sorrow and loss. The comparison, he had said, was heart-wrenching.

Rutledge stood in the back of the chapel, staring up at that face while Meredith knelt near the altar, head bowed, but not, he thought, in prayer. If she was looking for anything here, it was strength. Or courage.

Hamish had been there in the back of his mind ever since the night Meredith Channing had come to his flat. A dull, unceasing monologue of despair, the words nearly indistinguishable, but he knew them by heart.

Fiona. He could hear that whisper as Hamish lay dying before the blessing of the coup de grâce. *You took my happiness from me. I'll take yours.*

Rutledge had tried to shut out all feeling after Jean had walked out of his life in the spring of 1919. He hadn't wanted to feel again. He didn't want to feel anything now.

But he watched Meredith come to grips with what she had seen, and he wondered if she had wanted this man to be her husband. Or if he was. Either way, here was her chance for atonement.

After a time, she rose and walked toward him. There were no tears now, just the resolve he was dreading, and she said, "Will you take me back to the hospital now?"

It was too short a distance to say anything important, and so they walked in silence. When they reached the hospital with its frivolous roofline of chimneys, she asked that he carry her valise to the door. "They'll find somewhere for me to stay. Close by. I can visit every day."

He did as she asked, numbly, knowing he had already been shut out.

As he set the valise down with a click on the marble step, she said, "I'm so sorry. But this is something I have to do." Her voice was steady, but only just. A little deeper in note as well, from the tears she was holding back.

"Duty is bitter company," he said quietly.

"I don't know how long he will live. Months. Years. But I'll close the London house and live in Bruges for now."

"Meredith—"

"I wish I had met you then. I wouldn't have been so foolish as to marry without love." She rose on tiptoe and kissed his cheek. "Good-bye, Ian."

Someone opened the door, as if he or she had been waiting to admit Mrs. Channing. She stepped inside, and it swung shut again behind her.

He stood there for a moment longer, as if hoping she would change her mind. And then he went to the motorcar.

France was just miles away, and he knew where Hamish had died. His service revolver was in his valise.

It was time to end it.

22

Rutledge crossed the frontier between France and Belgium and soon after found a deeply rutted road through devastated countryside that led in the direction of the River Somme, approaching it from what had been the German lines. The land was healing, after a fashion, grass and weeds struggling to reestablish themselves. Nature seemed to find a way to cover up the scars of tragedy. But men had marched down this road to kill other men, and the land was rough and desolate, as if no one cared to live here where so many had died. He couldn't blame them. If ghosts walked anywhere, surely they did here, and he felt that nothing grown in such bloody soil would ever prosper again.

He could see across the twisted landscape to where he and so many others had fought, and yet he found his sector of that fateful night hard to recognize. Rains had washed down trench walls, the stench had gone, and somehow it all seemed so much smaller in scale now. Without the men who had served here among the wire, the hellish pits of shell craters, and the tools of war, whether guns or tanks or trenches, it seemed to have changed. He stopped the motorcar at one point and got out, listening. There should have been shouts and the cries of men, the whistle of shells and the chatter of machine guns, the deafening roar of battle, the deeper throb of aircraft overhead. Instead, there was only a light wind, hardly stirring the ridged and torn landscape.

He could still name the men he'd led to their deaths here. As he walked, he thought he could see their faces, but it was only the tightness in his throat and the tension across his shoulders that made him light-headed.

It wasn't long before he found the place he'd been searching for. He'd always had a good sense of direction, and even without markers he knew it was here.

Looking down, he saw the lace of a boot sticking through the soil next to a struggling clump of grass, and he felt ill. How many times had a heel or a buckle marked all that was left of a man who had been living and breathing seconds before? He'd been told that farmers in some places still dug up the dead with their plows. He'd seen them lying rotting in the sun, shrouded with the first snowfall, twitching in the pelting rain.

The revolver was heavy in his coat pocket, well oiled and loaded. He was not likely to miss. And Hamish, he realized, had been silent since he left the motorcar, waiting.

He took the weapon out and held it in his hand. Its feel and its weight were familiar, comforting.

He was raising the revolver, his head bowed for the shot, his eyes closed, when the image of that single boot lace came to him.

It would be obscene to kill himself here, he realized. To add one more body to the thousands upon thousands who littered this land. A desecration to fire a revolver here in this stillness.

Even France had failed him. After a time, the revolver still in his hand, he turned back toward his motorcar, and then drove back the way he'd come.

23

Rutledge landed in Dover and collected his motorcar from the bowels of the ferry. When his turn came to present his identification, he was asked to step aside, and waited impatiently as others behind him were cleared and sent on their way.

Eventually a uniformed constable from the Dover police came up to him.

"Mr. Rutledge, sir? Will you come this way?"

Wary after his last encounter with the Kent Constabulary, Rutledge left his motorcar where it was and followed the man.

Inside one of the dock buildings stood former Sergeant Bell. He looked at Rutledge and then smiled. "Yes, that's him, all right," he told the constable standing to one side. He added for Rutledge's benefit,

"You'd said to watch for certain names on ships' manifests. When yours showed up, we weren't precisely sure who was coming in from France. The constable here sent for me because I knew you by sight."

"Yes, good work," he told the two men. It was, in fact, reassuring that someone had taken him at his word. As he and Bell walked toward the motorcar, he added, "How is the Summers's dog?"

"Muffin?" Bell made a face. "Silly name for a dog, but he answers to it right enough. Still, he looks for someone every time I take him outside. And he sleeps by the door, as if to be ready if anyone knocks. Sad, really. He's devoted to someone. We manage well enough, mind you, but I can see where his heart is."

"Can I give you a lift?" Rutledge asked.

"Yes, thank you, sir. Have any luck in France?"

Rutledge realized Bell believed he'd gone there on police business. "No luck," he replied simply.

"And where are you off to now?"

"Sussex. I'll look in at Eastfield and at Hastings. Then back to London." As he ran down the road along the water, he said, "You know this coast, Bell. Where would you come in, if you didn't wish to attract attention to yourself?"

"There must be a thousand coves and inlets from the Scots border to the Welsh, rounding this part of

England. And none of them requires more than a boat sufficiently sturdy to cross the Channel—the smaller the better—and some knowledge of where one is heading. I doubt your man knows this coast. And so he'd have to ask some Frenchie to bring him over. During the war, we worried about the Germans setting spies ashore in the dark of night, sneaking in, like, where nobody was looking. The coast watch was all very well and good, but there was no way to prevent them if they got past the Navy. A good fog works wonders, if you know your landing."

"Our man could be here already."

"Very possible, if you ask me."

Rutledge left Bell at his door and continued down the coast toward Hastings. Vast stretches of marsh interspersed with habitation and villages that had been part of the old Cinque Ports trusted with the defense of England marked this road. He ran through Winchelsea and tiny Dymchurch, then detoured to St. Mary's in the Marsh, desolate and isolated, with its scatter of cottages. He went into the church itself and found it empty. At Rye, he turned inland and came eventually to Eastfield.

Constable Walker greeted him with some relief. "Constable Petty has been withdrawn, sir. I was told Tommy Summers is out of the country."

"He took the boat across from Dover to France, it appears. But for how long? He may already be in Sussex again."

"Damnation." Walker shook his head. "I'd never given that lad credit for being smart enough to outwit the police, the way he's done. I don't know what to make of it, and that's the truth."

"He's had a long time to plan his revenge, if that's what we're dealing with. He knew it would be a risky business. He must have considered every contingency."

"Shall I ask for Constable Petty to come again? An extra pair of eyes won't come amiss if you're right and Summers is on the prowl again."

"With any luck, we'll find him first," Rutledge said grimly.

But where to look?

He went to The Fishermen's Arms and paced his room, thinking.

"If I were Tommy Summers, what would I do?" he said aloud.

But Hamish gave him no answer.

The cottage where the man had lived before as groundskeeper for the Misses Tate School? But surely that would have been given to whoever had taken his place in the position?

Still, it was worth finding out.

Rutledge left the hotel and walked to the school. The property ran deep, backing up to pasturage on the outskirts of Eastfield. To one side of the main door was a small wooden gate leading into a tradesman's passage to the rear of the house. Here were the kitchen gardens, he saw as he rounded a corner of the building. A path led on between the beds to the barnyard and outbuildings. Behind these was a small walled orchard, apple and pear trees heavy with fruit. To the left of the orchard gate was another that opened into a small plot of ground with a smaller cottage set in it. Empty by the look of it, but all the same, Rutledge went up to the door and opened it after knocking.

There were two rooms and a tiny kitchen with a woodstove. The furnishings were simple and well worn. A table and chairs, a cluster of other chairs, their padded cushions faded with age. He could see the bedroom through an arch without a door. It contained a bed frame with a rolled mattress on it, some chests, another pair of chairs, one of them on rockers, and a cradle.

A patina of dust lay over everything, and as he walked to the bedroom, his own footsteps left faint impressions in the dust on the floor.

It was likely that the present groundskeeper lived not on the property but at his own home in Eastfield.

A wild-goose chase.

He went out and closed the door behind him and then latched the gate.

As he crossed the barnyard, he found himself face-to-face with Mrs. Farrell-Smith. She stood there, watching him approach along the path. There was something in the way she held herself that raised alarm bells in his head.

She said, "Policeman or not, you're trespassing."

"I'm sorry," he said, keeping his voice level. "If I'd known you were in the school today, I'd have asked permission to enter the grounds."

"What are you searching for? Something to identify the groundskeeper you believe was Tommy Summers?"

"I thought he might have come back here," Rutledge answered. "It's familiar, and that means safe. But it appears no one has been in the cottage for some time."

"The greengrocer's son has agreed to work for us. He still lives with his parents. Besides, I doubt Summers would even try to slip into the grounds. The staff know him by sight. Well. I suppose you must start somewhere." She watched a dove circle the barn roof and then perch there, its voice soft on the summer air. "Is it true? Is it this Tom Summers who has done these murders?"

"As far as we can tell. Yes. The trouble is, we can't find him. That's why I came to look in the cottage."

"You won't be arresting Daniel Pierce, then?"

"Are you in love with him?" he asked.

She sighed, and to his amazement, appeared to answer the question honestly. "I think I've always loved him. Sadly, he didn't love me. I thought perhaps in time—I was foolish, I know that now. I even thought I could use Anthony to make him jealous. But you can't make someone jealous who doesn't love you at all."

"You defended him fiercely enough."

She flushed. "I had a very good reason." After a moment she met his gaze and said, "Come with me."

He followed her back to the school building and through a side door into a shadowy passage. This led in turn to a staircase, and at the top he found that they were in the foyer outside her office. The door was standing wide—it was obvious she'd seen him walk to the school and go through the tradesman's gate. She had made a point to follow him to find out what it was he was up to.

Pointing to a chair, she went to her desk, and with a key on a chain around her neck, she opened a bottom drawer.

Looking up at him again, she asked, "Do I have your word that you haven't lied to me about Daniel or Tommy Summers?"

"You have my word," he replied.

She reached into the drawer and brought out a thick envelope, then closed the drawer again.

"You asked me to look into any event here at the school while members of the Eastfield Company were students. I couldn't tell you that I'd already learned something about one of them. It had been in my aunts' personal papers, and I stumbled across it in my first year as head mistress. Although it was rather shocking, it had no immediate importance then, you see, except for a personal interest in the child this once belonged to."

She upended the envelope, and something fell out onto her blotter. Rutledge looked at the tangle and then felt cold as he recognized what it was.

A garrote.

No, not really a garrote. A clumsy, crude imitation of one.

"Daniel," she went on, "was apparently very different from his brother. Anthony was a gentleman in every sense. Daniel was—he was more at home with the sons of tradesmen. He fought with them, played with them, felt comfortable in their presence. My aunts referred to him as a little ruffian. He enjoyed the Army as well, I think. I've been told that he was very popular with his men."

Her fingertip touched the garrote. "According to my aunt Felicity's note, on the last day before the Pierce brothers were to leave Eastfield and go to the school in Surrey, Daniel brought this in, and during the morning, he threatened his classmates with it. The boys, that is, not the girls. Aunt Felicity was quite shocked when she overheard him swearing he'd slip into their houses in the dead of night and dispatch them, and she took the garrote away from him. She insisted on summoning his father, but Daniel begged her not to. He swore he'd done it to protect someone. It's all there in the file. The fear of God, he told my aunt, was nothing to the fear of death, and so he'd used the threat. In the end, she was dissuaded, against her better judgment. So she wrote an account of what had transpired, kept the garrote with it, and told Daniel that if he didn't behave himself in Surrey and become a fine example of the Misses Tate School, like his brother, she would go directly to his father. He gave her his solemn promise."

Rutledge reached for the garrote, picked up the length of rope and the two short, carefully whittled sticks tied at each end. Crudely made though it was, it was still too close to the mark for comfort. "Where the devil did a small boy Daniel's age come to learn about garrote?"

"Aunt Felicity wrote that Daniel had already made a friend at the new school and had been invited to stay with him one weekend. The friend's father had served in India and had books on Thuggee, the bandits who preyed on caravans. Quite the sort of thing a boy would read, if he had the chance. Daniel told my aunt that he had tried to make a garrote like the one described in the book, only he didn't have a man's head scarf or a handful of rupees to tie at each end. He only had some rope he'd found in a shed at the brewery and two sticks he'd been whittling."

Rutledge tested the rope between his hands, snapping it taut, but the threads of hemp were worn and gave under the pressure. "It wouldn't have worked, of course," he said.

"Ah, but the other boys weren't to know that, were they? No one locked doors—and Daniel's version of Thuggee would have been appropriately bloodcurdling."

"Who was he trying to protect? Which boy?" he asked

"Daniel refused to say. Of course my aunts weren't blind. According to Aunt Grace, it had to have been the Summers boy. Daniel defended him sometimes. Still, Aunt Felicity believed Daniel was showing off, just to be bloody-minded. Her word."

And in return, Thomas had discovered garrote, learned what it was, and then used one years later to kill his protector's brother. It was a measure of the feelings that drove him that Summers owed nothing to Daniel Pierce, not even a modicum of gratitude, and had used his name at The White Swans apparently without a qualm.

"Gentle God," Rutledge said quietly.

"Indeed," Mrs. Farrell-Smith agreed.

Hamish said, "In France Indian soldiers served."

Although the British had crushed Thuggee, these men would have known about it—some said it still existed in dark corners of the country—and very likely could have shown Summers what a proper garrote was, if he hadn't found sufficient information on his own.

"If you had learned of this report when first you came to Eastfield, you would have suspected Daniel. It was damning," Mrs. Farrell-Smith was saying. "I think his father must also have feared this would come to light—he must have been worried sick when Anthony was killed, for fear that in revenge I'd betray Daniel. My aunts would eventually have told him about the garrote. Still, he needed to *know* that one son hadn't killed the other. And so he had wanted Scotland Yard, less prejudiced than Inspector Norman, to investigate. Daniel was his favorite, and now he has only one son."

"But you weren't pleased that the Yard was brought in. Why did you think I'd uncover this? Why were you afraid of me and not of Inspector Norman?" He set the garrote back where he'd found it.

She smiled for the first time. "He has no imagination. You do."

Would it have made any difference if Mrs. Farrell-Smith had trusted him sooner?

Impossible to say. Still, Marshall might still be alive. He'd learned, as a policeman, that people held their secrets close, and the common good often failed to have any bearing on that need to protect them.

"Must this come out, if Summers is arrested?" she asked after a moment.

"I'm afraid so." And then he said, "Mrs. Farrell-Smith, where is Daniel?"

The shadow of an old grief settled over her face. "I wish I knew. He's loyal to my husband, you see. They were friends at school. He thinks my husband killed himself because he was jealous of me."

"Did he have cause to be?"

She shook her head impatiently. "You don't understand. Michael didn't kill himself because Daniel loved me. He killed himself because Daniel didn't love him."

"And you never told the police this?"

"I didn't mind suspicion falling on me. It was Daniel I didn't want to drag into the inquiry. Besides, it would have crushed any hopes I harbored in that direction."

"Did Anthony know you loved his brother?"

"Not in the beginning. When I did tell him, he warned me that Daniel wasn't the sort to settle down, and he wished me luck. I think Daniel still has the war on his mind, if you want the truth. But I've waited six years. I can wait six more if I must. And I'll be here, in Eastfield, if he ever decides to come home again."

She returned the garrote to the envelope and locked it away again. "Don't let me down," she said as she came around the desk to see him out. "Find Summers. I don't want another scandal keeping Daniel away. I don't want another cloud over our names."

At the door, Rutledge said, "If your aunts knew what was going on, why in God's name didn't they protect young Summers? Or punish his tormentors? Why did they allow the bullying to continue for so long?"

She frowned. "They were old-fashioned. They believed that a boy should be able to take care of himself. Sticks and stones and all that. They felt that it was important for him to develop a backbone, stand up to his tormentors. But when one is so young, one doesn't have the skills to face down a bully and teach him a lesson, does one?" She considered Rutledge for a moment, then added, "In my opinion there was something else as well. Their father— my great-uncle, the Frenchman who founded the school—would have considered Tommy Summers slovenly and unfit. He'd have taken him in hand and made a man of him. My aunts weren't capable of that, and they must have felt that Tommy was a rebuke."

And so five men had died.

He left, then, letting himself out, and as he walked back toward the hotel, Hamish said, "Do ye believe her?"

"I'll have the answer to that when I catch Summers. For all I know, she hates Daniel Pierce and sees this as a way to punish him for his rejection of her."

At the end of the street, he stopped and looked back at the school, feeling as if he were being watched.

Mrs. Farrell-Smith was standing at her window, as if to be certain he had left the premises.

He was about to walk on when out of the corner of his eye he saw a shadow at a window above hers.

He kept going, showing no sign of having noticed.

The school was closed for a week. Was it Daniel Pierce waiting for Rutledge to leave, or was it Tommy Summers back in Sussex and using the empty building to hide from the police?

Out of sight of the school, Rutledge stopped and considered how best to extract Mrs. Farrell-Smith without alerting whoever it was at the window above hers. Surely she would remain in her office a few minutes longer. He had a little time.

Moving quickly, he went down a list of people he could trust. Constable Walker would arouse suspicion, coming on the heels of Rutledge's visit. Mr. Ottley, from St. Mary's? Neither seemed to be the best choice. Summers would be on alert.

Coming toward him was Mrs. Winslow. She was walking with her head down, eyes on the road, but she carried a marketing basket over one arm.

He thought there was a good chance that Mrs. Farrell-Smith would let her in. But with what excuse? She had no children in the school. No reason to call.

Just behind her was Tyrell Pierce's clerk, Starret, hurrying in the direction of the brewery with an envelope in his hand.

Rutledge touched his hat to Mrs. Winslow and after she had gone on her way, stopped Starret.

"Sir?" the man asked, looking up at him.

"I need a favor, Starret. Will you go to the Misses Tate School and hand a message to Mrs. Farrell-Smith? She's there at the moment. I'd like it to appear that Mr. Pierce has asked to speak to her."

"But he hasn't, and I have this account to return to the brewery office."

Rutledge smiled. "I'd like to invite Mrs. Farrell-Smith to dinner. But we got off on the wrong footing, and I'm afraid she won't see me. Perhaps you'd help me lure her out of the school where I could speak to her. I'll explain the subterfuge when I see her."

"I really can't oblige you, sir. Mr. Pierce was most strict in his instructions."

Rutledge said, "And I am most strict in mine." He reached for the envelope in Starret's hand, and as the clerk expostulated, he wrote on it, *I must see you at once. Please come.* He signed it simply *Tyrell*, and prayed she couldn't recognize the man's handwriting.

"Inspector—"

Rutledge lost patience. "The sooner you deliver this, the sooner you can return to the brewery," he said. "And make it look as if you really came from Pierce. If you fail me, I'll have something to say to Pierce about your conduct."

The man gave him a reproachful look, and then walked on without a word. Rutledge watched him go.

Five minutes passed, time enough, Rutledge thought, to deliver the message. But neither Starret nor Mrs. Farrell-Smith appeared.

He thought, "If it's Summers, I've given the man a second hostage."

But there had been no choice, as Hamish was pointing out.

Another five minutes passed. Rutledge paced impatiently, ignoring the stares of passersby.

It was time to take action, he thought. And prayed that he hadn't sent two people to their deaths. He was just turning away when around the corner came Starret, with Mrs. Farrell-Smith at his side.

Rutledge breathed a sign of relief.

She saw him waiting, and at once called, "Did you speak to Tyrell? I thought I could trust you!" She was very angry.

He nodded to Starret, dismissing him, and when Mrs. Farrell-Smith reached him, he took her arm and led her toward the hotel. "Don't say anything more," he commanded in a low voice. "Just come with me."

She stared at him, about to pull away from his grip on her arm, and then something in his face alerted her.

"You've found Daniel," she began, anger fading, hope taken its place.

"I'm afraid not. At least I don't think I have. When I left the school, I saw you standing in the window. There was someone else by the window on the floor above you."

She stopped stock-still, and he urged her on.

"Not here. The hotel. We've drawn enough attention already."

She relented and said nothing more. He took her into the hotel lounge and found a chair for her.

"Are you sure?" she asked, keeping her voice low. "A trick of the light, perhaps? I'd have sworn the school was empty. I'd have heard someone walking around. I know every sound!"

"I'm not mistaken. Are you certain there's no one else in the building? And the greengrocer's son isn't working today?"

"No one should be there. The only reason I was there was to return some papers to my office, and then I decided to spend half an hour working." She shivered. "What if I'd encountered him when I went to Sixth Form for the marks? My God, he knows the school inside and out, doesn't he?"

"How many doors are there in the main building?"

"Let me think. There's the main door, of course. And the side entrance you know about. The door to the kitchen gardens. The terrace, with French doors, where we hold our teas, and of course, one into the coal cellar. That's too many—he'll be out through one as soon as you enter another in force."

"We must wait until dark. It will take that long to collect enough men from Inspector Norman to cover the school."

"Will there be—damage to the school? I answer to the trustees, they'll hold me accountable." She twisted a ring on one finger. "My aunts thought I was too young to have sole responsibility. And I was. But now . . ."

From Reception came the sound of voices, and he looked up. It was Inspector Norman in search of him.

Rutledge excused himself and went to intercept him.

"We've just finished searching the tunnels beneath the castle ruins, but he's not there. Still, I think you ought to come and see what we've found in one of the caves."

"Yes, give me five minutes." Rutledge returned to Mrs. Farrell-Smith. "I must go. Is there someone you can stay with? Where you'll be safe? I don't think it's a very good idea to go home."

She was frightened, her face pale. "Surely you don't think he was in the school to kill me? I wasn't even there when he was taunted."

Rutledge said, "Under the circumstances, it's best if you come to Hastings with us. If you don't mind sitting in the Inspector's office, you'll be safe if not precisely comfortable."

Relief washed over her face, and she went with him to where Inspector Norman was waiting.

"I'll explain on the way. At the moment, Mrs. Farrell-Smith is in protective custody."

Norman said, "Just hurry, that's all."

They left for Hastings, and after dropping his charge at the police station, Rutledge went with Inspector Norman to the caves that ran under the cliff on which William of Normandy had built his first castle. There was a warren of the caves, spreading out from shorter tunnels, and Rutledge was reminded of what lay under Dover Castle in Kent. Nature had contrived them, but man had made use of them.

At the mouth of one such cave, a man had set up a sideshow to accommodate the curiosity of holiday-makers looking for something to do on a rainy day. A painted donkey, crudely made from wood and plaster of Paris, was harnessed to a wooden cart laden with packets of silk and tobacco, kegs of whisky, and other contraband. On the wall behind was a painted canvas drop showing smugglers off-loading an array of goods from the decks of a French fishing boat drawn up close into the shore. Goods were passed from hand to hand by men standing knee-deep in water, then shouldered to carry to similar carts waiting to take the contraband to the caves.

Norman led Rutledge quickly past the other exhibits, continued beyond a barricade blocking the way, and soon came to a small offshoot of the main cave where a constable stood guard over a lamp-lit scene.

A small camp bed, a flat-topped chest bearing a lantern, and a chair stood out against the surrounding gloom. The smell of damp mixed with the cave odors of stale air.

Norman stepped forward into the shallow area and opened the chest. It was obvious as he shone his torch at the contents that he'd seen them earlier, before summoning Rutledge. Dark workmen's clothing, a pot of what appeared to be black grease paint, rags, and a Thermos of water lay inside. A pair of chimney sweep brooms stood in a corner, and a workman's lunch pail hung beside it.

"He could come here, change his clothes, and go out again as a different person," Norman was saying. "A laborer on his way home, a sweep with brooms over his shoulder, whatever little vignette he chose. Not a very clever disguise."

But effective. Rutledge could feel his claustrophobia mounting, but he held up a shirt, gauging the size. "Yes, it could be the man I saw. Medium height, medium build. How does he come and go?"

"I shouldn't think it would be too difficult after dark to get through the lock the showman has put on the grille across the entrance. This exhibit isn't officially allowed, but the man does no harm, and his presence here deters others from using these tunnels for more nefarious pastimes."

Rutledge turned to leave, fighting down rising panic. "Summers could hardly walk into The White Swans in these garbs. But he'd be equally suspicious wandering about Eastfield in a gentleman's clothing. Did you find the garrote?"

"No, damn it. He'd be a fool to leave it in plain sight."

"More importantly, he probably has it with him."

"For that matter," Norman pointed out, "there are no identity discs here. Blank or otherwise."

"He must have taken those as well. I think he's preparing to kill again. At the end of the war, he was on burial detail. Did you know? He'd have seen enough of the discs then to copy them exactly. As for names, he could have collected them from any soldier he met. He didn't want the names of the dead—ghosts don't kill. And he wanted us to search half of England looking for those men. Dust thrown in our eyes. But I think I know where he is. And I'll need your help getting to him."

Norman nodded to the constable on guard, and the three of them left the shallow depression.

Back into the sunlight again, Rutledge told Norman what he suspected.

"I can bring enough men to cover the entrances. But who's going in? We don't know if he's armed. I wouldn't be surprised if he is."

"I'll go in. I think he wants to garrote me, not shoot me."

"By the way, there's a message for you from the Yard," Norman said after a moment. "Mickelson is feeling better, and he's pushing the doctor to release him. He wants to take the case back from you."

"Wanting is not having," Rutledge answered. "And with any luck at all, if I'm right, we'll catch our elusive friend tonight."

But in the back of his mind, he heard Hamish's words. "What if he's cleverer than you?"

24

Rutledge escorted Mrs. Farrell-Smith back to Eastfield, and she sat beside him in the motorcar in pensive silence most of the way.

She had already agreed to take a room at The Fishermen's Arms as a precaution, but now she said, "There must be something else I can do. After all, some of this is my fault."

"Do you know where Daniel Pierce is?" he asked, not looking at her.

It was some time before she replied. "When he came to tell me that he was leaving Eastfield for good, that he was never coming back, I was so angry I picked up the first thing to hand and threw it at him. It was the paperweight from my desk, and it actually hit him in the face. I was appalled. I stood there unable to say anything. And he just turned and left my office." She coughed, to ease the constriction in her throat. "I tried to tell myself it was the war, the danger he lived with every time he went into one of those abominable tunnels, or perhaps it was blowing up so many men. I don't know. But he needn't have lied to me."

Rutledge was wary, now. Had Daniel Pierce told this woman about Peggy Winslow? Or had she guessed the truth?

"What lie did he tell you?" he asked when she didn't go on.

"It was ridiculous. Daniel, the most exciting man I'd ever met, always a scapegrace, always fun, never dull—in France even his men adored him. And he stood there in my office and told me he was converting to Catholicism and becoming a lay brother in a contemplative order. If he didn't love me, if he didn't want to marry me, I could understand that. If he needed to put the war behind him, I'd have done everything in my power to help him. What was even worse, he thought I'd *believe* him. It wasn't until the killing began that it all made sense. I'd found the garrote of course, and I thought, he left me because he was starting to lose his mind and didn't want me to know. And I thought, if I can find him before the police do, I can still save him." She turned to him, grief in her face, wanting to hear

Rutledge make light of the lie and tell her that Daniel loved her as much as she loved him and would come back one day.

"That explains why you told the police it was my motorcar you saw by the rectory gates, when you thought it must be Daniel's."

"Yes. I'm so sorry. But I'd do it again, if I thought it would protect him."

Rutledge considered what she'd told him, and he thought Daniel Pierce must have given this woman the literal truth. That he was withdrawing from a world he couldn't face—not because of the war as she wished to believe, but because of the ill-found marriage of Peggy and Virgil Winslow, about which he could do nothing. It would explain too why the Yard had failed to find him. The police had looked in the wrong directions all along.

He said, "He may have told you the truth, you know. That he was looking for a peace that you couldn't provide. An—absolution."

He had meant the carefully chosen words to give her a little peace as well. But she was blind to what he was saying, seeing it as a reaffirmation of her own belief.

Mrs. Farrell-Smith sat back, reassured. "Then he was letting me know he'd be all right, wasn't he? And that I must try to be patient until he's healed."

Rutledge let it go. She would be happier living with forlorn hope than with bitter truth. It was obvious how fiercely she could love, and he had a feeling that she could hate just as fiercely. And Peggy Winslow was vulnerable. Time was not always a healer—as often as not, it was just a measure of how long someone had waited.

As they turned into the hotel yard, she said, "Please. Find something for me to do. I'm responsible for the school. What if he decides to burn it down? Who knows what he could do, to try to cover his escape? I'll be worried sick until it's over."

After she had been given her room key, Rutledge asked the desk clerk for paper and pen, and told Mrs. Farrell-Smith what he wanted. Then he went to find Constable Walker.

He would have given much to put a watch on the school long before this, as soon as Mrs. Farrell-Smith was safely out of it. He had learned a grudging respect for the man they were after, well aware that Summers was capable of circumventing any plans the police chose to make. But Walker agreed with Rutledge that there was a greater risk of losing their quarry altogether if he got the wind up and slipped away. Besides, in daylight, there was no way to guard the rear of the property without being seen—the pastures beyond were flat and empty of shelter.

"If he thinks you saw him, he's already gone away," Constable Walker pointed out. "What I'm counting on is that he wants his revenge so badly, he'll take a chance that you didn't notice him."

Rutledge tried to picture the street in front of the school. "There's the first floor in the greengrocer's house."

Walker was skeptical. "You can see the main door from those windows, but there's not a good view of the alley."

"Then we wait until dark, and box him in."

With an eye to that plan, there was something else Rutledge needed to attend to. He spent quite some time closeted with an assistant at the ironmonger's shop, and left there well satisfied with their knowledge of what he wanted.

Restless now, with nightfall still hours away, Rutledge patrolled the village and outlying farms on foot, staying well clear of the school but covering as much ground as he could. There was no indication that Summers had left the school building, but Rutledge spoke to every man whose name might appear on the killer's list, telling them to be alert. He found all of them save Tuttle, whose mother informed him that her son was in Hastings until the morrow. "There's a girl," she'd said. "He can't stay away from her."

All the same, as a precaution, Rutledge ordered Walker to be on the lookout for his nephew, in the event he came back to Eastfield earlier. The course of true love seldom ran as smoothly as expected.

At length night fell, and Inspector Norman and his men arrived in Eastfield in the sunset's afterglow, that soft light that was always slow to fade. They went directly to St. Mary's Church, as agreed, where they were not as likely to draw attention to themselves. He had brought a sergeant, Constable Petty, and two other constables whom Rutledge hadn't encountered before this. Both were sizeable and quiet.

At Rutledge's request, Mrs. Farrell-Smith had spent her afternoon sketching maps of the school and marking the exits clearly. After each man was assigned to guard a specific door, Constable Walker explained how to reach their posts unseen, carefully describing landmarks to help them find their way in the dark. The main door was the most difficult to reach, even using the shadows for cover. It was decided to leave that to the last, once the other men were in position.

"You'll have only a few minutes to reach your destination. I want you in place by the time it's completely dark. Mark me, don't go inside the school, no matter what happens. The point is to bottle him up. I'll do the rest," Rutledge told them. "This is a dangerous man.

You're not to take any chances if he comes your way. Use your truncheons to stop him if need be. Here are your signals. One long blast of your whistle if he comes your way. Two short if you need help. One short and one long if you see he's got out of the building. Understood? Good. Any questions?"

Rutledge led them outside to the apse of the church, to accustom their vision to the gathering dark, then saw them off. He turned to Inspector Norman, who was taking the main door. "I'm going in that side door I showed you on the map, because I know my way there. Your task is to back up anyone who gets in trouble. But stay outside. If anything moves in that building, I'll be assuming it's the killer. You don't want to get in the way."

"You ought to be armed."

Rutledge said grimly, "I am."

He watched Inspector Norman disappear into the dark shadows of the churchyard and then heard the squeak of the rectory gate as he passed through it.

There was nothing to do now but wait until his men were in position. Five minutes passed. It was time for him to move.

The squeak of the gate reached his ears again. It stopped almost at once.

Hamish said, " 'Ware!"

There was no reason for Norman or his men to come back to the church.

He had been standing not far from the church tower, facing the rectory, and now he moved toward the gate, picking his way through the heavy summer grass and the scattering of tombstones. It was as dark as the back side of hell in the churchyard, and there was no way to know whether someone had been coming into it or going through into the rectory grounds.

Misdirection.

Rutledge knew then that he'd been right. Summers had seen him leave the school, had seen him turn and look back at the windows. Shortly afterward, someone had come for Mrs. Farrell-Smith. That had had to be done, Rutledge had had no choice. But his quarry, taking no chances, must have slipped out the back way, across the kitchen garden, the barnyard, and out through the orchard before Mrs. Farrell-Smith had even reached safety.

And now he was loose. But here in the churchyard or at the rectory?

Rutledge's hearing was acute, but Hamish's had always been far sharper.

"On the steps of the rectory."

Rutledge could just make out the soft footfall. And then it came down the steps again and was lost in the

grass. After a few seconds Rutledge realized that someone was moving around to the side of the rectory, facing
the church.

Where was Mr. Ottley, the rector? At this hour, in
his bed, most likely. But was he? For now Rutledge
could see that although the drapes had been drawn,
lamps were still lit in his study.

Just then, the rectory door opened, throwing a shaft
of light across the lawn, and Mr. Ottley was saying, "I'm
glad you came, Tuttle. I think you've made a wise decision. If Miss Lang accepts your proposal, I'll be happy
to post the banns and marry you when the time comes."

Tuttle. Constable Walker's nephew. And what the
hell was he doing in Eastfield? He must, Rutledge
thought, have arrived at the rectory while it was still
dusk and the police were gathered inside St. Mary's.
Damn and blast the man!

"Thank you, Rector," Tuttle responded. "I'm that
sorry to have come so late, but we lost track of time,
didn't we, Nan and I?" He laughed lightly. "One good
thing about getting married, I shan't be traveling all
the way to Hastings and back of an evening."

Mr. Ottley laughed with him, and then they said
good night.

The door closed, and the shaft of light vanished,
leaving Rutledge blind for several seconds. But he
could hear Tuttle moving down the path from the

rectory door, and then turning toward the gate into the churchyard. A shortcut to his house—Rutledge had spoken to his mother only that afternoon.

A lorry rumbled down the Hastings Road, and its headlamps swept the churchyard wall as it passed the main gate.

As if in a tableau, Rutledge could see Tuttle stop, his head turned toward the vehicle. And in the shadows by the rectory wall, he could just discern the outline of another man frozen in place not ten yards from where Tuttle was standing.

Tuttle was the victim this time.

And Rutledge had two choices—to call out a warning, and risk losing Summers, or to put himself between Tuttle and the killer.

Tuttle was opening the rectory gate, whistling to himself as he stepped through it and paused to shut it behind him.

Something—some tiny movement—caught his attention, and he turned to stare at the rectory wall, now in darkness again. "Who's there?" he asked sharply.

A voice said softly, so as not to disturb the rector behind his closed doors, "Do you remember me, Tuttle?"

The low churchyard wall was between them now. Tuttle said warily, "I don't know your voice. Who are you? What do you want?"

"To say hello. For old time's sake."

"You've got the wrong man, then," Tuttle answered and began to walk swiftly toward the far gate and the better-lit Hastings Road, careful to keep on the smoother ground between rows of gravestones.

He passed within ten feet of where Rutledge was standing, but his attention was wholly on the man behind him as he listened for the telltale squeak of the rectory gate. He began to pick up his pace now, anxious, clearly beginning to realize the danger he was in. The Hastings Road was safety—doors he could pound on, people who would hear him shout for help. Even the sanctuary of The Fishermen's Arms, if he was quick enough.

Behind him, Rutledge saw the killer vault the wall rather than use the gate, landing lightly, in a crouched position. Then he straightened and started forward.

Rutledge turned his head. Tuttle by this time was some fifteen feet from the main gate, and he cast a worried glance over his shoulder, unable to see where in the shadows his hunter could be. The wind up now, he made a frantic dash for the gate and was through it, into the Hastings Road, running for the hotel.

" 'Ware!"

It was Hamish who saved him.

In an instant, Rutledge realized that Summers must have caught a glimpse of him there amongst the trees watching Tuttle walk on, and on the spot changed course, altering his intended target to the one at hand.

There was a fleeting movement of air, a sound that had barely registered, before Rutledge dropped to his heels, out of reach of the garrote intended for his throat. It scraped across his head, and he heard the man behind him swear.

Rutledge surged to his feet again, catching Summers off balance, and the two men fell hard against a footstone, flailing at an adversary neither of them could see in the thick shadows of the church tower.

For an instant Rutledge had a solid grip on the man's upper arm, spinning him as they got to their feet, but his boots slipped in the bruised grass, and Summers broke free. He ran, only to fall headlong over something underfoot. Rutledge lunged forward, missed him, and saw him race toward the church porch and the deeper shadows of the apse beyond.

Rutledge gave chase, launched himself at the figure just ahead, and brought Summers down, knocking the wind out of both of them.

Rutledge was the first to recover, but the other man was fast, and breathing hard, he set off again, back the way he had come, toward the west door of the church.

He got it open before Rutledge could stop him, and then tried to slam it shut, catching one of Rutledge's hands as he did.

Setting his teeth, Rutledge pulled at the edge of the door, bracing himself, and when Summers suddenly let the door go, it opened so fast that he was flung against the carved stone arch. He nearly cracked his head against the protruding foot of a saint, but using the wall as a fulcrum, rebounded with such speed that he was inside the entrance to the church before Summers could manage the inner door into the sanctuary. Something brushed his face, and he grunted with shock at a touch so close and so human. Then he realized that it was not a hand but the frayed end of the bell rope. He caught it again somehow, and leapt high on it, coming down with all his weight on it.

High above in the tower, the bell clanged with a deafening discord.

Two short blasts of a whistle—it was the nearest he could come to the signal for needing help. But before he could ring the bell again, Summers was on him, knocking him to one side. Rutledge whirled as he crashed into the wall, expecting Summers to be in front of him now.

He judged it wrong.

The garrote this time brushed his ear and he jerked sideways, knocking against the low table where church information and items for sale were usually kept. It went over in a crash, and Summers yelled in pain as one of the legs unexpectedly clipped him, and he went down.

They were fairly equally matched, although Rutledge had the advantage of height. He felt for the wildly swinging bell rope, caught it, and leapt high a second time. But Summers reached up as he was scrambling to his feet, and seized Rutledge's ankle, pulling him back. Still, he managed to keep his grip on the rope, and again the bell sounded a harsh note, rocking on its cradle to ring a second and then a third time before Summers could stop him.

Kicking out with his free foot, Rutledge caught Summers in the throat, for he choked on a cough and released his hold.

Letting go of the bell rope, Rutledge dropped to the stone flagging, trying to pick up movement and locate Summers. But he waited a second too long, for something brushed his shoulder, then a fist slammed into the edge of his jaw. Rutledge's head snapped back, and he saw stars.

The other man was on him then, pinning him half against the wall, half against the door into the sanctuary. Shaking his head to clear it, Rutledge broke the hold, lashing out in his turn, and Summers stumbled backward over something that had fallen from the overturned table, sending it bouncing across the floor, and he went down. It was the break that Rutledge was looking for, and he caught at the fabric of the man's lapel, held on hard with one hand, and with the other, went for where he guessed the man's body would be. The blow sank into yielding flesh, and he heard the whoosh of air as Summers fought to breathe again.

Rutledge was on the point of following up his advantage just as the outer church door scraped open and the beam of a torch swept them.

Both combatants froze, then turned as one to stare into the brilliant light as Mr. Ottley said sternly, "This is a house of God. Get out of here now."

The man in Rutledge's grasp, using all his strength, broke free, spun the rector into Rutledge's arms, and was gone.

The rector lost his balance and went down, taking Rutledge to one knee as the torch went skittering across the stone floor like a wild thing, the spinning light blinding both of them. Rutledge heaved Mr. Ottley away and was out the door after Summers, unaware he had not gone far.

This time the garrote didn't miss. It whipped over Rutledge's head and drew across his throat so quickly he was helpless to stop it.

And Summers pulled hard, with a force that was backed by anger and an intense will.

Rutledge spun, jerking his revolver from his pocket and raising it in the same motion. The barrel caught Summers with such force across the temple that he went down, the garrote slipping through his hands.

Just then the church door opened and the rector barreled out, torch in hand, shouting Rutledge's name. The beam caught Rutledge in the eyes, and Ottley stopped short.

"At my feet, damn it," he snapped, and the torch swept downward.

"Who is that?" Mr. Ottley asked, peering at the slack, unconscious face. "I've never seen him before!" There was astonishment and relief in his voice.

"At a guess, one Thomas Summers."

The rector moved closer, frowning. "Are you sure? That doesn't look like the Summers lad."

"You haven't seen him in fifteen years. He's changed. He's a man now, not a boy."

Ottley pointed to the blood on the side of the unconscious man's face. "Did you kill him?"

"No. But he'll have one hell of a headache when he comes to his senses," Rutledge said with some satisfaction, shoving his revolver back into his pocket.

His tone brought the flashlight upward, so that Ottley could study his face, but it stopped at Rutledge's throat. *"What in God's name—"*

"The garrote. He tried to kill me."

Ottley was about to say more when they heard shouting from the direction of the Hastings Road and Norman came charging into the churchyard. "What the hell is happening?"

As he reached the small tableau picked out by Ottley's torch, he added, "We heard the bell, but from where Petty stood, he could see a light in the school. He was certain someone was moving around in that room. Finally I went inside myself. We found a candle lit and a piece of paper on a string, hanging over it. When the candle flickered, the paper moved. We came here—" Norman ran out of words, staring from Rutledge to the rector, and finally noticing the third man lying in the shadows at Rutledge's feet.

"He left the school before we got there," Rutledge said. "He's been following Tuttle. From Eastfield to Hastings and back to Eastfield, I should think. I got in his way."

Norman stepped across to take the torch from the rector's hand and shine it down at Summers.

"Hold it steady," Rutledge said, and stooped to go through Summers's pockets.

There was no identification in any of them. Only, in a breast pocket, a single identity disc intended for his next victim's mouth.

Rutledge looked at it, saw the name, and said nothing. He passed it on to Norman, who brought the torch up to see it more clearly. "Well. We needn't ask if you're this man. Bertie Grimes, corporal, the Yorkshire Rifles."

As he handed it back to Rutledge he saw what was around his neck.

"What the hell did he do to you?" Constable Walker asked, stepping forward for a closer look.

Rutledge unwound the garrote and passed it to Inspector Norman. "The murder weapon."

"Yes, that's the garrote," Walker was saying as he took it. "But what's that around your throat?"

Rutledge reached up and touched the flanged band that encircled his throat. It was what he and the ironmonger's assistant had spent most of the afternoon devising: the only thing he could think of to protect against a garrote. "A gorget. Of a sort. It's meant to be similar to the armor a knight wore around his neck and shoulders to protect them. The ironmonger will have to cut it off. And the sooner the better. Meanwhile, we ought to take Summers to Dr. Gooding. In the event I hit him harder than I meant to."

But as they trooped toward Dr. Gooding's, carrying Summers on a table the rector brought from the church, the man came round, dazed and at first hardly coherent. And then finally aware of where he was, he started to struggle, only to be forced down by the ungentle hands of the constables carrying him. Subsiding, he lay there with one arm flung over his eyes.

Gooding, roused from sleep, pronounced Summers well enough to be taken to Hastings and charged with multiple counts of murder. Rutledge looked at the men surrounding the patient and said, "Norman, if you'll contact Dover police, and ask that a former sergeant named Bell bring the witness he has in his keeping to Hastings at his earliest convenience, we'll have one more piece of our case settled."

"Who is Bell? And what's the name of the witness?" Norman asked. "This *is* Summers, isn't it?"

"Yes. That's Summers. Bell will explain. Will you give me five minutes alone with the prisoner?"

After a moment they did as they had been asked, but it was clear that Inspector Norman was not best pleased.

When they had shut the door behind them, Rutledge said to Summers, "Is your wife still alive? It won't save you from hanging if you tell me. But there is someone very much interested in her condition."

Summers was staring at him, his eyes intent. "Why should I help the police?"

"Do you hate her as much as you hated the others?"

"I didn't hate her at all. I needed her money," he said coldly.

"You can't inherit any of it, if you've killed her. If she's still alive and you haven't treated her too badly, she might be induced to pay for your defense."

"Not bloody likely," he said harshly. "I killed her confounded little dog. As good as."

Which told Rutledge that Mrs. Summers was still alive. Where?

"I'll give you until nine o'clock in the morning to think that over and tell me where she is."

Summers gingerly touched the side of his head. A red welt marked where Rutledge's revolver had struck him. "You needn't have hit me so damned hard."

There was almost a whining note in his voice.

"Your fault for trying to garrote me," Rutledge said unfeelingly. "Why didn't you stop the killing when you could? Why not let Hopkins take the blame? Did your revenge matter so much that it was worth hanging for?"

"At first it was vengeance. I'd thought about it long enough. I decided it was time to show I had the backbone to do it. When they died, they were as alone as

I was all my childhood. A lonely death in return for a lonely life." Summers's face changed, something in it that gave Rutledge pause. At length he said, as if it was unfathomable to him, "Then I found I liked planning and stalking and killing my victims. It brought the war back again. I hadn't realized it then, but it was probably the happiest time of my life. I felt so *alive*." He considered Rutledge. "You were in the war, at a guess. Do you know what I'm talking about? Did you feel it?"

There was an eagerness in his voice, a need to hear that others had been caught up as well.

Rutledge remembered the trenches, the stench of war, the broken bodies of the living, the torn, bloated corpses of the dead. The nightmare of trying to survive against all odds, and watching those under his command decimated day after day.

"No," he said. "I never did. And I thank God."

Turning on his heel, he left the room, telling Norman that the suspect was all his.

"What did you talk about?" Norman demanded. "I want to know."

"About the war," Rutledge said, and walked out of Dr. Gooding's surgery.

25

They brought the little dog into Inspector Norman's office the next morning. He had already sent for Summers, who was sitting in a chair, stubbornly silent now.

Bell dropped the lead as Rutledge opened the door, and Muffin ran in, stopped short, cast a glance at Summers, and then rapidly swung around the room, frantically searching for the one person who wasn't there. Summers stared at him as if he'd seen a ghost, but as the dog came full circle, he stopped in front of the man's chair and began barking, surging forward and then back again, head down, neck outstretched and taut.

Bell, watching, said, "My God."

"Get him away from me!" Summers demanded, drawing his feet under the chair, out of reach. "The bloody dog *bites*."

Rutledge spoke over the ferocious display of anger as Muffin all but attacked Summers, teeth bared, ears back.

"Where is she? Or I'll lock him in the cell with you."

"Damn it, call him off."

But Rutledge stood there, grimly watching as Muffin leapt closer, challenging the man in the chair.

Desperate, Summers kicked out, and Muffin got his ankle, holding on with the tenacity of his terrier ancestors. Summers screamed, stood up and tried to shake the dog off, but it was impossible. Bell, just behind Rutledge, started to step forward, but Rutledge put out an arm to stop him.

Summers cried, "All right, for God's sake, I'll tell you. Get him away from me—she's in the Convent of the Claires. South of Paris. I swear it. Please—"

Meredith Channing had said something about convents.

"Why is she there?" Rutledge asked, holding up his hand to stop Bell.

"I told them she suffered hallucinations after a head injury," he said rapidly. "That what she remembers is confused, erratic. There was never a pet dog, we were never in Sussex—they pitied me."

Bell hurried forward and caught the dog by its collar, his voice firm, pulling Muffin back. It took some doing, and Summers's ankle was bloody by the time Bell had separated them. Summers reached down and gripped it, swearing.

Bell turned reproachfully to Rutledge. "That was not right."

"It was the only way," Rutledge answered harshly. "He killed with impunity. He'd have left her there. She was no further use to him. Nor was her money, now."

He turned on his heel and walked out of the room while Bell soothed the dog and carried him down the passage to the motorcar that had brought him from Dover.

Norman left Summers slumped in his chair and followed Rutledge. "You're a cold bastard when you want to be. And you've put Mickelson's nose out of joint, bringing the suspect in. He's to be released tomorrow—Mickelson—and sent to London to finish healing. He refuses to clear you, you know. He claims he's uncertain. But we've found Summers's motorcar. It's very like yours. Mrs. Farrell-Smith was right on that score. I don't think you'll have much trouble over that business."

"It doesn't matter," Rutledge said, refusing to admit to Norman or anyone else that it did.

Norman said after a moment, "I'm curious. When did you bring your service revolver to Eastfield?"

Rutledge said, "I took it to France with me. Force of habit." With that, he walked away, leaving Norman to stare after him.

A fortnight later, when Rutledge had given his testimony at the inquest and returned to London, he asked Chief Inspector Cummins to meet him for lunch at a quiet restaurant where they could talk.

Cummins came in, sat down, and greeted Rutledge cheerfully. "I'm glad to see you survived. It must have been touch and go, according to my sources."

For an instant Rutledge thought that Cummins was referring to that moment in the wasteland of the Somme, when he'd considered his future and decided against dying there. And then he understood. The reference was to Eastfield. "It was a close-run thing— whether I'd be hanged for murder or would bring in the real killer."

"Why did he target Mickelson?"

"Apparently he'd seen Inspector Mickelson standing in the churchyard by his mother's grave. He was afraid Mickelson was looking into his family's past. It wasn't true, of course, but it nearly got Mickelson killed, all the same. By the time he'd retrieved his motorcar and stopped Mickelson by the rectory gates, there was no opportunity to garrote him, and so he used a spanner."

"I hear Mickelson is being bloody-minded about clearing you of any role in his attack."

"He's had an epiphany. So I've been told. The KC trying Summers—Julian Haliburton—has informed Mickelson that the Crown takes a dim view of muddying the evidence. Inspector Mickelson's statement has officially exonerated me of all blame." Rutledge didn't add that it would be some time before his arrest on a charge of attempting to murder a fellow policeman had faded from the collective memory of the Yard. That anyone believed him capable of such an act still stung.

Cummins chuckled. "Yes, Haliburton is a stickler for accuracy." His amusement faded. "You understand that you won't be promoted to fill my shoes? Bloody stupid of Bowles, but there it is."

"I hadn't expected it," Rutledge said. And yet he knew that he would have liked to follow a man like Cummins.

"On a more interesting subject than the Chief Superintendent, I haven't thanked you for your help with the Stonehenge murder. This is more information than I'd ever hoped to find."

"There's something more," Rutledge replied. "I think I know the name of the murder victim."

Cummins was aghast. "I don't believe it. How in hell's name did you ever get to that?"

"We'd wondered why the knife was left in Hastings. It occurred to me that there must be another connection. At least a name to be going forward with. And what's the most popular name in Hastings?"

"Robinson? Turner? Johnson?"

"William the Conqueror. The first of the Norman kings of England. There's an Inspector Norman there, as well. While I was there giving evidence at the inquest, I asked one of his constables if there was anyone in the Inspector's family who had gone missing in 1905. At first Petty thought I was trying to cause trouble with the police in Hastings, but then he told me that there were several families named Norman in that part of Sussex. And one of them, a William Norman, was lost in Peru in 1906. He was a schoolmaster who was eager to find another lost city of the Incas. As it happened, an American, Hiram Bingham, actually did find a lost city. Machu Picchu. This William Norman sailed for Peru on the twenty-second of June, 1905. The family was told he'd reached Peru safely, had gone into the jungle, and was never heard from again. He was declared dead seven years later."

"To reach Peru, he'd have had to take passage on a ship going out there. Did he?"

"Yes. Apparently he did. Someone did."

"Well, then, he isn't our William Norman, is he?"

Rutledge signaled the waiter to bring their menu. "The report said that the captain of the S.S. *Navigator* had described Norman as the worst sailor in Christendom. He never left his cabin throughout the voyage, he was as green as anyone the captain had ever seen, and when he stepped off the ship, his legs would barely hold him upright. But he insisted that he was all right."

"A great disguise, seasickness," Cummins said dryly.

"You forget, the ship's captain had never seen Norman. He was nothing more than a name on the manifest, and the few glimpses anyone had had of him."

"Hmmm. Who then took his place? The killer?"

Rutledge said, "I expect we'll never know. But if it was the killer, then he's dead." He paused. "He was a schoolmaster in a prestigious public school in Dorset. Norman. Not so very far from Stonehenge."

"What was his field?"

"History."

"Was his journey to Peru carefully planned or spur of the moment?"

"It was apparently arranged some months before his departure."

Cummins shook his head.

"Where did the schoolmaster who planned the Druids' trip to Stonehenge teach?"

"You've seen the file. At a public school in Dorset."

"Coincidence?"

"He was cleared. He couldn't have killed the man nor roped him to that bloody stone. He was within sight of his fellow Druids at all times."

"No, possibly not. But perhaps someone knew about his adventure to Stonehenge and thought it a very good idea to take an inconvenient body there."

"But what about Wheeler? He was identified."

"You know how uncertain identifications can be. At a guess, the Edinburgh police were happy to see the end of Wheeler. I've done some research. There was a Wheeler from Orkney killed at Gallipoli. He'd immigrated to Australia from Belfast in 1904."

"Did he, by God!"

"Where is your schoolmaster, now? Do you know?"

Cummins made a wry face. "Dead of cholera in India. Hindsight is a wonderful thing, Rutledge, but it doesn't solve crimes."

He himself had said much the same, one day in Eastfield.

Cummins took up his menu. Without opening it, he said, "I was so sure about Wheeler. Even so, we could find no motive to explain why he'd been killed. And without the identity of the victim, we were still stymied as to motive. It was a vicious circle. That's what bothered me all these years. In spite of the loopholes in your arguments, I expect you've come closer to finding answers than I ever did."

"How do you suppose someone discovered your grandfather's name was Charles Henry?"

Cummins gave it some thought. "There was a solicitor connected with the case. His name was Charles Henry. I remember remarking to someone that my grandfather's name was Charles Henry. Charles Henry Cummins."

"Who overheard you?"

"Oh, I know who was there at the time. Our Druid leader, the schoolmaster." He smiled. "Before you leap to conclusions, that Charles Henry—the solicitor—was up in years. In fact, he died soon after the inquest. He was probably dying at the time and no one realized it. Weak heart." He set aside his menu and raised his glass. "I always knew you were a very good policeman, Ian. Bowles is a fool, damn his eyes."

The waiter was hovering, and Cummins looked up at him. "Yes, yes, all right. How is the fish here?"

When Rutledge returned to his flat at the end of the day, he found a letter waiting. It was from Rosemary Hume, and it was brief.

It's time, Ian. Can you come?

He left a message for the Yard, and set out straight-away for Chaswell. When he got there, it was late, but

Rosemary was waiting up for him. Even as he walked through the house door, he could hear Reginald's forced breathing. Rosemary took him directly up the staircase to the room her husband's cousin had been given.

"He asked to see you alone," she said as she turned back toward the stairs.

Reginald was in a chair, leaning forward, struggling for breath. He greeted Rutledge with a weary smile and a nod.

"I'm sorry to see you in such straits," he said, sitting down by the invalid chair. "Is there anything I can do?"

A paroxysm of coughing nearly doubled Reginald in two, and afterward he lay back against his pillows, drained. But he lifted a hand and pointed to his desk. It was a tall affair with bookshelves above, and then the drop-down front that formed the writing surface. Rutledge walked across the room, opened the desk. It was all but empty, and he turned to Reginald.

"Left."

There were cubbyholes on either side of a small central alcove, and Rutledge looked in the left one. He saw an envelope pushed deep into the narrow space and hardly visible. He pulled it out. Maxwell Hume's name was scrawled across it in a firm hand, and then, more recently, that had been crossed out and his own name had been written above Maxwell's. From the state of the envelope, Rutledge realized that Reginald must have written this some years earlier, for the original ink was already fading. "This?"

Reginald nodded.

Rutledge went back to sit by him. "Shall I open it now?"

Reginald said briefly, "Later."

And so they sat together for the rest of the night, mostly in companionable silence, although at times Rutledge talked quietly about their lives, about the war, and about Max.

Shortly after dawn, Reginald put out a clawlike hand and gripped Rutledge's arm with surprising strength. Rutledge gave him his own hand, and waited.

"Forgive me." The words were hardly more than a whisper.

He said, "You're forgiven. With all my heart."

"Truly?"

"As God is my witness."

After a time, the room fell quiet, the struggle to breathe finished. Rutledge held the thin hand for a while longer, and then laid it gently in his friend's lap and closed Reginald's eyes. He took the letter, then remembering, put it in his pocket where Rosemary wouldn't see it.

And he went down the stairs to where Rosemary, her eyes red with crying, was drinking tea. She passed a clean cup to Rutledge, and he poured his own. It was lukewarm, but he drank it for her sake.

A little later she said, "I finally slept. And then I awoke with a start. I didn't know where I was. It was then I heard the silence."

"I'll speak to Mr. Gramling soon."

"He didn't want a priest at the end. He said it would be wrong to ask for anyone to save two souls, his as well as Maxwell's." She hesitated. "Did he kill himself, Ian?"

"No. God, no, Rosemary. He—simply stopped breathing."

"I thought that was why he wanted a policeman at the end."

"I wasn't a policeman upstairs tonight. I was a friend. I've sat with the dying before this."

She reached out and put her hand over his. "I'm sorry. Thank you."

Half an hour later, he left her still sitting at the table and went out to find Mr. Gramling.

Rutledge didn't read the letter until much later that day, when he had gone to visit Maxwell Hume's grave.

Max,

I hesitate to put this on your conscience as well as mine. But I face my first battle tomorrow, and if

I die, I don't want to carry this with me into what-ever hell I find. And so I'm writing to you, and when you read this, you will know I'm dead and out of any man's reach. I must tell you that when I was much younger, I killed a man. I should have taken my chances with the courts. But I was very frightened, and the people I turned to told me that given the circumstances, I would ruin the rest of my life if I went to the police. I listened to them, not because I really believed them but because I wanted to believe them. And so through circum-stances that aided us and the careful planning of two other people, we carried it off.

The victim was William Norman. Do you know the name? He went exploring and never came back. Only it was a poor man who worked for the school whom we dressed as William Norman and sent to sea with the promise of a return ticket two weeks after he landed. For our sins, he died of a fever instead and never came home. I blame myself for that as well.

William Norman was a schoolmaster who hurt people for his own pleasure. Sadistic and clever, he forced his boys to make choices. Lie about a friend or he would tell the headmaster a worse lie in its place. Steal money and swear that it was one of the servants, who would then be sacked without a reference. Or he would fail someone we liked whose marks were already poor, and see that he was sent down. When it was my turn, the choice was particularly heinous. I refused, I said I'd die first, and he told me he could arrange for me to die, and showed me the knife. He also told me who would be blamed for my death. I didn't know where to turn. He told me he'd leave me for a quarter of an hour, to make my decision. I did. I took the only course I could see. I picked up the weapon from his desk and then bent over it as if weeping. He came in, took my hair in his hand and pulled my head up. I drove the sharp blade into his body. By some fluke, it nicked the great artery and he died. I don't know where I found the strength or the courage to watch it happen. I cleaned up as best I could and went to find my housemaster. He and one of the younger masters and I sat there and decided to cover up the crime. I asked if William Norman's family would suffer, and they thought not. He'd been estranged from them for some years. That was all I needed to know.

If I survive this war, I'll burn the letter. Don't blame the others, will you? They hadn't known what he was doing, but when I told them, they believed me and did their best to save me. I was always grateful.

And below Reginald's signature was a postscript.

Forgive me, Ian, for exacting a promise once I discovered you were a policeman. In truth, our friendship was genuine. And I have tried to make up for that night, short of confessing. Does that mean William Norman won after all?

Rutledge read it again, then folded it and returned the sheet to the envelope.

Would he take it to Cummins—who knew much of the story already? He himself had been zealous in search of a truth not for the sake of that truth but because he was a good policeman and it was his duty to pursue the guilty. What truth would be served by closing the case, when the principals were beyond the law's reach?

Rutledge didn't know. Just now his duty was to bury the recent dead and mourn them with honor.

Hamish said, "Do ye regret giving your forgiveness before ye knew why you were being asked?"

Rutledge said, "I don't. God knows, I need forgiveness of my own."

He walked back to the house. Rosemary was ready, and it was time to follow Reginald to his final rest.

HARPER LUXE

THE NEW LUXURY IN READING

We hope you enjoyed reading
our new, comfortable print size and found it
an experience you would like to repeat.

Well – you're in luck!

HarperLuxe offers the finest in fiction and
nonfiction books in this same larger print size and
paperback format. Light and easy to read, HarperLuxe
paperbacks are for book lovers who want to see
what they are reading without the strain.

For a full listing of titles and
new releases to come, please visit our website:

www.HarperLuxe.com

SEEING IS BELIEVING!